Rhis felt her hand on his throat, the fingers probing gently for a pulse. Her voice was tense in his ear. "Don't you *dare* die on me, you ungrateful son of a Pillorian bitch! I'm in enough trouble already. I—"

He moved with unerring precision. One hand clamped tightly around her neck. He clasped her left wrist with his other and yanked her arm up behind her back. Thrown off balance, she fell forward and was crushed against his chest.

He brought his mouth down to her ear. Her light, flowery scent drifted over him. "Try anything, *anything,* and you are dead." He could feel her pulse beating frantically under his fingers.

"You really"—her voice came out in gulping gasps—"don't have to do this."

"Move!" He shoved her toward the hatchway and stopped at the opening.

A searing, stabbing heat shot up his neck. He drew in a sharp breath. He had no time for this. He focused his mind. Tensed his body. And felt the softness of her hair against his chest. The firm swell of her behind against his . . .

Bloody hell! He was completely naked.

His plans of forcing her to the bridge and commandeering her ship suddenly took a sharp turn. . . .

FINDERS KEEPERS

LINNEA SINCLAIR

BANTAM BOOKS

FINDERS KEEPERS
A Bantam Spectra Book / May 2005

Published by
Bantam Dell
A Division of Random House, Inc.
New York, New York

All rights reserved
Copyright © 2005 by Linnea Sinclair
Cover illustration copyright © 2005 by Dave Seeley
Cover design by Jamie S. Warren Youll

If you purchased this book without a cover, you should be aware
that this book is stolen property. It was reported as "unsold and
destroyed" to the publisher, and neither the author nor the
publisher has received any payment for this "stripped book."

Bantam Books, the rooster colophon, Spectra, and the portrayal of a
boxed "s" are registered trademarks of Random House, Inc.

ISBN 0-553-58798-6

Printed in the United States of America
Published simultaneously in Canada

www.bantamdell.com

OPM 10 9 8 7 6 5 4 3

With thanks to:

Rob Bernadino, husband of infinite patience who
    believes in me . . .
Nancy "Kate" Gramm, author extraordinaire, friend
    first, patient mentor . . .
Kristin Nelson, incredible agent, and her Wonder
    Dog Chutney . . .
Anne "Send Chocolate" Groell, enthusiastic editor
    and accomplished author . . .
All my Intergalactic Bar & Grille regulars, especially
    Carla, Lynne, Debbie, Cy, Celia, Mike, Dawn,
    Charapa, Karen, Chris, Melissa, Sue . . .
Special thanks to the very talented and supportive
    Robin D. Owens, Susan Grant, Catherine Asaro,
    and Jacqueline Lichtenberg . . .
and as always . . .
My furpersons and typing assistants, Daq and Dooz,
    thanks FUR all your help!

FINDERS KEEPERS

The *Careless Venture*'s intruder alarm erupted through the cavern with a harsh wail. Trilby Elliot shot to her feet, knocking over the makeshift repair table. Sonic welder and integrator cables clattered against the cavern floor.

She bolted for her freighter's rampway. Overhead, a nest of sleeping bloodbats burst out of the rocky crevices like small, leathery missiles. The panicked bats spiraled in front of her. Screeching, they fled through the wide mouth of the cavern into the lavender twilight.

She reached her rampway just as a silver object flashed across the sky behind them.

"Damn. Double damn." Another ship here meant big trouble. And even a little trouble was more than she could handle right now.

She sprinted through the air lock.

Coils of black conduit snaked down the freighter's corridor, humped over the hatch tread into the bridge. She sidestepped the cables and reached for the alarm, slapping it into silence. A flick of her thumb activated the intraship. "Dezi, we got incoming! Take the bridge."

"On my way, Captain." A reassuring reply came from three decks below in maintenance.

But then, Dezi couldn't see what she could.

Lights blinked in a crazed staccato on the scanner console. Data, ominous and irritatingly incomplete, spilled down the screen. The incoming ship was small, but Trilby's malfunctioning equipment refused to pin down its origins. It could be a Conclave scout ship; it could be a pirate probe. It could also be the first of a squadron of fighters from the-Gods-only-knew-where.

She grabbed her binocs and laser rifle from the utility locker, tabbed the intercom back on. "Main scanner's still not cooperating. I'm going outside for a visual."

A second acknowledgment came, calm as the first.

Good ol' Dezi.

A wave of late-afternoon heat assailed her as she passed under the cavern's high arch. She crouched down between a nest of scrub palms and moss-covered boulders, scanned the sky with her binocs. The bright rays from the setting sun flared painfully into her eyes.

"Damnation!" She flicked her thumb against the autofilter. Nothing happened. The filter was stuck—again. She smacked the binocs hard against her thigh, then brought them back up.

They hazed for a moment then adjusted. She panned the horizon, looking for movement, listening for something other than the jungle's thick silence and the pounding of her own heart. Five minutes passed. Sweat stained her drab-green T-shirt in dark, uneven patches.

Then a flicker, a metallic glint. She locked the binocs on it. The image came into focus and her sweat-dampened skin chilled as she recognized it. It was a Trahtark, a 'Sko high-powered fighter, its distinctive slant-winged shape silhouetted against the sun's final flares.

Quickly, she panned a three-sixty. The rest of the squadron must be there, somewhere. Which also meant a mother ship in orbit. Somewhere. And somewhere, when it involved the 'Sko, was a place much too close for comfort.

But the darkening violet skies showed nothing. Nothing but the lone Tark.

The fighter blinked in and out of the purpling clouds, skittering like a frightened mizzet on a sheet of ice. Trilby knew that, even blind drunk, she could fly better than that. Then the fighter veered out of a cloud bank, and she saw the unmistakable signs of laser damage scoring the portside flank. Now the fighter's seesawing motions made sense.

It wasn't the lead attacker, but the prey.

She took another quick scan of the sky. A Conclave border squadron in pursuit of the Tark might pick up her own energy signature. She'd have a bit of explaining to do then. And no doubt a handful of fines to pay with money she didn't have. But the scan revealed nothing.

Then the Tark dropped so close to the top of the jungle that she held her breath, waiting for the sound of impact.

It came with a grinding, screeching, snapping

sound—metal against damp wood—then metal against rock. The Tark screamed to a halt on one of the few areas of jungle floor that wasn't submerged under Avanar's infamous swamps. Trilby was already on her feet, surveying the area with her binocs now set on night-watch. The first glimmer of orange flame licked into the night sky. A few minutes later she smelled a hint of acrid smoke, invisible in the diminishing light.

She panned another three-sixty. A Conclave patrol would have been here by now. But the skies were empty, quiet.

Her breathing and heartbeat slowed to normal. And a wicked smile crept across her face. The Tark's status had just shifted from threat to profit.

She judged the crash site to be about two miles to the south. A safe distance but clearly workable. Not for a rescue; a Conclave ship in distress would've had her already hollering at Dezi to load a 'scooter with a med-kit.

This was 'Sko. Which was, as far as she and every other Independent freighter captain were concerned, just another word for intergalactic garbage.

Pricey—and dangerous—intergalactic garbage, but garbage all the same.

She cataloged her options. The sun had slipped away as she watched the ship, and the night air wrapped around her bare arms like a damp and heavy cloak. The first of Avanar's three moons had risen, pale and sickly.

Not the ideal conditions in which to perform a salvage attempt, especially on a fire-damaged 'Sko fighter. If she waited until morning, the flames licking at the starboard wing of the Tark would have died, the metal cooled. And the 'Sko pilot, if injured, would be weakened, or preferably dead. Dead would be nice. Everyone knew an injured 'Sko could be even more blood-crazed than a healthy one. She probably should wait until morning, although she'd be battling sweltering temperatures then.

But the fire flickered out as she watched. Doused, she assumed, by an emergency extinguisher system.

That was good. In fact, it could be more than good, she told herself, realizing she'd already made the decision to inspect the downed Tark in spite of the encroaching darkness and unknown status of the pilot. It was the answer to her problems. With minimal fire damage, there was sure to be something salvageable, something to sell at Port Rumor or Bagrond. 'Sko components were rare and brought more than decent money, even at salvage rates.

Decent money was something Trilby was a bit short of right now. And her supply of indecent money was running perilously low.

She caught the glint of Dezi's metallic, somewhat humanoid form as she turned around. The DZ-9 'droid waited at the base of the *Venture*'s rampway. The bulky freighter loomed over him, almost protectively. They'd been in the middle of repairs when the alarm had wailed in warning.

"Looks like we got a keeper," she told the 'droid as she trotted toward the slanting metal rampway. "Bring out two AGSs with loaders. I'm going to grab some more firepower, just in case we've got company." She patted his tarnished shoulder as she passed by. "Thanks, Dez."

"You're quite welcome, Captain. It's always my pleasure to be useful."

She ducked through the air lock, grinning, as Dezi's voice trailed off behind her. Four months ago that small courtesy would've sparked a big dissension. Jagan had always found her habit of thanking Dezi annoying. 'Droids were one of many things that didn't require appreciation, in his way of thinking.

But she was no longer concerned with Jagan Grantforth's way of thinking, and so was free to revert to her impulsive and irresponsible ways. Or however it was that Jagan and his mother had termed how she lived her life.

She could still see his handsome and haughty face on his last transmit: "Mother was right. You are nothing but low-class trash from Port Rumor."

Better than high-class trash from Bagrond, she'd wanted to tell him, but never did. He wouldn't have understood. By that point in their relationship, she knew, they didn't even speak the same language.

She shook off the bad memories, plucked her faded service jacket from her closet, then went in search of an extra laser pistol that worked.

She stepped off the ramp to find Dezi complaining about one of the AGSs.

"I do believe, Captain, that the support stands for these units must be replaced very soon. You can see here where this bar is completely rusted. Should something of a greater weight than I be seated—"

She sighed. "We'll add it to the list, okay? But the AGSs are going to have to wait until we get the comm pack back online and my portside scanner replaced. AGS stands aren't going to be a whole lot of help," she said, straddling the bulky scooter, "in avoiding 'Sko nests between here and Port Rumor."

"I was only making the suggestion for future reference."

"You're very thorough. I do appreciate it, believe me."

"Well, thank you. I always try to—"

"Dezi."

The 'droid cocked his tarnished head in Trilby's direction. "Yes?"

"Let's go. There's a wreck waiting for us."

"Oh, yes. Right. I was just about to—"

But Trilby had already gunned her scooter, activated the antigrav unit, and dropped over the ledge and out of sight by the time Dezi reached the point of explaining just what he was about to do. And doing it.

She set the AGS down as close as she could to the smoldering wreckage. The 'Sko fighter had flattened an area in the jungle at least twenty feet wide and three times as long before it ended up in a grove of gnarled harelnut palms. One of the bronze giants tilted sideways, its long, drooping fronds sooty and brittle from contact with the remains of the Tark's fire-blackened engine. Her headlamp flooding the scene before her, Trilby flicked the safety off her pistol.

The sleek fighter was skewed into the soft ground, its starboard wing ripped from the fuselage. The port wing impaled the thick fronds of another tightly packed grove of palms. But other than that, it was surprisingly intact. She didn't know if she should give credit to the pilot or the autoguidance system.

She placed her headlight on wide-beam, throwing a swath of light over the wreckage. Dezi followed suit.

"You start aft. I'll take a look up here." She grabbed a hand beam from the AGSs utility compartment and played it over the cockpit area. The canopy had sheared off, leaving the cockpit open and exposed. She steeled herself for the inevitable mangled remains in a flight suit; she'd seen no chute deploy prior to impact, so obviously the pilot didn't have a chance to eject.

But the cockpit was empty. A jolt of fear roiled queasily in her gut. "Oh, great," she said softly, then, louder: "Dezi. Over here, now."

She heard the thudding of his feet on the ground. "Can I be of assistance?"

"Watch my back." She transferred her beam to her left hand and brought her pistol, primed, into her right. "Our 'Sko pilot's disappeared."

The 'droid stepped closer and inspected the empty cockpit. "Highly unusual."

"Tell that to the pilot when we find him. 'Cause he's not in there. Which means," she played her beam in a slow, wide circle around her, "that he—or she—is out there. Somewhere."

The night seemed to close in on her. The pale light of the moons elongated the shadows, and they danced and wove eerily in the periphery of her high beam.

Someone or something was out there, and it was 'Sko armed and 'Sko trained. She listened carefully, hearing only the sound of her own breathing and the slight squeak of Dezi's joints as he moved in the opposite direction. She damned herself for not latching the datalyzer onto her utility belt. But the life-form sensor had been relegated to her growing pile of nonfunctional equipment.

Well, live and learn. She hoped she would manage the former long enough to do the latter.

She swept the area with her beam again, probing the recesses of the night, searching for the telltale red of the 'Sko uniform. Blood red, like the carnage they caused devastating trade depots, mining colonies, cargo freighters. The 'Sko acquired, butchering whoever stood in their way—including their own wounded.

She shivered slightly, in spite of the hot night air.

You'd better be dead, you motherless son of a Pillorian bitch. After all, she didn't ask for the 'Sko to crash right in her front yard. But the fact that he did—and the fact that Trilby was, as far as she knew, the only sentient being on a world that most of civilized space wanted nothing to do with—gave her the unalienable salvage rights.

Finders keepers. It was worth the risk.

Plus, she desperately needed the money. And only someone as desperate as she was would be crawling around in the Avanarian jungle at night, looking for a—Gods willing and luck with her—dead 'Sko.

She found his boot heels first and froze in her stance. A male, from the size of the boots. Her beam traveled up the length of his uniformed legs. Black uniform. Not red.

The black-clad form lying in the deep grass wasn't moving.

"Dezi!"

The thudding steps came quickly this time.

"You appear to have found him." The 'droid's beam played up the length of the man's back and over a head covered with dark hair. The pilot had fallen face-first, his arms extended crookedly over his head.

"He's dead, isn't he?" Trilby asked hopefully.

Dezi bent closer to the pilot's head. "Actually, no. There is evidence of slight respiration."

"Damnation." Trilby hunkered down next to the pilot, the light from her beam illuminating his pale profile. The long grasses hid all but one dark brow and a closed eye. A purplish bruise had already formed on his cheekbone.

She pulled at the dark cloth of the jacket collar, revealing a black shirt and a collar with a distinctive gray diamond-shaped design. Beneath, she found the pulse she was looking for. It was strong.

Again, she swore. Softly. "I can't . . . we can't just leave him here."

"Captain. I strongly advise against bringing an Ycsko—"

"He's not 'Sko." For one thing, he was obviously human. The 'Sko . . . well, no one was really sure what the 'Sko were. "He's Zafharin, judging from the uniform."

"The Empire. Well, yes. That's different."

Was it? Trilby asked herself as she and Dezi carefully loaded the unconscious form on the expanded pallet of the AGS. The Empire and the Conclave, in which she claimed a loose citizenship, were rivals, maintaining a trade relationship with only the barest sheen of civility. But they had been enemies in the past. The Imperial–Conclave War had ended about three years ago.

She wasn't political, but neither was she stupid. The Zafharin Empire was very powerful. If it hadn't been for the advent of 'Sko aggression, they probably would have annexed all of Conclave space years ago.

A three-year-old truce declared she could no longer look upon the man on the pallet as her enemy.

But she could still be careful. Very, very careful.

He had, she reminded herself, been dumped on her doorstep courtesy of the Ycsko. That alone would take some explaining.

The medistat in the *Venture*'s small sick bay logged in her guest as Unknown Male Humanoid, but not much more. Trilby watched Dezi review the data from the barely functioning unit.

"How bad is he? Just an overview," she quickly added before Dezi could begin. "I know we can't get the details."

"Minor lacerations externally, but I don't believe there's been substantial blood loss. A mild concussion. And either some oddly random internal bruising or the unit is misreading again. But vitals are strong."

"It's the damned unit. Any clue who he is?"

Dezi tapped at the panel. "Humanoid male in his early forties. Six feet three inches in height. Two hundred fifteen pounds. No tattoos or subcutaneous identification chips."

"A man of mystery, eh? Unstrap his boots. I'll get his jacket and shirt off." They were in worse shape than their owner, with laser burns on the jacket's left side and a long tear down the front of the shirt.

"His pants too. The regeneration needs to—oh! Would you prefer I undress our patient, Captain?"

"I've seen naked men before. But thanks for defending my virginity." She grinned at the 'droid. "You're a tad late, though."

She pulled off the black jacket, then the shirt, as carefully as she could. A harsh line of darkening bruises started at the pilot's left shoulder and continued under the soft mat of curly black hair sprinkled across his torso. The bruises marred a well-muscled body that seemed younger than the age the medistat had assigned. She'd seen enough spacers and company-freighter officers in her thirty-three years to know that long hours seated at flight controls—and even longer 'tween time seated on a bar stool in station pubs—weren't conducive to a flat stomach and muscled shoulders.

Even Jagan, at thirty-eight, had gone soft around the middle. Though she doubted he'd ever had a body quite as nicely defined as this.

She and Dezi slid the regeneration cylinder over the pilot's body and latched it in place. Maybe the medistat was wrong. Maybe he was a younger crew member and not an officer as his uniform suggested. Fewer responsibilities and smaller salaries often meant grunts spent more time in a ship's gym than in high-priced bars and eateries.

But no. The lines around his eyes attested to a familiarity with tension and stress. His face, with its square jaw and thick dark brows and mustache, was strong and almost stern. But not unattractive. Still, she had a feeling that it was the sternness most people would remember. Smile lines were noticeably absent.

She moved a lock of hair from his forehead. There was more bruising to match the welt on his cheek. He stirred slightly. Quickly, she withdrew her hand, surprised he'd sensed her touch. Or had he? The regen unit had already tranked him to mask any pain. His reaction might just be coincidental.

She considered adjusting the sedative dosage manually. That would leave him in an unconscious state longer. But her curiosity right now was stronger than her fear of this Zafharin officer, her former enemy.

After all, it wasn't as if he were going to come bounding out of sick bay, naked, and chase her around her ship.

Still, a bit of precaution was advisable. Especially as she had some quick work to do back at the wreck. She removed the rifle strap from around her shoulder and tossed the weapon to Dezi. The 'droid caught it gingerly.

"Keep him tranked up as long as you can," she said. "But if he wakes, make sure he knows you mean business."

"Of course, Captain." Dezi drew himself to attention as Trilby stepped past him. His voice followed her out into the corridor. "But what business am I supposed to be in?"

The deep-night hours on Avanar, home to a variety of lethal nocturnal reptiles, were inhospitable to further salvage work. She gunned the AGS in the darkness, its pallet heavy with bulky components, and headed back to her ship. There was still time, however, for her to clean up, then stop briefly in sick bay just to make sure their guest was still alive.

He was. Satisfied, she returned to her bridge and perused the latest shipping-quote requests she'd managed to download before her comm package had gone off-line.

Requests were dwindling. Only four this past septi, eleven for the month. She could remember over forty per month this same time a year ago.

The small-freighter business was in bad shape. A series of recent raids by the 'Sko had all but obliterated any decent contracts. No one wanted to risk shipping goods on short-haul freighters with antiquated navigational systems and inadequate defenses. Nor ship them through a quadrant like Gensiira, where the Conclave border patrols were out of funds and, at best, merely decorative when they were in the lanes.

So business had moved to the pricier, but well-protected, large freighter companies, like Rinnaker, Norvind, and Grantforth Galactic. They could afford to hire private security escorts to protect their ships and cargo. And put small traders like her out of business as a result.

It flitted briefly through her mind how eerily the situation mimicked her relationship with Jagan. They'd met when business was good, contracts coming in at a nicely profitable pace. He'd demanded as much of her attention as the shipping agents had. But then the raids had started, and little by little those same agents avoided her transmits.

And Jagan canceled dates.

Then four months ago the bottom had fallen out.

"We can't work with independents," the agents had said.

"I'm marrying Zalia," Jagan had told her.

She leaned back in her chair, pinched the bridge of her nose. *To hell with Grantforth. And the 'Sko.* Then, as an afterthought, she added: *To hell with the Zafharin.* The war with the Empire, her government announced, had drained their budgets. But it didn't keep them from slapping more taxes onto the already high dock fees at the station depots off Quivera and

Bagrond, or dirtside ports like Rumor. Nor from levying heavy fines on any small trader who was found with illegal weapons-systems upgrades. Like the set of LD-5 torpedoes she had her eye on. Word of that, spread quietly through the trading community, could improve her chances for contracts.

But Lady-Fives wouldn't do her a bit of good if she couldn't get her communications package working again. Even her customizations there were illegal: range boosters and transmit scramblers were frowned upon but essential to survival in Gensiira.

And she needed them; her customers depended on her ability to stay one step ahead of the 'Sko and the government. The Techplat contract was proof: they had a good-size pickup ready for her at Bagrond as soon as she finished her repair work here.

That run would pay for the auxiliary drive feed she installed last month. She didn't want to think about who or what was going to pay for her new comm package.

For the next twenty minutes she tried to cajole her ship's failing comm system to handshake with her new range boosters. It was an effort that only produced more problems, including a cramp in her leg.

She slid awkwardly out of the narrow maintenance tunnel and limped toward sick bay.

Dezi was still diligently on guard.

"Anything new this hour?"

"No, Captain. He's still improving. Vital signs appear to be stronger."

"That's encouraging. But I was wondering if we should—"

"*Nav! S'viek noyet.*" A deep male voice rasped over her words.

Trilby watched the man's head move slowly side to side. His respiration rate was increasing. He murmured again, but more softly. On the panel covering his chest, a series of lights danced first green, then yellow, then green again.

"He's still having nightmares."

"It could be a reaction to the trank. The regen does not indicate anything threatening."

"To him, maybe not, Dez. But I know Zafharish when I hear it. And it never, ever sounds good. Even if I don't have the damnedest idea of what he's saying."

More proof of the Conclave's lack of concern for its citizenry, in Trilby's estimation. The desperately needed Zafharish-to-Standard translation programs, required by the Conclave to conduct business in the trade lanes bordering the zone, were two years behind in distribution.

"I regret I have no extensive knowledge of Zafharish either. However, I do believe *nav* indicates *no*."

"And *vad* means *yes*, and *dharjas taf, viek* is what you'd say to get a cold beer. But unless he speaks Standard, I doubt my pub-crawling vocabulary is going to help me find out his name. Or his rank. Or how in the Seven Hells he ended up here in a 'Sko fighter."

Trilby glanced at the tattered black uniform draped in the closet opposite the diag bed. She'd already turned it inside out, hoping to find some clue to his identity. The slight possibility of a reward hadn't escaped her notice. And the higher the rank, the greater the reward. That is, providing the Empire wanted him back.

But any ship's ID patches were conspicuously missing.

In the hours that followed, she and Dezi played

with theories as to how a Zafharin pirate could end up with a 'Sko Tark.

It couldn't have been easy.

The two factions probably hated each other almost as much as Conclave trading companies hated them. If not more. Yet since the war's end, there had been rumors of a power shift. Of individuals high in the Zafharin Empire who were willing to sit down at the table with certain other individuals in the Ycsko.

For the most part, the rumors were disregarded. The two were incompatible. The Ycsko were as lunatic in their organizations as they were in their raids. Both Niyil military parties fought with the Dakrahl religious faction who plotted against all six Beffa trading cartels. High Rulers were crowned almost as frequently as Trilby filed flight plans.

The Zafharin were more organized, though no less deadly. Theirs was a linear society, patriarchal. Clan name bestowed rank and status. The House of Vanurin had reigned for more than eight centuries; Kasmov, its emperor, for the last thirty-one years. His eldest son and daughter sat in positions of power in the Council of Lords.

Vanurin blood also ruled in the Zafharin Fleet. First High-Commander, Lord Admiral Neville Vanushavor, was Kasmov's cousin. Two of his sons held the rank of Senior Captain. Even more powerful than Vanushavor's sons was Senior Captain Tivahr. Port gossip tagged him to be a brilliant but arrogant, cold-blooded man who knew nothing of fear. Or compassion.

Cooperation between the 'Sko and the Zafharin seemed unlikely. Still, both factions had the same goal: the acquisition of Conclave goods and, it was said, the eventual domination of Conclave space.

Neither of which was encouraging to Independent traders like Trilby Elliot. Political machinations, border disputes, and the constant games of spy versus spy between the 'Sko and the Zafharin were just more aggravations on a struggling freighter captain's already long list. Whatever funds she could grasp from salvaging the Tark were, as far as she was concerned, way overdue.

And if the Zafharin Empire had the decency to throw some reward money her way as well, those Lady-Fives she desperately needed might just become her ticket to happiness.

If she didn't decide to hunt down Jagan Grantforth and use them on him first.

2

He knew where he was. He recognized the pitted gray metal walls, the filthy stone floor. His cell on Szedcafar.

But this time Rafi was there, in full dress uniform. Gold braid on one shoulder, medals glinting on his chest. And Malika, in a provocative black skinsuit. Gemstones dangled from her ears and wrists.

And another woman, smaller than Malika. She had silvery-blond hair and was dressed in faded green fatigues. She wore no glinting medals, no gems. Yet her very simplicity made Rafi look pompous, and Malika harsh and tawdry.

The red glow of a force field pulsed all around them. They were prisoners. He knew they had to escape but Malika wouldn't listen. She laughed at him and stroked his face, taunting him.

He batted her hand away, annoyed, then again saw the woman in green. She stood on the other side of a wide chasm in the floor, reaching out to him. She

*reminded him of the air sprites in his childhood sto-
ries. Or the Gelfaia, legends from the Faytari Drifts,
worshiped by the 'Sko for their fragile beauty.*

*He called to her, but she didn't seem to understand
his words. Yet she wanted to help. Somehow he knew
that. He was moving toward the edge of the chasm
when Malika grabbed his arm.*

*"She is common." Her voice hissed cruelly. "Low-
born. Do not soil yourself with her contact."*

*"She can help," he said to Malika, and looked at
Rafi for assistance. But Rafi only shrugged and
looked away.*

*Suddenly, the Ycsko were there—seven of them, al-
most skeletal in appearance in spite of their billowing
red robes. The air sprite spoke quickly to him. Her
words sounded like a warning.*

*Next to him, Malika laughed again, higher now,
almost hysterically. She handed something to the red-
robed Ycsko. A cylinder. A hypospray.*

*He watched it come closer, knowing once it
touched his neck the pain would start, flooding his
body, burning his mind. He tried to will it away by
sheer force of thought . . .*

His eyes shot open. The stark whiteness of the
walls rushed in, almost blinding him. He flinched in
pain, but silently. Always silently.

Then the darkness engulfed him, and he slept.

After a while his eyelids fluttered again, more
slowly this time, letting his pupils adjust to the light.
It didn't seem quite as bright as before but still stung
his brain like a thousand needles.

He forced himself not to hurry his surreptitious
scrutiny, yet his body was on alert. The memory of his
short-lived captivity by the 'Sko came back, with the

pain of their drugs and interrogation attempts. His ears took in the low whoosh-and-hum of something around him. It didn't sound or feel like the high-ceilinged, brightly lit interrogation room he remembered.

Through slitted eyes he glanced around, aware of the diagnostic cylinder fitted over his body.

He was in a medical unit, a small one. Ill-equipped too: his regen bed was the only one.

He longed to move his head, flex the aching muscles in his arms and—damn!—scratch that insistent itching over his wounds. But his senses had alerted him to another presence. He wasn't yet ready to make an official appearance. Not until he knew exactly where he was, and why.

Years of intense training allowed him to feign sleep. Not even the regen bed registered any change in his heart rate or respiration. Yet he was completely aware of all his surroundings. By habit he began calculating the distance between his left side and the wall. Three feet six inches, roughly. The wall to his right was five feet from him, perhaps two inches more. It contained a small ship's diagram, illuminated icons showing emergency stations and fire equipment locations.

He memorized the diagram.

There was a doorway, a hatchway about seven feet from the line of his right shoulder.

A metallic-skinned 'droid, an old DZ-9, he noted with mild surprise, stood by the hatchway, laser rifle in hand. Its joints squeaked every so often as it changed position to glance down the corridor or at the panel on the wall.

Since when, he wondered, had envoy 'droids been used in security? And by whom?

If that were the only impediment . . . but then there was a sound. Quick footsteps approaching on a metal floor. The steps echoed, solitary, telling him the walker was alone in the corridor. He heard no other noises, no other people but the walker and the 'droid.

He listened to the cadence of the steps, mentally timing their separation. Whoever was coming toward him was light in weight and short in stature. Probably female.

She was. As the woman entered the room, the dim overhead lighting caught the glisten of gold in her short cap of pale hair. Rafi would have described her face as winsome, sweet, with large, long-lashed eyes. And a mouth with just the right touch of poutiness. But Senior Captain Rafiello Vanushavor was an inveterate lady's man, well versed in cataloging a female's charms.

Unlike Rafi, his own expertise lay more with weapons and strategies. A woman's allurements were inconsequential. His exposure to Malika had taught him just how shallow those outward observations could be. And how painfully wrong.

"How's he doing this morning?" The woman's question drew his attention. She spoke Standard. He knew immediately he was on the wrong side of the zone.

"Still unconscious," the 'droid replied. "Though the nightmares have stopped."

"I don't understand why he's still out cold. When's the last time you ran a diagnostics?"

"Ten minutes ago. But internal diagnostics is off-line again. I can bring up the data manually, through the medistat, if you want to look at it."

She sighed tiredly. "Maybe I should."

The 'droid turned to interface with a small console near the door. "The medistat will relay test results on its screen in forty-three seconds, Captain."

Captain? She was too young to hold such rank. Perhaps in her twenties? He found it difficult to judge her age through his narrowed eyes, but the outline of her form was clear against the room's white walls. The top of her dark-green shirt hung open to her waist, its sleeves rolled up. The tight sleeveless ribbed T-shirt underneath hugged her breasts. The curve of her hips and rear filled out the baggy pants. A wide utility belt sagged around her small waist from the weight of a laser pistol and several spare charger clips. It wasn't the uniform of a med-tech.

She stepped closer, studied the screen on the diag cylinder. A sweet, musky scent of flowers and perfumed powder drifted to him.

"Think we should risk a stim? I don't see anything here that tells me why he's still unconscious."

"His level of pain may be too great."

It was. He used the pain as a point of focus. He'd lived with pain, and the discipline it brought, almost his whole life.

He'd also lived with the knowledge of his power, his control. He'd be there again. Soon. He just needed for her to come a little closer.

He slowed his hearbeat, his breathing, using methods he had been taught over thirty years ago. Just a few more seconds. Just a little closer . . .

A red light flashed in warning on the cylinder.

"Damn, what's happening?" There was a note of panic in her voice.

"A cardiac irregularity." The 'droid stepped quickly to the other side of the unit. "I cannot tell if it's serious enough—"

The diagram and diagnostic panels blinked off in one swift motion. The cylinder went dark.

"Shit! What'd you do?"

"I did nothing. I was merely attempting to calibrate the unit."

"He's stopped breathing, damn it!" She quickly unlatched the lock on the unit, sliding it down the bed.

He felt her hand on his throat, her fingers prodding gently for a pulse. Her voice was tense in his ear. "Don't you *dare* die on me, you ungrateful son of a Pillorian bitch! I'm in enough trouble already. I—"

He moved with unerring precision. One hand clamped tightly around her neck. He clasped her left wrist with his other and yanked her arm up behind her back. Thrown off balance, she fell forward and was crushed against his chest.

Her cry of terror vibrated against him like a personal warning siren.

"*Yagash!* Quiet!" He quickly amended his harsh command into her language. To control her meant control of the 'droid. He'd deal with any other crew later. His fingers expertly splayed across the base of her throat, finding the vulnerable artery. "Make a move and she's dead."

The 'droid appeared stunned, his metallic arms making small, jerky movements. The laser rifle rattled in his grasp.

"You really don't have to do this, you know." Her

voice was small, muffled against his bare chest. He inched her arm up further. She yelped in pain.

"Please, do not hurt her." The 'droid's plea almost reached a whine.

"Drop the rifle." He pulled himself upright, holding the woman against him in a crushing grip. "Drop it and kick it toward the door."

There was a clank of metal as the rifle hit the decking and then the scraping sound of it clattering across the floor.

"Now, come here."

"Sir?"

"Here, damn it!" He stood, leaning on the edge of the bed. He spun her around so she faced the 'droid. "Her belt and holster. Undo it. Now!"

"Wait!" The woman squirmed against him, then tried to look up. "You don't have to—"

He briefly clasped her jaw in his fingers, wrenched her face back to the 'droid. "Tell him to undo your belt."

"Look, you don't understand!" Her words came out in a pain-filled rush. "Dezi, tell him—"

"Captain, perhaps now is not the time to argue. My memory banks are not one hundred percent accurate, but it appears he is holding your throat either in the paralyzing *G'zhen Dai* grip used by thirty-second-century warrior-monks on Dakrahl—"

"Dezi!"

"—or the fatal *Tah Fral* employed by the Order of Despi Guild assassins. Unfortunately, my graphic overlays for both files are rather vague."

"But he doesn't—"

"The belt," he repeated harshly. "Undo it!"

The 'droid stepped gingerly toward him. Metal

fingers unthreaded the clasp. The belt clattered to the floor.

"Kick it toward the door."

The 'droid did as he was ordered and looked back expectantly.

"Now, get on the diag table."

"But, sir, I'm not injured and these units don't work on—"

"Get on the table! Now!"

The 'droid climbed stiffly onto the bed.

"Lie down and pull the cover over you."

There was the slight hiss as the cylinder was drawn up on the rails.

"Good."

In a swift movement, he released the woman's arm, locked the cylinder in place, then yanked her back against his chest. One hand still cupped her throat. The other pinned her arms at her waist. He brought his mouth down to her ear. Her light flowery scent drifted over him again.

"Try anything, *anything*, and you are dead." He could feel her pulse beating frantically under his fingers.

"You really"—her voice came out in gulping gasps—"don't have to do this."

"Move!" He shoved her toward the hatchway and stopped at the opening. "Now. I am going to release your arms. For a second. To pick up the weapons. But I still have one hand on your throat. Do not try anything stupid." His fingertips dug more deeply into her skin. "Do you understand?"

She inhaled painfully, barely able to breathe out an affirmative.

He reached down, dragging her with him, and

snatched up the rifle and her utility belt. He quickly slung the rifle's strap over his shoulder as he straightened, then, making sure his fingers were still firmly digging into her throat, pulled the pistol from her utility belt. He dropped the belt to the floor and yanked her firmly back against him.

The series of movements cost him. A searing, stabbing heat shot up his neck. He drew in a sharp breath. He had no time for this. He focused his mind. Tensed his body. And felt the softness of her hair against his chest. The firm swell of her behind against his . . .

Bloody hell! He was completely naked.

His plans of forcing her to the bridge and commandeering her ship suddenly took a sharp turn. He took a half step back from her, self-consciously, and pressed the hard muzzle of the pistol into her back.

The reality—and analogy—of what *had* been pressing against her wasn't lost on him. "Take two steps forward." Discomfort gritted in his words.

They faced the wall. The wall and the small utility closet.

"But—"

"Now!" He pushed her forward. She stumbled, and he thrust the closet door aside. "Pants!"

She grabbed them and started to turn, but he forced her another half step forward. He had no desire to see her reaction to his unclothed state. Or his body's reaction to her. "Move when I tell you to, and only then."

She offered the pants from over one shoulder. He ripped them from her grasp. Making sure she was trapped against the half-open closet door, he balanced precariously first on one leg, then the other, as he pulled on his pants.

She followed his orders in the same manner with his jacket and his boots. He shoved his bare feet into them without bothering to secure the straps.

Now. Shall we try this again?

He grabbed her arm, yanking her backward. But she surprised him and used his own force to spin around and face him. Her eyes blazed in anger.

"I don't know what you think you're trying to prove—"

Fool, he thought. Then: *gutsy little fool.*

"Silence!" He swiftly bent her arm around her back. She yelped, stumbled against him. He made sure she felt the muzzle of the pistol in her side.

"Now. Move!"

She swore at him in response. But very quietly.

He dragged her into the corridor and stopped, looking quickly left and right. The corridor was stark, gray, with flat metal bulkheads and decking common to most freighters. Conduit and piping snaked overhead. The light strip along the top of the wall glowed in broken patches where burnouts hadn't been replaced. A square intercom speaker was duct-taped to the wall a few feet away.

His mind replicated the image of the emergency diagram in the sick bay. What he saw now supported his theory. The ship was probably an old Circura IV, minimum crew complement of five.

Well, he knew of two.

With a rough shove, he propelled her in the direction of the bridge. A diffused glow at the end signaled the open hatchway. He stopped. "How many others?"

"Other what?"

"Do not be insolent. I have no tolerance for it."

She tried to turn in his grasp to look up at him. He grabbed a handful of pale hair and forced her head back against his chest. "How many others?"

"Other 'droids? None."

"Crew?"

"Just Dezi. Just the 'droid. That's it. Just me and the 'droid."

"When do they get back?"

"Who?"

He tightened his arms across her midsection and heard her gasp. He could crush her ribs easily, with little effort, in spite of his own injuries.

"Do not be insol—"

"What do you want to know, damn you? Who are you looking for?"

"The rest of the crew!"

"There is no rest of my crew! That's all there is. Me and Dez. Dez and me. It's the whole show. Gods damn you, that hurts!"

He pushed her again, yanking on her hair. "You cannot run a Circura Four with just two people. The ship's too big for—"

"She's not a Four, she's a Two."

He hesitated. A Circura II? By the Gods, the ship had to be an antique! If she even still flew.

The hatchway to the bridge loomed ahead. He stopped by the opening, listening for any sounds of life, and, hearing none, dragged her up and over the hatch tread.

What he saw on the bridge and through the large viewports confirmed the worst. It was an old Circura II. The bridge was small. Antiquated comp boards were patched into newer systems, none of which seemed to fit quite right. A torn cushion on the captain's chair was repaired with duct tape. Thin black cables, tied together with red ribbon, snaked over the forward command console. A tiny plush toy resembling a felinar, wide-eyed and whiskered, dangled from another length of the same red ribbon attached to the ceiling conduit.

And they weren't in space. They weren't even berthed in any known station or spaceport. They were dirtside in the mouth of what looked to be a large cavern that, judging from the steam rising in the early-morning air, overlooked a thick, tropical jungle.

There wasn't another ship, not another soul around.

It made absolutely no sense.

He pulled his hand from her hair and spun her about, grasping her roughly by the elbow. He shoved the pistol against her ribs. *"Kazat merash! Gdro deya?"*

"What?"

It took him a moment to realize he'd barked at her in Zafharish again. He was getting sloppy. Inexplicably. "Where in the Seven Hells are we?"

"Avanar. At least, I call it Avanar." Her eyes narrowed. "Where did you think you were?"

"Av-an-ar?" The name meant nothing to him.

"Yes."

"And where is this Avanar?"

"Quadrant 84-YC-7 on my charts. Gensiira System. About a trike from Port Rumor. It's a small H-4 planet, uninhabited. Unless you count the bloodbats and vampire snakes."

He remembered now. A sweltering, inhospitable world briefly used by the Conclave to house a defensive sensor array during the war. But before the

Empire could formulate plans to destroy it, the planet's high humidity and corrosive environment disabled the equipment. It had rotted into the swamps under one-hundred-twenty-degree temperatures.

From the steamy brightness visible through the forward viewports, it looked to be approaching that now.

He looked back down at the small female before him. The top of her head didn't even reach his shoulders.

She tried to angle her body away from the pistol digging against her ribs. He tightened his grip on her arm, pulling her closer. "How much did they pay you to bring me here?"

She gave him a hard look that clearly questioned his intelligence. "I didn't bring you here. And nobody paid me anything. You brought yourself here in a 'Sko Tark, which you, without so much as a by-your-leave, dumped on my doorstep. I went down to salvage it, expecting at worst a dead 'Sko, which I could handle. I found you, alive. What did you expect me to do? Leave you there as a feast for the local flora and fauna?"

He saw the rows of flattened palms, like a large, long footprint in the jungle, through the viewport behind her. "You were not taking me back to Conclave Security on Quivera Station?"

"That would be damned stupid of me. Considering there're at least two arrest warrants with my ID on them there."

"Warrants? For what?"

She sighed. "The usual shit. Code violations. Manifest documentation violations. A couple of drunk-and-disorderlies. Things all low-budget short-haulers run into."

"And you are here because of a . . . code-violation warrant?"

"Of course not," she replied indignantly. "I'm here because I finally scrounged up a booster that would interface with my comm pack. I needed someplace to do an install."

He stared blankly at her. His mind seemed to be moving very slowly all of a sudden. Why would a mercenary working for the Conclave use this un-known hell as a repair station? Quivera had excellent facilities in their docks.

"You work on your ship here?" He nodded to the jungle behind her.

She wriggled her shoulders again, clearly uncom-fortable. But he had no intention of releasing her un-til he was sure of his situation. At the moment, nothing made sense.

"Yeah, here," she said. "It's cheap. Free rent. With no poke-noseys breathing down my neck, logging vi-olations. Or handing me slap-wrists on my 'illegal customizations,' as they call them. That way I don't end up getting pissed off and taking a swing at them, so that my ass lands in min-sec for a deuce while they're charging me dock rental the whole time."

He listened to her words, heard the lingo that flowed down seedy freighter docks in the Conclave as freely as cheap beer. A poke-nosey was a govern-ment inspector. A slap-wrist was a government fine. Min-sec was the minimum-security jail, usually filled with freighter crew sleeping off their latest binge. And a deuce was two days.

It finally clicked in his mind. The little spitfire glaring up at him, struggling against his grip, wasn't a threat, wasn't even capable of being a threat. She was simply a low-budget freighter captain who got a bit more than she bargained for when she rescued him from the jungle floor.

Abruptly, he released her elbow and pointed the pistol toward the chair at the nav station. "Sit down."

She sat and gingerly arched her neck and back.

He ran his hand over his face, feeling an unaccustomed twinge of guilt. "It . . . it seems there has been a misunderstanding," he said slowly. He wasn't used to apologizing. But then, he wasn't used to making mistakes.

"Misunderstanding? No shit. You could've killed me."

"I thought . . . I was under the impression you were a bounty hunter taking me back to Quivera."

"The war ended over three years ago, Mister Wizard. Or haven't you noticed?" She didn't disguise the irritation in her voice. "The Conclave and your Empire have a peace treaty going. And even if I were capable of taking you back to Quivera, which I'm not, it certainly ain't worth killing me over. I mean, the food sucks and the government makes sure all the public bars water the booze, but it ain't worth killing me over."

Her flippancy infuriated him, momentarily eclipsing his regret at his actions. "My position is a bit more delicate than your impudent remarks—"

"Don't you dare call me impudent!" Her voice shook. "I've earned the right to be impudent! I bring you on my ship, try to save your life. And you lock my 'droid in the regen bed and damn near break my ribs. Plus, I've got a headache so bad that my hair hurts. So don't you dare tell me I can't be impudent!"

And with that she swung the chair away from him and plopped her boots up on the nav console, as if signaling to anyone and everyone within range that there was no more to say on the subject.

Anger surged through him. Ignorant little fool! He wanted to grab the back of her chair, spin her about, force her to face him. Thoughts and emotions churned in disarray, not at all helped by the low but constant throb of pain in his body. No one spoke to him like that without suffering the consequences. He was the one who should be rightfully indignant, who should remind her just who she was talking to.

Except that she didn't know.

That stopped him cold. Made him open the fist he'd clenched in his fury and drop it to his side. She didn't know. Oh, from the uniform she had to assume he was Zafharin. It was an officer's uniform, there was no denying that. But his name and his rank were not apparent.

He should tell her. Now. She'd be fearful. Obedient. Controllable. She'd never dare turn her back on him in such an insulting manner.

In such an interesting manner. Intriguing manner.

He brought his breathing under control. And felt an unexpected twinge of fascination that surprised him.

There was something amusing in the absurdity of it all—this jungle world, this derelict ship, this little green-eyed spitfire . . .

A corner of his mouth quirked into a small, unaccustomed smile. He flicked the safety back on the pistol, shoved it into the waistband of his pants. He took a moment, rubbed his knuckles over the damned itching on his side, reconsidered his options.

Perhaps it would be better, just for now, if she didn't know who he was. If she thought she could trust him. Strictly for security reasons, of course.

But security reasons did dictate that he determine her identity.

"What's your name?" He leaned against a sensor panel partition and folded his arms across his chest. When she didn't reply, he added, "How may I apologize if I do not know your name?"

She touched a button on the armrest and reclined the back of the chair before swiveling around to face him.

"I think you owe me more than an apology." She held out her hand, palm open.

He hesitated, weighed his instinctual desire to retain the weapons against his need for her cooperation. And his own need to appear cooperative. He pulled the pistol from his waistband and handed it to her. She shoved it through her belt, then grabbed the stock of the rifle as he held it toward her.

"That's good, for starters." She lay the rifle across her lap. "Now, who are you?"

He shrugged, lightly, moving easily into his new role. "My clan name is Vanur. My given name, it is a long one, in my language. But it can be shortened to Rhis."

"R-e-e-c-e? And you are Zafharin."

His heritage wasn't a question and he knew that. He made no attempt to hide his accent. And his uniform spoke for itself. "Rhis with an *i*. R-h-i-s. That's how my people spell my name. And obviously I am

Zafharin. I'd have no value to your security people if I were otherwise."

"Oh, they'd love a live 'Sko," she commented absently, then: "Elliot. Two 1s, one *t*. Captain Trilby Elliot."

"And your ship?"

She let her gaze wander around the meager bridge as if in mock inspection. "Umm. You first."

"Me?"

"Yeah, Rhis. You. What ship were you assigned to, before you decided to take a joyride in a Tark?"

His mind worked quickly, knowing delay would be interpreted as prevarication. "The *Razalka*. You know of her?"

"Hell, everyone in civilized space knows the Zafharin's prized huntership. Tivahr's the captain, isn't he?"

"As far as I know, he still is. Or was, three weeks ago, when I . . . when my team and I ran into . . . problems near Szedcafar."

He saw her eyebrows raise and immediately regretted the admission. Szed was a 'Sko world that housed a large military base. It was not a place the Zafharin were known to frequent, uninvited. He thought quickly. "We were part of a war-games exercise. I was the designated target, in a Tark we captured a few years ago." He kept talking, wanting to sound cooperative. "Somehow we crossed the border, became disoriented. I played decoy so they could get back."

"Dangerous game."

He shrugged. "It's part of, what is your expression, my job description?"

Another quizzical raising of eyebrows. But he expected her reaction, wanted it. As well as her next question, which would help solidify his assumed identity.

"And your job is?" she asked.

"Lieutenant. B-Squadron."

"Lieutenant. But—"

Rhis held up one hand. "My turn, I believe. Tell me about your ship."

She hesitated. "Fair enough. She's the *Careless Venture*. Independent starfreighter, registration out of Port Rumor, currently."

"You're an Indy?"

"When I pay my dues."

He nodded, closed his eyes briefly. He knew the thin line many small-freighter operators walked, both financially and legally. "How long have you had her?"

"Five years, give or take a few months."

"You don't see many of these around anymore."

"You mean how do I keep this rust bucket in the space lanes?" She sighed tiredly. "With spit and a prayer, that's how. And to answer the rest of your questions, yes, I told you the truth about there being no other crew. And yes, a DZ-Nine isn't a usual freighter 'droid. But he was part of the bargain when I got the ship and, as with you, I didn't have the heart to leave him to the scrap heap.

"And yes, when I'm allowed to finish the repairs on my communications system, I'm headed for Port Rumor, where I have a one-up to Bagrond waiting for me. You're welcome to come along. Or you're welcome to stay here with the remains of your prize 'Sko fighter and play tiddlywinks with the bloodbats. Frankly, I don't give a mizzet's ass what you choose to do."

He started to reply, but she raised her hand, stilling his words.

"As for right now," she said, standing, "I'm going back down to my sick bay and releasing Dezi." She slung the rifle strap over her shoulder. "And then I'm going to pour myself the biggest glass of iced gin I can find. Because I have a splitter going and my eyes are refusing to focus. And I haven't even had breakfast yet. So if you'll excuse me . . ."

He stopped her progress at the hatchway with a hand on her arm.

"Elliot—" His voice sounded harsher than he wanted it to be. He didn't even know why he'd stopped her, only that he'd reached for her before he was aware of doing so.

She glared up at him. "Look, if you're going to try to kill me again, would you please just be done with it? Because if you're not, you're keeping me from a much-needed drink."

"Go pour yourself a drink. I'll release the 'droid."

She thought over his offer for a moment, then shrugged.

"Be nice to him," she said as he followed her into the corridor. "He's terrified of you."

He nodded tersely, his face again impassive. "I will explain everything." He watched her disappear down the circular ladderway and ignored an illogical desire to trail after her.

The 'droid's head jerked in Rhis's direction as he stepped into the sick bay. Dezi was still locked in the regen bed. His limbs twitched as if someone had poured antifreeze in his circuitry.

"Oh, no. Please, sir, tell me you didn't kill her. Tell me she still lives. She's a good girl, truly she is. A bit wild at times, but—"

"Captain Elliot is pouring herself a drink," he said over Dezi's pained pleadings. He flipped the latch off the cylinder and slid it back. "It was just a misunderstanding," he added as the 'droid scrambled awkwardly to his feet.

Dezi clanked down loudly to the floor and looked up at Rhis. "A misunderstanding. Yes, of course. It had to be. But the captain—Captain Elliot is fine?"

"She's fine." He spied his shirt still hanging in the utility closet and grabbed it. A sharp pain shot down his shoulder. He ignored it. "She said something about pouring herself an iced gin—"

"Ah, yes. In the lounge. It really isn't a lounge, not a true ship's lounge."

"Belowdecks?" he asked, trying to stem the tide of what appeared to be an unending dialogue.

"Belowdecks. Next to the captain's quarters. More exactly, it once was part of the captain's quarters. She—"

"Dezi. Lead the way, I'll follow."

"You want me to . . . ? Oh, yes, of course. This is my ship. That is, it's Captain Elliot's ship. But you are the guest. And . . ." Dezi shuffled quickly out of sick bay, his voice echoing in the empty corridor of the ship.

Rhis followed a pace behind, shaking his head.

Trilby braced her arms against the countertop flanking her small galley and sucked in large gulps of air. She'd almost died. That son of a bitch had almost killed her, all because he'd mistaken her for some Conclave-kissing bounty hunter. She knew that when she stopped shaking she'd find something hilarious in that misidentification, but at the moment nothing seemed funny.

Least of all that she might jeopardize the Techplat contract because of the repair time she'd wasted while arguing with that lunatic.

That naked lunatic. Who'd pressed his admittedly gorgeous body against hers in sick bay, leaving little doubt as to his masculine charms.

Good thing she hadn't made a quip about the proverbial pistol in his pocket. A hysterical giggle rose in her throat but she choked it back. It would be too easy for her laughter to change to tears, for the tension of the past few hours to underscore once again that she was stupid and trusting of all the wrong people.

Like shipping agents who promised her business, then canceled contracts.

Like a man she thought was in love with her. Who married someone else.

Like a Zafharin she thought was harmless, who tried to kill her.

Three for three? She hoisted herself onto one of the two stools bolted to the lounge decking, pulled the laser pistol from its uncomfortable position in her belt, and laid it on the counter. Well, maybe not quite three for three. At least with the Zafharin, she'd obtained 'Sko parts for salvage. A gift from the Gods, that one! She might be able to make a payment on her ship. It would be nice not to have to worry about the repossessors for a while.

She drew the rifle strap over her head, propped the weapon against the bulkhead. Her fingers massaged small circles over the ache in her temples. It would be nice not to worry about anything for a while. Not dwindling business and empty bank accounts. Malfunctioning equipment. Lying bastards of ex-boyfriends. 'Sko pirates. Half-crazed Zafharins—

—wandering around her ship doing the-Gods-knew-what while she sat here in the middle of a pity party. Damnation!

She jerked upright, twisted around, and slammed against something tall and unyielding.

Strong hands caught her firmly by the waist as she tumbled off the bar stool. She lurched forward, grabbed a handful of heavy black fabric with one hand and the ridge of a wide shoulder with the other.

She jerked back, releasing Vanur's jacket as if the

fabric were on fire. "Son of a Pillorian bitch! What do you mean by sneaking up on me like that?"

"I didn't realize you didn't hear us come in. You are all right?"

"I'm fine." Exhausted. Overworked. Jumpy as hell. And no doubt overreacting. But fine. Or at least getting there. Her momentary flare of anger dissolved under the concerned expression on his face. And the fact that she didn't have to go looking for him or Dezi. She saw the 'droid amble through the hatchway, her utility belt in his hand.

She splayed her hands against the front of his jacket and pushed. "I said I'm fine. You can let go now."

His only response was a narrowing of his eyes, as if she were a specimen under scrutiny. An unknown and unexpected specimen.

She hoped he wasn't having flashbacks, thinking she was some kind of Conclave spy. She didn't have the energy or the patience to go through the whole routine again. "Let go, Vanur."

He released her so abruptly that she tottered unsteadily and grabbed the countertop just as he reached for her again.

"Sorry." He seemed as startled as she was.

She brushed away his offered hand. "Dezi?" He looked none the worse for being locked in the regen bed.

The 'droid handed her the belt. "Would you like me to resume the sensor calibrations?"

Calibrations that should have been completed hours ago. "Please. And put this back in the weapons locker." She gave him the rifle. Good ol' Dezi. Her last link to sanity. She strapped the belt around her waist and shoved the pistol back into its holster.

"Thanks, Dez. Be sure you shut down at 0900, for at least a half hour. There'll be more than just this ship to repair if you don't get some downtime soon."

She hazarded a glance at Vanur as Dezi left. He'd retrieved his shirt and put it on. It hung open, his bruises looking dark and ugly. "And I should probably send you back to sick bay."

"There's no need." He squared his shoulders, but his mouth was a tight line, his dark eyes shadowed. Whatever painkillers the regen bed had pumped into him were probably out of his system by now.

"Well then, sit." She motioned to one of the stools. "I still need a drink."

And better control of her emotions. She had no real cause to be angry at him, she decided as she stepped behind the counter. After all, how would she feel if she woke, disoriented, on a Zafharin ship?

She knew she'd keep a smile on her face, and the safety off her pistol.

His smiles might be a bit strained, but he *had* handed her weapons back to her. She gave him a bonus point for that one. Yet something about the Zafharin unsettled her. He was too damnably good-looking, with his dark eyes and thick black hair. Which could also account for the underlying arrogance she sensed.

Of course, the quadrant was full of good-looking arrogant men. Like Jagan. Good-looking and arrogant, but also wealthy and powerful, holding himself up before the rest of the universe like some little plasti-weight God . . .

But Vanur was only a mere lieutenant, a flyboy, she

reminded herself. She thumbed the latch on the utensil rack and pulled out a squat hard-plastic tumbler. His kind were used to taking orders, not giving them. Still, her head pounded again, like two discordant drumbeats that said, *Grantforth. Vanur. Grantforth. Vanur.*

The sooner she got back to Port Rumor, the sooner she could request some compensation for her troubles. And be rid of him.

Her headache she could handle right now. She unlatched a second cabinet, reached up, and took out her last bottle of gin. When she turned, he was leaning against the countertop, peering up at the open cabinet behind her.

Time to play hostess. "Want something?"

He stepped around the counter, reached easily over her head for a bottle of Bagrondian whiskey.

"I can make coffee, if you'd rather," she offered. "Or do you need something to eat?" But he was shaking his head.

"Glasses are here." Their arms collided at the cabinet door. His fingers slipped around her wrist as he pulled her against him, and for a crazy, totally insane moment she thought he was going to kiss her.

His face tilted down toward hers, his other arm slid around her back . . .

And then he was gently nudging her out of the narrow galley. "I can do this for myself." He gave her a slightly quirky smile.

She backed away slowly, eased herself onto the stool, and uncapped the bottle of gin. He poured a short drink of whiskey, recapped the bottle, and secured it in the galley rack.

By the Gods, a man who cleaned up after himself!

She awarded him another bonus point. Jagan would've left the bottle out for either her or Dezi to secure.

She sipped the gin, let the fire burn down her throat.

He sat on the stool next to her, turned his glass in his hands. "You said something about Port Rumor?"

"It's about a trike from here." She leaned her elbows against the countertop and tried to assemble her features into her best "professional captain" demeanor. Better he learn the bad news now. "I've still got about ten hours' worth of hard work ahead of me before we can leave, though."

"Ten hours? I can be of assistance, cut your time down on those repairs."

His offer was tempting but not totally feasible. "Only if we worked separately."

"Yes, of course, but—"

"No offense, Vanur, but I'm not sure I'd trust whatever you'd do to my ship when I wasn't looking."

"Your ship is also my only means back. I would not be so foolhardy as that." There was a slight hint of disdain in his voice, made even more pronounced by his Zafharish accent.

"Oh, I'm not worried about your sabotaging the *Venture*," she said smoothly. "At least not while you're still on board. It's what you'll have her do *after* you leave that I don't trust. It'd take me days just to ferret out whatever wogs-and-weemlies you'd be able to set in place."

"Wogs-and-weemlies?" That small, quirky smile was back. "I do not do wogs-and-weemlies, Trilby Elliot. Especially now, when I'm hard-pressed to

return. I don't even have time for you to go to Port
Rumor."

She was about to remind him that the decision
wasn't his to make when he continued: "What we do
have time for is perhaps ten hours' worth of work,
which, with my help, can be reduced to six. Then we
head for the border, where I can contact an Imperial
patrol ship. And that is the *only* thing we have time
for." He raised his glass as if to punctuate his words.

"No way." She shook her head emphatically as he
downed the contents of his glass in one mouthful.
"I've got a good-size one-up run waiting for me on
Rumor. I'm not about to let that slide just because
whatever games you were playing out there by Szed
went sour."

"You do not understand. Three days is a delay I
cannot afford."

"No, you don't understand. This is my ship. We're
going to Port Rumor. You don't like that?" She motioned toward the viewport and the long gash of broken palms. "Go back to your Tark. I'm sure the 'Sko
will come looking for it, sooner or later. Or you can
work under my supervision and in three days pick up
a freighter headed for the border and be on your way
home. Understand now?"

It took a moment before he answered. "Understood."

"Wonderful." She secured the gin bottle, tucked
their empty glasses into the sani-rack. The gin had
kicked in. Her headache was starting to recede. "In
that case, Rhis-my-boy, let's get you settled. Then I
suggest you allow me to acquaint you with the problems you're going to face in this pet project of yours.
If you think you can get it done in less than ten hours,
then the Gods be praised. Because that is the *only*

way you're going to get this ship fully functional in that time—with divine intervention."

She stomped off toward the corridor but stopped in the doorway when she didn't hear accompanying footsteps. "Well?" she asked with undisguised impatience as she turned.

Something sparked in the short distance between them. It was like a small explosion of the emotional energy that had been building since she'd fallen off the stool and into his arms. An almost primal magnetism. She didn't know if he felt it, or saw it, but she did. She inhaled quickly as anger and nervousness mixed together inside her with something else she didn't want to identify.

Rhis's breathing seemed to match hers. He took a step toward her. His gaze moved over her in a possessive, almost predatory way.

Then his expression blanked out, his mouth suddenly a thin line. "Move it, Elliot! We've work to do. I do not have time to waste with your games."

"My—?" She gave him a look of incredulity before she turned and, swearing softly under her breath, marched down the *Venture*'s narrow corridor.

So much for Lieutenant Nice Guy. She rescinded one of his bonus points.

Rhis followed her down the corridor, damning his infamous temper. And damning the dull throb of pain in his side that had made him forget that he needed her cooperation, not her enmity.

He also needed her ship. But his plans to take it by force quickly changed when he realized they weren't in the space lanes. And that she was in the middle of repairs.

A fully functioning ship in the lanes was easy. All he had to do was override her primaries and change course. But dirtside repairs hinted at something more involved than a course change. And he didn't like surprises. They always meant unexpected problems. He had a feeling an old Circura II would be replete with problems that might slow even him down.

Control would be gained, but through deception. He had to appear harmless, amiable, sympathetic. Everything he wasn't. Or everything he'd risked his life for would be threatened.

He saw the distrust in her eyes when she turned to him in front of a closed cabin doorway. "Your cabin code is four-seven-eight." She tapped at the entry pad.

"You can't palm-code it?" he asked as the door slid open.

"If you're worried about your privacy, it's only Dez and me. Neither of us has the time to disturb you. But if I need to know where you are, I don't want to waste time decoding a locked door."

So her ship had no Crew Locator System, no internal sensor grid. That was good. But her lack of trust in him wasn't. Time to do some damage control.

He stepped inside, took a cursory glance at his cabin. Small. Basic. But clean. "I'm still a bit unsettled from everything. I didn't mean to sound so angry."

"Apology accepted, if that was one." She gave him a wry smile. "But I'm still not letting you lock this cabin."

She brushed by him. A scent of powder and flowers lingered, stirred something within him, lightly. Not like the unexpected sparks that had flown ten minutes ago in the lounge, flooding his body with a long-forgotten heat. That was a totally irrational reaction, startling him. He'd turned his anger at himself into anger at her. A clumsy move, yet effective. There was too much at stake here for him to be distracted.

But even now his gaze followed her, took in the soft curves of her hips and thighs as she walked. There was a narrow gray door on his right. She twisted its latch.

"Sani-fac," she said, pushing the door open. "Need more towels, let me or Dezi know." She pointed to the opposite wall. "Closet and drawer space in there."

"Useless, at the moment." He shoved his hands into his pants pockets and grinned sheepishly.

She tilted her head in momentary confusion, and then a slow smile crossed her face. "I might be able to help out. I've got some stuff in one of the storage lockers."

No hard-goods replicator on board then, either. "Don't go to any trouble—"

She waved away his comment. "No big deal. Besides, you might be rather ripe by the time we hit Rumor if I don't."

"I will bathe daily. I promise."

She smiled, more warmly this time. He saw the tension in her shoulders relax.

So this is how we do it. Light quips. Keep it friendly. Play on her concern. Maybe he should learn to let his pain be more evident. She'd judge him to be less threatening then. An injured man. Alone.

It was all arguably true. He'd just never showed weakness, in any form, before.

He motioned toward the corridor. "And now, your ship. You have repairs I can help with." He let his arm fall back to his side and, for the first time, didn't suppress the wince of pain.

"From the looks of you, you need a couple hours downtime first. Dezi and I can start—"

"It's just some soreness. Besides, much of the delay is my fault. You'll finish more quickly with my help."

She hesitated, crossed her arms over her chest. He could almost see distrust warring with compassion in her eyes. He had always avoided any awareness of human emotions before. But suddenly they interested him. Or rather, Trilby Elliot's interested him.

Her expression softened. Compassion won.

"Okay," she said, nodding. "I've got a problem with a booster interface you can tackle."

She was testing him. It was a minor problem, a booster interface. He could solve that in twenty minutes. Getting her to trust him might take a little bit longer.

He was forced to revise his twenty-minute estimate as he sat in the boxy maintenance cubicle on the hyperdrive deck, paging through the schematics screens. The room was little more than a converted storage closet. And when she leaned on the console, peering over his shoulder, he found himself increasingly distracted by her presence.

It was just because, he told himself, he wasn't used to having his work scrutinized.

He was staring at a particularly troublesome configuration when it finally dawned on him what was missing. "I need to see the data for your primary systems interface."

"Sorry. That's on a 'need to know' basis, Vanur. And right now—"

"I am familiar with the phrase." He arched an eyebrow. There were those in the Empire who'd been known to wonder if he had a patent on the expression.

"Well, so am I, so we have something in common, Rhis-my-boy," Trilby was saying. She laughed lightly. "I've heard stories about you, you know."

For a moment his gut tensed. Then he realized she was speaking in general terms. *You* meant the Zafharin Imperial Fleet and its reputation. Not one Zafharin in particular. He brushed off her comment. "We Zafharin pride ourselves on our discipline."

A discipline that demanded a masking of pain, though, try as he might, not of annoyance. He returned to the data on the screen, fingers toying impatiently with his lightpen or pulling distractedly at his mustache.

Her ship's analytical equipment was in a state of disrepair that was blatantly unacceptable. He called her away from her own work on a relay panel in the corridor behind him, counted to ten while he framed his request.

"I need a datalyzer. One that was manufactured in at least the past twenty years. Please."

Wordlessly, she handed him a unit from her tool kit. He flipped it on. The small screen flickered and died.

His facade cracked. He swore in Zafharish. "How you work under these conditions is a—"

Trilby grabbed the small unit, smacked it against

her thigh, then flipped it on again and handed it to him. The screen glowed brightly.

He glared at her. "This is ridiculous."

She left, inexpertly hiding her laughter under a coughing fit.

Imperial arrogance. No, maybe that wasn't quite right, even if the Zafharins were famous for it. Even if Rhis seemed to have his fair share. It was probably more accurate to lump Rhis's struggles with her ship's components as something more generic. Something Shadow had taught her long ago, in Port Rumor.

Incompetence bred by authority.

Jagan had it, enough to fill a black hole. She'd just lost sight of that under his pretty words, fancy presents.

And the Conclave had it. Hell, that's what the Conclave was. Authority, governmental authority. Incompetence by committee.

As for Rhis Vanur, he couldn't help that he worked for a government. He understood *need to know* because he'd probably been told more than once that he didn't qualify for that need.

Fighter pilots rarely did. Go there, shoot that, try to bring the hardware back in one piece.

With a soft sigh she realized Rhis was probably more interested in getting back to the Empire than the Empire was in getting him back. Her scanners, myopic as they were, showed that no one had come looking for the Tark. If they were concerned about the fate of their pilot, they would have looked.

But Trilby knew from firsthand experience that

people were expendable to governments and corporations. Hardware could be recovered at any time.

She had to remember that, had to stop lumping him in the same category with people like Jagan, or the trip back to Rumor would be hell for them both. He was only a lieutenant. He took orders; he didn't give them. His arrogance was cultural; Jagan's was cultivated.

Twenty minutes later, she stepped into the corridor and saw him swaying in his seat. He clearly belonged back in sick bay, not in the small, stuffy maintenance room.

At the sound of her footsteps he turned. The shadows under his eyes had darkened. She put out one hand, tentatively. He glanced at her offered hand with disdain, his spine straightening at the last moment.

"Why don't you go lie down? A few hours' delay won't—"

"I am fine." His right hand lay flat against the console, his arm braced. His body language spoke out loud and clear: *I am Zafharin. I can deal with pain.*

"You're a liar," she replied easily as he glared at her. "If you collapse here you'll block the doorway. So get your ass down to your cabin. I'll wake you in four hours or so."

"No, I—"

"The cabin has a comp." She stepped over the raised door tread, leaned her arms against the high console. "Read in bed if you like. But right now I don't think you should be sitting up. Or standing."

He pushed himself to his feet. "There is nothing wrong with—"

She caught him as he staggered against her, her

arms encircling his waist as he pinned her against the bulkhead. "Whoa, flyboy, whoa!"

She felt his weight sag, his face hot against her hair. She reached out blindly for the intercom panel by the door. "Dezi! Get down to maintenance, now!"

He struggled slightly. "*Nav, vad yasch*—I'm okay. I'm okay." His voice was strained, soft. But he didn't pull away from her.

When Dezi grasped him under the armpits, Trilby had the fleeting impression he was reluctant to let her go.

He woke, climbing out of a very soft, Trilby Elliot-scented dream to find himself in a small darkened cabin. Alone.

"*Lutsa*. Lights." His voice cracked, dry. He stumbled into the adjoining sani-fac and gulped down a glass of cold water, then splashed some on his face. His Trilby-dream had faded, though he could still remember the pale silk of her hair against his face. Her arms around him—

—had not been a dream. The close confines of the sani-fac brought back the shape of the maintenance cubicle. And his less-than-impressive collapse against her.

So much for his infamous Zafharin discipline. So much for his infamous control. Both faded like a vapor trail whenever he was near her.

He was probably just overtired. He'd strained his physical limits with this last mission. Even *he* needed time to heal. But his current situation hampered that.

Still, tiredness was not an excuse for the way he was handling this situation, this Trilby Elliot. He knew that. Her unlikely combination of sarcasm and softness rankled him and intrigued him at the same time. He couldn't remember the last time he'd felt his control slip through his fingers as easily as silken mist.

But then, his current situation didn't permit him to be who he was. He was born and bred for command. He'd never had to repress his finely honed instincts before. It unsettled him—almost as much as Elliot's presence did—and he took another mouthful of cool water while he rearranged his attitude.

His *infamous* attitude. He ran one hand over his face. Playing at being nice was draining him, tearing away at the hard-assed, arrogant son of a bitch he was supposed to be. Had been for over thirty years, until fate and the 'Sko had dumped him on the doorstep of one Captain Trilby Elliot.

He sat on the edge of the narrow bed, rolled up his shirtsleeves, and tabbed on the comp screen. The skin over his wounds no longer itched. And the pain in his body had quieted to a dull roar. He let that be his focus. That and his mission. Not her smiles or soft laughter. Or her sympathy. She didn't know who she was offering it to. She didn't know what it was doing to him.

Time to get back to work.

His self-proclaimed sixth-hour deadline came and went while he was flat on his back in the *Venture*'s cramped maintenance tunnel later that morning. Repairs on an erratic datafeed line weren't going well. Sweaty and exasperated, he sent Dezi scurrying out of the tunnel in search of "a Gods damned splicer that will work at least half the Gods damned time!"

A few minutes later, a scuffling noise in the tunnel told him that Dezi had returned. It was the captain's orders, he knew, that he not be left alone for long. But at least with the 'droid, he could be himself.

"About time!" he snapped. He reached over his head, his fingers grasping the thin cylinder of what he hoped was a more efficient crystal splicer.

The splicer wasn't what he was used to, but it was better than the first one. It still took him five minutes to repair the hairline fractures.

He flicked off the power on the splicer with a snap and closed his eyes, letting his head fall back against the hard floor of the tunnel. A dull ache throbbed between his shoulder blades from working in the tunnel's cramped quarters. But that didn't make him half as uncomfortable as the fact that, even here, in the bowels of her ship, he was still aware of her presence. He could almost smell the sweet muskiness of that perfume she wore. It was as if she were haunting him.

"Ridiculous," he said.

"I tried to warn you," replied a soft female voice in his ear.

His eyes flew open. He saw the object of his troubled thoughts kneeling beside him.

"Bloody hell!" He sat up abruptly. His head made hard contact with a low ceiling tile. The large gray square teetered on rusty hinges. He reached for it just as Trilby did. Their arms collided, throwing her off balance. She collapsed onto his chest.

He heard the sharp crack of the metal hinge snapping, saw the blur of movement out of the corner of his eye. Instinctively he clasped her tightly against him and rolled away, placing his body protectively over hers. The tile slammed against him, then slid to the decking with a loud clang.

He felt her rapid breathing against his chest. "You all right?"

"Umm, yes." She tilted her head, bumping her nose on his chin. She was sandwiched between him and the tunnel's curved wall. "You?"

His head hurt. His back ached. The crystal splicer dug an uncomfortable gouge into his left hip. But his body blithely ignored all of this discomforting physical information and chose instead to focus on the softness and the scent of the woman beneath him, in his arms.

Somehow in their grappling, her T-shirt had pulled up at her waist. His left hand rested on her bare skin, his fingers on the swell of her breast. His right hand lay against her neck, his thumb on the line of her jaw.

He was acutely aware his mouth was only inches from hers. And that if he spoke, if he were to answer her question, his lips might just graze against her own.

Startled, he realized that was something he desperately wanted to do. He needed to taste her, to feel the heat of her mouth on his. To brand her with his own heat, his own scent.

"Sure you're okay?" she repeated.

"Wonderful." He whispered his answer against her lips.

She was all softness. He rubbed his mouth against hers, feeling her lips part, feeling her body press into his—

She gasped, her hands pushing against his chest. She turned her face abruptly away. His mouth ended up, moist and hot, against her cheek for a moment before he finally understood what her hands were frantically trying to tell him.

He lifted himself stiffly off her.

"Just what in the Seven Hells do you think you're doing?" She squirmed, shoving her shirt back into the waistband of her pants.

He knew what he'd been doing, but had no explanation for it. It was a mistake. Another mistake. Like the one he'd made . . . was it only this morning? When he'd assumed she was a mercenary, taking him to Quivera.

But that mistake had been understandable. This was damnably incomprehensible, to lose control so easily because of a winsome face, a soft mouth, a mesmerizing scent of powder and flowers.

"The, um, tile came loose." It was a lame answer, but it was all his mind could come up with. He still tasted their kiss, the sweetness of her skin. And he still felt the warmth of her body where it had touched his, creating an even more intense warmth. Creating—

"A tile. Came loose." Trilby repeated his words as if he'd uttered gibberish. She was breathing hard, but some of the glitter of anger was gone from her eyes. "A tile came loose and that gives you the right to stick your hand under my shirt?"

"I didn't stick my hand under your shirt. I tried to pull you out of the way. We—"

An access hatchway slid open overhead. Dezi's metallic face filled the small square. "Captain! We're back online. Communications is back online. We can—oh. Pardon. Am I interrupting something?"

Trilby didn't seem to hear the question. She glared at Rhis. "Don't do me any more favors. Okay?" She glanced up at the 'droid. "I'll meet you on the bridge, Dez. Now." She shoved herself away and crawled hastily toward the tunnel's exit.

Alone in the tunnel, Rhis closed his eyes and lay his head against the flooring. Something had happened . . . something *was* happening to him. He didn't understand it. He was acting like Rafi, for the Gods' sakes! He'd been in this female's company less than one full day and here he was panting after her like some gelzrac in heat.

"Ridiculous," he said. But his tone wasn't overly convincing.

"Insolent, arrogant, insufferable, Imperial bastard!" Trilby's hushed but angry litany echoed the slap of her boots on the decking. She could have added "brilliant" and "too damned good-looking for his own good," but she was still working herself into a frenzy over his negatives. She didn't intend to even touch on Rhis's positives until they parted company at Port Rumor.

She stomped onto the bridge, then let herself collapse into her seat.

Communications were back online. A long list of messages waited for her, not the least of which was the confirmation of the availability of the Bagrond run. That made her feel better. She quickly sent off her acknowledgment. Then, boots resting on the bridge console, she leaned back in her chair and brought up the armrest screen to review just what everyone had to say to her this septi.

Neadi's face appeared. Her skin was the color of deep golden coffee; her dark eyes sparkled. "Hey,

Tril! Hope you get this." There was the usual "working our butts off slingin' beer and booze," and then her friend's jovial demeanor became serious.

"Something's going on. Yeah, I know, business has dropped off in the past few months, but hell, when haven't the Indys had their ups and downs?"

Neadi knew the deep-space transit business as well as Trilby did. She'd been raised on short-haulers, though ones larger than the *Venture*. But it was her and her husband's pub adjacent to the spaceport that put them in a good position to hear what was going on in the traders' lanes between Rumor, Bagrond, and Quivera.

"Talk is that someone's in bed with the 'Sko. Yeah, I know, I know." Neadi held up one hand as if she could hear Trilby's disbelieving snort. "Who sleeps with the 'Sko? The Zafharin, maybe."

Trilby's mind flickered to a tall, dark-haired man one deck below. A small mental warning bell jangled softly.

"We're hearing whispers of an under-the-table agreement with one of the Beffa cartels. It's got people thinking about the 'Sko attacks recently. If the 'Sko stop the small trade, then only the big guys, like GGA or Norvind, will work Gensiira. Which is big profits for them.

"But it's also big losses if the 'Sko's real purpose isn't to take out the small haulers but to entice the big traders into an area that's been long known for its lack of patrols. The 'Sko will profit if Gensiira falls to them. But the Zafharin will profit even more if the 'Sko drive out you small operators and then the Empire moves in to annex us.

"We might just be the incentive for the Empire to stop harassing the 'Sko out by Szed.

"So be careful. Watch who your runs come through and what flight plans you file. It could be nothing more than jump-jockey gossip, but I know that you've been looking to spend some money on upgrades. Screw that, girl. Go for weapons. A new ion cannon'd be nice. A set of Lady-Fives even better. I've got contacts if you don't."

Trilby swiveled in her seat for a while, thinking. The Bagrond run had come through a reliable agent, an old friend. She stopped swiveling, pulled it up again on the comp, and tried to read between the lines. Nothing. At least, nothing that shouldn't be there.

But there'd been other requests. Not to her. But before she'd left Rumor she'd seen a couple of the pricier bottles of gin being poured.

And then there was Rhis. The Zafharin pilot. A lieutenant. Off the *Razalka*, he said. Who just happened to be in possession of a 'Sko fighter. Captured years ago, he told her. Used now only in war games. Malfunctioned and landed in her front yard.

That fit, to a point. She'd seen no other craft, 'Sko or anything, in pursuit. If the Tark were stolen, the 'Sko would obviously have been on Rhis's tail.

But maybe it wasn't stolen. Maybe it was a gift. A thank-you. For that other rumor Neadi alluded to.

Who else but the Zafharin would be sleeping with the 'Sko?

She left the bridge, her mind more on Neadi's warnings than where her feet were taking her. It wasn't as if running trade in Gensiira was easy to begin with. But at least the enemy was known: the government, mostly in the form of customs inspectors. And generally visible in one place: dockside. But the 'Sko—and the Zafharin, for that matter—made their own rules. A little caution might be advisable at this point with her business. And her onboard guest as well.

Shame she had no inbred distrust of Zafharins. Port Rumor had always been indiscriminately eclectic in its populace. She knew several Zafharin freighter operators. And more than a dozen half-Zafharin merchants, including Neadi's husband. Port Rumor was a busy place now, and had been even before the war ended.

But to have an Imperial military officer dumped in her lap, courtesy of a 'Sko Tark—a fully armed 'Sko

Tark—wasn't quite the same as sharing a beer with a half-Zafharin drive tech in Flyboy's.

She stopped walking and stared at the door in front of her. Cargo Hold 3. She had intended to head for her cabin, one deck below the bridge. Not all the way down here.

Brilliant, Tril, just brilliant. She resisted the urge to pound her head on the door.

She turned quickly instead, flinging her arms wide in a gesture of frustration. And smacked Rhis Vanur firmly in the chest with the back of her hand. "Damnation! Sorry."

He grabbed her arm, steadying her as she looked up at him in surprise. And something flared, sparked again. Something primal. Intense. Urgent.

She shook off his hand, stepped away quickly. "You following me, Lieutenant?" She tried to add ice to her voice, her body needing it.

He hesitated. "I've been looking for you."

"Down here?"

"I called the bridge. You didn't answer. And your ship has no CLS."

Trilby tamped down her newborn paranoia. He was right; she didn't have a functioning crew locator on board. Dezi used his thermal grid to find her on the ship. When she wanted Dez, she used the comm. She belatedly realized she'd never told Vanur to do that. "What's the problem?"

"Problem?"

"I don't think you're down here looking for a copy of my potato-and-cheese casserole recipe. So what's the problem?"

"Oh, yes. Well, not a problem. Just a modification

I thought you might consider for the booster." He shrugged.

"I thought you finished that yesterday." She fell in step with him as they headed toward the companionway.

"I did. At the time, I didn't think it would work with your equipment, but I've been playing with the idea. I might be able to customize—"

"Wogs-and-weemlies?"

He turned at the bottom step, smiled down at her. "Ones you would like, I think. Our ships use it on border patrol. I guess you could call it an invasive filter."

She followed him up to the next deck in silence, stopped just short of the open lounge hatchway. "You mean, you can grab messages that aren't meant for you."

He hesitated only a fraction of a second. "Yes."

"Nice modification." And one she could sell in Rumor for a pretty piece of change, once she unraveled the program and found how it worked. "How long will it take you?"

"An hour, perhaps less. I can work on it on the way to Rumor. Right now I want to finish calibrating the sensors with Dezi."

"I want to see the program before you install and run it."

"Of course."

Of course. And this from a man who just yesterday had held her throat in the paralyzing *G'zhen Dai* grip used by thirty-second century warrior-monks on Dakrahl. Or was it the fatal *Tah Fral* hold employed by the Order of Despi Guild assassins?

She shook her head as he headed belowdecks to the drive room.

She stepped into the lounge. Her stomach had been rumbling for a while. She removed the large casserole of stew from storage and placed it in the processor. That's what she was supposed to have done ten minutes ago. Instead, she'd been wandering on autopilot on the cargo deck. If she hadn't bumped into Vanur—

A thought struck her with the same high-voltage intensity as his touch had by Cargo Hold 3.

What was Vanur doing down by the holds?

Looking for her, he'd said. She didn't know what bothered her more: the fact that he was following her, or the fact that he was following her and she'd been blissfully unaware of the fact.

The processor chimed. She thumbed the door open, let the spicy aroma pour over her for a moment.

Maybe she was being paranoid. Or maybe she didn't want to face the real reason she was so jumpy around him. She just didn't know if it had more to do with his heritage or his gender.

He was terribly male. Terribly, wonderfully male. That might be something worth exploring if she weren't still smarting over Jagan. And if Rhis weren't also walking around her ship in a Zafharin uniform. Six months ago she wouldn't have cared. Now she was doubly cautious.

She secured the stew in the server, then tabbed on the coffeemaker. When he came in for dinner she was still on her first cup. But it was cold. She stirred it halfheartedly and pretended to stare out the viewport at Avanar's lengthening shadows. Two moons were rising. She could see Rhis's reflection—dark-haired and dark-shirted—outlined on the viewport as he sat at the high counter that separated the galley area, a bowl of stew before him. The glint of one of her ship's portable datapads was next to that. He was working on a sensor glitch that Dezi's diagnostics couldn't unravel.

Or so he said.

For all she knew, he was working on plans to help the 'Sko conquer all of Conclave space.

Neadi's words haunted her, but her thoughts kept being sidetracked to the heat generated between them in the maintenance tunnel earlier. She was surprised the insulating plates hadn't melted after falling on their bodies.

It exasperated her how he'd caught her off guard. But then, maybe what she thought had happened really hadn't. Maybe they did only fall against each other by accident, her shirt riding up, his hands simply landing in a logical spot.

But that kiss, that kiss had been no accident.

So she watched him now without watching him. Tried to watch the "him" that was Zafharin Imperial Lieutenant and not the "him" that was broad-shouldered with strong arms. And night-black hair, the only soft thing on his body. Like the soft hair matting his chest—

She stood suddenly, irritated at her train of thought, forgotten coffee cup still in her hand. "We'll be ready to go at 0600?"

"Absolutely. We could depart tonight, within the hour."

Trilby shook her head. "No. I need some sleep, Dezi needs some downtime, and you're still recovering from some good bumps and bruises."

He glanced down at where his shirtsleeves were rolled up, exposing the faded purple gash on his arm.

"I know, I know," she said with exasperation, seeing him start to reply. "You've got a hot date waiting for you back there across the zone. Well, even if we leave at sunrise tomorrow, we're still ahead of schedule. We all need a good night's sleep."

She moved around him to place her cup in the sani-rack.

He handed her the empty casserole dish. "I could start—"

"Thanks, but no. I need you on the bridge at 0545. I want to run a complete systems check before we blow this pop stand."

He pushed himself away from the counter, tucked the datapad under his arm. "Then 0545 it is."

She let out the breath she'd been holding as she watched him leave, then hurriedly finished securing the galley. With Rhis in his cabin, she'd have some time to poke around in her ship's systems undisturbed. Find out just what Mister Friendly Lieutenant had been doing near her cargo holds.

And while she worked on it, she'd try not to think about what it felt like to kiss him.

He saw it the minute the door to his small cabin slid open. His black jacket, cleaned and patched, draped across the back of the only chair. He picked up the jacket, caught the light scent of her perfume, then saw something else.

A long-sleeve white shirt, large enough for him. It felt new and didn't smell of powdery flowers. He wondered where she'd gotten it. Replicator? But no, her ship didn't have a hard-goods replicator on board.

Her consideration surprised him, yet it didn't. He was learning she could be brash and flippant one minute, warm and beguiling the next. She made it clear she didn't trust him. And, of course, that she didn't particularly like him.

The last he was used to. Not many people did.

But then she'd patched his jacket, found him a shirt, and made sure there was always hot soup, or coffee, within his reach. Asked if he needed another blanket. If there were enough clean towels in his sani-fac.

And a couple of times had teased him in such a way that made him think maybe he was wrong. Maybe she might like him, even if only a little bit.

That worried him. Because he didn't know what he'd do if she did.

He tossed the jacket back onto the chair, thrust all thoughts of her from his mind. He had to remember who he was, why he was here.

He set his alarm to wake him at 0130. He still had work to do.

The first thing Trilby did when she stepped through the door of her quarters was to set the alarm for 0530. The second was to pull the comp around on its swivel arm so that it faced her bed. She sat on the faded purple quilt, legs crossed, elbows on her knees, and put the *Venture* through a little-used series of paces. Little-used because she'd not had to deal with an intruder on board before.

The program was one she'd created with Shadow,

one of their best. His young, lanky form floated into her mind. She could still see his unruly mop of muddy-brown hair, forever being pushed out of his eyes with long fingers. But his face blurred in her memory. It had been almost seventeen years since he was killed.

She'd just turned sixteen when it happened. Shadow was about two years her senior. He'd picked up a skim job on a Herkoid long-hauler. Three months later, Trilby followed. Herkoid knew where to find cheap labor.

Port Rumor. The junkyard of civilized space offered not only spare parts but spare bodies. Orphans, bastards, by-blows. Thousands of children, living in storage sheds, working illegally on transports and freighters. Jobs, food, clothing were snatched from discards and castoffs. First to see it owned it. Finders keepers.

That was Port Rumor in those days.

Now Shadow was gone. He'd been on the bridge when 'Sko lasers had sliced through the hulking freighter. Sliced first the bridge, then the drive room, aft.

But the cargo holds were spared. Sacred. The 'Sko never damaged the cargo. Didn't shit where they ate, as Shadow used to say.

Trilby and three others had been in the holds. Two containers had unstrapped as they'd come out of jumpspace and shifted. Her stint on cleanup detail, and the arrival of a Conclave squadron, had saved her life.

Trilby pinched the bridge of her nose with two fingers. Tiredness washed over her as the memory receded. She shook her head, stared at the data on the screen. Saw the patches Dezi had made and the ones

Rhis had made. Everything within acceptable parameters. No wogs. No weemlies.

She'd deliberately stopped staring over his shoulder just to see if he would try something. Because if he was going to, she wanted him to try it before they hit the lanes.

Her fears, however, appeared to be unfounded. Looked like Rhis was being a good boy.

She stripped off her green T-shirt and lay her utility belt, laser pistol attached, over the nightstand that jutted out from the wall. Her pants she balled up and tossed into the hamper in the corner. She'd have plenty of time to do laundry on the trike back to Rumor.

Or maybe she'd assign that duty to Mister Friendly Lieutenant. In spite of his obvious helpfulness, she could tell he had no experience in the domestic end of shipboard duties. That tagged him as a career officer in her book. Career officers, especially Imperial ones, didn't do their own laundry.

Perhaps it was time someone filled in those gaps in his training.

She fell asleep, a smile still on her lips.

He woke a few minutes before the alarm chimed and lay in the darkness of the small cabin. It seemed unnatural to be on a ship and not moving, not feeling the thrumming of the drives through his body.

He pulled on his clothes, then slipped into his jacket. The new white shirt would shine like a beacon in the *Venture*'s dim corridors, and he needed to be part of the shadows for a while. To do what he had to do. To work his "wogs-and-weemlies." He heard

Trilby Elliot's voice say that in his head, a voice wary yet laced with sarcasm.

Wogs-and-weemlies.

He retraced his steps to the auxiliary systems and communications backup panel recessed in a small storage closet just before the holds. He decoded the lock, careful of tripping any alarms. Then it was a good half hour's worth of work, aided by the pilfered datalyzer, before he was into the ship's primaries.

All her illegal customizations floated before him. Trilby Elliot's handiwork. He didn't know if he was more surprised by the sophistication of her methods or just her downright crazy creativity.

There was a talent there. The brash little air sprite had a real knack. Had she been raised in the Empire, schooled through the Imperial Academy, she probably could have run circles around half the chief engineers he knew.

He could learn a few things about wogs-and-weemlies from her, though he doubted she'd want to teach him. But he should be able to find some answers in her Master Program Templates. It might be interesting, later, to run her patch methodology through the *Razalka*'s computers.

He tapped at the pad, trailed down a datafeed to her personal files, the most likely place for her templates to reside.

But found the *J* files first. It took him a few minutes to understand *J* was for Jagan Grantforth. Grantforth Galactic Amalgamated. The Empire had taken enough of their ships that he recognized the ID stamp in the transmission code. What tugged at his curiosity was the regularity of the entries over the past year and a half that had ended abruptly about four months ago.

Grantforth was a well-heeled outfit. New money, it was true, but then most of the Conclave was built on new money. Not like the long clan heritage of the Zafharin.

He couldn't imagine why a high-profile export firm like GGA would utilize a short-hauler like Trilby Elliot. Or why she hadn't profited from the relationship.

Except the relationship hadn't been business. He discovered that as the messages scrolled by on the small screen. And his real reason for accessing the *Venture*'s primaries, as well as Trilby's intriguing patch templates, slid from his mind.

Wealthy, influential Jagan Grantforth had thoroughly bedazzled, and seduced, an unsuspecting, gullible Trilby Elliot of Port Rumor.

He watched Jagan's vid transmissions with growing distaste. The well-tanned blond-haired man on the screen dished out compliments with a sugary sweetness. A few later transmissions were also the same; only the last two were obviously different.

"But, Trilby, little darling," Jagan's miniature image said on the screen. "You know I adore you; you know no other woman can make me feel what you do. But there are differences in our lives and that can't be ignored." The image looked down at the half-empty wineglass in his fingers for a moment, then back at the vid lens. "Sorry you had to find out about my engagement to Zalia that way. I didn't mean to hurt you. But there's no reason why we can't keep on with this beautiful relationship we have. You just have to understand I'm going to marry Zalia out of . . . well, duty. Her family's wealthy, well connected. And I am, after all, one of *the* Grantforths."

The final transmission was a bit more heated. Jagan still pleaded that he wanted her, but there was an anger there as well. Evidently Trilby had given him his walking papers and he didn't like having his sweet little setup so peremptorily disrupted. And, judging from his closing remark, she had also been less than diplomatic in her ending of their affair:

"Mother was right." Petulance clouded Jagan's handsome features. "You *are* nothing more than low-class trash from Port Rumor."

An unexpected bolt of hot rage shot through Rhis's chest. With surprise he realized that had Jagan Grant-forth been standing in front of him at that moment, he would've gladly flattened the man against the nearest bulkhead.

Trilby glanced at Rhis as he strapped himself into the copilot's seat and saw shadows under his eyes. It was 0542. He looked like he could use another few hours of rest.

She should have forced him to spend another day in sick bay. But her need to get the *Venture* function-ing quickly had taken precedence over his medical condition. She felt slightly guilty about that now. "You want a light trank?"

"Of course not! I am fine." He tugged on the strapping with a show of force.

"Yeah, yeah. I heard that line before, Rhis-my-boy. That's what you said just as you passed out in—"

"You said something about a full systems check?" He overrode her comment, focused on the screen flickering to life on the console.

She chuckled, swiveled her datapad into position.

"Okay, tough guy, have it your way. Full power active. Let's run down the list. Life support."

"Power levels optimum. Filters online."

"Got it. Auxiliary generators?" It was odd hearing Rhis's voice, not Dezi's reply to her routine questions.

"On standby."

They went back and forth for the next five minutes, making a small adjustment here, a slight change in levels there. Several times Trilby noted Rhis almost issuing the command before she did, as if he were about to take over the captain's prerogative. She doubted that Senior Captain Tivahr would have tolerated that on the *Razalka*'s bridge.

But evidently a lowly Zafharin lieutenant felt himself more qualified than an Indy freighter captain. Well, she'd show him a thing or two yet. "Do much heavy-air flying, Rhis?"

"Enough."

"Keep in mind that this is a cargo freighter, not one of your sleek, high-performance Imperial toys, okay? Try to let me handle her 'til we clear dirtside gravity." She tapped at his hand resting on the throttle and command pads. "I do know how to fly this ship."

He snatched his hand away.

"That's better. Now, let's get this bucket of bolts in the air."

As the bulky ship strained upward, Rhis grudgingly admitted she'd been right about one thing. His heavy-air time had all been in high-performance and high-priced Imperial toys. Toys that had better gravity buffer systems than the *Venture* did. His side twinged again. He worked on his breathing, brought his mind out of his physical frame and focused on the instrument readouts before him.

A half hour, twenty-nine minutes . . . his focus changed from the readouts to watching Trilby Elliot at the controls. She was breathing a little harder, her own body fighting the strain. But her hands moved flawlessly, correcting rotation and axis, fiddling with a thruster.

"The starboard auxiliary is always fritzy," she said when she saw him watching her. "That's my safety valve. Some damned fool tries to steal my ship, hell, he'll find her skittering out of control before he can begin congratulating himself on his prowess." She gave a small chuckle. "If I thought the Zafharin had any interest in old junkers like mine, I wouldn't be telling you this."

The Zafharin never had much use for small freighters. Warships, scoutships, large-cargo conveyors, yes. But an old Circura II wouldn't be worthy of their attention. He, however, would never be able to see one without thinking of a certain pale-haired air sprite. But perhaps air sprite wasn't the proper analogy for her. Her fragile appearance was all a sham, a trick of nature that had given her the face of a princess and, he was beginning to understand, a life of privation.

A very wrong number on the console caught his attention. "Your ascent angle's too steep."

Trilby raised her right hand over her head. The plush toy felinar bumped against it. "Nope. Just fine."

He looked at the long-tailed toy, at the red-tinged readout, then at Trilby. "Don't tell me you're serious."

She grinned.

He understood. "Another theft-prevention device?"

Dezi answered for her. "Captain Elliot has always stated that pirate factions intent on capture or sabotage would overlook the simplistic. Begging your pardon, Lieutenant, for of course the Zafharin's high rate of success reveals that your people are more thorough than most. For example, the *Razalka*'s ambush of GGA's sharvinite convoy five years past certainly showed tremendous—"

"Thank you, Dezi," two voices said simultaneously. But for different reasons.

"Would you check incoming messages, Dez?" Trilby disengaged the heavy-air engines and primed her ship's hyperdrives.

Rhis realized his training had him anticipating her movements like a slightly fractured shadow. He folded his hands to keep them from wandering to the controls. "Waiting for confirmation on your Bagrond pickup?"

"Got that already." The ship had pulled free of Avanar's gravity and leveled out easily. The forward viewport filled with the dark elegance of deep space.

Rhis relaxed back into his seat.

"Waiting," she continued, "for some news from Neadi Danzanour."

"Danzanour?" It was a Zafharin surname.

"Neadi's husband, Leonid, had a Zafharin father. But he was raised here, in Gensiira, on Marbo. He and Neadi run a great little pub near the spaceport. Good people," she added, almost as an afterthought.

"You've known them long?" Other than stumbling over her personal letters from Jagan Grantforth, Rhis had no other source of information on Trilby. And working on her ship's systems hadn't provided for the time to ask such questions. But the next three days— a "trike," as she termed it in her freighter lingo—had no demands on them. Other than to babysit the *Venture* on her journey.

Trilby was nodding. "I met Neadi when I worked for Norvind Intergalactic."

"Norvind hired you out of the Merchant Academy?"

She glanced at him, then at the scanner at her right. "I thought I saw something," she began. "Probably just interference. Now, what? Oh, yeah, Norvind. You would've heard of them, I guess, wouldn't you?" Referring, he knew, to the fact that Norvind had lost its share of cargo to the Zafharin during the war.

"No academy. That, Rhis-my-boy, costs money. Worked in a tool shop in Rumor since I was, I don't know, twelve or thirteen. Learned enough to sign on with Herkoid a few years later. But they folded, just before the war, you know. Rinnaker bought some of their ships. Norvind took over some of their routes, personnel. I was just part of the package." She turned to Dezi. "Got any new messages?"

"Transferring them to you now." His metal fingers tapped at the keypad.

The data light on her screen flashed. Trilby pulled up the first message.

Rhis saw the face of an attractive woman fill the screen; her deep-golden skin and thick curly hair indicated her Bartravian heritage. She was probably in her late forties. The lines on her face were those of a woman who laughed often, and easily. But she wasn't laughing now.

"Good to hear you're back online, Tril. And glad I reached you in time about Rinnaker. There's been more bad news. I hope you get this before you make Rumor. Send me your ETA." She hesitated, pursing her lips. "It's about Carina. Carina's missing."

Trilby tensed visibly.

"I sent her the same warning I did you. But you know how her brother is, how her whole crew is. It's profit first, all else be damned.

"Looks like they were hijacked. They were hauling a shipment of Grade-Two sharvinite. Gensiira patrol found *Bella's Dream* not far from the border at Q Eighty-four. Next thing after that's Szed."

" 'Sko." Trilby breathed the word quietly.

"Ship was ram-boarded, bridge trashed. Cargo was gone. Two crew, left for dead. Carina and Vitorio are missing."

He'd seen the carnage wrought by the 'Sko too many times not to recognize the description. But it was the location at the border that set off his internal alarms. This was not an average 'Sko strike. Not there. Not now. He listened more carefully.

"Patrol's trying to reconstruct the logs. As soon as we hear more, I'll let you know. Be careful out there, little one."

The screen blanked out. Trilby covered her eyes with her hand, then pinched the bridge of her nose.

Dezi's joints squeaked as he stood. "I'm truly sorry to learn this news." He patted her head in a clumsy yet strangely endearing fashion.

Trilby nodded. "Thanks, Dez." She drew a deep breath and raised her face, her eyes bright with unshed tears when she turned to Rhis.

He felt as if something were tearing him in half. The information he'd just heard was vital. He had to investigate it, act on it. But he found all he could think about was the pain of the woman before him.

He heard himself telling her he'd take the helm. "Pour yourself a drink, Elliot. And send an answer to *Dasja* Neadi," he said, using the Zafharin word for *Lady*. "She needs to hear you're safe."

He expected her to protest, to bluff that she was all right. But she didn't. The meekness with which she accepted his offer and the quiet way she left the bridge bothered him. Bothered the arrogant, insufferable, Imperial hard-ass who had never been bothered by such things before.

"Captain Elliot and Carina have known each other since they were very young."

Rhis turned toward Dezi and found the 'droid looking at him. Envoy 'droids were supposed to be adept at interpreting human facial expressions, even the most minute ones. He wondered just what had played across his face and how much he had given away. Enough, evidently. He nodded for Dezi to continue.

"They grew up in Port Rumor together. Captain Elliot has often told me of the games they played to circumvent capture by the Iffys—"

"Iffys?"

"Indigent Family and Youth Authorities, I believe. All unclaimed children were to be placed in orphanages. However, Captain Elliot—"

"Trilby was an 'unclaimed' child?" To a Zafharin, the terminology was appalling. It was one of the first things he'd learned as a child. Lineage and clan history formed the essence of a person's identity.

"Yes." Dezi's optical sensors blinked. "As were Carina and her brother, Vitorio. That is why I believe this news is so upsetting to Captain Elliot."

"This is more than losing a friend, then. This is as if she lost someone in her family."

"I believe that would be a correct analysis, Lieutenant."

Rhis thought of Rafi. Not family, but the closest thing he had to it. How would he react to news of Rafi's capture by the 'Sko? "Perhaps I should go check on her."

"I find that advisable. Be assured I can handle the helm. I've done so for many years now."

Rhis watched the message transit light on the comm panel. He knew she needed time to compose a message. And herself. The light blinked out. He unstrapped the restraints and stood.

And again, for a moment, duty warred with a part of him he didn't know existed. Duty decreed her personal concerns were not his problem. He was an officer in the Imperial Fleet. She was just a low-budget freighter operator. She—

She was hurting. Of all the Godless, soulless creatures in civilized space, he should be the last one to offer her comfort. He wasn't even sure he knew how.

He only knew he had to try.

Trilby wrapped the faded purple quilt around her shoulders and leaned against the padded bulkhead. She could still feel the slight vibration of the interstellar drives, a reassuring, familiar feeling. She needed that right now. The one swallow of gin she'd managed to get down was little comfort. The tall glass on her bedside table had tiny droplets of water speckled on its exterior like clusters of elongated stars. The ice cubes shifted, tinkling, cracking.

Her cabin door chimed. The overhead readout was blank. With only herself and Dezi on board there never had been a need for her to activate the ID system, even if it had worked. And when Jagan had been there, her cabin was his as well.

Now there was her Zafharin lieutenant, though her visitor could just as easily be Dezi.

Her Zafharin lieutenant. He was not, she admonished herself as she trundled to the door, *her* lieutenant. More than likely he was some Zafharin female's lieutenant. One he was obviously anxious to get back to. He probably saw her mourning as a tactic to delay him.

She tapped at the access pad on the wall. The door slid to the left. Light from the corridor spilled into the dim cabin and she looked up, blinking. Tall. Broad shoulders. Definitely the Zafharin lieutenant.

At least she had the presence of mind not to call him *hers* again.

She took a step backward, snagged her heel on the edge of the quilt, and stumbled, arms flailing. She was abruptly caught up in strong arms and drawn against a familiar black jacket and white shirt. Was she, she wondered as his arms wrapped around her, going to spend her life with her nose forever in this man's chest?

Women usually didn't throw themselves into Rhis's arms. Rafi would've no doubt approved of the way Rhis caught Trilby tightly against him, and taken it as a positive sign of things to come.

But Rhis was a realist. It wasn't his charm but a bulky purple quilt snaking around Trilby's boots that had precipitated their current embrace.

"Are you all right?"

She pushed away from him and gathered the tangled quilt in her arms. "I'm not drunk, if that's what you're thinking. Clumsy. A bit . . ." She paused, then sighed loudly. "A bit off balance, in more ways than one. But no, not drunk." She motioned to her glass as she plopped down on her bed. "One swallow made it down. Any more and I think it might decide to come back up."

"I'm not—it would be okay if you were drunk." Rhis recognized the defensiveness in her tone. That dismayed him, though it rarely had before. People's feelings were unimportant. But this wasn't just people. This was Trilby Elliot. "It's not easy to hear such news of someone you've known almost your whole life." He glanced around for something to sit on. Next to her, on her bed, was an inviting option, and for that very reason he rejected it. He still had this urge to take that small, purple-swaddled form back into his arms.

He sought an alternative. He'd never been in her cabin before. It was about the size of the one she'd assigned him, with a double bed along the back wall. Shelving, six drawers, and a closet were on the left. Her quarters lacked any semblance of luxury, just like the rest of her ship.

Unless you counted the purple quilt as a luxury. The muted glow from a small bedside lamp and from her computer screen, which was swiveled toward her, showed it wrapped around her like a protecting cocoon. The square shaft of light from the corridor highlighted the threadbare spots in the thin gray carpeting. As his eyes finally adjusted, he saw a larger plush toy felinar that lay on its side on the bed next to her. And in the corner, a single metal-back chair clipped to a deck lock.

He stepped on the release to unlatch it from the floor and dragged it over, straddling it as he faced her.

"This won't cause you any delays, if that's what you're worried about." She drew her knees up under her chin. "I'm not in a position to go chasing after Carina. Or the 'Sko. We'll make Rumor on time."

"That's not why I came to talk to you. Tell me about Carina."

"Why? Do you think you know her or something?"

He responded with a small shake of his head. "I think it might help for you to talk of her."

She was silent, and he could read the distrust in her eyes. No doubt she was wondering who had named Rhis Vanur chief psychiatrist.

"I've known her for years. But you knew that, didn't you?" Again a silence, but a thoughtful one this time. "Dezi," she said knowingly.

"I probably would have guessed anyway."

"Yeah, well, Carina is someone Dezi categorizes as one of my 'wilder' friends."

Rhis remembered how the 'droid had described the now-subdued woman before him: *She's a good girl, truly she is. A bit wild at times . . .*

"More wild than you?"

"Yeah. Wilder than me. Couple of years younger than me too. She's really a stunning girl. Woman," she corrected herself, and rummaged through a drawer in her nightstand. "Here." She handed him a thin holograph, then tabbed the light up a notch so he could see.

Five people filled the picture taken in a bar. Neadi's bar, he assumed, recognizing the golden face of the woman standing behind the counter. A taller dark-haired man was on her left. Potted plants quivered overhead from an unseen breeze, green fronds and a variety of brightly colored blossoms trailing down on the right side, almost touching the shoulder of a portly, red-bearded man with bright blue eyes. The man's shirt had a GGA logo on the front. Next to him, perched on a stool, was Trilby, laughing, batting away the hand of an exotically beautiful woman on her right who was trying to pour a glass of clear liquid on Trilby's head.

The woman had to be Carina. Her glossy brown hair was long, curling about her shoulders and, as she moved, falling in more curls to her waist. Without her high cheekbones and full mouth, her face would appear almost too thin. But the combination, and her large, almond-shaped dark blue eyes, gave her instead a mysterious, almost regal look.

He immediately pegged her as vain, though he recognized he had no valid reason to do so. But there was something in her face that reminded him of Malika. Something in the way she looked at the people around her, appraising them, categorizing them.

She had a beauty not unlike Malika's as well: dark and sultry. Trilby, next to her, was so different. Like a ray of light, or a bright moon in a dark sky.

Trilby sparkled. When he'd first seen her, through a haze of pain in sick bay, he'd thought she was pretty. Sweet.

Truth was, he admitted with some reluctance, she was more than that. She was enchanting. Enchantingly beautiful.

He felt a heat rise in his body, brought his concentration back to the problem at hand. Carina.

"Carina is the mischief-maker, yes?"

"Carina is the mischief-maker, yes." She mimicked his accent, lightly rolling the *r*, drawing out the *i*. "*Vad,*" she added.

His surprise was genuine. "You speak—"

"Only *yes, no,* and *another beer, please.* Plus an assortment of useful curses." She grinned. "All the necessaries, courtesy of Leo." She pointed to the dark-haired man next to Neadi.

She was smiling now. The quilt had slipped from around her shoulders and she released the tense grip on her knees. Something warm stirred inside Rhis's chest. He'd made her feel better. Odd how that also made him feel different too.

"And what was *Dasja* Carina trying to do?" he asked, bringing her attention back to the holo.

"*Dasja* is Miss?"

"Lady. But as in a title, not as in a gender. It can be a title of heritage, or of graciousness." He'd not had to explain his language in a long time. "Honored woman," he said finally. "*Dasjon* is for a man. Lord. Honored man."

Trilby nodded. "*Dasja* Carina would probably laugh her ass off if you referred to her as a lady. She was trying to water me. To get me to grow." She pointed to the lush green plants. "She's always bringing plants to Neadi and Leo. She's got a pretty good hydroponics section on the *Dream*—" She stopped. "Well, that's probably gone now."

The small, bright glow faded from her face. Rhis felt the lack of its warmth, wanted it to return.

"So she waters you?" He forced a smile. "And this? Who is this with the beard?" It wasn't Jagan Grantforth. He'd known what Grantforth looked like even before he'd seen Trilby's files. Jagan Grantforth's well-groomed form was frequently seen on the televid next to his politically well-placed uncle, Garold, now Chief Secretary of Trade in the Conclave.

"That's Chaser. He's a med-tech at GGA HQ on Bagrond. He comes back to Rumor once in a while. Carina, Chaser, and I grew up together there. In Port

Rumor." She took the holo from him, studied it again. "Seems like a long time ago. Growing up, that is. Not this holo. This was only a few months ago."

"A birthday?" Rhis guessed, trying to fit the holo into the timeline of Trilby's *J* files.

"Hmm? Oh, no. I had—well, it was just another wild party."

He heard her stop mid-sentence, heard the attempted lightness in her tone. There was a reason for that party, one she wasn't willing to share. He had a feeling it had to do with Grantforth. Or, rather, Grantforth's absence.

"Where was Dezi?"

"Getting more liquor, where else?"

"So *Dasja* Neadi does not have him tend bar?"

"*Dasjon* Leonid," she said, and Rhis nodded at her use of the term, "takes Dezi back to the kitchen to teach him to cook. That's been an ongoing project. You probably noticed I do most of the cooking on board."

"A food replicator would be easier, no?"

"A food replicator would cost money, yes." She held up one hand and ticked items off on her fingers. "I need a new long-range sensor optical diffuser, new short-range optical filters, and my portside scanner's on its last legs. I only have one really working crystal splicer—"

"That I know well," Rhis cut in dryly.

"—and the main cargo door needs to be removed and rehung because some fool crashed a forklift into it last month, and if it falls off on my way to Bagrond I'm in deep shit. My AGSs need to be completely overhauled and have new stands put on, and," she added, giving him a wary glance, "I probably shouldn't be telling you this, but only one of my laser rifles works and my ion-cannon reservoir is down below half.

"And you ask about a replicator?" She exhaled a sharp laugh. "Rhis-my-boy, talk to me about a fully charged complement of Lady-Fives instead. Then I wouldn't be worrying about the ion cannon."

He knew the *Venture* was in bad shape. But her lack of defense options startled him. Only one working laser rifle and a dying ion cannon. "I thought your Conclave outlawed LD-Five torpedoes after the war."

"Oh, they did. But they're not out here in the lanes, I am. And when they cut back on funds and manpower for patrols in Gensiira . . ."

She didn't have to finish her sentence. Rhis knew. The Conclave was turning its back on a region that had little to offer in the way of profits or pleasures. Not like the inner worlds of Quivera or Bagrond. All part of the Lissade Quadrant. Lissade was the United Intergalactic Conclave's home base and as different from Gensiira as the *Venture* was from the *Razalka*.

Then something that had bothered him about Neadi's message came back into mind. "How did *Dasja* Neadi know to warn you and *Bella's Dream*? Yes, I know, in a spaceport bar she would hear talk. But talk so specific?"

"How do you think Port Rumor got its name? Not because of Neadi's bar, which is called Flyboy's, by the way. It's because we're close to where the borders of Gensiira, your own Yanir System, and the 'Sko's Eilni intersect. Conclave. Zafharin. Ycsko." She touched three invisible points in the air as she said the names. "That's the only place that happens. And Port Rumor's the closest cold beer."

The star charts played through Rhis's mind, show-

ing that same intersection. And now, from what he'd
learned from her ship's charts, traders' lanes he'd not
been aware of.

"There are 'Sko expatriates who jump ship and
look for refuge on Rumor, though not many," Trilby
continued. "Lots more Zafharin expats who don't
want the formalities of your Empire. And the usual
assortment of bastards that results when the Conclave is thrown in. You may think your Empire is a
safe distance away on Verahznar, Rhis. But believe
me, anything you know there, we know of, sooner or
later, on Rumor. And very often sooner. Freighters
carry more than cargo, you know."

He did. It had never been brought home quite so
well before. "And so Neadi hears . . . ?"

"What Quivera or any of the political higher-ups
are not yet willing to release. Or admit. And she
heard that someone in the Conclave is looking to
make some real profits. Knock out all the short-
haulers like me. With 'Sko help."

Rhis straightened, his hands curling tightly around
the top metal bar of the chair. Suddenly duty took on
a very personal meaning. "Tell me," he said, his voice
suddenly serious, almost flat. "Tell me everything
Dasja Neadi said."

Rhis sat in the lounge, waiting for the teakettle to
chime. Life without a replicator. Life without a comfortable bed and soft, thick carpeting in his cabin.
Life with a patched comm system, temperamental
scanners, and only one ion cannon, half-dead at that.

Life with Trilby Elliot, air sprite with only one
working laser rifle. And a missing friend.

Rhis thought he was beginning to understand how that friend was missing. And why.

He'd listened to Trilby tell him of Neadi's warning. Then, with her permission, he reviewed Neadi's message itself. And he'd told Trilby a small part of what he had heard about the 'Sko—though not his part in verifying those rumors. It was still necessary for her to believe his 'Sko Tark was leftover from war games, his appearance on her doorstep due to mechanical failure.

He couldn't tell her of his being on Szedcafar. He heard Neadi question who, besides the Zafharin, would sleep with the 'Sko. And he knew Trilby wouldn't believe his story.

One man was simply not capable of infiltrating the 'Sko military base.

But then, he was not one simple man.

He'd been three days overdue at the recon point and had left strict orders with his command staff *not* to wait more than twelve hours for his return.

He hadn't anticipated the Ycsko removing him from their compound on Szed to one of their mother ships. Looking back, he realized he should have. But as *Dasjon* Admiral Vanushavor had liked to point out, he'd become reckless of late. Not careless. Reckless. It was as if he didn't care if he lived or died.

He didn't. At least, at the time the infiltration of the compound on Szed was proposed, the success of the mission meant more to him than his life. And the mission had been a success. He did infiltrate the military base and relay the critical stolen data back to the *Razalka*. It was his own rescue that had been botched, and he'd been forced to take actions that were nearly fatal.

Might have been, if not for Trilby. Avanar's vampire snakes would've found him eventually. And he would have faded into the swamps and not be here now, piecing together information that made what he'd learned on Szed even more urgent.

And he would not be here now, waiting for the kettle to chime so he could deliver a cup of hot tea to one Trilby Elliot, air sprite, freighter captain, and finder of lost Zafharin officers.

As if on cue, a soft but shrill pinging sounded in the lounge.

He performed his duty and headed for the ladderway.

Trilby was back in command of her bridge. Dezi's knee joints squeaked as he vacated the copilot's seat and returned to navigation. Rhis handed her the steaming tea and placed his own mug in the holder on the copilot's console.

She pointed to a screen to his right. "Dezi and I worked up a list of all the short-haulers gone missing in the past two months, ones that fit Neadi's profile. Departure, pickup, and cargo are all noted."

There were seven, including *Bella's Dream*. Four had contracted through Rinnaker. Two from Grantforth. One from Norvind.

He turned the list into data and the data into pinpoints on a star-chart grid. On the *Razalka*, that grid would be projected, suspended in a holograph over the large polished table in the ready room aft of upper level of the bridge. The best minds in the Empire would scrutinize it, tear it apart.

Here his grid was flat on a comp screen. He absently tapped his lightpen on the table, waiting for his tea to cool, wondering just how much he could share with his air sprite and an old envoy 'droid.

"Well?" Trilby asked.

"I can understand why *Dasja* Neadi sees a problem."

"And?"

He shook his head, took a sip of his tea. It was a good, strong brew, pungent. Almost Zafharin quality. "I have more questions than answers, Trilby Elliot."

"We've got two days yet before we reach Port Rumor. Neadi may know more then. Flyboy's has been busy lately."

Rhis glanced at her. His air sprite had lost some of her sparkle again. The pleasant memories she'd shared with him in her cabin had led to more serious things. Things that led him to the conclusion that he was going to have to do those wogs-and-weemlies after all. The ones she was so worried about. The ones finding her files on Jagan Grantforth had halted.

She was not two days from Port Rumor. She was three, perhaps five days from the *Razalka,* or the closest Imperial outpost, whichever he found first.

Trilby Elliot wouldn't be happy when he took control of her ship. That thought uncharacteristically rankled him.

But he had to take control of something at this point and had a little over twenty-four hours in which to do so. The *Venture* presented a much easier prospect than controlling his inexplicable reactions to her captain.

He had a feeling that both of his problems were going to let him get very little sleep again tonight.

Transit time on a run had a predictably boring routine. Like most freighter operators, Trilby tried to pattern her hours after the old dirtside rhythms. That meant at least six hours sleep at a time she designated as night. A large mug of coffee within fifteen minutes, first thing in the morning. And the rest of the day tending to little things to fill the time as the ship went from point A to point B.

She pulled on her last clean T-shirt and pinged Dezi on intraship. "I'll be on the bridge in ten. See Rhis yet?"

"He's not been to the bridge this morning, Captain. However, the galley was activated about an hour ago."

"Got it. Thanks."

Rhis was seated at the counter, portable pad on his right, coffee on his left. She took a quick glance, saw the freighter schedule data on his screen. "Anything?"

"More questions." He looked tired.

She heard the frustration in his voice. Frustration over a problem that wasn't his. That touched her, made her think about awarding him another bonus point. She refilled his coffee. "Please don't tell me you were working on this all night. I told you to get some sleep. How's your side?"

He stretched his left arm. "Better."

Liar, she thought. *I should've tranked him and locked him in sick bay.* Of course, she'd have had to strip off his clothes again. That was a pleasant thought. She needed pleasant thoughts right now to chase away her worries over Carina.

"I'm going to play captain on the bridge for a while. Give Dezi some downtime."

"I'll be all right here."

She grabbed a large plastic mug, filled it with coffee, and snapped on a protective spill cap. She was often lax about loose items in the lounge, but never on the bridge. Everything was strapped down, sealed, and secured.

"You know where to find me if you need me."

Dezi came back on duty at lunch.

"Seen our lieutenant around?" she asked.

"He was not in engineering when I left. And I didn't see him in the corridors. However, it's possible he's in the lounge. After all, it's approaching your lunch hour, and—"

"That's where I'm headed, Dez. Then I've got to get some chores started." If she didn't keep busy her mind would keep drifting back to *Bella's Dream*. One more thing in her life she could do nothing about. "If you see him, tell him I'm looking for him."

She didn't run into Rhis on the forward ladderway

or in the corridor. The lounge was empty, spotlessly clean. She grabbed a swamp apple from the fridge and crunched on it on her way to her cabin. The crisp fruit was one of the few benefits of her excursions to Avanar.

She was sorting laundry in her cabin when her door chimed. Dezi wouldn't leave the bridge without advising her. So she knew with relative accuracy who stood on the other side even before she heard the muffled Zafharin voice call out. "Trilby?"

She stepped around a pile of towels to slap at the panel. "Come on in." And then caught his expression of bewilderment when he took in the state of her cabin.

"Redecorating?"

She waved one hand at him and then realized, as he averted his eyes, that what she also waved at him was her scanty flowered bra. Pillorian silk. Lace trimmed. She chuckled. "It's either this," she said with a sweeping motion, "or next shift I'm on the bridge totally naked."

Rhis opened his mouth then clamped it shut, and she was surprised to see the color heighten on his cheeks. She'd embarrassed him? She hadn't thought it possible.

She couldn't resist. "Well, actually, if you remember, that was the way you and I started our relationship."

"That was not of my choosing." He shoved his hands in his pockets and looked anywhere but the floor. Her empty closet seemed to have a particular fascination for him.

"Don't do much laundry duty, do you, Vanur?"

Something distasteful flashed across his face, and

his dark brows slanted into a frown. Ah, Pampered Imperial Arrogance. Slumming.

"It'll all be over soon." She tossed the last towel on the pile. "Port Rumor's about forty-eight hours from now. Then you can be on your way back to the much-improved, much-preferred Empire."

"Dezi doesn't cook and now does not do laundry, yes?"

"Not if you want to eat and have something to wear, no." She grinned. His Zafharin accent and phrasing still sounded quaint to her. It gave him a unique, almost endearing quality. "Don't they teach you about proper utilization of personnel in the Imperial Fleet Academy? Or is it just true that everyone in the Empire is perfect at every task, like those rumors I've heard?"

"Rumors?" he asked in mock indignation. His eyes sparkled playfully. "You have known me now, what, three, four days, and you do not know that everything produced by the Zafharin embodies perfection?"

Well, I have seen you naked, she almost said but then stopped, knowing that only proved his claim. Ah, well. She chuckled again, then, on a whim, grabbed a pile of towels from the floor. "Okay, Lieutenant Perfection, here you go." She shoved the towels against him. "Some of them are yours, anyway. Glad to know they'll all be spotless and perfectly folded within the hour."

He stared at her, his arms overflowing, clearly not expecting her demand. "This is not—"

"Enough?" she cut in, grinning broadly. She snatched at the pile of silk and lace next to her. "Want more?"

Rhis backed up a step. "No."

"Good." She motioned down the corridor to her right. "Laundry is the third door on the left. Says L-One on the wall. Three cycles, all sonic, but only two work and you may have to smack the microdryer a few times to get it to kick on."

He switched a look from her to the towels in his arms. Then back again. A small furrow dug into his brow. "Elliot, this is really not—"

"One more word of complaint out of you, Vanur, and you will get my bras and panties too."

Again his gaze zigzagged back and forth. What was going on in that aristocratic head of his? Then he swore under his breath in Zafharish and turned, almost stumbling over the door tread as he strode down the corridor.

A towel escaped from his grasp, falling onto the decking. Trilby saw it when she followed him. Laughing, she threw it after his retreating figure. "I like 'em nice and fluffy, Vanur. And neatly folded!"

He glanced over his shoulder at her with an unreadable look. Trilby leaned against the bulkhead and laughed until her sides ached.

Gods, it felt good to laugh. She wiped her eyes, then went back to her cabin to get the rest of the laundry, stuffing it into a canvas duffel. In her brief exchange with Rhis she'd forgotten for the moment her concerns for Carina, her hurt over Jagan, her worries of how she was going to pay for everything she needed just to survive. She knew he had enjoyed the light verbal game as much as she had. She'd seen the sly smile on his mouth, the mirth dancing in his eyes.

More than enjoyed it: he'd encouraged it. He could have shut her down with a quick, biting comment. Or just walked out. She felt he would have two days ago. But now . . .

Now things were different. Or starting to become different. There was a camaraderie. Maybe this was the real Rhis Vanur, not the arrogant, demanding, cold man who had lunged at her in sick bay, almost ending her life. That man had been in physical pain and no little amount of fear. She could see that now.

She lugged the rest of the laundry down the corridor, thinking maybe her Zafharin lieutenant wasn't quite that bad, after all.

She waited an hour before checking his progress. How much damage could he do to a load of towels? She found him smacking the front of the dryer with the flat of his hand. Pounding it with his fist, he informed her, didn't have the same positive result. The unit whined and grumbled as if in agreement. She grabbed a stack of freshly folded towels and hid her laughter in their softness.

The corridor suddenly resounded with a loud, discordant wail.

She dropped the towels and spun toward him.

He held his hands in the air in supplication. "I was only doing what you told me to—"

She grabbed his arm. "Incoming. Damn it! That's my short-range alarm. We've got incoming!" She bolted down the corridor.

He caught up with her on the ladderway to the bridge. "Short-range?"

"Long-range is fritzed. Can't ID." Their boots hammered up the metal stairs. "Short-range is all we've got to handle unfriendlies."

Trilby was first through the hatchway. "Who's there, Dez?"

"Ycsko. Three Trahtarks." The 'droid relayed their speed and distance without any of his usual, meandering dialogue.

Trilby slid into the captain's seat, her fingers already keying queries into the ship's systems. The wailing ceased. "Okay. I see 'em. Weapons online. Shields at max."

"Affirmative."

She raked the safety straps across her chest. "Anyone else in the neighborhood?"

"Negative. I have sent out a broad-channel Request for Assistance."

Rhis stood, scanning the data at the copilot's station. The Tarks were about twenty minutes behind the *Venture*. Then he grabbed for the navigator's chair. A light flashed on her panel, showing his station was online. She went back to her work with Dezi.

"Fifteen minutes. Still closing," the 'droid intoned.

Something odd flickered on one of Trilby's data comps. It came from the navigation. She shot him a look over her shoulder. "Vanur! What the hell—?"

"The 'Sko have started filtering their energy emissions. This grants them some invisibility. Unless, of course, your scanners know to look for them."

Trilby saw the large blip flash on her long-range screen. Somehow he'd gotten it to work again. Her anger at Rhis died and was replaced by a moment of amazement. And then a growing feeling of dread. "Cloaking device?"

"Not exactly."

"Eleven minutes," Dezi stated.

"Shit! That's a mother ship." Part of Trilby's mind acknowledged Dezi's countdown. The other part focused on data now streaming next to the ominous blip. She glanced again at Rhis, saw him frowning at the weapons data on the screen on his left. He evidently had the same thoughts she did. A half-dead ion cannon was no match for a 'Sko mother ship.

Her stomach tightened in fear. Neadi's warnings played through her mind. But she wasn't on a cargo run. Her holds were empty.

"Dezi, amend that RFA to a Code-Three SUA!" A Request for Assistance could be ignored. A Ship under Attack advisory could not.

She shook her fist at the blip on the screen as if it could see her. "Gods damn you. I don't have any cargo!"

"That will not be their concern until it's too late."

"Thanks for the encouraging words, Vanur."

"Nine minutes."

Trilby's fingers flew back to the command controls. "Tarks are in attack formation. Retract cannon hatch."

"*Nav!*"

Trilby's chair tilted back. A broad arm shot in front of her, knocking her hands from the controls. He yelled words at her as he keyed in a course change from her station.

She swore back at him. "Speak *Standard,* Gods damn you!"

"The abandoned miner's raft in the asteroid belt. There!" He pointed to the data now on her screen. "We can get there. We can lose them in the debris field."

It just might work. Trilby hesitated only a second before throwing the ship hard to starboard.

The freighter shuddered as the Tarks' weapons laced the shields. The auxiliary interface panel behind Rhis sizzled, showering sparks through the small cockpit. Two data screens flickered. The *Venture*'s engines whined, straining. Power readouts sagged, then spiked.

Rhis worked in a course adjustment. "We have to outrun them."

Trilby tapped quickly on a datapad on her left. "Dezi, get down to engineering. Disconnect the A-Five bypass. I'm going to run everything we got to the drives. That should give us what we need." Though what condition they'd be in when they got to the rafts was up for grabs.

Rhis slid into the seat Dezi vacated just as Trilby banked the ship to port to avoid incoming fire.

"Missed me, you bastard." There was a grim note of glee in her voice.

A critical-status light blinked red. "You're disconnecting life support?"

"Only belowdecks. I'll seal the bridge on Dezi's signal. What do you think, we've got reserves? That extra power has to come from somewhere."

It took five more long minutes of ducking and diving, of skittering through the blackness before the asteroid debris field was in sight. Two more comp panels sizzled as the *Venture*'s shields tried to handle the impact of the 'Sko weapons. Trilby ran through every evasive maneuver she knew, then invented a few more. She trusted Rhis to keep one hand on the cannon's targeting controls and prayed for a lucky shot.

He grazed one Tark. It fell back behind the other two, damaged but not disabled.

"Good shot, flyboy."

The *Venture* defied all safety parameters, pushing her components beyond their specs. Circura II short-haulers weren't built to maneuver like this one did.

But even the best of patches couldn't hold up forever under enemy fire.

She announced the problem before he did. "Starboard shields down forty percent."

They were just skimming the first debris from the asteroid field. Already several shots from the Tarks exploded off target, shattering the small asteroids instead.

"We'll make it."

She wished she had his confidence. She checked the scanners, saw the two lead Tarks and one behind. Her stomach clenched. "They're still on us."

"When we get into the larger debris field, it'll force them to loosen formation. I should be able to get a clear shot then."

"That big debris will get through my starboard shields eventually."

"Logged and noted, Captain."

"Unless I—" Trilby spun out of her seat. "Take over, Rhis. I might be able to do something here."

He reached over and transferred control just as she wrenched the lower panel off the auxiliary power console on his right. She hunkered down, a crystal splicer already in her hand. But she kept a vigilant watch on her screen.

The Tarks started to change formation. Then the weapons sensors showed incoming fire. He banked, maneuvering the freighter around several larger groups of debris.

Trilby braced herself against the edge of the access panel as her ship veered sharply. "Don't forget my starboard aux thruster's a bit oversensitive."

Aft shields showed two grazing hits from the Tarks. Then a readout on the main console went suddenly from red to green.

"Got it!" Trilby pushed herself upright. "Just bought us about ten minutes more on the shields, Rhis-my-boy."

"Good. Our friends are starting to get careless."

Trilby lunged for her seat, rehooked her straps, and swung the armrest controls in front of her. The debris fields on the viewscreen were tightly grouped, with boulder-size asteroids trailing away from one almost as large as her ship.

Rhis wove the freighter through the fields with practiced precision.

Trilby saw a brief opening ahead and poised her hand over her controls. "I'll take her back when we get there."

"We're not going there."

"We're not?"

Rhis banked the freighter without warning, sending the bulky ship into a narrow space between two asteroids. Smaller debris pinged off the shields. Proximity alarms wailed in complaint.

Trilby ignored what her eyes told her and worked the data from her navigational systems. Rhis flew her ship as if he'd been born in the captain's chair. She patched in small corrections, playing with attitude and yaw as he sloughed off their speed.

"Use the braking vanes," she told him, but he was

already tabbing them down to fifteen percent, then twenty.

She caught his swift, questioning glance in her direction. He was no doubt wondering how she knew that trick. And she was wondering who taught him.

A flare on the aft viewscreen drew her attention.

Rhis's smile, when she looked back at him, was almost feral. "A Trahtark's main flaw. Increased power means decreased stability in tight quarters."

They emerged with only two Tarks on their tail. Trilby retracted the vanes quickly.

"They're persistent, though." She saw the splattering of their lasers on the port shields now. There was an ominous hissing and popping noise from a console to her right.

"Let them be so." Rhis magnified the viewscreen until a large angular object came into view. "There. The Drachnar mining rafts. Should be two of them."

"One and a half," Trilby corrected as she scanned her data.

"Let's take our friends for a tour."

"We might be able to do better than that." Trilby brought up a file from her nav charts. "This ship used to dock here. I've still got the codes."

She caught his brief look of appreciation. It meant more to her than she wanted to admit. "Head for the red launch tower," she told him. "I might be able to release the maintenance 'bots from those bays below. Drachnar always staffed at least sixty to a bay. If even half are left, that should play hell with their targeting sensors."

The lead Tark got in two good shots before they got to the raft. "Starboard shields down twenty percent!" Trilby hung on to the armrest as the freighter shimmied in response.

"Two minutes, Trilby-*chenka*."

"Got a leak in the compression feed."

"One minute, forty-five."

Another alarm wailed overhead. Trilby slapped at the panel, silencing it. "I'm not getting a response from Bay Eighty-Seven. Affirmatives from Eighty-Five and Ninety-Two."

"One minute." The console behind Rhis continued to hiss and spark.

Trilby ignored it. She focused on the weak signals from the mining raft. "I'm getting a readout on Eighty-Seven. It may open and discharge. It may not."

"Forty-five seconds."

"Remember my ascent indicator is wrong."

Rhis reached over her head and tapped the plush felinar.

"You learn quick. For an Imperial."

He flashed her a conspiratorial grin. "Twenty-five seconds."

"Sending release codes. Bays Eighty-Five and Ninety-Two responding. Bay Eighty-Seven—" Trilby took her eyes from the data scanners and glanced at the aft viewscreen. It looked as if a hundred metallic balls suddenly shot out of a gigantic pinball-machine tube. She gave a short whoop of delight. "Eighty-Seven's decided to party!"

Both Tarks banked sharply as the maintenance 'bots bounced off their shields. The pilots' attentions and targeting computers suddenly overloaded. Rhis targeted, locked on, and fired the ion cannon.

The lagging Tark, the one he'd damaged earlier, exploded into a ball of debris and escaping gases.

"Damned good shot, flyboy!"

Several thousand tons of plasteel gridwork loomed ahead. One Tark followed behind, closer now, firing more insistently.

"Aft shields down another twenty percent. I'm going to pull power from the port shields, Rhis. Aft is critical now." The ship's drives were in the aft section. The drives and Dezi.

"I can compensate." He made some quick adjustments, keeping the Tark targeted to starboard.

The *Venture* hugged the perimeter of the larger raft, proximity alarms again screeching. It was a close, dangerous maneuver.

Rhis banked the ship sharply, cutting power.

The Tark's view of the raft was blocked by the larger freighter in front of it. The pilot tried to pull up abruptly at the last moment but slammed into a protruding launch tower, shearing off one wing. Jagged chunks of metal wheeled through the airless void toward the raft's empty launchpad.

Trilby hollered with joy again, reached for Rhis's hand in a congratulatory handshake. His clasped his large hand around hers, grinning, but there was something more than the thrill of victory in his eyes.

Just as she had no doubt there was in hers.

His hand tightened around hers. Warmth flowed up her arm. Flustered, she plastered on her "professional captain" mien. "We did good, flyboy."

His fingers squeezed hers. "We did very good."

Not "we." Rhis was the hero, and not only because he'd just saved their lives. But because he cared about Carina's plight. Pored over shipping logs rather than sleeping. Poured her tea and brought it to her. Folded the towels, nice and fluffy, just as she liked them.

Damnation! She pulled her hand back. She had to stop touching him. Next time she might not be able to stop.

She feigned a proprietary look and keyed control of her ship back to her station. She guided it between two large storage depots, but her heart was still pounding. Which reminded her of the larger problem: the 'Sko. "Anyone else out there?"

They were too deep in the asteroid field for the mother ship to come after them. But another set of Tarks, if diligent, might find their trail.

Rhis looked up from the scanner and wiped one hand over his face. "No. The mother ship seems to have pulled out of range."

She heard his emphasis on "seems" and grudgingly acknowledged her scanners were often myopic, at best. And they were not at their best right now.

"Well, we'll keep out eyes peeled." She keyed open intraship. "Dezi? All clear, for now."

"I am pleased to learn that. Shall I reconnect life support?"

"I want to do a systems check first." She nodded to Rhis. "We took some damage."

He leaned forward, bringing the data online as Dezi acknowledged her request. "I have begun repairs on the compression feed already."

"Get back to me when you're done. Captain out."

A low exclamation in Zafharish was followed by a few curse words she recognized. Her heart stopped for a moment and she glanced at her long-range scanner. But it showed no intruders, 'Sko or otherwise.

Then she remembered she'd started a system check. He probably was compiling a damage report. "Tabulating repair times for me?"

He raised his gaze from the screen, and for a moment she thought she saw something hard glitter in his eyes' dark depths. Something more than annoyance at her ship's mounting ills. Then he shook his head, his mouth twisting into a cynical half smile.

"Have you ever had the feeling," he asked her, with an aimless wave of one hand, "that the Gods are conspiring against you?"

She burst out laughing. "My whole life. Don't be so sure it's you. Could be the Gods don't want me to make a nice profit off that Bagrond run."

"Or maybe the 'Sko don't," he put in quietly.

Trilby's smile faded. "You can't be serious. They were purposely waiting for the *Venture*? There's no way they'd know my schedule. It's not as if we departed from a controlled port where I'd have a flight plan filed." Like *Bella's Dream* had, coming out of Marbo.

"You're right. Of course," Rhis said quickly. "I was thinking of something else."

"That they knew you were on my ship? How? Nothing came by to check out where your Tark went down. Not a seeker 'droid. Not even a flyby."

He ran one hand through his hair before answering. "Sorry. It is only that . . ." He paused, then quickly, almost harshly: "I don't know what it was I was thinking."

Her comp screen chimed twice softly. She turned from him, paged down the data from her systems check, then sent it to Rhis's screen. He wasn't going to like the results, but then, she didn't like what she was hearing. Or his sudden evasiveness, his hesitancy with his words. "Okay, so we've got problems. Why all of a sudden do you think it's personal?"

"I don't. It is just that . . ." He shrugged. "I've been in Fleet for too long. Paranoia is part of my job description. We most likely came across the Tarks by happenstance. A routine patrol."

It was a totally believable explanation. And she totally didn't believe it.

"In Conclave space, nowhere near any trade lanes? As soon as we get up and running, I'm sending out an advisory." She didn't think for a minute the Conclave would investigate. But at least a warning would be posted. The kind of warning that could have saved *Bella's Dream*.

"We're close to the border. By the time you contact a patrol base, the 'Sko will be long gone. Besides," Rhis added with a shrug, "your people may ask what you were doing out here."

True, but the gain seemed to outweigh the risk to Trilby. "I'll take that chance."

"I advise you not to."

It was the first time she'd heard that sharp tone from him since he'd grabbed her in sick bay. She leaned back in her seat, was about to ask him just who he thought he was to dictate to her, when he touched her lightly on the arm.

"Sorry." And he sounded sorry. "I'm not giving you orders. But I am trained to deal with security issues. If the 'Sko have left this area, your report will generate nothing. But if they've not, your report will help them trace us again."

He had a point. She nodded, slowly. The light touch on her arm changed to a reassuring and not at all unpleasant clasp. Warm, almost possessive. But his evasiveness rankled at her. She leaned away from him. "Okay. But I'm filing as soon as we pick up Rumor's outer beacon."

"Agreed."

"Can I have my seat back now? That routine patrol poked some holes in my ship. I want to get her into one of the raft bays so we can patch her up. Just in case they're still waiting for us when we leave this asteroid field."

"Of course." He unsnapped the harness strap. "Let me know what you need me to do."

Be honest with me, Trilby thought, but said nothing. Her disquieting sense of unease about her "hero" was back. She hated being kept in the dark. Bad things always seemed to follow. Like Jagan's marriage. Her agent's desertion.

She guided the *Venture* into an abandoned bay, worrisome thoughts trailing through her mind like the debris floating through the wreckage behind her.

The *Venture*'s landing struts locked onto the docking rails with a loud clank that reverberated through the ship.

"Would be nice if the gate fields still worked." Trilby motioned to the darkened ring of lights at the wide docking-bay entry. "Then we could all help with outside repair." She kept her voice level, professional. Rhis seemed to have the uncanny ability to get her emotions seesawing, and she was, frankly, tired of it. She had to remember he wasn't "her" hero. He was her passenger. One she'd never see again after Port Rumor.

"As it is," she said, unsnapping her straps, "best this raft can do for us is let us filch power from its solar grid."

Rhis turned. "You don't have EVA suits?"

"One. Mine. Doubt it'll fit you." She paused in the hatchway to glance at the life-support lights above the door. The *Venture* was back to normal, at least where that was concerned.

She reached for the palm pad, but Rhis's voice stopped her. "How much experience do you have with zero-g repairs?"

He sounded concerned about her. Troubled by whatever it was he wasn't telling her, she didn't want him to be. His concern felt false, somehow. She leaned back against the hatchway. "Funny thing about EVA suits. Bigger they are, more they cost. Herkoid found that out a long time ago. Wasn't a kid in Port Rumor, 'specially a girl, who didn't get lots of training in zero-g repairs. And I don't mean in sims."

She saw his eyes close and bit her lip. Her answer had been sharp. But if he were truly concerned about her, then he had to be honest. All she could think about when the Tarks showed up was survival. She never questioned for a moment why they were on her tail. It had taken Rhis and his Fleet-issue paranoia to do that.

It bothered her that she didn't have an answer. But it bothered her more that she thought he did. And, in spite of the way he held her hand and looked at her with a dark fire in his eyes, he wasn't willing to share it.

That hurt her, just as Jagan's lies and polished subterfuge had. Just as the supposedly wise social workers in Port Rumor had. Everyone seemed to know better than she how to run her life. And none ever saw fit to tell her. After all, who was she? Nothing but another cast-off kid to the Iffys—*the* Iffys—and nothing but a low-budget jumpjockey to Jagan Grantforth. *The* Jagan Grantforth.

She slapped at the palm pad. The door whooshed

open, letting in the tinny smell of a ventilation system that had just kicked on.

"It'll take Dez and me about two hours, I figure, to patch what we can. I'll be on intraship." She pointed to a small overhead speaker in the corridor. "I'll tell you what we find. And you tell me the minute you see any hint of visitors on my screens."

He put his elbow on the armrest, then covered his mouth with one finger. After a moment, he nodded.

Talk to me! She wanted to yell at him. He was flatlining. Withdrawn. She could only figure it was because of the 'Sko patrol.

"Understood," he said finally.

She wished she knew just what it was he understood.

Rhis listened to the cadence of her boots descending the metal stairs. *Short. Probably female.* He remembered coming up with that appraisal as he lay in sick bay.

Definitely female. He ran his hand over his face and turned back in the seat. He felt like the Gods had plugged his name into the number-one slot on their shit list.

He had to tell her the truth. Now. Who he was and what had brought him here. And that they were returning to Imperial space. He'd hoped to take over the *Venture* about six hours from now. They'd be close to a jumpgate he'd used before for a quick transit back to the Empire. He needed more time as well to finalize the wogs-and-weemlies he'd added to her ship's systems, so that with one signal, all controls would be his. But the bits of coded transmissions he'd snagged from the 'Sko mother ship had forced him to accelerate his plans.

The 'Sko were looking for him. Waiting. He should have known they'd try to trace the energy signature from his Tark and then position patrols at the most likely coordinates. Anticipating, no doubt, a rescue by an Imperial ship.

But the patrol by Avanar had seen only an old Circura II starfreighter, which they almost let slip by.

Except for the second bit of data he pulled from their transmission.

The *Careless Venture* was flagged in their files for immediate destruction upon sighting. His air sprite was marked, targeted. And the kill order was tagged with the code symbols *Dark Sword*.

Dark Sword. He didn't have to translate it from Ycskrite to Zafharish. He'd seen the symbols enough during the war to recognize it immediately. Dark Sword was the 'Sko code name for their contact in the Conclave. An anonymous, but well-placed, double agent, from the little the Empire had been able to discern.

He clenched his teeth. The data obtained from his near-fatal mission to Szed alluded to this same high-placed contact in the Conclave. A transport corporation was also involved, as a conduit for funds and information. Both Rinnaker and GGA could fit the profile of the latter. But there were too many possibilities for that crucial government contact. And no new clues.

Until now.

But why would Dark Sword want his air sprite dead? Rhis drummed his fingers on the armrest. He had no answers to that one. But this much he did know: the 'Sko and their spy would have to kill him first to accomplish that part of their mission. And take out the *Razalka* as well.

Because that's where he was taking her. And that's where she was going to stay.

He listened to her chatter to Dezi as they welded patches on the ship's hull. She was working with an array of tools as threadbare as her ship. And as sparse as her closet.

That had shaken him. He'd stared at her empty closet because he couldn't look at the few items of clothing on the floor. He'd always prided himself on his spartan lifestyle. But he had seven daily uniforms in his closet, three dress uniforms, and a workable collection of off-duty clothes.

Trilby Elliot had almost nothing. His closet, his quarters, his entire lifestyle was lavish in comparison.

He had more than one working EVA suit. And he'd been chosen for his assignments because of his qualifications, his intellect, his physical strength.

Not because he took up less space. Or because he was expendable.

Trilby was expendable. Not only to Herkoid but to Jagan Grantforth. Both had shamelessly used her. Both had carelessly endangered her. The thought made him want to punch holes in the bulkhead with his fist.

He settled for answering her question in a sharper tone than he intended. "That scanner disk is still not receiving, no!"

"Well, hell, Vanur, don't bite my head off." Her voice sounded hollow on intraship. But he could clearly picture her rolling her eyes in frustration at him. "We're doing the best we can."

"Of course. Sorry."

"But long-range is okay?"

"Long-range is clear." He hadn't taken his eyes off it. Couldn't afford to. The *Venture* was uncomfortably vulnerable right now, for all the protection afforded by the asteroids and the rafts.

"We've got one more patch to try. If that doesn't work, then it's going to be a slow, careful ride back to Rumor."

No. A slow, careful ride to the border.

The time spent on repairs had been productive, not only for the *Venture* but for Trilby's attitude. Some of her disquiet had abated. The ache between her shoulder blades had far more of her attention at the moment than Rhis's elusive comments. She heard the buckle on his safety strap snap into place as she powered up her ship's engines. Maybe it was time to let things get back to normal. "With no more surprises we'll ETA at Rumor in about forty-three hours."

"Unlocking landing grapples," Dezi intoned.

"Affirmative," she replied. She angled the thrusters, felt the ship shimmy slightly. "You hear me, Vanur? Forty-three and you're free."

"Will you miss me?"

His comment startled her. That and the playful tone in his voice. His evasiveness seemed to have dissipated along with her annoyance at him.

She'd thought about it while she wrangled with the repairs. Maybe he'd told her the truth when he said it was just a routine patrol. She had to admit he had a lot more experience in that area than she did. If the *Venture* jumped through hyperspace as quickly as she jumped to conclusions, she'd have to apply for a patent for a miraculous hyperdrive.

She shot a quick grin over her shoulder and found him looking quizzically at her. "I'll miss you every minute of every hour of every day. Now stick your nose back in your station and holler like hell the second anything even farts out there."

"Captain." Dezi tilted his tarnished head. "I don't believe this ship's sensors are calibrated to detect the discharge of organic digestive—"

"Long- and short-range on full sweep," Rhis said loudly.

"Then we're out of here." She increased power. The *Venture* glided smoothly away from the raft.

Trilby watched the first coordinates flow across her screen. She let Rhis plot a course out of the asteroid field. He had, after all, gotten them in rather skillfully, and in one piece. There was still a bit of weaving to do before they could head for Port Rumor.

At the eight-minute mark the asteroids became smaller and more widely spaced. She gave her ship a little more power and was pleased with the way she handled. Maybe getting knocked around a bit had done the old girl some good.

At fifteen minutes they were at the outer edges of the last bands. At twenty, completely clear.

"Log notes we have cleared the belt at nineteen minutes, thirty-one seconds, and—"

"Thanks, Dez. Got it." She looked back over her shoulder and caught Rhis slowly shaking his head. She grinned, then settled back, her smile fading. It might be about forty-three hours until they reached Rumor—and she was sure Dezi would be glad to give a more precise estimate of the time—but the next two hours were the most critical. If the 'Sko mother ship was still around, she'd make her presence known before the *Venture* cleared Quadrant 84 and was back in Conclave patrol range.

It was one of the reasons she'd used Avanar for so long. No one, not even the Conclave, liked to come this far out. Except now her little secret had been discovered by the 'Sko.

One hour out and the engines were purring at max. Long-range and short-range were blissfully silent. They were still too far from the trader lanes to see any merchant traffic on the screens.

Rhis had to be right. It was only bad timing that'd made them cross paths with the 'Sko. Nothing was out here now. It was almost peaceful. Trilby relaxed a bit more and realized she was hungry. Soup sounded good. She unsnapped her buckle.

"Take the con, Dez. I'm going to see what I can scare up in the galley. Soup for dinner okay with you?" she asked Rhis as she stood.

"Need some help?"

"Nope. I'll bring a couple mugs up here."

She found two large packets of vegetable soup in the food locker and set the timer for three minutes. She turned and was looking in the galley lower racks for two mugs when she heard footsteps coming down the corridor.

She raised her head over the counter just as Rhis walked in. His hands were shoved in his pockets. His face wore the look of a small boy who knew he was about to get into big trouble.

"I need to talk to you." His voice had the tight tone of a grown man who knew he was in trouble.

Damn, double damn. Her heart plummeted just as

unease raced up her spine again. Her mind raced over several things. First was the location and status of her hand weapons. She had never given him the codes to the weapons lockers, but then, he was Zafharin. Still, his hands in his pockets didn't appear to conceal a laser pistol.

The second was a reappearance of the 'Sko. But her alarms were silent. And Dezi would've been on intraship long before Rhis could make the trek down the ladderway.

Then for a brief moment she wondered if he was ill. The crash of the Tark was no child's play. And he had bounded—quite naked, she remembered—out of the regeneration unit long before he was completely healed. Her gaze raked him head to foot. No, he looked fit, disgustingly fit. If he dropped dead now he'd be the best-looking corpse she'd ever seen.

So it had to be about that evasiveness that had settled over him after the 'Sko attack. And his cryptic comments. Maybe there was something to his paranoia after all.

And maybe, just maybe, he'd finally realized he should share that information with her. A bonus point, if he did. She patted the high counter. "Have a seat. Soup's almost ready."

The timer pinged while she was placing the mugs on the counter. He climbed onto a stool but was silent as she poured the thick, fragrant liquid full of sweetroot and goldbulb. Crisp chunks of greenlace floated to the top.

She perched on the stool next to him and wagged her spoon in his face. "Talk."

He took a spoonful of the soup first, sipped it

thoughtfully. She wanted to smack him with her spoon for the minor delay but stirred her soup instead.

"I wasn't involved in war games," he said finally. "I was part of an infiltration mission. The 'Sko took me prisoner. I stole the Tark and escaped."

She let out the breath she'd been holding. That was it? Hell, she'd figured as much. There was no reason why she, or anyone in the Conclave, wouldn't have been sympathetic to that situation. "Why did you lie to me?"

"I will explain that in a moment."

"So those 'Sko *were* looking for you—"

"Trilby, please. Hear me out."

She tapped her spoon on the edge of her mug, barely disguising her impatience. "Go ahead."

"They were looking for you too."

The spoon trembled in her fingers. "But that makes no sense. Why me? I've never even had a cargo contract worth more than—"

"It might have something to do with Grantforth."

She dropped her spoon. It clattered against the countertop. "Jag—What in hell are you talking about?"

"I recognized a transmission signature from the mother ship during the attack, locked it in a capture feed." He waved his hand. "Yes, I used that program I mentioned. Please. Let me finish."

Trilby closed her mouth.

"What I snared was a coded transmission from the mother ship to the Tarks. But I couldn't run a decode until we destroyed them. There is only so much," he said, splaying his hands on the counter in a depreciative gesture, "that I can do at once. Survival was more important."

"No shit."

He let out a short sigh. "But I decoded it while you started your systems check."

And swore loud and long, Trilby remembered. And became evasive, not to lie to her, but to protect her.

"The mother ship was sent to look for me. But your ship was listed in their kill file. As soon as they ID'd you, they changed course to follow."

Kill file. Trilby knew about 'Sko kill files. Anyone who worked the lanes did. But kill files were usually for revenge. You take out a 'Sko squadron, a 'Sko station, you're in their kill file.

"But I never did anything to them!" she protested. "Look at me. I'm a small hauler. I'm broke. I don't go running raids on 'Sko colonies, or—"

"I don't know why you're in the file. But you are. And the order, the code that I picked up from the mother ship, also held a code that I know from the war. It relates to a double agent in your government, someone the 'Sko call Dark Sword. And it relates, we now think, to this same agent using a Conclave transport company to help them. GGA is one of the possibilities."

She sat back. Grantforth Galactic Amalgamated. Not Jagan. When Rhis said "Grantforth" she automatically assumed he meant Jagan, personally. But why would he? There was no way he'd know about her fiasco of a relationship.

"GGA would never work with the 'Sko," she protested. "I mean, hell, Garold Grantforth's on the Trade Commission. Are you saying his family's betraying him? It would ruin his political career, to say the least."

This time it was Rhis who stirred his soup. "The

message didn't specifically mention GGA. But tell me about Garold Grantforth. Do you know him?"

"Sort of," she admitted after a moment. *What was it, one or two cocktail parties? Three? A year ago, maybe.* "I met him at a couple of social events I went to." She saw something odd in Rhis's expression but couldn't peg it. No doubt he was wondering where a low-budget hauler like Trilby Elliot would meet up with a high-powered politician.

Oh, Gods, she thought. *He thinks I was a prosti.*

She waved her hand quickly. "Not those kind of parties. I knew his nephew. Jagan. Jagan Grantforth. He introduced me to his uncle. That's all."

Rhis's spoon clunked hollowly against the sides of the plastic mug. He was staring at her, his silence urging her to speak. But she didn't know what he wanted her to say.

"I dated Jagan Grantforth, okay? I know that's probably hard for you to believe. I mean, he's got money, right? A name. Position. But we dated. We—" and she stopped and had to look away from the intensity in his eyes. It wasn't disbelief she saw there. It looked like pity.

Gods damn him and his Imperial arrogance! She might as well have a sign plastered on her forehead: *I'm nobody and let somebody rich and powerful use me.* She could see it in the way he was looking at her. *Poor, stupid Trilby. Did you really ever believe someone like the Jagan Grantforth would want you?*

"So you dated Grantforth."

She turned back to him, raised her chin a little higher. "Yeah. So what?"

"So what did he learn from you?"

"I beg your pardon?" Her voice dripped icicles.

"No, no." He wiped one hand over his face. "About your routes. Your cargo runs. The things you told me that Neadi hears all the time in her bar. What did he learn from you?"

The icicles moved from Trilby's mouth to her brain. Her thoughts froze, seized up like a clogged sublight drive.

"I . . . I don't know. Lots of things. I never thought . . ." She turned her face away, then propped her elbow on the counter and dropped her chin in her hand. How many times did Jagan go to Neadi's? How many things did he hear? What could he possibly have gleaned from them that GGA or the 'Sko would find useful? "I don't know," she repeated softly. "Are you sure about this?"

"I wasn't. Until I went to Szedcafar looking for proof."

It took a moment for the import of his words to register. She swiveled her face around. "*To* Szed?" She must have misheard. Last time his story was that he'd ended up *near* Szed, by mistake. When dealing with the 'Sko, the difference between *near* and *to* was usually life and death.

He nodded. "I, my team and I, managed to infiltrate a Syarian depot a few months ago."

First Szed, now Syar. "That's Conclave space!"

He shrugged. "We were following a trail of information. That trail went from the Syar Colonies to Szed. In a roundabout way. But it went there."

Port Rumor was in Gensiira, more than halfway across the Conclave from Syar. She couldn't see the immediate connection. "What do the Colonies have to do with Neadi's bar?"

"Nothing, directly. But Grantforth has significant ties to the Colonies—"

"So do lots of people. Rinnaker and GGA both have small shipyards there." Jagan had promised her a tour. That tour, like a lot of his promises, had never materialized. "And Grantforth money—specifically Garold's money—backs two of the mines and half a dozen other industries."

Something hovered at the edge of Trilby's thoughts, something deep and dark and ugly. She couldn't quite see it, though. It was still too illusive, shadowy. "But why would GGA care about my shipping runs, or the schedules of freighters like Carina's?"

"I don't know. But the 'Sko do, though why is not yet clear. We have a connection, but not a reason. That's what we were looking for in Szed."

Where he was captured, and escaped. From what she'd heard of the 'Sko, escape from Szedcafar was a near-impossible feat. She might have to revise her opinion of Rhis Vanur and of the kind of training mere lieutenants received in the Zafharin fleet. *Hero* might not quite cover it.

"And the information your team found . . . ?"

"Pointed to a relationship between a Conclave official, a transport operation, and the 'Sko," he said softly. He held up one hand, ticked the items off on his fingers. "GGA or Rinnaker. The 'Sko."

Trilby stared at him, at first in disbelief. Then, as her mind sorted through the information, a chill crept up her spine. "You're saying that Jagan's uncle's a traitor? Or that Rinnaker's sold out to the 'Sko?" Carina was missing. Chaser worked for GGA. She knew others at Rinnaker. Were all her friends now at risk?

He shook his head. "I'm saying there is significant evidence that something is going on between the 'Sko and someone in the Conclave. All the data is not in yet."

"Why not?"

"Because, Trilby-*chenka*, I think some of that data resides on your ship. Remember that transmission I snared? This is why I can't be delayed at Port Rumor." He hesitated a moment. "This is why we're now heading back to Yanir, to Imperial space."

His tone was so soft, so kindly, that his words almost slipped by her. *We're heading back to Yanir.*

Then reality kicked in. Hard. The 'Sko wanted her dead. And her ship was headed for the Empire. Without her permission.

Someone other than Trilby Elliot was in control of the *Careless Venture*.

Anger surged through her. "Wait one damned minute!"

He caught her hand as she made a grab for his arm. "Listen to me. Please. I have risked my life for this. The 'Sko tried to kill me. They have a kill order out on you. Doesn't this tell you that this is something beyond the profits of a one-up run?"

There was a pain in his voice, as vivid and raw as the bruises she'd seen on his body. Bruises inflicted by the 'Sko. Who had issued a kill order on a destitute freighter captain because of something someone in the Conclave told them about her.

The import of his words hit her like a battering ram. She clung to Rhis's hand as if he were her lifeline. *Her* hero. And more than just hers. Either GGA or Rinnaker was involved with the 'Sko, trading dirty.

That put everyone who had ever raised a beer at Neadi's in a Tark's targeting sights.

Uncovering that information had almost cost Rhis his life. And all she could think of was getting to Port Rumor and refilling her bank account. Shame colored her words. "Why didn't you tell me this before?"

"Tell you of corruption in your Conclave?" He stroked her fingers reassuringly. "Would you have believed me? A Zafharin? A naked one, as I remember, who threatened to harm you?"

She recognized the little quirk of a smile under his mustache, saw how he was trying to add levity into the situation, take the sting out of his words. He had a right to chew her out. Jagan would have. But he made it sound like none of it was her fault. "Maybe not right away, but—"

"You wouldn't have. If I were in your position, I wouldn't believe my story. But I didn't make up what happened to *Bella's Dream*. And I didn't invent the 'Sko by the rafts. You must see that I'm telling you the truth."

A very disturbing truth that gave new meaning to Neadi's rumors. The 'Sko were infiltrating the Conclave. She clearly understood Rhis's urgency, his need for her cooperation. Or rather, her ship's cooperation, which he'd facilitated without her assistance. Her earlier anger drained from her. "How'd you get Dezi to—"

"I showed him the transmission from the 'Sko."

Dezi's linguistic files on Ycskrite had to be as meager as on Zafharish. But she knew that certain key sequences, like a kill-file order, he'd be able to translate. She nodded, suddenly grateful for her 'droid's usually aggravating overprotective tendencies.

And to Rhis. His Imperial Arrogance notwithstanding, he'd been nothing but helpful since she'd rescued him. And all she'd given him was grief, lumping him in with the likes of Jagan, thinking his only reason to get back to the Empire was because of some sloe-eyed beauty waiting for his return. "I feel like an idiot. I wish you'd told me—"

"I wanted to." He brought her hand to his lips, brushed her fingers with a lingering kiss. "*S'viek noyet.* I am sorry."

She had to remind herself to breathe. A thousand delirious sensations ran up her arm when his lips touched her fingers. And that heat that had sparked between them without warning over the past few days suddenly hung, thick and sweet, in the air.

Startled, she focused on his large, strong fingers clasped around her own. There was a faded white scar across his knuckles. A small example of his sacrifices for his Empire and, in a way, for her.

Maybe that's all she was feeling: gratitude. She sought a distraction from the warm tingles radiating through her body. "Did your team try to rescue you?"

He hesitated. "They were under orders not to. That is one of the risks of my position. The information they had, and the ship we'd used in the mission, were more important."

Lives were expendable. But make sure the hardware comes back in one piece. And the Zafharin—no: Tivahr. Rhis was assigned to the *Razalka*. Senior Captain Tivahr had taken the possibility of Rhis Vanur's death as an acceptable loss. It fit with everything she'd heard about the man.

"So they abandoned you to the 'Sko?" Her voice shook. She had seen what the 'Sko could do when she was contracted to Herkoid. Those few that survived were little more than broken minds in misshapen bodies, now haunting the dark corners of Port Rumor.

Rhis leaned forward and framed her face with his hands. "I'm fine. I'm alive. Not even the vampire snakes," and he traced her mouth with his thumb, "had a chance to get to me. Because of you. Everything is going to be all right, Trilby-*chenka*. When we get back to my—"

She launched herself against him. Her arms locked around his neck, her right foot hooked into the rung of the stool so she didn't topple over. Her mouth pressed hard against his. He tasted slightly salty, a little like soup. And when his mustache scraped against her face and he groaned her name, she knew she was lost.

And she didn't give a mizzet's ass.

She wanted him. She wanted to give in to that primal heat that erupted every time they got within a few feet of each other. She wanted to dive into the seductive looks that made his eyes glitter like an explosion in a reactor chamber. She wanted to explore every inch of him, kiss away the pain of every scar on his hard and perfect body. She wanted to show him that life was worth living, even if his infamous commanding officer, Tivahr, didn't think it was so.

So when his hands fumbled with her T-shirt, she didn't stop him. She nibbled on his ear instead.

And when he pulled her off the stool and into his arms, she didn't stop him. She kissed his neck instead.

And when he carried her into his small cabin and lay her down on his small bed, murmuring things in Zafharish she didn't understand but that sounded awfully wonderful, she didn't stop him. But let her hands slide slowly down the front of his shirt, undoing it. And, as he kneeled over her, she unfastened his pants, ran her hands over the hard planes of his body. And let her mouth take over where her hands had been.

He rasped her name and drew her face up to his. "No," he said. "I want . . ." His mouth covered hers, his tongue probing. Then he pulled back, sucking lightly on her lower lip before he slid his hand underneath her, pressing her up against him.

"I want," he repeated. He trailed hot kisses down her neck, across her breasts until she was shivering. His other hand cupped her breast, then stroked one taut nipple, but gently, teasingly. His tongue followed.

Then, just when she thought the explosions of delight in her body could get no better, he kissed her again. Hard, this time. A molten wave of passion rolled over her.

"I want you. *Yav chera*." His hoarse whisper filled her ear. "*Yav chera*, Trilby-*chenka*. Tell me you want me."

She turned her face slightly to look at him. There was a softness in the lines of his face she'd never seen before. An openness. A vulnerability. It tugged at her heart.

"*Yav chera*," she replied softly.

His thumb covered her lips. "*Yav cheron*. If you want me, it is *yav cheron*. When I want you, which is all the time, it is *yav chera*."

He moved his thumb and brushed his lips against hers.

"*Yav cheron*," she told him. She laced her fingers through his hair and pulled his face back to hers.

He returned her kisses with a hungry passion, pressing his hardness against her. She arched against him and wrapped one leg around his thigh. He murmured in Zafharish. She understood only her name, though his hands and his kisses spoke a language that needed no translation.

Then he was inside her. She clung to him. He was trembling, his kisses intense as he thrust into her. She felt a long ripple of passion surge through her, felt his body respond in kind. And the heat that had been building between them mushroomed into a fireball.

He held her tightly, his face buried against her neck. And whispered those damned Zafharish words of his over and over against her skin.

They sounded wonderful.

Trilby thrust her head through the neck of her dark-green sleeveless T-shirt, wriggled her arms through the straps. But another pair of hands pulled it snug down her body, then moved up to lightly trace the outline of her breasts underneath.

She sucked in her breath, laughed nervously.

"Hmm?" Rhis's face was warm against her neck. His fingers had found the edge of her underpants and smoothed the lace against her hipbone. "Going somewhere?"

"I should check in with Dez on the bridge," she said. *I should've checked in an hour ago.* She glanced at the clock inset in the wall. *Two hours ago. Damnation!*

Rhis snaked his arms around her waist. She could feel the heat from his bare skin against her back, through her T-shirt, and against her own bare legs.

The sensation alternately thrilled her and mortified her. What in the Seven Hells had she done?

Well, she knew exactly what she had done. And it had been delicious. She just didn't completely understand what had prompted her to do it.

He was a stranger! A Zafharin. She knew nothing about him other than he was a lieutenant on the *Razalka*—her stomach clenched at the name—and he had a great body that she had unashamedly explored for the better part of two hours.

"Trilby-*chenka*?"

Half the time he didn't even speak Standard! All those passionate-sounding words could be nothing more than a recitation of a navigational checklist. Or a recounting of his family's genealogical chart. The Zafharin were famous for their pride in their families.

Families. She closed her eyes for the moment. Oh, Gods, he might even be married!

She pulled out of the steamy warmth of his embrace. Her pants were crumpled on the floor. She grabbed them. "I really have to—"

"You did not want this, with me. Did you?" His voice was soft. She thought she heard an echo of dismay.

Shit!

She turned. He sat on the edge of the bed, his dark hair mussed, the bedsheet halfway around his waist. He looked magnificent.

And confused.

"No. I wanted . . ." She remembered just what it was she wanted. And he wanted. And he'd taught her to say it in Zafharish.

Yav cheron.

She let her pants slip through her fingers, came and sat down next to him on the bed. "No, I wanted this.

With you. I just would've liked it under different circumstances."

He touched her face. "So would I. But sometimes the universe does not listen, even to me." He offered her a small smile. "You're afraid."

She nodded.

"So am I."

His admission bolstered her dwindling confidence. She had to smile back. "You don't seem like someone who's ever been afraid of anything."

He stroked her cheek. "I never was. Before. But this . . . this . . ." He shook his head. "This has me *dravda gera mevnahr*. What you might call 'ass over teakettle.' "

"Because?"

"Because if you were to talk to all the people who know me, and tell them that I have this beautiful air sprite in my bed and that I cannot stop thinking about her—or touching her—they would all not believe you."

"Rhis?"

"Hmm?"

"Are you married?"

Dark brows slanted over startled eyes. The fingers stroking her cheek halted. "No."

Ah, the feared M word. Gets 'em every time.

"I'm not husband hunting." She leaned away from him, grabbed her pants again. "So don't get jumpy." She shoved her foot through one pants leg. "But I also don't get involved with married men."

She hazarded a glance at him. His hands had dropped down to his knees and his face wore a slightly sheepish expression.

She pushed her foot through the other pants leg, then stood. "Have you seen my socks?"

She peered under the chair. He lifted the blanket that had fallen to the floor. His socks were there. Hers weren't.

He reached over and grabbed the pillows and flipped them over. Then he turned back to her. "No. They're not in your boots?"

She had a very distinct memory of clothes flying. She didn't think either one of them had stopped to tuck socks into boots. She tried to convey that in the look she shot him.

He chuckled.

She picked up her boots, wriggled her fingers inside just in case. "I'm not going to the bridge barefoot. I'll meet you up there in five?"

He stood. The sheet was knotted at his waist. "In five," he said, reaching for her. He pulled her back against him, kissed her soundly. She melted against his warmth for a moment, then with a sigh stepped back.

"You know, if you'd done that in my sick bay," she said as she backed toward the door, "instead of grabbing me by the throat, the past couple of days would've been a whole lot nicer."

"Recommendation logged and noted. Captain."

She grinned as she strode toward her cabin. Captain. For the first time, he said her title with a definite note of respect. This was getting better and better.

Rhis stood in the center of his cabin and closed his eyes. The scent of perfume and powder rose off the heat of his skin. The sheet was slipping out of its knot around his waist. Slowly, deliberately, he exhaled. Then just as slowly, just as deliberately, he drew in another deep breath.

When he found his heart still pounding, every muscle of his body still twitching with energy, and his thoughts still racing in an almost giddy delight, he knew it was true.

He was crazy. Unequivocally, undeniably crazy. He'd lost his mind. His control was shattered. His discipline nonexistent.

And he didn't give a damn.

He opened his eyes, turned his face just enough to catch a glimpse of himself in the mirror.

He didn't look any different. Except for the wide grin plastered across his face. That was different. That was . . .

Trilby. His air sprite. His gutsy little fool who infuriated him and enchanted him and mesmerized him. Who delighted him.

When she haltingly said, *Yav cheron,* he thought his heart was going to explode.

Which would probably have shocked most of the Empire, as most of the Empire knew he didn't have a heart.

He didn't. He'd given it to her. Which was, he grudgingly admitted as he pulled on his clothes, one of the wisest things he'd ever done.

Now all he had to do was save civilized space from the 'Sko and life would be wonderful.

"I need to tell Neadi where I am," Trilby said as he eased into the copilot's seat. He clicked the straps around his chest.

"And," she continued, "I have to get someone to pick up my Bagrond run."

He leaned over, enfolded her hand in his. A slight blush rose on her cheeks. That pleased him. "I agree. Both must be done, but not here. The security of your communications is not . . ." He hesitated. She may be his lover, but this was her ship he was criticizing. Even lovers had to tread that ground carefully.

"The best?" she asked. "I'd even agree to nonexistent. This is a freighter, not a military ship."

He squeezed her hand. "My point. And we've just had an encounter with the 'Sko. And are still two hours from my border at Yanir. When we get back to the *Razalka*—"

"You sound so sure we'll find her."

He nodded. "Of that I am, yes." He knew standard procedure would be followed in his absence. He knew—barring an all-out war—her most likely locations, who she'd be in contact with. Finding the *Razalka* was simply a matter of going down the list.

"An Imperial patrol isn't going to try to shoot my ass off when we cross the border?" She pulled her hand from under his and cocked her fingers at him, mimicking a gun.

"No. Dezi, did you upload the program I created?"

"Yes, Lieutenant." Dezi's metal fingers ran down a series of touchpads at his station. Data flashed on a small screen on his left. "We commence broadcasting an Imperial ID when we are forty minutes from the Yanir border."

Lieutenant. For a moment he thought he'd misheard. Then he remembered. He hadn't told Dezi, wanting to tell Trilby first. And he'd never gotten around to telling Trilby.

He turned back to her. His timing couldn't be worse. He wondered where to start and found her staring at him, her eyes wide.

"You hacked into my system!" Her tone was accusatory, but she was grinning.

This wasn't the topic he had intended to discuss. But something in her amazement fed that part of his ego that took pride in the wogs-and-weemlies he could create. And she, the queen of wogs-and-weemlies. "Well, yes. I mean, no. But, Trilby, I have—"

"What do you mean, no? You can't change a ship's ident code. It's illegal. That's a sealed program. How in the Seven Hells did you hack—"

"I do not hack." He let a haughty tone return to his voice. "I professionally amend system codes to perform at an optimal level."

She reached over, playfully punched him in the arm. "You promised me no wogs-and-weemlies!"

"They're only wogs-and-weemlies if you don't know they're there. You know. And I will show you how it's done. And undone. Fair?"

She nodded. "Fair."

He looked forward to that. Working with her, challenging her, teaching her. Learning from her. There were a few fail-safes on the *Razalka* that needed attention. He'd throw the problem at her, see how creative she could get.

He glanced at their coordinates. It was "night" by their bodies' biological clocks, but they still had a ways to go. Freighters weren't known for speed; an old Circura II even less so. Dragging his air sprite back down to his cabin would be a nice way to pass the time, but it would be too easy to fall asleep afterward, and there were other things to attend to. Once they got back to the *Razalka,* things would start happening quickly. He wanted to be in a position to take action.

He swiveled the comp screen up from the armrest, motioned for her to do the same. "I think you should see what we've learned from the 'Sko. And I want to play this against that chart we created on the missing ships. Including *Bella's Dream.*"

And there was something else, something he needed to discuss with her. But then the data he'd entered into her ship's memory banks flashed on his screen and everything but the 'Sko left his mind.

Trilby listened to Rhis translate the 'Sko data, watched him overlay schedules and coordinates from the missing freighters. She was alert to coincidences, spotted one he missed. But he didn't miss many.

He was, she decided, brilliant. And dedicated. He attacked the problem before them as if he were personally responsible for saving the universe from the 'Sko. Not just an officer who, when they got to the *Razalka,* would become part of the team again.

Lieutenant Rhis Vanur. She glanced at him, her heart doing a little flip-flop. She was suddenly glad he was a mere lieutenant. He knew what it was like to be on some CO's shit list. Knew what it was like to have his life often controlled by powers other than his own.

Rhis was someone with whom she could share her frustrations. Jagan only bragged about all the lives he controlled. How people jumped when he snapped his fingers.

Like she had.

But Rhis was different. Oh, he had that Imperial arrogance, but she understood it. It was pride. Not unlimited power. He didn't snap his fingers. Bark orders. Change people's lives without consulting them.

He held her hand. Worked with her by his side. A tiny hope flared in her heart. She thought of Neadi and Leonid. Would Rhis give up a military career for the freighter business?

You're getting ahead of yourself, she warned. But it was a tiny hope she didn't want to let go.

The 'Sko symbols for Dark Sword blinked at her on her screen. Rhis was frowning at them. She tapped at the symbols. "You're sure this has something to do with me?"

"I wish it were otherwise, but yes."

"And that it's tied in to Rinnaker, or GGA?"

He closed his eyes briefly, nodded. "Tell me again about Secretary Grantforth. How many times did you meet him?"

An image of Jagan's lean-faced uncle flitted through her mind. The man's reputation was impeccable. Rhis had to be wrong.

"Three times. Three different parties. One on Bagrond. That was the first time. The other two were on Quivera."

She saw his eyebrow arch. Both worlds oozed money. "But Jagan was the reason I was there. Not Garold Grantforth."

"Then perhaps we have to start with him. How did you meet Jagan?"

The thought that Jagan might be involved with the

'Sko made her feel equally unsettled. He might be a cad and a womanizer, but she thought he hated the 'Sko as much as she did. She couldn't imagine anyone in the Conclave who didn't.

"I had a three-month contract with Norvind to Crescent City on Bagrond. That was a bit over a year and a half ago. Grantforth has a depot in Crescent. One day Jagan just showed up at my loading dock." She shrugged.

"And?"

"And we got to talking. Just little stuff. I don't know. I think he came at me with some stupid line. What's a nice girl like you . . ." She waved her hand. "You know."

It really sounded stupid now. She wondered why it had seemed so cute then. Probably because it had been uttered by Jagan Grantforth. *The* Jagan Grantforth. She made a mental note to never again fall in love with any man who could have *the* plastered in front of his name.

"And he asked you, what? To dinner?"

"Lunch. At GGA's executive club."

"And he never said why he was interested in you?"

That sounded like an inane remark from someone who'd just spent two hours ravishing her body. She knew he was trying to uncover Jagan's real motives, but the question still piqued her. She glared at him.

"Trilby-*chenka*." He grabbed her hand again.

She'd ask him later what this *chenka* business was all about. First she wanted to see him wriggle his way out of this one.

She waited.

"Don't deliberately misunderstand," he said. "But I know much of Jagan Grantforth's reputation. And yes, I want to know what a lovely woman like you was doing with something like him."

"I know. I'm sorry." She patted his hand, then pulled hers away. "And yeah, I thought about things like that too. Or rather, I tried not to. I was just so flattered that *the* Jagan Grantforth was showing an interest in me. Saying nice things. Telling me he loved me." She glanced at his face to see if he had any reaction to her words. He was scowling. Good.

"Which I later found out he didn't. At least, that's what I have to assume, since he married someone else."

"Zalia Auberon."

"How'd you know that?"

He gave a quick shrug. "I think someone mentioned it. We do keep tabs on what GGA does from time to time."

"So okay, he married Zalia. But that doesn't make him a spy for the 'Sko." Still, she thought about his transmits in her files. She had intended to delete them. But maybe there was something in them that might now make sense. Maybe his secretary, or one of his assistants at GGA, had access to her transmits to him. She wouldn't discount that Jagan might leave one on-screen in his office, in a boastful fashion. She'd have to go over them, but privately. No use airing her dirty laundry any more than she had to.

"How often did he go with you to Neadi's?"

"At least ten times with me, on the *Venture*. But then sometimes he'd use a GGA shuttle and meet me there."

"He worked runs with you?"

Worked? No, Jagan didn't work. "He'd do a trike, or a one-up from time to time, when . . ." And she let her voice trail off. She wasn't completely comfortable discussing her past sexual exploits with the man she'd just spent two hours making love to. But there were larger issues here.

She looked away from him, toyed with the tail of her safety strap. "You have to understand, Jagan and I were pretty involved. I mean, okay, maybe it was stupid, but there was a point in the relationship when I really thought we had a future together. A real future.

"But our schedules were different." Hell, their entire lifestyles were different. But she didn't want to see that back then. "So sometimes he'd hang with me, for a trike, on board. But he never really got involved in the mechanics of my runs. He was here strictly for . . . my company."

She glanced back at him.

"I can understand that," he offered quietly.

"Yeah, well, I can and I can't. He had . . . he has this attitude, you see. He's better than everybody. Has all the answers. He's way up there," she said, raising one hand, "and I'm way down here. Eventually he made sure I knew that."

Rhis started to reply but Trilby turned away. Her admissions to Rhis hit a raw spot she hadn't realized was still so sensitive. "Hey, Dez. Can you check logs for me? How many times was Jagan on board recently?"

"Of course." The 'droid accessed the data quickly. "Sixteen times in the past twenty-one months."

"Send that to my terminal here, okay?" She turned back to Rhis. "Crazy thought. Jagan's assistants and secretary always knew when he was with me. They had to. Maybe this contact you're looking for is one of them." That made more sense to her. "Let's play those dates against shipping schedules out of Rumor. While you do that, I'll try to pull up all the times he met me at Neadi's as well."

Rhis nodded. "That could bring up something interesting. But the ships haven't been missing during your entire relationship. Only the last two months."

"True, but if they also had access to my transmits to him, we might be able to see a pattern. I always gave him my run schedule ahead of time. And we sometimes talked market gossip."

Rhis held her gaze for a moment. "Excellent suggestion." He sounded slightly amazed.

She grinned. "I do come up with one on occasion."

"It must be my influence."

She groaned, then swiveled her comp screen and pulled up her files of Jagan's transmits.

It was about two and a half hours later, just a little after midnight by Trilby's biotime, that the *Careless Venture* confirmed contact with an Imperial outpost. She glanced at the time–date stamp on the top of her screen as the unfamiliar Zafharish words scrolled by. And realized she'd known Rhis Vanur for five days.

A full hand, in freighter lingo.

And in five days her whole life had been spun around.

Rhis's fingers flew over the console in front of him. "Should be able to initiate voice contact . . . yes." A series of lights in the center panel blinked from red to green.

She heard a male voice from the outpost identify himself and the name of his station, she assumed. She understood very little of the ensuing conversation between Rhis and the outpost, other than a few *vads* and *navs*, and common terms like *dock* and *schedule*. And *Razalka*. That name she caught, along with Tivahr, and Vanushavor. Those were mentioned frequently as well.

But as to putting it all together in a sensible fashion? She leaned back in her chair and waited.

Rhis seemed relieved, calmer, when he ended his communication. "This is good." He was nodding, not at her but at nothing in particular in the dark viewport of the bridge. "Fortuitous. A tactical team has been on Degvar Station for the past trike. Lieutenant Gurdan is in command. I know him."

"You're not thinking of trying something against the 'Sko now? I thought you had to wait for the *Razalka*."

"Of course. But Gurdan has much experience, and with the facilities at Degvar I can go deeper with this information." His fingers drummed absently against his mustache.

Deep enough to save Carina? Reluctantly, Trilby held out little hope for that. More likely, the Imperial Fleet would be looking for links and patterns between this Dark Sword and the 'Sko—the loss of Carina didn't really concern them, and she doubted they'd listen to a mere lieutenant if he suggested it should.

No, all they'd be looking for were answers to who and when and how.

She wanted to know that too. Then additional questions surfaced. More-personal ones. Like what would happen to Trilby Elliot and the *Careless Venture* once Rhis got back to the *Razalka*?

The war was over. She had no fear of being taken prisoner. So that meant only one thing: they would part company at Degvar. She'd be free to go back across the border.

But she knew a part of her would forever reside with the Empire and a certain mere lieutenant. So much for finders keepers. She'd found him, but there was no chance she could ever keep him.

Lieutenant Gurdan was a thin man, almost as tall as Rhis, but his hair was a sandy brown color and he was clean-shaven. Trilby halted in her conversation with a Degvar dockhand and watched the two men salute each other. She thought they would've clasped hands, exchanged a few hearty thumps on the back. Rhis had intimated they were friends or, at least, as she recalled his words, that he knew Gurdan. And seemed pleased Gurdan was here.

Oh, well. Military. Trilby shrugged it off, turned back to the problems of securing a Conclave ship—a nonmilitary one at that—to an Imperial docking system.

"I think we're set now," she told the dockhand. All rampside-panel lights finally flashed green.

"I am pleased I could be of help." His round face creased with a smile. His accent was thicker than Rhis's. He motioned to her ship, tethered to the docking rim of the station. The *Venture* was visible through the large, square viewports. "She is not common, no? Many years she has served, *vad?*"

You mean how do I keep this rust bucket in the space lanes? She remembered saying that to Rhis. It was a quip she was used to making. "She's a good old gal. Not too fast, but reliable."

"Not what he is used to." The dockhand made a short motion with his chin to where Rhis stood talking to Gurdan. Trilby glanced at Rhis just as he turned in her direction. He nodded at her, held up his index finger. He wanted her to wait.

Well, it wasn't like she knew anywhere else to go. She needed to send a message to Neadi, but every damned sign she'd seen so far was in Zafharish. She could easily end up in the commissary instead of communications.

She realized the dockhand had said something about Rhis and her ship. Oh, yeah. The man probably knew Rhis was assigned to the *Razalka*. "A little slumming is good for the soul."

"Slum-ming? I am not familiar with this term."

She grinned, waved off his comment. "It means . . . well, point is, we made it. He made it."

"Well, yes. Of course he did!"

Imperial arrogance, Trilby thought as she logged out at the rampway pad. It must be a compound they put in their drinking water.

She heard Rhis shout something to Gurdan. He was headed her way. The dockhand finished his work and backed up abruptly, saluted.

Rhis returned the salute crisply but with noted disinterest. Trilby saw that the smaller man didn't seem perturbed, though he scurried away quickly enough. *Military!*

"Everything's okay?" he asked, with a quick glance at the ramp pad.

"*Vad.*" She grinned up at him. "And that's all I can remember of your language right now, tired as I am."

"I have a few hours ahead of me with Gurdan. Then I will be back. But you don't have to stay up. Why don't you—"

"I'd like to send Neadi that message. Can I use the comm system here, or is that restricted?"

"It's restricted, but, yes, I'll make sure you can use it."

"Do you have time now?"

He shook his head. "I wish I did, Trilby-*chenka*. But there have been some additional moves on the part of the 'Sko in the past trike. Serious moves. The information I have is vital."

She knew what it meant when the 'Sko went on the offensive. It wasn't a thought she wanted to dwell on. "Go do what you have to with Lieutenant Gurdan. I'll wait—"

"No. I'll get someone to take you to communications. I know you understand the necessity to be not too detailed in what you send to Neadi? Our system is secure, but it is not foolproof."

"She just needs to know I'm safe. Especially after Carina."

Rhis hesitated, glanced over his shoulder to where Gurdan and two other officers stood. "Trilby-*chenka,* there is something . . . I need to talk to you. But I—" The sharp trill of a comm badge interrupted him.

Trilby was startled. She hadn't noticed the metal disk on his jacket until now. Gurdan must have given it to him.

Rhis had already tapped at it, listened to a short spate of Zafharish words. He replied, tapped it off, and turned back to her. "I'm sorry. Something urgent. Go send your message to Neadi."

Loud footsteps approached from behind him. Gurdan and the other officers.

"I will be back in two, three hours. Yes?" He started to reach for her but Gurdan said something. His hand came out toward the thin officer instead. He replied to Gurdan's comment with several short commands.

He turned back to her. "Major Mitkanos will be here shortly to escort you to communications. I must go."

She leaned against the docking-ramp console and watched him stride down the corridor, flanked by the tactical team officers. *Yav cheron,* she said silently. *In a few more hours, I'll tell you in person, again.*

Major Mitkanos was a muscular man in a gray uniform. His short-cropped black hair was sprinkled with silver, his jaw was ruggedly square, and his nose had a slight bend that told of more than a few fistfights. His appearance was gruff, until he smiled, his wide mouth softening the hard, chiseled edges of his face.

He shook Trilby's hand with a firm grasp. "Be glad to help. I have heard something of your adventures. That he stole that Tark. Takes your ship. Then you find that you have the 'Sko in pursuit again."

He didn't quite take my ship, Trilby wanted to say. *Was more like a cooperative agreement.* But then, she knew how stories changed as they filtered through the ranks.

"It's been a bit harrowing," she agreed, and followed him down the corridor. Except for the signs in Zafharish, Degvar looked similar to most other stations she'd seen, though more utilitarian. The constant blinking, flashing, chirping, and trilling adverts that floated through most Conclave stations' commercial corridors were missing.

Degvar had nondescript gray bulkheads and gray decking. Door frames on the dock level were red; when they exited the lift three levels up, they were yellow. Entry palm pads were larger, with a series of touchpads on the left. And on this level, armed personnel were more conspicuous.

Most were in gray, like Mitkanos. Only a few wore the black that Rhis and Gurdan's team did.

She was about to ask why when he halted in front of a set of double doors, yellow-ringed. He lay his hand on the pad, then tapped three touchpads with his thumb. The doors cycled open.

Two officers in gray uniforms, one male and one female, sat at the consoles. The woman turned, nodded to Mitkanos, and spoke in Zafharish. He grinned, tapped her playfully on the shoulder.

"Corporal Rimanava will help you," he told Trilby. He motioned for her to sit next to a young woman whose long dark hair was pulled back into a thick braid. Mitkanos turned to the other officer, leaned on the back of his chair, and dropped into a low conversation.

"Corporal Rimanava." Trilby offered a handshake before she took the chair. "I'm Trilby Elliot. Captain of the *Careless Venture*."

"Farra Rimanava." She accepted Trilby's hand with a wide smile. "Sit, please. I understand you need to send message to Gensiira. In Conclave, *vad?*" She spoke haltingly, as if searching for the proper words in Standard.

Trilby relayed Neadi's transit code. That Farra Rimanava, or rather the Empire, already had the codes for Gensiira and Port Rumor didn't surprise her.

Farra showed Trilby how to activate the holocam in the console. It wasn't so different from other comm systems she'd seen, except that everything was labeled in Zafharish.

"This ends message," Farra said, pointing to a square touchpad. "If you wish, I will get cup of tea while you record. So you have privacy, *vad?*"

"That's okay." Trilby motioned with her hand. "It's only a short message."

"Then I will wait. This is okay? We will get tea with Yavo when you are finished. It is end of shift for me."

Trilby activated the holocam and started her message. There was good news and bad news, she told Neadi. She'd run into a 'Sko nest. But she was safe, across the border in Yanir. "I'm going to have tea with two Imperial officers in a minute," she said, with a smile to Farra, "so everything's fine. Have Leonid's cousin take my Bagrond run." She gave the details and contact name.

"I don't have an exact ETA on my return. They're real interested in what happened to Carina. They think the nest I found might have something to do with that." She didn't want to reveal anything more.

"I'll be in touch. Don't worry. Tell Leonid and Chaser I'm okay. Dezi sends his love."

* * *

She was tired, but the tea was excellent, pungent with a spicy aroma. It shook some of the cobwebs out of her head, fed some life back into her veins. There were still a few hours before Rhis would return. If he finished his urgent meeting early, she felt sure someone on station would know where to find her.

She sat with Farra and Yavo Mitkanos at a table in the far corner of the officers' lounge, a long room that curved along on the outer frame of the station's ring. The floor-to-ceiling viewport showed the immense blackness of space. The lights of a small maintenance craft winked out of view as she watched.

No one else was in the lounge. She counted eleven tables and six stools at a bar. A bank of food replicators was adjacent to it.

The tea tasted freshly brewed. She sipped it appreciatively as Mitkanos answered her question about the gray uniforms.

"Ground forces. Like your marines," he said, plucking at the insignia of crossed swords on his chest, "but we call ourselves *Stegzarda*. *Stegzarda* means perhaps *strength command* in your language. We assist the Imperial Fleet when it comes to border outposts."

Farra nodded. "Especially with recent *jhavedzga*—"

"Aggression." Mitkanos corrected her.

"*Vad*. Aggression by the Ycsko. That is why Gurdan's team is here. And now the *Razalka* comes."

Mitkanos snorted.

"Uncle!" Farra slapped his arm playfully.

"Niece!" he replied, grinning. And Trilby saw the same wide mouth, the same lines in the jaw of Farra Rimanava and Yavo Mitkanos.

"He's your uncle?" Trilby asked.

"*Vad.* Yes. And the reason I am here." She blew him a kiss.

"What, you think I let my sister's child join the Fleet? What the Fleet teach my Farra-*chenka,* eh? To think? No. To follow orders, from Tivahr the Terrible. Or maybe she spends her time running away from the admiral's son, who cannot keep his hands from women."

"There are hundreds more ships. The Fleet is large." Farra was trying to sound serious, but a few chuckles slipped out. "My beloved Uncle Yavo. He has no love for the Fleet."

"Arrogant rimstrutters!" Mitkanos made a dismissive wave with his hand, then pointed at Trilby. "Ask her. She knows. Probably complained about her ship from the moment he walked on board."

"He didn't walk. He was carried," Trilby said, not without some mirth. Perhaps Rhis's Imperial Arrogance did come from something the Fleet put in the drinking water, as she suspected. But she didn't discount that Mitkanos had his share of arrogance as well. More likely she was listening to the usual rivalry between military branches. She'd known many a Norvind crew to trade verbal insults with crew from GGA.

"Carried?" Mitkanos's eyes widened. "He permitted this?"

"He was out cold. Flat on his face in a jungle swamp. But, yeah, when he woke up, he made it pretty clear my ship was a lot less than what he was used to." She grinned. All Rhis's blustering, which had so infuriated her, now seemed almost endearing.

"It is easy to get spoiled on a ship like the *Razalka,*" Farra said in a conciliatory tone.

Mitkanos snorted again. "The *Razalka* is not a ship. It is a kingdom. Tivahr's kingdom. He is emperor and, yes, sometimes executioner."

Trilby heard the anger in his voice. What did he call the *Razalka*'s captain, "Tivahr the Terrible"? No wonder it had taken Rhis so long to loosen up, to smile. "But he's just the captain," she said.

"Senior captain," Mitkanos interjected. "Most of the admirals fear him. For good reason."

"Why do they tolerate it? If he's such a tyrant—"

"They created him." Mitkanos folded his hands on the table, leaned toward Trilby. Farra shook her head but said nothing.

"You know it is true," he said to his niece. He looked at Trilby. "They created him. Forty . . . what, forty-two years ago? I know you have rumors of this in the Conclave. He is, what you call it, a crècheling? An experiment. Bred in a genetics lab like a recipe for *boulashka*."

Trilby nodded. She vaguely remembered some whispers during the war. Tivahr was rumored to be some kind of superhuman. Stronger. Smarter. But genetic manipulation had long been illegal on both sides of the Zone. And, Leonid had pointed out, immoral in the Empire. Clan history and lineage were sacred. A crècheling, a test-tube-formed human of unknown genetics, had no definite lineage.

She'd forgotten that conversation until now.

"Some say Vanushavor blood runs in his veins. Some say even Vanurin," Mitkanos said quietly. "But the list is much longer than that. So they don't know what he is. Or who he is. But he came out smarter and stronger than they wanted him to. And now they can't stop him."

"Nor can the Ycsko," Farra pointed out.

"I have fought the 'Sko many times and won."
Mitkanos thumped his hand on his chest. "The victory
record of my platoon is glorious. All the *Stegzarda* are
known for bravery."

"And so is the Fleet. We work with them here, on
Degvar, Uncle."

Trilby began to suspect that Farra might have a
tender spot for someone in a black uniform. Well,
she knew the feeling. She didn't think many of her
friends back in Rumor would be any happier about
her involvement with a Zafharin Fleet officer than
Mitkanos would.

He said something to Farra in Zafharish. Trilby
recognized a few words, but her brain was too tired
to try to translate them.

Mitkanos turned to her with an embarrassed grin.
"I apologize. I forget, you do not understand. I tell
my niece, we are brave because we are a . . . what is
the word? A unit. A family. We are bound by mutual
trust. Loyalty. But the *Razalka,* she operates on fear.
It is different, no?"

Trilby thought of Grantforth Galactic Amalgamated. Jagan's opinion of his family's employees as
"underlings" became apparent to her as she'd come
to know him. It was one of the things that had unsettled her about him, one of the things that had made it
easy to walk away from his flattering words and his
lavish gifts. She'd given them all back. It hadn't been
a pretty scene.

She nodded. "We have our share of tyrants too,
Major. I try to avoid them as best I can."

Mitkanos patted her hand. "Well, you had only to
deal with him a short time, yes? Now you can go

home and tell your friends you survived what, four, five days with Tivahr the Terrible on your ship. They will be impressed."

But Tivahr wasn't—Trilby started to say, and stopped. Something ominous, something cold and fearful suddenly wrapped around her like an icy blanket. Something about Mitkanos's surprise that Rhis had been carried on board the *Venture*. And before that. *He* took your ship, Mitkanos had said. It was the way he said *he*. With a capital *H*. Underscored. In lights. As if *the* resided before his name.

The Senior Captain Tivahr.

She closed her eyes for a moment, her head spinning. She felt Mitkanos's large hand on her arm. "Niece, we have tired her. This has been much stress. She has had Captain Tivahr on her ship and now me, frightening her."

Tivahr. On my ship. Tivahr.

She opened her eyes. "He told me his name was Vanur." Her voice sounded thin. "Not . . . Tivahr. Rhis Vanur."

Farra and her uncle exchanged quick glances. A low, guttural curse passed Mitkanos's lips.

Trilby leaned back in her chair. Mitkanos's hand fell away. A few choice curse words of her own tumbled through her mind, but she didn't have the energy to voice them.

"Khyrhis Tivahr," Mitkanos said quietly. "I saw him come down your rampway on my security screen."

Farra shot a question at him in Zafharish.

"I do not know," he answered in Standard. "Captain Elliot. It appears now perhaps we have been too forward in our talk. But there was no indication from him," and he looked back at Farra, "that you did not know who he was. He identified himself properly many times when your ship made contact with the station. I was in ops. I heard him myself."

All the conversation she'd listened to on her bridge came back to her. She understood little of it. Only basic words like *dock* and *schedule*. And the names: *Razalka*. Vanushavor. Tivahr.

She shook her head. "You heard him in Zafharish." She gave him a weak smile. "Other than *vad, nav,* and *dharjas taf, viek,* I don't understand very much of it." *Except for yav cheron,* a small voice reminded her. She pushed it away.

Farra asked something else.

"No," Mitkanos said. "He did not put her under any security restrictions."

Trilby frowned, not comprehending his answer.

"My niece said that perhaps he felt he had to protect his identity from you, because you are Conclave. But you would have been confined to your ship then. Not permitted access to this station. You would have a Level Three, or more, status. He said to me Level One. And yes," he nodded to Farra, apparently anticipating her question, "I clarified. I have not been *Stegzarda* Chief of Security for three years and not know this."

He sat back, folded his arms across his broad chest. "Tivahr was very clear when he spoke to me on the comm. 'Level One,' he said, for *Dasja* Captain Elliot."

"Then is not a problem, Uncle." Farra lifted her cup, drained the last of her tea. "Is nothing more than oversight. Or perhaps Captain Tivahr did not want Captain Elliot to be afraid of him."

"He would not be so considerate of her feelings,

no," Mitkanos disagreed. "He lives for fear. More likely he knew that was the easiest way to get her to cooperate with his plans. He is a master at that, manipulating people.

"But regardless," he said, standing, "what he has given you is an interesting tale to tell, no?" He took her empty cup, and Farra's. "Come. My niece and I will walk you back to your ship, and we will talk of more pleasant things. For Tivahr is our problem now. Not yours. Your trouble now is over."

But it wasn't more pleasant things that ran through Trilby's mind as she wrapped herself in her purple quilt and propped herself up against the headboard of her bed.

It was everything she'd learned about Tivahr the Terrible. Emperor and sometimes executioner on his own ship. And a master manipulator of people.

She glanced at the chair in the corner, secured to the floor with the decklock. It would feel real good to unclip it and throw it at something right now. Like the bulkhead.

Or *the* Captain Tivahr. If he dared walk through her cabin door again.

It was with that pleasant thought that she fell into an exhausted sleep, purple quilt wrapped tightly around her, catching her tears of anger as they fell.

The words on the screen in front of him blurred. Rhis reached for his tea and, as his fingers closed around the mug, realized it was cold. He'd been sifting through the data Gurdan supplied him for, what, two hours now?

He sought the time stamp on his screen. Two and a half.

Bloody hell.

Since all the changes he'd quietly made to the *Venture*'s systems, he'd had little or no sleep. He felt it now, as his side began to ache again. Even he had his limits. Forty-eight hours with only two hours' sleep was one of them.

"Run a comparative on my analysis. I need about four hours downtime. Have it ready for me by then."

Gurdan looked up from his own screen and tabbed at the touchpads on his right. He was quiet for a moment, his gaze moving rapidly over the data now streaming down his screen. "We may need more than four hours, Captain."

Rhis stood, leaned his fists on the edge of the briefing-room table, and glared at the thin man. Gods, he was tired. And he needed to sink against something Trilby-soft and Trilby-scented.

"Four hours," he repeated. "Do I make myself clear?"

Gurdan's mouth tightened but he nodded. "We will do what we can in four hours."

"No. You will supply me with a thorough and complete analysis in four hours. Or I will find someone to replace you who can."

His boots echoed sharply as he strode down the corridor. The situation with the 'Sko had worsened considerably, factions merging with factions, even in the few days he'd been absent. No, it was more than a few days. He'd spent five on the *Venture*. Two in 'Sko captivity. And two and a half weeks before that, slowly infiltrating the Ycsko system with his team. He'd been away from the *Razalka* for almost a month.

He'd been away from Trilby Elliot for a little less than three hours. He wasn't sure which discomforted him more.

Trilby, he decided as he hit the call button for the lift. But Gurdan's lackadaisical response to his analysis request ranked right up there on the discomfort list as well.

Hell and damnation! Was he the only one able to elicit results in the Fleet?

Gurdan's team was good, but his team on the *Razalka* was better. Had to be. Or they wouldn't be there.

He sagged tiredly against the metal wall of the lift, thankful no one else occupied it. His thoughts drifted back to the 'Sko. The information he'd stolen from Szed. The movement in the Niyil parties and the Beffa cartels. The tie-ins with Rinnaker, and now, with the attack on the *Venture,* with GGA. He had an uneasy suspicion Garold Grantforth might be involved. The man was power-hungry. But his political success and well-known image made it difficult to see how he'd worked it, if he had. Or how Rhis could prove it.

Jagan Grantforth, or someone in his office, as Trilby suggested, could well be the key. He'd have to look further into that, follow the same kind of trail in Rinnaker as well. The Empire wasn't in the position to openly criticize the Conclave. Not yet.

That was something else he had to attend to.

That and . . .

His mind fogged. He had the disturbing sensation he'd forgotten something. Something important. But that was ridiculous. He never forgot anything important. He tolerated lapses in himself even less than he tolerated them in his crew.

The lift slowed smoothly, easing to a stop at the dock level. It was good to be back with Imperial technology again. He remembered some of the public lifts in Syar and Bagrond. Shuddering things, swaying and jerking. Outdated. Antiquated. Quite useless. Typical Conclave technology.

He stopped just short of the *Venture*'s rampway. The aging freighter's rounded bow was visible through the viewport. In the dim light on her bridge, he saw a small movement, recognized Dezi's tarnished form.

A wry smile played across his face. One of the

more entertaining examples of Conclave technology. He'd talk to Trilby about getting the 'droid a complete overhaul. His tendency toward verbal ramblings was, if nothing else, a waste of energy.

He strode up the rampway, some of his lassitude abating. It was almost 0330 on his biotime. His and Trilby's. His mind filled with a dozen different ways to wake her. He could almost feel the softness of her skin against his mouth, smell the intoxicating powdery scent of her. He imagined her saying *yav cheron* in a shy but passionate voice. He laid his hand against the *Venture*'s palm pad and realized his hands were sweating, the front of his uniform pants uncomfortably tight.

He heard the lock cycle, then click twice. But the hatchway door stayed closed.

Conclave technology, he reminded himself, but wiped his hand down his sleeve before trying again. *Conclave technology and hormones.*

It cycled, clicked twice, and went dead. The red *entry denied* light glowed brightly.

He frowned. Perhaps an interface glitch? The ship was segued into Imperial technology now.

He stepped back to the docking podium at the foot of the ramp, activated the intercom. "*Venture,* the hatch lock is not responding."

He waited. Nothing happened.

"*Venture,* there is a problem with the hatch lock. This is Rhis."

Nothing. He checked the status lights on the podium. Everything showed green. Maybe Trilby was asleep and Dezi involved in some maintenance function that prevented his responding.

Several more minutes passed. The ache in his side

resurrected itself. He punched the intercom button again. "Trilby? Dezi? Open the—"

It opened.

Trilby Elliot stood in the air lock in her faded green T-shirt and baggy flight pants. Her service jacket, embroidered with the *Venture*'s name on the sleeve, was tied around her waist. Her pistol, holstered but not locked, hung from underneath it.

The strap of her laser rifle looped over one shoulder. She cradled the weapon in her hands, and as he took a step forward, he heard the distinctive snick of the safety being unlocked.

He stopped. Her face was pale, her lips drawn in a thin line. There were smudges down her cheeks but her eyes were dry, steady, penetrating. And as cold as the glaciers on Chevienko.

His throat felt hot in comparison. He rasped out her name. "Trilby-*chenka*?"

"This," she said in an eerily quiet voice, "is one of the rifles that works." She tilted the barrel slightly upward. If she pressed the trigger, the charge would hit him in the throat.

"I don't understand."

"But I do, Tivahr. You're a lying, manipulating bastard."

Lying? He hadn't lied—

Tivahr. She called him Tivahr. Some of Chevienko's icy chill gripped his chest. He now knew what he'd forgotten.

Once he explained, surely she'd understand. The precariousness of his position. The urgency of the situation with the 'Sko. The way that his feelings for her had so completely obliterated everything else from his mind.

She raised the rifle, braced it against her shoulder.

"Get. Off. My. Ramp." She activated the target lock. He saw the thin red beam flick on, knew without looking down that it highlighted the center of his chest.

"Bastard," she hissed.

He backed up a step. Anger surged through him. Anger and a sense of loss, of desolation so complete that it took all his strength not to double over. It sucked the air out of his lungs, the life from his body, would have stopped even his heart from beating.

But he didn't have a heart anymore. He'd given it to her.

"Please. Trilby." His voice was raw. "Let's discuss this. Calmly."

"Discuss?" She laughed harshly. "Yeah, that's what Jagan said too. Let's discuss this, darling. Fucking liars. Both of you."

Her comparison stung like crazed firewasps against his skin. Jagan's duplicity and smooth words surfaced, prickling against his conscience. "I am not Jagan Grantforth," he protested.

"No. You're Tivahr. *The* Senior Captain Tivahr. You say 'jump' and the entire universe says 'how high and when.' Well, I'm not jumping anymore. And you have ten seconds to get off my ramp. Nine." She shifted position, locked her fingers on the trigger. "Eight—"

"We will talk tomorrow. I can explain everything, I promise."

"Six . . ."

He turned, shoved his hands in his pockets, and made sure he held his head high as he walked away.

* * *

Rhis stared at the ceiling of the small barracks sleeping room and realized he didn't even know his cubicle number. Nor did he care. Just as he didn't care about the odd look the quartermaster in ops gave him when he'd demanded a sleeping room. Nor about the raised eyebrows of two of Gurdan's team he'd stormed past in the corridor. He'd made it clear he was going back to the Conclave freighter. What in hell was Tivahr the Terrible doing on the barracks level?

What in hell, indeed.

He swallowed hard. This was hell. Worse than his interrogation by the 'Sko. Because the 'Sko he could fight against. The 'Sko he could hate.

He didn't want to fight with Trilby. He wanted to make love to her. And he couldn't hate her. Because she was right. He had lied, not so much to protect himself but to ensure her cooperation. He wanted her—

Yav chera.

—for selfish reasons. And he saw her flirt and laugh with Rhis Vanur in ways that he knew she never would with Khyrhis Tivahr. Tivahr the Terrible.

He knew what people called him, not only here but in the Conclave. Saw the fear that had flickered in her eyes at the mention of the *Razalka.*

And so Rhis Vanur was born. Rhis, who could be everything that Khyrhis was not. He shed the legend, the superstition, the rumors. And the truths. And reinvented himself. Into someone he hoped Trilby Elliot might love.

And she had. Hadn't she?

Yav chera.

* * *

He woke hungry, edgy, and with the unaccustomed feeling that his life had somehow spun out of control. The crowd in the officer's mess annoyed him. What in hell were all these people doing eating at this ungodly hour of the morning? The lines at the replicators were long, and trays were heavily laden with portions.

Morning. The numbers on the time panel caught his eye: 1830. It was dinnertime on station. But to his body, it was almost 0600—0545 to be exact. He'd lain in the sleeping room for two hours, slept maybe twenty minutes.

He stepped away from the line, headed for the coffee dispensers. A broad body blocked the panel in front of him. The gray-uniformed man filled a mug, then turned. Something flickered in the man's eyes, then he nodded. "Captain Tivahr."

It took a moment for Rhis's brain to register the rank on the man's collar. "Major." He shouldered brusquely past the man, grabbed a mug, and held it under the spigot.

There were no unoccupied tables in the lounge. The gray-clad *Stegzarda* filled most of the room. Fleet personnel sat by the door. He saw the burly major— Mitkanos, he remembered now, recognizing the wide mouth, the bent nose—at a table with a young woman. Security Chief Mitkanos. He had turned over the problem of Trilby's message to Neadi to him.

He was standing at Mitkanos's table before he realized he was there.

Mitkanos and the young woman were staring at him.

"I assigned Captain Elliot to you last night."

Mitkanos leaned back in his chair. "That was this afternoon. Sir."

He blinked. Station time. Of course. "I'm aware of that, Major," he snapped. "Was her request handled?"

"Rimanava sent Captain Elliot's message herself." Mitkanos nodded to the young woman, whose hands tightly clenched her mug of tea.

Rhis saw the apprehension in her eyes, just as he saw the defiance hinted at in Mitkanos's casual posture. He'd never met the man before last night—this afternoon, he corrected himself. But the battle crests on Mitkanos's sleeve told him the older man had been around awhile. Long enough to remember when the *Stegzarda* held power in this sector. Long enough to remember when the Fleet had taken it away from them.

He turned to the young woman. "What's your rank, Rimanava?"

"Corporal, sir."

"You on duty now, Corporal?"

"No, sir. Not until tomorrow morning."

"I don't have that kind of time to waste. Send a copy of Captain Elliot's message to me in Briefing Room One. You have five minutes."

He turned and strode for the door, ignoring the table of Fleet officers who rose and saluted as he stormed by.

He saw alarm flash in Gurdan's eyes when he stepped into the briefing room. The lieutenant stood up, stiffly. "You're early, Captain."

"There's work to do, Lieutenant. And unless I'm around, it doesn't seem to get done." He took his seat at the head of the conference table, tabbed on the screen. It blinked into solidity in front of him.

He scanned the files. "How far have you gotten?"

"We should have a complete analysis within the hour."

"Should? Should is unacceptable. You will."

"Yes, sir." Gurdan nodded briefly, then bent over to speak to one of his team at a wall console.

Rhis tapped the screen, opened one of the files he'd taken from the 'Sko. Dates and coordinates spilled past him. But now ship names and cargo overlay the data. Good. Good. Gurdan's people had picked up on the patterns he'd found, fleshed them out.

He drummed his fingers against his mustache. His mouth was dry. Coffee—

He glanced to his right. Then his left. Coffee. He'd left his coffee at Mitkanos's table.

The briefing-room doors slid open. Corporal Rimanava walked in. She put a cup of coffee on the table next to him, then clasped her hands behind her back and stood, waiting.

Waiting for what? Surely she didn't expect him to thank her for bringing his coffee. "Yes, Corporal?"

"I sent that copy you requested three minutes ago, sir. I wanted to make sure you received it."

Copy? Oh, bloody hell. He touched his screen, moved the analysis data, saw his message box flashing. His fingers reached for it before he could stop them. The transit ID grayed out, then Trilby was staring at him, her large green eyes sparkling, her mouth pursed in a small smile.

He knew that mouth, knew what it felt like, knew what it tasted like.

"Captain Trilby Elliot here, Independent freighter transit ID 1015–2711." She paused after the requisite ID. "Hello, Neadi, old friend—"

His fingers darted to the screen, freezing the message, halting her greeting. But her face still looked at him, her lips slightly parted to begin her next word. Or to entice a kiss.

He blanked the screen, but he could still see her. See her smile. The way she wrinkled her nose. He swallowed hard. He thought her message to Neadi might give him some clue as to how to reach her, to get her to talk to him again. But it only made him want to bolt out of his chair and take the maintenance stairs two at a time down to the station docks. Outrun even the lifts.

But he couldn't do that. She still had one laser rifle that worked.

He slumped back in his chair, covered his eyes with one hand. And then remembered the efficient Corporal Rimanava was still standing there.

Bloody fucking hell.

Fatigue washed over him. He wiped his hand down his face, turned to her. "Thank you, Rimanava. I got the message," he said quietly.

"You're welcome, sir." She nodded curtly, spun on her heels, and walked out.

He turned back to his screen but saw Gurdan first. The lieutenant's thin face was expressionless. Rhis read volumes in it.

"Reports are ready?" He forced a harsh note into his voice.

"Compiling the final tabulations now, Captain."

"Advise me when they're done." He touched the report he'd been working on when Rimanava had walked in, dragged it back to the center of his screen, concentrated on it.

But he was drawn to the time stamp on his screen:

1845. To Trilby's body, it was more like 0600. She might be awake. Maybe he should try to reach her. But if she were, then she'd had almost as little sleep as he had.

No, let her sleep. Let her anger die down. They were both overly tired. Tempers were thin. Brains were foggy.

Let her sleep. The *Venture* wasn't going anywhere. At least not until he said so. And not just because of the docking clamps securely locked onto her ship.

But because of another of those wogs-and-weemlies she'd been so afraid of.

He'd amended all her command codes. Her ship would respond to maintenance, life support, communications. But her engines, for all intents and purposes, were dead. Unless he was on board to input his overrides.

He initially intended to use the program if she refused to return to the Empire. He'd left it in place when he became worried she'd go dashing off into 'Sko territory, looking for Carina. Keeping her safe was becoming a passion for him.

It never occurred to him to mention the program when they made Degvar. He'd done nothing to make her feel like a prisoner. If she wanted to leave, she most likely would request permission to depart through Degvar ops, which would come to him.

And they would . . . discuss it.

Then he remembered the way she'd stared at him down the barrel of her rifle.

He hoped she wouldn't try something crazy, like breaking dock and bolting off station. There wasn't enough juice left in her laser banks to even singe the docking clamps. And besides, when she went to bring the engines online, they weren't going to respond.

And that, he knew, would really piss her off.

He leaned back in his chair, realized with mild surprise that Gurdan was gone. He hadn't noticed him leave. But his message file was flashing. The report was done.

Good. His gaze drifted out the viewport. His mind traveled down seven decks and halfway around the station. He drummed his fingers on his mustache.

No, not his air sprite. She wouldn't be that crazy.

Lieutenant Gurdan rose stiffly from one of the well-worn chairs in front of the lounge viewport and nodded to Trilby.

"I appreciate your time, Captain Elliot." He closed his datapad with a snap, tucked it under his arm.

Trilby stood also, the strap of the laser rifle trailing through her fingers. Gurdan was polite and professional during their entire one-hour interview about *Bella's Dream,* Rinnaker, and GGA. He never once mentioned the weapon lying casually on the small table next to her. Nor that the small green indicator lights showed it was fully primed.

She hooked the strap over her shoulder, offered him her hand. "I appreciate your thoroughness, Lieutenant. *Bella's Dream* is just another Indy freighter to you. But Carina and her brother are my lifelong friends."

"*Bella's Dream* is symptomatic of a much larger problem. One that threatens not only the Independent freighter trade and your Conclave, but our Empire as well. Every incident must be looked at very closely right now."

She walked him to the air lock, her hand tightening on the rifle as the hatch slid open. But only a Degvar dockhand lingered in the waiting area. She relaxed. "Is there anything else you'll need from me?" she asked.

"I cannot think of anything." He patted the datapad. "Your logs are very complete."

"Then I'm free to go?"

He stepped through the hatchway and turned back to her. "I personally do not know of any further information my team needs from you. But perhaps you should check with Captain Tivahr. He's most likely still in Briefing Room One. The *Razalka* is due in at 0200. Station time," he added.

That was about six hours from now. Middle of the afternoon for her. Middle of the night for Degvar. "Why would that delay me?"

"The *Razalka* has her own personnel working this problem. And this is their sector. They may want to view your logs and schedules."

"Can't they just use your notes?" She pointed to his pad. "You have everything right there."

"The crew of the *Razalka* prefers to conduct their own investigations."

Well, then this was just a phenomenal waste of time. Trilby secured the hatch door behind Gurdan's retreating figure and stomped down the corridor to the bridge.

She braced her arms against the back of her chair and stared out the wide forward viewport. Degvar curved off to her right. She could see various lights winking from the viewports on the different levels, and large darkened areas where the space station's outer hull hid recessed weapons bays. Another docking ramp spiked out in front of her, about six ship lengths away. It was empty. She wondered if the *Razalka* would dock there or if it were too large and would simply hang in geosynchronous orbit, utilizing shuttles.

She heard Dezi's footsteps as he clanked over the hatch tread. Her fingers smoothed down a wrinkled piece of duct tape that patched an old tear on the headrest. "I need you to plot me the shortest course to the border."

"We've received clearance to depart?"

"No. And I doubt we will." She traced the frayed piece of tape, her mind working. "The docking clamps Degvar uses are similar to the ones on Bagrond. Remember the time their main system fritzed out? We were all stuck. But I had that real good trike run to Quivera waiting. We had to go."

"I remember the incident well, Captain."

She turned, a wicked grin on her lips. "So do I, Dez. So do I. I'm going to get my tool kit and drag out the old EVA suit. If anyone asks where I am, I'm in the shower. Or napping."

She trotted down the forward ladderway, whistling.

It took her less than five minutes to suit up and exit from the *Venture*'s portside airlock. She lectured herself while she worked, dangling in zero g from the side of her ship not facing Degvar Station. *All bad things happen for a good reason, Trilby-girl! There you were, locked onto the station, the Quivera run dwindling before your eyes. So you got pissed off enough to get out there and gut the damned clamp locks—and learn a thing or two about station mechanisms.*

Little knowing, she continued as she spliced a datafeed cable, *that two years later that source of frustration would become a source of freedom.*

It was easier this time to create a bypass around the station controls. She could now unlock the docking clamps with a signal from her ship.

She tabbed her helmet mic, set for short-range private channel. "Reel me in, Dez."

She stripped off her EVA suit and grabbed her service jacket. Her skin felt clammy and cold from working outside. She thrust her arms through the sleeves as she trotted up the ladderway to the bridge.

She slid into her seat, clicked her safety strap over her chest, and looked at Dezi. "We're back in control of our lives again." She tapped her touchpads, brought her course on screen. "Priming sublight engines."

She brought up her codes, entered them, then started the auxiliary thruster sequence. "We'll be halfway into next septi by the time they figure—"

"Engines are not responding, Captain."

Her hands froze over the controls. "Impossible." She dumped her sequence string, started over. "Gods, I knew I should've replaced that thruster board before we worked on the communications system."

She tapped the pads.

Nothing.

"Damnation!" She reached over, ran a quick diagnostic on the thruster boards. All lights showed green.

She unsnapped her safety harness. "I'm going down to the engine room to see if something's rotted out. Again."

She pounded down the stairs. Twenty minutes later, she was back. She almost threw the datalyzer across the bridge.

"Everything is optimal, I take it?" Dezi asked.

"Too damned optimal. Let's try again." And again. And again. After the third again, Trilby swiveled around, yanked her harness off, and thrust herself from her chair. She stopped just short of the open hatchway, braced her hands on either side of the door frame. "Damn him, damn him, damn him!"

She kicked the bulkhead. Hard. Her foot throbbed.

"Ships are usually referred to as 'she,'" Dezi said.

She spun around. "I'm not talking about the *Venture*." Her words were clipped, terse. "I'm talking about that ungrateful, arrogant, motherless son of a Pillorian bitch."

"Oh. Lieutenant Vanur."

"Recently reincarnated as *the* Captain Tivahr. Master manipulator. Boy genius. Gods damned hacker!"

"I was under the impression you were rather fond of him."

"Fond?" Trilby gasped. "Of that Ligorian slime weasel?"

"He appears rather fond of you."

"That's the operative word, Dez. *Appears*. He's a pro at appearances. Especially false ones." She crossed her arms across the back of her chair and leaned her forehead against them. "Damn. Damn. Double damn."

She closed her eyes, listened to the quiet click and hum of her ship, the slight squeak of Dezi's joints. And to the small voice in the back of her head that chanted, *Stupid, stupid, stupid.*

She raised her head. "Dezi."

"Yes, Captain?"

"He had you run a program. The one that changed the *Venture*'s ID codes."

"That's correct."

"You still have it?"

"He retrieved his original, but I did make a copy that I believe he was not aware of."

She turned her head. "Have I told you lately how much I love you, Dez? You are the joy of my life. The song in my heart."

"I am not programmed to respond to human emotions, but I do appreciate the sentiments. I take it you would like to view the copy of the program?"

"You're a veritable mind reader as well." She slid into her seat, swiveled the screen up from the armrest. "Let's see just how good this son of a bitch really is."

He was good. Beyond impressive. She looked at what he'd done, how he'd circumvented certain code requirements and fooled others, and thought of Shadow.

Shadow could've done this. Would be doing this, if he'd lived. He'd been gutsy enough, and crazy enough, to use some of these same tactics.

She felt a twinge of regret. Damn him for lying to her! For being Tivahr and not Rhis Vanur. A man who could be this creative, this downright devious, could hold the key to her heart. Just as Shadow had, but they'd been children then. She'd never told him, and he would've laughed if she'd made mizzet-moon-eyes at him anyway.

She exhaled a long sigh of frustration. She had no doubt he'd hacked into her primary system codes and either deleted hers or amended his own. And she had no doubt that *that* program was as beautifully convoluted as this ID-altering one before her.

She could undo what he'd done. It wasn't impossible. But it would take time. A long time. A trike, maybe a septi. He had traps, fail-safes. Tweak something wrong and ten other key functions would scatter, attach themselves to alternate functions, and there'd be a worse mess.

It would be like plucking hairs off a felinar, one silky strand at a time.

She didn't think there was enough gin on her ship to get her through it.

She leaned her head back, stared at the ceiling of her bridge, at the toy felinar dangling from its red ribbon. He had to know she'd find this wog-and-weemly. He surely didn't think she was going to abandon the *Venture,* spend the rest of her life on Degvar. Therefore, he must have put this program in place while he was still pretending to be Rhis Vanur, still pretending he cared about her.

She couldn't think why he would've done it, then. Except as a silent but incredibly well-crafted parting gesture to show how little she meant to him.

If she weren't so busy hating him, she could have admired his handiwork more.

Rhis made five copies of Gurdan's report, one for each member of the *Razalka*'s tactical team. He highlighted certain sections, based on what he knew each officer's analytical strengths and weaknesses to be.

Then he bundled them and sent them to his personal file, to be uploaded when his ship arrived.

In four hours.

He'd feel about four hundred years old when they got here.

He rose, wincing as pains shot through his back. *Make that five hundred years old,* he thought, and reached for his empty coffee mug.

He ran into Gurdan in the corridor, datapad under his arm.

"The debriefing with Captain Elliot is completed. Report filed."

Debriefing? It came back to him. Gurdan's team needed Trilby's impressions for their files. Plus information on Neadi Danzanour. And *Bella's Dream.* He'd okayed the interview when they first arrived on station. Then forgotten it was scheduled.

That meant she was awake. He glanced at his time cuff. Of course she was. It was damned near their lunchtime.

"Will you be needing a copy of my report, Captain?"

"Yes, I will. Code it to my transit file on the *Razalka.*" Which should be arriving. Soon. He hoped soon. He hadn't slept in his own bed in a month. He hadn't slept in any bed for more than an hour in a trike.

". . . and she did request permission to depart. However, I told her to speak with you first."

"She . . ." Gods. Trilby was leaving. No. She couldn't. But she wanted to. She might try.

But ops hadn't called him.

"When did she request this?" He tried to marshal his scattered thoughts, put some firmness back in his voice, which was starting to sound distinctly hoarse.

"I left the *Careless Venture* two hours ago."

Two hours. Ops hadn't called him.

Bloody hell.

He shoved his empty coffee mug into Gurdan's hand and strode purposefully down the corridor to the lifts.

He arrived just as one opened. Three dock techs exited. He stepped inside. "Dock Level!" The doors closed. He leaned on the safety rail and tapped his comm badge. "Tivahr to ops."

"Ops. Lieutenant Gramm," a female voice replied.

"Has the *Venture* requested permission to depart?"

There was a moment of silence. "No, sir."

He slapped the badge again. "Tivahr to security."

"Security. Mitkanos."

"Any unexplained explosions on Dock Level? Unusual activity?"

"None reported, sir. Monitors show nothing unusual."

The doors opened. He ran halfway around the ring, only slowing as he came to the *Venture*'s rampway. Her round, pitted bow was still clearly visible through the viewport.

Her bridge was dark. Empty. But the ship was still there.

He keyed in his access codes, slid back the cover on the rampside docking controls. Everything looked normal. He tapped in a status verification request. Dock clamps were secure.

Then something flickered across the screen and disappeared. If he hadn't been so tired, if he hadn't been leaning against the control podium, his chin almost in his chest, he never would've seen it. The small flicker was gone now. But he'd created enough of them to know what they looked like.

A hidden bypass.

Someone had altered the clamp-release codes. And not from this terminal.

Out of everyone on Degvar, he knew of only two people who could've done that.

And *he* hadn't.

He activated his comm badge. "Tivahr to ops. Patch me through to the *Venture*."

He waited, wondering how many requests it would take this time to bring her to the air lock.

"This is the DZ-Nine 'droid."

Hearing Dezi's voice so quickly startled him. He began to reply in Zafharish. "*Yaschjon Tivahr*—this is Rhis. Let me talk to Trilby. Captain Elliot."

"I regret Captain Elliot is not available at the moment."

"Where is she, in the galley? Put me through, Dezi."

"I'm sorry. She's not on board."

Maybe she left right after talking to Gurdan. Or maybe . . .

He sprinted to the viewport, scanned the perimeters of the ship for a small figure in an EVA suit. That's how he would have accessed the clamp controls. He saw nothing.

"Where is she, Dezi?" His tone was insistent.

"I do not know, Captain."

"I have to talk to her. There were some programs I installed on the *Venture*. She might not understand—"

"If you are referring to the one that invalidates her primary command codes, she is already aware of that."

He closed his eyes briefly, leaned his forehead against the viewport's thick glass. "She is."

"Yes. And she's not very happy, Captain Tivahr."

He didn't think she would be. "You have a penchant for understatement," he told the 'droid.

"Sir?"

"Where is she?"

"I do not know."

"Dezi!"

"She did not relay her destination to me."

And he'd given her full clearance on the station. No required escort. No check-in. And no trackable badge.

Damn! He pushed himself away from the viewport. "If you should hear from her, I need you to give her a message from me."

"Of course, sir."

"Tell her, tell her I said *yav chera*."

"Yav . . . ?"

"*Yav chera*. Tell her I said *yav chera*."

"Yes, sir."

"Tivahr out."

Trilby swiveled the chair away from the console and looked with surprise, and gratitude, at the burly man seated behind the desk. It had been a risk coming here. But she realized she had two problems to solve when, overwhelmed with frustration, she'd stalked down the *Venture*'s ramp. The first was that her tinkerings with the dock clamps had probably been caught on security cameras. She needed to provide a reasonable explanation for her actions before someone stumbled on the truth.

The second was that she needed an ally.

She took a chance that Mitkanos was the answer to both.

He was Chief of Security on station. And her earlier conversations with him hinted that he was not a fan of *the* Captain Tivahr.

The conversation she'd just overheard had been in Zafharish, but some of the words Leonid had taught her had come back to her. Plus she knew *his* voice.

"You didn't have to do that, but thank you. It was uncommonly kind toward someone you don't know."

Yavo Mitkanos shrugged. "I did nothing extraordinary. I was asked a question about explosions on Dock Level. Had there been any, I would have reported them."

"But unusual activity?"

"I saw, on my monitors, a captain conducting an exterior inspection of her ship's hull. I do not find that to be an unusual activity. Do you?"

She'd done it dozens of times. But only once before for that very reason.

"You also," she continued, "didn't tell Tivahr I was here."

Another shrug of his broad shoulders. A comically innocent expression played across his gruff features. "He did not ask me."

"You know," she said softly, "I think you're the first security grunt I've ever liked."

He grinned broadly.

"Thank you," she said again. She glanced at the screen behind her. Save for herself and Mitkanos, the security office was empty. Whether this was the usual state of operations on Degvar, she didn't know. But it had been damned convenient, and damned lucky, for her.

"I gather the *Razalka*'s within shouting range." She motioned to the data on the screen.

"Five hours, though she'll make it in four. Her crew knows well their captain does not like to be kept waiting."

"Then he'll leave?"

"That is what I have been led to believe."

"Gurdan said I have to talk to the team on the *Razalka* now. If that's all he wants, he should've told me." She was annoyed, embarrassed, and angry over her current situation. But she still held on to the small hope that something she knew might help find Carina. For that she was willing to tolerate annoyance, embarrassment, and anger. And *the* Captain Tivahr, although in limited doses. "He didn't have to disable my ship for that."

"Captain Tivahr has not shared his objectives with me."

"Then you have no impound order on the *Venture*?"

"*Nav.*"

"So this is strictly Tivahr's doing?"

"Unfortunately, yes."

She didn't miss his choice of words. "And you don't know if he'll let me go after I talk to his team?"

"As I said, he has not shared his objectives with me. But I am aware, of course, that you have recently found your ship's engines to be inoperative. Perhaps you took damage from the 'Sko attack you were not aware of. Should I hear of something that would assist you in better allocating your repair time, I would be obliged to inform you."

She stopped in front of his desk as she headed for

the door. "Major Mitkanos," she said, holding out her hand. "I have no idea what your pay grade is here. But whatever it is, the *Stegzarda* don't pay you enough."

He shook her hand firmly. "It is a good thing, then, that I love my work, *vad?*" He glanced at the monitors on his desk. "Go get a cup of hot tea. You need it, and he is back on Barracks Level now. No one will bother you."

12

He awoke with a jolt. He didn't know if it was the sharp trill of the cubicle intercom in his ear or his own internal sense of impending urgency. The two things happened almost simultaneously. He sat up, snagging his boot heel on the blanket. He'd fallen asleep fully clothed.

"Tivahr here!" His voice rasped. But his body, and his mind, felt marginally better than before his—he glanced at the time panel—one-and-a-half hour nap.

One and a half hours. The *Razalka* was due in a half hour from now.

"Captain, we've received confirmation that the *Razalka* has cleared the outer beacon."

Make that fifteen minutes.

"Acknowledged. On my way."

Not even time for a cup of tea. He snatched his jacket off the wall hook, slipped it on, then fumbled with his collar. He ducked his head, caught his reflection in the mirror. He still wore the white shirt Trilby had given him. No wonder the collar seemed wrong.

Trilby. More than his collar was wrong.

He sealed his jacket, ran his hand through his hair. His uniform betrayed the fact that he'd worn, slept in, and, thanks to Trilby, washed the same one for a month. His white shirt was nonregulation. His jacket held no ship's insignia, no bars signifying rank. His comm badge bore Degvar's emblem, not the *Razalka*'s.

And he was way overdue for a haircut.

Hell. It was just his crew. They'd seen him come ragged off missions before.

Eleven minutes.

The door, sensing his presence, opened. Light from the corridor glared in his face. Gray uniforms hurried past him, blending in with the gray bulkhead.

There was a queue at the lift. But when the doors parted, the gray line waited. He stepped inside first.

"Ops," he said.

Two of the *Stegzarda* crew were going there as well. The remaining four gave other destinations.

He clenched his fist by his side as the lift sped up the levels. He fought the urge to tap his comm badge, to see if Trilby was back on the *Careless Venture*. Not that he could make time to talk to her right now. Probably wouldn't be able to for at least two hours after his ship arrived. But he wanted to know. Needed to know.

But not in a lift full of *Stegzarda*.

There were more black Fleet uniforms on the Operations-Center Level. The *Stegzarda* worked the station. But Fleet personnel ran it. He returned several salutes and strode through the wide doors as they irised open.

Ops was fully staffed, even though it was the station's red-eye shift. The approach of the Empire's premier huntership required nothing less.

The room was a large half circle that encompassed two levels, with a viewport spanning its height and breadth. He entered on the upper level, which was half the width of the lower. Degvar Approach Control was immediately in front of him.

"Status?" he asked the young woman who turned upon his arrival.

"The *Razalka*'s just locked onto our escort tugs."

He nodded, took the ladderway to the lower level. There was a small landing at the halfway point, where the stairs angled to the left. The landing overlooked communications and the large viewscreen bordering the far edge of the viewport. He didn't stop there, as he could already see the *Razalka*'s upper bridge on the screen—his bridge. And, standing at perfect attention, his executive officer.

The silver-haired man saluted as Rhis reached the last step. He was younger than indicated by the color of his hair. His dark eyes were bright and there was an air of amiable trustworthiness about him. "Captain Tivahr."

"Commander Demarik." Rhis returned the salute crisply. "Tell Jankova I need her full team in my ready room in twenty minutes."

"Acknowledged, Captain. However, Lord Minister Kospahr has been using it as his office."

"What—?"

"Captain Tivahr." A portly man in an elegant dark suit pushed himself out of the chair behind Demarik.

The *captain's* chair. Rhis clenched his teeth, felt a muscle in his jaw begin to throb.

Kospahr. What in hell was that egotistical bureaucrat doing on his ship? In his command chair? Why in hell hadn't he been warned about this?

He saluted Kospahr, wishing he could offer a different hand gesture instead. "Lord Minister. What a surprise."

"You're out of uniform, Tivahr. You look a disgrace."

"I don't think you've come all the way from Council Chambers on Verahznar to tell me that."

"I came all the way from Council Chambers because you've been absent for over a month. Captain." Kospahr took a step forward. Demarik took a step away from him, a brief flash of distaste on his usually pleasant features. The shorter man didn't seem to notice. "My cousin the emperor needed answers."

His cousin the emperor. Kospahr always said those four words as if they were one. More likely his cousin the emperor—who was in truth his second cousin—was tired of listening to him whine.

Rhis inclined his head with the barest semblance of respect. "I've already prepared a detailed report for Emperor Kasmov."

"Good. I'll review it before you send it to him."

Demarik moved across the bridge behind Kospahr, leaning over shoulders, conferring with various bridge crew. Rhis recognized the familiar procedure. The *Razalka* was preparing to lock into synchronized docking orbit with the station. She was too large to use any of the ramps.

Rhis purposely looked past Kospahr. "Mister Demarik."

Demarik turned. "Sir?"

"Get Jankova's team in my ready room. Minister Kospahr will have to find someplace else to have his tea party. I'm on my way to the shuttle now."

He strode toward the lower-level doors and was glad when they shut behind him, cutting off Kospahr's sputtering protestations.

He strapped himself into a seat on the left side of the shuttle, knowing that as the small ship pulled out of the station's bay, he'd have a clear view of the *Venture* through the viewport. The freighter was dwarfed by the station, looking small and battered. Her bridge lights were still dark. No reason to sit on the bridge if the engines were dead.

The long, deltoid form of the *Razalka* came into view as the shuttle turned. Spiky with weapons turrets and braking vanes, she was an example of Imperial technology at its best. Her hull sparkled with lights. All departments were active. The captain was on his way in.

Demarik and the *Razalka*'s chief medical officer were waiting in the air lock when the shuttle docked in the large bay. Overhead lights blinked green twice as enviro kicked on.

He returned Demarik's salute, then held up his hand to stop his CMO's anticipated order. "No, I am not going to sick bay right now. I need to change my uniform and meet with my team in my ready room."

"Your report indicated you suffered injuries." The CMO rocked back on his heels and eyed Rhis from head to toe. He wasn't a tall man but stockily built, with a round face that looked even rounder under his balding head.

"And my report also stated I am suffering no ill effects from those same injuries."

"And if you were, you wouldn't tell me anyway."

"Very astute, Doctor." Rhis handed Demarik a small packet. "There's some classified data in there I'd like you and Jankova to review. After the meeting," he added over his shoulder as he headed for the air lock. Demarik hurried to keep up with Rhis's long strides.

"Additionally," he said as they proceeded into the corridor, "I need an explanation from you regarding Kospahr's presence on my ship. I need to know how long he's been here, what he's done, who he's spoken to." They halted in front of the lift. "I don't like surprises, Demarik."

"Yes, sir. I'm sure you know I did everything I could to prevent this."

"Not enough, obviously," he said coolly. "Not enough."

Rhis rested his chin in his hand and watched Commander Jankova and her team pull his data apart. On one end of the conference table in his ready room, a multilevel holograph of the shared border regions of the Empire's Yanir System and the Conclave's Gensiira rotated slowly just above the small projector set into the tabletop. Cosaros and Bervanik argued quietly, adjusting the projection's parameters as it turned.

At the center of the long table, Hana Jankova stood in front of a thin screen, her copper-colored hair glinting as the room's overhead lights played down on it. Her arms were crossed over her chest. Her brows were drawn into a frown over her bright blue eyes.

Standing next to her was Lieutenant Osmar, a lightpen in his hand. He stabbed at a line of data. Jankova shook her head in disagreement.

Rhis watched, listened, and, at least for now, said nothing. He knew where the problems were, knew the locations of gaps in the data, the glaring inconsistencies. But pointing these out to his tactical team wasn't the same as letting them find and follow the trails themselves.

For the trails, he knew, would eventually lead to the source.

The Ycsko.

And GGA.

The ready-room doors slid open with an almost-silent hiss. Rhis glanced to the left, saw Demarik enter, and give a small nod to Jankova. The slightest upturn of her mouth was her only answer.

Rhis had known about their relationship for over eight months. Had tolerated it only because Demarik was the best exec in the Fleet, and Jankova had one of the sharpest tactical minds in the Empire.

He'd said nothing to either of them when he realized what was going on. He didn't have to. He'd worked with Zak Demarik for more than ten years. He'd mentored Jankova for five, since she'd come out of the academy at the top of her class. His opinion of "emotional entanglements" as a waste of valuable time and energy was well known not only to them but to every one of his crew.

Malika had taught him that well, twenty years

ago. It was a lesson he'd never forgotten. Until he met Trilby.

He turned his face toward the room's high viewport, letting his hand drop from his chin. He rested it on the arm of his chair and clenched his fist. Maybe it was a lesson he now had to remember. His air sprite had already skewed his life, deprived him of sleep, muddied his thinking. She was giving him an out, with her lone working laser rifle. He should be thankful. Let her go. Forget her.

Something squeezed his chest, hard. Painfully.

In his mind, he saw the kill order in the 'Sko transmit. It was his duty to protect her.

But another part of his mind argued, *Let the Conclave protect her.* She was an Indy trader. She was their responsibility, not his.

He had to let her go. She'd do all right. She was bright, gutsy. A survivor. They hadn't really become involved. They'd made love one time. A response to the stress of the situation. It had made them both overly sensitive, overly emotional.

There was no place for emotions on the *Razalka*. She wouldn't fit in here. She was unorthodox, impulsive. Distracting.

Enchanting. Enticing.

Damn it!

He had to forget her. He had to let her go.

"Captain?" There was a note of urgency in Jankova's voice.

He sat upright. "What is it?"

She hesitated only slightly before answering. "You've cut your hand."

He looked down, saw the thin stream of blood flowing down his wrist. In his fingers were the shards of his lightpen. He didn't remember grabbing it from the table. He didn't remember snapping it in half.

He pushed himself to his feet, saw the looks of concern and confusion on Jankova and Demarik's faces. Osmar's eyes were wide. Cosaros studied the holograph with a new intensity.

Bloody hell. Literally.

"It's nothing. I'll go clean up." He tossed the broken pen on the table, belatedly remembering the units were supposed to be indestructible.

So much for Imperial technology.

He strode through the ready-room doors, his fist still clenched.

She had tea by herself, though both Fleet and *Stegzarda* personnel wandered in and out of the mess hall during the twenty minutes she sat, steeped in the game of hurry-up-and-wait.

With every heavy footstep she heard Rhis. She steeled herself, forced herself not to turn but to stare at the darkened viewports, looking for the reflection of a tall, broad-shouldered form.

Degvar was filled with a goodly assortment of tall, broad-shouldered forms. But none set off her internal warning sirens nor made her heart skip a beat. She didn't have to turn around. She'd know if he were walking toward her.

He never did.

She damned him, damned herself, and finally shoved her empty mug in the disposal and trudged back to her ship. It was the middle of the afternoon on her bioclock, but she was exhausted. The hot tea, instead of reviving her, made her lethargic.

She wrapped herself in the purple quilt and told her cabin lights to dim. The *Razalka* was due in shortly. Might already be sitting out on skim, for all she knew. If someone needed to talk to her, they'd know where to find her. It wasn't like she could go anywhere else.

Damn him.

The plaintive tones of her cabin's intercom woke her. She climbed out of a muzzy-headed sleep, aching and disoriented. It took her a moment to slap the touch-pad on the wall next to her bed.

"Elliot," she croaked. She kicked the quilt off her legs.

"Captain, I have a Corporal Rimanava at the air lock." Dezi's voice was irritatingly chipper. "She would like to know if you care to join her for breakfast."

Breakfast? The red numbers on her time panel showed ship's time of 1800 hours. Dinner, her stomach told her.

She pushed her hand through her hair. She'd slept over six hours. "A minute, Dez." She muted the intercom. "Lights."

The illumination in her cabin increased, flickered, then steadied. Damned generator! What next?

She tabbed off the mute. "I fell asleep," she told him. "I'm . . ." She peered in the mirror. Gods. She looked like she'd slept in a windstorm. But she was hungry.

"I'll be a few minutes. Hell. Send her down to my cabin." Farra Rimanava looked like an understanding sort. After all, she'd survived with Mitkanos as her uncle.

She'd dragged a clean T-shirt over her head and managed to do something with her short mop of thick hair when her cabin door chimed. "Come."

Farra walked in, her long hair neatly braided, her gray uniform spotless.

Trilby grabbed her service jacket. Dark green and frayed on the cuffs. She returned the young woman's smile.

"Welcome on board the *Careless Venture*. Sorry I didn't meet you at the ramp. I just woke up."

"Uncle Yavo says it takes full day to get body and station on same time, *vad*?"

"Usually I ignore station time. I hit too many of them." Which was why spaceport pubs like Flyboy's and stations bars in places like Bagrond prospered. Someone was always coming in, hungry and thirsty and looking for a good time. Or trouble. Which often turned out to be the same thing.

"You have seen many places, then? This I find fasten-ing. No." Farra shook her head.

"Fascinating," Trilby supplied, pulling on her jacket.

"Ah, yes! Fascinating. I need much to learn Standard. We have breakfast, share tea. You talk to me in Standard. Uncle Yavo says I learn much."

"I'd like that, thanks." She stepped into the corridor, motioned Farra ahead of her. They climbed the ladderway to the bridge corridor and found Dezi waiting by the hatch lock.

"I'm going with Corporal Rimanava to have some dinner. Or breakfast. If anyone comes looking for me—"

"Captain Tivahr was here several hours ago," Dezi said.

Trilby froze. "While I was sleeping?" She'd given Dezi strict orders not to permit Tivahr on board. But she doubted that the DZ-9 would be able to stop him, if *the* Senior Captain of the *Razalka* really wanted access. So that meant he'd left of his own accord. She wondered why Dezi hadn't called her.

"No. Before you returned," the 'droid said. "But when you came back on board you said to hold all messages for at least two hours."

Yes, she did. She remembered that now. Her eyes had been rapidly closing.

"And then when I checked on you, you were asleep. May I say I think you needed the rest? Besides, Captain Tivahr's message did not appear to be urgent."

"What message?"

"He said, '*Yav chera.*' " He looked at Farra. "Did I pronounce that correctly, Corporal? My linguistic chip does not contain many Zafharish parameters."

Trilby leaned against the bulkhead and closed her eyes briefly. Her throat felt suddenly tight. She swallowed hard.

"Bastard!" she hissed.

"No," Farra said, with a slight frown. "It does not mean that. It means—"

"I know what it means," Trilby said hurriedly. She pushed herself away from the bulkhead, slapped at the hatch-lock release. The hatch slid sideways, letting in a gust of cool station air. "It means," she said, as Farra stepped onto the ramp beside her, "that he's not only a bastard, he's a lying bastard."

They threaded their way past station technicians and dockworkers in silence. But they were the only ones waiting for the lift. Farra spoke after the doors closed.

"He said this, when he pretends to be this Vanur person? He tells you, '*Yav chera*'?"

Trilby stared at the numbers flashing on the overhead readout. "Yeah," she said after a moment, feeling her cheeks starting to burn.

Farra shook her head knowingly. "Maybe not tea then, Captain Elliot. I think, no, you need something stronger. Coffee? Or you like to try a glass of our famous Yaniran *fedka*?"

The Yaniran liquor was highly potent. Leonid let her try a sip once. It had made her eyes water.

"At breakfast?" Trilby asked with a wry smile.

"We have saying on my home station. When mizzet farts in air duct, high and low suffer stink." She clasped her hand on Trilby's shoulder. "Come. We go see Uncle Yavo. Drink a toast to farting mizzets. Then we go eat. Breakfast. Dinner. No matter."

Drink a toast to farting mizzets? What the hell. It was the best offer she'd had in a long time.

Trilby folded the thick slice of bread in half and dunked it in her soup. "Looks like we got here just ahead of the crowd." She motioned to a large group of black-uniformed personnel coming through the doors of the officers' lounge.

Farra's knife hesitated over her breakfast as she glanced up. "Not our people."

"I know. Fleet."

"*Razalka*," Farra said. She stabbed a thick chunk of fried fruit. "They are *Razalka* crew. See their . . ."

And she shoved the fruit into her mouth, her free hand circling the emblem on her uniform.

"Insignia," Trilby said. So this was crew from *his* ship. Interesting. After two glasses of *fedka* with Yavo Mitkanos, that information barely fazed her.

She nibbled on her bread. It was deliciously soggy.

"In-sig-ni-a." Farra tested the word.

"How long have they been docked here?"

"Not docked." Farra's hand circled in the air this time.

Trilby nodded. "Synchronous orbit. We call it 'sitting out,' or 'sitting out on skim.' The big tri-haulers have to do that a lot. And if they're in for more than a trike, we call them 'shuttle sluts.' "

"Sluts?" Farra giggled wickedly.

"You know. Big ships have a lot of personnel. They suck up all the available shuttles."

"Good language, your Standard!"

Trilby studied the group waiting at the replicators. She could see the difference now. It was more than just the design of the insignia. It was their spotless uniforms, their unmarred boots. Their datalyzers, weapons holstered perfectly as if they'd all been stamped out by the same machine.

It was also in the way they held themselves, backs straight, shoulders level, eyes straight ahead. Arrogance on the hoof.

And not a one of them was smiling.

Poor bastards. She sipped her coffee.

Three more Fleet officers strolled in, and she immediately recognized they weren't off the *Razalka*. For one thing, they strolled. For another, the two men and one woman were talking animatedly. They had

Degvar emblems on their chests. And smiles on their faces.

They headed for her table, and only as she saw the widening smile on Farra's face did she realize this wasn't a chance meeting.

Farra introduced them. "My friend Lucho, his sister Leesa. And cousin Dallon."

Lucho had a shy smile and the same thick brown hair as his sister. He unclipped two chairs from an empty table and dragged them over, locking his into place next to Farra. *So this,* Trilby thought, *is the reason she defends the Fleet to Uncle Yavo.*

She shook his hand, then Leesa's, while Dallon unclipped an empty chair from a table farther away. He hooked it to the decking between Trilby and Leesa.

"*Dasja* Captain." He took the hand she offered, but instead of shaking it, brought it to his lips and brushed it with a light kiss.

His hair was a richer glossy brown than his cousins' and he wore it long, pulled back into a tail and tied with a black cord. He was several years older. Mid thirties, Trilby guessed. Not boyishly cute—and she had to admit Lucho was cute—like his cousin. But attractive, in a rugged, almost roguish way.

"*Dasjon* Dallon." She smiled and pulled her hand away.

He grinned, the craggy planes of his face softening. "You speak my language?"

"Badly."

"We talk Standard," Farra said. Trilby noticed she'd slipped her fingers through Lucho's. "I need practice. I learn new word just now. Shuttle slut!"

"A useful term to know," Dallon said. His accent

was light compared to Farra's, and he spoke Standard easily. "Especially if you want to get a good bar fight going." He chuckled.

"Sounds like you've worked the Conclave." Or else maybe the freighter lingo she knew wasn't that unique after all.

Dallon winked at her. "I've worked many places."

Lucho laughed. "Our illustrious cousin just gets promotion to supply-ship captain."

He was, Trilby realized, somewhat her counterpart in the military. She turned, interested in learning more.

"It's a good job," Dallon said. He lay his hand on her left arm, leaned toward her conspiratorially. "You know why? Because no one shoots at a supply ship. And everyone wants to be my friend, to see what little goodies I have this trip."

She could imagine Dallon at Flyboy's. With his easygoing, good-natured personality, he reminded her of Chaser. It wouldn't take long before everyone was his friend. Even there.

"I'll bet the free samples you hand out make even more friends," she said. When the cargo wasn't solely your responsibility, it was easy to have a case here or there turn up missing. Later found, of course, in the captain's personal quarters.

He chuckled, winked at her again.

"Captain Elliot."

The lounge was noisy. She didn't hear his approach. But she heard his final footstep, saw the tall shadow fall across the table. Heard the cold, authoritative tone in his voice.

Her heart thudded hard against her ribs for a few beats, then slowed to normal, as if the potent *fedka* had kicked in again. She drew a deep but quiet breath, pasted on her best professional captain smile, and looked up to her left. "Captain Tivahr."

His face was impassive, and for a moment it was if she could find nothing of Rhis Vanur in him at all. But then something flickered in his eyes, something loosened the rigid line of his mouth. He was Rhis again. And he looked disappointed, like a child learning the circus had come and gone and he'd missed it.

Just as quickly, the rigidity was back. His lips thinned.

"Commander Jankova will need to talk to you. You will make yourself available at 0730."

She bristled at his tone. Pompous bastard! What had Mitkanos called him? An arrogant rimstrutter. Try to intimidate her, would he? She tilted her face, let her mouth curve into a sly smile, didn't bother to prevent the impudent tone that had annoyed him more than once from lacing her words. "Your place or mine?"

She saw the startled look in his eyes before they narrowed. "Commander Jankova will be at your ramp at 0730. Any delays on your part will not be viewed favorably."

She almost rose to her feet and clocked him one across the mouth right then and there. Would have, if Dallon hadn't been holding on to her arm.

"Let's talk about delays," she said, anger simmering under her words. "Let's talk about who raped my ship's primaries and totally disabled my engines. It wasn't me, Tivahr. You want my cooperation? Then give me the Gods damned release codes."

"This is how you help your friend Carina?" he countered harshly. "This is how much you care?"

Trilby sucked in her breath as if she'd been

slapped. "Don't you dare." Her voice was deathly calm. "You lying, manipulative son of a bitch. Don't you dare question my motives. Or by all I hold holy, you will regret the day you slithered out of that test tube and thought you could ever be a real man."

He held her gaze for three very long, tense seconds. Then turned on his heels and strode stiffly for the doors.

"Do you think that was wise?" Farra Rimanava asked softly. She glanced at Lucho, then back to Trilby.

Trilby sagged against the hard back of her chair, let some of the roiling emotions drain out of her. "Of course not." She gave Farra a wan smile. "But then, wise people don't run freighter businesses with no funds and only a dilapidated Circura Two." Nor do they, she knew, try to play finders keepers with a Zafharin officer dumped in their laps courtesy of the 'Sko.

She glanced toward the wide entrance of the lounge to see if he was really gone. He was, and no one around seemed to notice or care. Her brief verbal exchange with him hadn't been audible to anyone other than those at her table.

"He has much power," Leesa put in, with a nod to Farra.

"He also has some codes essential to Captain Elliot's ship," Dallon added.

Trilby looked at him. He'd removed his hand from her arm and now had both hands folded in front of him on the table. His jovial demeanor had turned serious.

"Or did I not hear correctly?" he asked her.

She nodded. "He hacked into my primaries. He told me, promised me, the only thing he changed was my Conclave ID to an Imperial one." He'd promised her other things as well. Things she didn't want to think about right now.

"And you thought that was all someone like Tivahr would do?" Lucho asked.

"He did not tell her he was Tivahr," Farra answered, before Trilby could figure out where to start. "He told her his name was Vanur. And not a captain, no?"

"Lieutenant," Trilby said. "He said getting back to the *Razalka* was urgent because of information he found on the 'Sko."

"So he changed your primaries, forced you to come here?" Dallon asked.

"No, that's not it at all." She glanced at the frowning faces around her. Was it so inconceivable that she'd cooperated? "I came willingly. There never was any coercion"—well, at least, not after the incident in sick bay—"once he explained he'd been captured. Then, just after we left Avanar, I received a report that a friend's freighter had been attacked by the 'Sko. She's still missing."

Leesa sighed softly. "That is the Carina mentioned?"

"Carina and her brother, Vitorio, of *Bella's Dream*. He told me that the Empire might be able to help. So, no, he didn't force me here, didn't take over my ship in some wild gun battle. He . . ." *Seduced me. No. I seduced him.* "We worked together," she amended, and damned the heat rising to her face again.

"Then why did he change your primaries?" Dallon asked.

"Damned if I know."

"And why did he not give you the release codes when you arrived?" Lucho added.

Trilby shook her head. Then noticed Farra looking quizzically at her. But the young woman said nothing until they were alone in the corridor, her friends having departed with promises to get together again later.

"I go on duty shortly. But first I need to ask something, Captain Elliot."

"Trilby. And what do you need to know?"

"*Vad.* Trilby. I need to ask, but you not need to answer, okay?" She stepped back against the bulkhead. They were a few feet from the entrance to the lounge and station crew filtering in and out in small groups. "These words, this message Tivahr left for you."

Yav chera. Trilby nodded hesitantly.

"This has special meaning. Between man and woman. It is not like 'I want cup of tea.' For that we say *yav chalka* about something. You know this, or not?"

"Sort of."

"So a man does not say *yav chera* and then talk to that woman so cold the way I see now. At least, not in so short a time. You understand? It is not my business, but . . ."

Trilby crossed her arms over her chest and drew a deep breath. "If you're asking if something happened between us, yes. But this Tivahr you see here isn't the man I knew as Rhis Vanur."

"Uncle Yavo thinks he force you." Farra ducked her head a bit shyly. "To bed."

"No, it was—Why would your uncle think that?" Why was Mitkanos even aware that something had happened between Tivahr and herself? Farra had only learned of Tivahr's message an hour ago. And they'd seen Mitkanos, but spoken only in Standard. Had Tivahr said something, bragged about his sexual conquest?

"Because of several things. Because of what I tell him I see when Captain Tivahr watches the message you sent to your friend."

"He viewed my message to Neadi?" Great! He probably suspected her of broadcasting Imperial secrets all over civilized space.

"He had big sad look on his face. And Lucho's older brother works with Lieutenant Gurdan. And he hear Gurdan say Captain Tivahr has much concern for this Captain Elliot."

Farra wagged her finger in Trilby's face, as if reprimanding her. "Everything must be perfect for *Dasja* Trilby Elliot. Gurdan, he say other crew take you to communications to send message, *vad?* But Tivahr, no. He want top person. Who is security chief, he ask. He give orders to Gurdan. And Lucho's brother, he hear this. *Dasja* Trilby has much value."

Trilby bit her lip. "Because I know Jagan Grantforth?" she ventured.

Farra shrugged. "I know the Grantforth name, but not this person."

"His family is GGA. His uncle's a politician in the Conclave."

"The way Tivahr looks at your face on screen, this does not look like politics." Farra grabbed Trilby's hand, gave it a reassuring squeeze. "I must go. We will have tea later, *vad?* And things work out. You have friends here, Lucho and myself. Dallon. Leesa. And of course, Uncle Yavo."

Trilby returned her friendly gesture, watched as Farra headed for the lift and merged with a small group of *Stegzarda* crew waiting there. Farra turned, waved as she stepped into the lift. Then the doors closed, and Trilby was left alone.

The time panel in the corridor read 0722. She had eight minutes to get back to the *Venture* for her meeting with Jankova. The *Razalka*'s commander, she knew with irritating certainty, would no doubt be early.

Two things surprised Trilby about Commander Jankova. The first was that Jankova was female. The second was that she was a genuinely pleasant person. Not stiff like Pavor Gurdan. And not overbearing and arrogant like Tivahr.

The interview went quickly. Forty minutes passed and Hana Jankova was standing, offering Trilby her hand.

"Your valuable time is appreciated, Captain Elliot."

Trilby wasn't one to whine, but she also wasn't one to let an opportunity slip by. "It's not like I have anywhere else to go. Your captain's locked me out of my own primaries. My ship's dead. I'm stuck here until he decides otherwise."

They stopped at the door to the *Venture*'s lounge.

"I wasn't told anything about that."

"Then he didn't give you my release codes?"

"No."

"Do you know if he intends to release me? Or should I start looking for work on a maintenance crew?" She didn't bother to hide the bitterness in her voice. "I've already lost time, and the Gods only know how many cargo runs. I've got a ship to keep up and pay for. I'd appreciate it if you'd remind Captain High and Mighty Tivahr about that fact."

She saw Hana Jankova's mouth twitch into a small smile at her description. "I will inform the captain of your request."

Trilby leaned against the open hatch lock as Jankova descended the short ramp. Maybe if enough people on Degvar learned what a bastard Rhis really was, they'd support her in a mutiny. The thought of rallying the *Stegzarda* and the Degvar Fleet techs temporarily cheered her. Maybe she'd even commandeer the *Razalka*. Mess around with a few of his command codes. Teach him what it felt like to have everything important in his life ripped away. To be at the mercy of someone who didn't give a damn about his needs or existence.

She slammed the side of her fist against the hatchway rim and wished it was his smug face she hit instead.

Rhis slammed the side of his fist against the top of his desk. He wished he could slam it against Kospahr's face, but he knew that action wouldn't sit well with Emperor Kasmov.

"You are not in charge of this ship," he told the portly man sitting diffidently in the chair in front of him. "I'm the captain. The senior captain, may I remind you. You have no authority—"

"And I'm Second Lord Minister of Defense, Senior Captain Tivahr. My cousin the emperor has empowered me to examine this situation. I have done so. I've read your report, and Gurdan's. I've yet to see Commander Jankova's, but that doesn't matter." He waved a fleshy hand. "I doubt it'll change my mind. This Elliot woman can be used to bait the Ycsko faction. And trap Secretary Grantforth. And maybe even that weakling pup Jagan Grantforth. We're looking at tearing open the Conclave, Tivahr. Breaking open GGA."

"We have no definitive proof Grantforth, or GGA, is behind this. To take actions now based only on suspicion could risk—"

"This is worth any risk! We're talking about accomplishing what even a war against the Conclave could not. You'd deny the Empire this victory? What kind of officer are you? Where are your loyalties?"

Rhis folded his hands on top of his desk, clenching them tightly. "I'm the best captain in the Fleet, and you bloody well know that. I've given my life to the Empire. But Captain Elliot is a Conclave citizen. You can't demand she risk her life to take down her own government."

"I can and I will. Her government is corrupt. And she's in a position to expose that."

"And if the 'Sko get to her first?"

Kospahr shrugged. "At that point, she'll already have dragged Grantforth, or whoever is involved, out into the open. If the 'Sko get her, well, she's only a bloody Indy. Of little value, other than she was Jagan Grantforth's whore."

Rhis shot to his feet. Blood pounded in his ears. He wanted to leap over his desk, throttle the man. "Don't push me, Kospahr. You won't win."

His office comm trilled. He jabbed the touchpad. "Yes?" he bellowed as Jankova's face appeared on the small screen angled into the top of his desk.

"Sir. I have my report on Captain Elliot."

"Perfect timing," Kospahr said smoothly.

"Send it here. To my private files," he told Jankova, then flicked off the screen.

He glared down at Kospahr. "Get out, Lord Minister. I have work to do."

He wondered if Trilby appreciated the fact that he was trying to save her life. He brought Jankova's report on screen, paged past the requisite opening.

No, she probably didn't appreciate it. She hated him. If he had any doubt of her emotional state before, that was gone after their conversation in the lounge on station.

Well, it wasn't really a conversation. He'd ordered her to talk to Jankova, knowing damned well how she'd react. But he hadn't liked that man's hand on her arm, or the way he'd leaned so close to her. He'd glimpsed an insignia on the man's black uniform. He was assigned to a Fleet supply ship. There were two in Degvar Station at the moment.

More than that Rhis didn't know, didn't care to know. Except he wanted that glorified shit-hauler away from Trilby.

Even if she hated him for doing so.

Jankova's report was good. He could tell by Trilby's answers that they'd gotten along. She was

more open with Jankova than she had been with
Gurdan. It might just be because Jankova was a
woman, but he didn't think so. People felt comfortable with Hana Jankova. She didn't let her brilliant,
incisive mind overshadow her heart.

Like he did.

But then, Jankova hadn't, as Trilby so succinctly
put it, slithered out of a test tube. She had a large,
supportive family. A clan heritage.

And now Zak Demarik.

Rhis had a report to read. And an interfering second lord minister of defense to appease. And a whole
other list of problems mentally filed away under the
heading of *Trilby* that he couldn't afford to look at
right now.

Then he found the addendum to Jankova's report.
Captain Elliot would like to remind Captain High
and Mighty Tivahr that he still had her release codes.
And she had a ship to pay for.

The release codes. Kospahr wanted to use Trilby
and her ship. But if Captain Elliot and her ship were
no longer on station . . .

He slapped at the desk comm. "Prep my shuttle.
Five minutes." He made it in three and a half.

He listened as Dezi identified himself and the ship,
then said the only words he knew would guarantee
Trilby's appearance. "Tell Trilby I have the release
codes for her primaries."

It didn't take her long. The hatch lock slid open.
She had the rifle slung over her shoulder. "This better
not be some kind of game. I'm not in the mood."

He recognized the T-shirt she was wearing as the

one she'd worn that first day in sick bay. She had only five, all dark green. He knew that well. But this one had a small tear in the shoulder, and the strap of the rifle now pulled on it.

He dragged his mind back to more-pressing matters. Like getting her the hell off station as quickly as possible. "Requesting permission to come aboard, Captain," he said quietly.

Her eyes narrowed. He knew she didn't trust him. "You brought the codes?"

He tapped one finger against his head.

"Oh, terrific." She hesitated; she'd clearly been hoping he was simply going to hand her a coded disk. Clearly didn't want him on board. For a moment, something ugly gripped his gut. What if she had that supply officer in her cabin?

He'd be obliged to kill the man. But he'd give her the codes first. "This won't take long."

Reluctantly, she stepped back and held out her hand toward the corridor behind her. "After you. Captain."

He sat at the copilot's station, brought up the initialization primaries. Her scent of powder and flowers surrounded him. The toy felinar dangled over his head. Behind him, Dezi's joints squeaked.

He locked the moment in his memory. It would be the last one he'd have of her for a long time.

"You might want to record this," he told her before he brought up his program. "You might need it sometime."

Surprise flashed through her eyes, then she nodded at Dezi. He heard the 'droid's metal fingers tap the touchpads at navigation.

It took him three minutes to undo his program, to

reinsert her codes, align her commands in proper order. It would have taken him longer, but she'd already been working on it, he saw. Done pretty damned well. He saw the two minor errors that had stymied her, kept her from unraveling it further. Had she known about those, she would've been gone long before now.

He sat back, motioned to her controls. "Go ahead."

"Not until you answer one question."

This surprised him. He thought she'd toss his ass and get the hell away from Degvar at her first opportunity.

"If I can."

"Are you schizophrenic?"

"What?"

"You're a rude, arrogant son of a bitch. You've got an ego half the size of civilized space and a temper to match. You don't give a damn about anyone or anything. Other than yourself. And then, every so often, you're actually a nice person. Like now." She reached over, tapped her finger on his armrest as if to get his attention. "You really ought to see a doctor. I'm serious."

He pulled himself out of the chair. She was too close to him. He needed something between them, starting with the metal and padding of the copilot's chair. And then, eventually, the vastness of space, of the Empire and the Conclave.

"I appreciate your advice. And ask now that you follow mine. It is important." She swiveled around to follow his actions. He looked down at her.

"Two things, Trilby-*chenka*." The affectionate term slipped out before he could stop it. He saw spots of color form on her cheeks. But her eyes flashed in anger.

He held up his index finger. "First, do not use the *Venture*'s ID until you reach Port Rumor. Use the Imperial code I created. The 'Sko kill order is keyed to your Conclave ID. Change the name of your ship, get a new code when you get home."

He raised another finger. "Second, you have ten minutes to depart Degvar. After that, my real evil self will reappear and I will once again be that arrogant, loathsome bastard intent only on crushing everyone and everything in his path. Do you understand?"

She nodded. Her fingers flew to the controls. "Bringing sublight engines online." Green lights flashed and he felt the familiar, out-of-synch trembling under his boots.

Her voice stopped him at the hatchway to the corridor.

"Tivahr."

He looked back into the bridge, saw her turn around in her seat. "I never said you were loathsome. Now get the hell off my ship."

He tapped his comm badge as her rampway sealed behind him. "Tivahr to ops. Emergency departure clearance for the *Careless Venture*. My authorization."

He didn't wait for a reply. No one on Degvar would dare question a command from *the* Senior Captain Tivahr.

Trilby held her breath when she contacted Degvar departure for clearance. It was entirely possible Rhis was up to something. She didn't know what, but the fact that she was back in control of her ship made her feel a bit more confident. Whatever it was, she could handle it. Now.

Degvar departure cleared her, even withdrew the docking clamps. She didn't have to use her own wog-and-weemly after all.

She powered the thrusters as the ship dropped away from the station. She would've loved to crank the engines to full power, blast a few holes in the Imperial outpost's outer hull. But she didn't wish all Imperials to hell. She thought kindly of Farra and Mitkanos. And Farra's friends.

Only Rhis . . . *Khyrhis* Tivahr, she corrected herself. She'd reserve judgment on Tivahr until she was safely back in Port Rumor.

She banked the *Venture* and headed for the Degvar

inner beacon. Twenty minutes later, she cleared the outer beacon and cranked her drives up to full power.

All lights showed green. All conditions were go.

"Let's get the hell out of here," she told Dezi, and retracted the vanes flat against the *Venture*'s hull. No one out here to complain about her energy wake. She had a clear path to the border.

Three hours. Three hours, thirty-one minutes, and seventeen seconds, according to Dezi. Three hours, thirty-one minutes, and sixteen seconds. She'd be back in Conclave space, could pick up the first jumpgate. She could forget all about *the* Captain Tivahr. It'd be a trike to Port Rumor from there. She could forget all about Rhis Vanur. She could—

—bring her weapons systems online. Alarms wailed through the small bridge. Her short-range scanners went into overload.

"What in hell we got, Dez?" she shouted over the din. She slapped at the alarm cutoff.

"A full squadron of attack fighters. ETA ten minutes."

" 'Sko? Out here?"

"Imperial."

Imperial? "We're broadcasting that Imperial ID!"

"Affirmative."

"Hail the bastards. Something's wrong!"

"Hailing frequency open."

"This is Captain Elliot. I've got clearance through your space from Degvar."

"Maybe they're an escort," Dezi posited.

She glanced at the scanners. The fighters were armed and under full power. "Fat chance."

"Captain Elliot, this is Imperial Squadron Leader." She turned toward the speaker at the sound of the pilot's voice. It was a stupid habit. She couldn't see him. She'd have to break herself of it one of these days. Right after she broke herself of the habit of trusting Gods damned arrogant Imperials.

"Power down," the pilot said. "Or we will be forced to take aggressive action."

"Look, I've got clearance—"

"Power down, Captain. Or—"

She cut off his transmission, whirled toward Dezi. "I need a jumpgate. Any jumpgate."

"Captain, this ship's guidance system isn't reliable in an Imperial—"

"Get me a Gods damned jumpgate!"

"Locating a jumpgate."

She banked the *Venture* hard to starboard, away from the fighters. They followed, effortlessly. "Anything?"

Three coordinates flashed on her screen. "Shit." They were far away and she didn't even recognize the energy signature on the closest one. She changed course for it anyway.

The fighters pulled closer.

"Dezi, disconnect life support. Or we're not going to make it."

The 'droid ambled quickly off the bridge. She sealed it behind him. "Damn you, Tivahr," she murmured. "Damn you, damn you."

She knew now what he'd done. He'd set her free so he could arrange a convenient "accident." No record of what happened on Avanar, or her unwise conversation with him on Degvar. No one to have to pay reward money to. Probably wouldn't even be enough left, after the fighters were finished with her, to line a mizzet's nest.

Her ship bucked as the drives surged with the increase in power. Life support was off-line. All power was cut off except for the bridge and the drive room.

She searched frantically for signs of the jumpgate. Imperial energy signatures were different. Her equipment was all Conclave issue. Incompatibilities were rampant. But they might not be fatal.

The fighters racing up behind her looked damned fatal, indeed.

Then the familiar three-tone chime pinged from her console. She had a lock on the jumpgate. Five minutes, they'd be in range.

Its outline coalesced on her screen, shimmering. She had to reach it before the fighters intercepted her. There was no guarantee they wouldn't follow her in, but it was, she hazarded, a fifty–fifty chance. And as long as she stayed in the gate, they couldn't fire their weapons.

She'd be going hell-bent for the-Gods-knew-where, but they couldn't kill her. And it would give her time to send out an RFA. No. An SUA. Somebody, somewhere, would have to hear her.

"Four minutes," she told Dezi. "Bringing hyperdrive engine online. Secure—"

She slammed against the bulkhead panel beside her chair. Her safety straps dug into her ribs. She screamed an angry, hoarse cry of fear. Sparks erupted behind her. The bridge plunged into darkness, and the horrifying sound of metal tearing and buckling was the last thing she remembered.

It was a flawless plan. Perfect. If what he suspected was true, it would bring Dark Sword out into the

open. It would expose that agent's dealings with the
'Sko. It would show how he threatened Rinnaker, un-
less they followed his orders. And it would destroy
Jagan Grantforth and GGA.

Rhis sat back in his office chair, justifiably pleased
with himself. It had taken him only two and a half
hours to draft it. He'd throw it at Demarik and
Jankova, let them tear it apart, and then put the final
touches to it.

Then all that was needed was about six months to
implement it. Six months and nothing in the Conclave would be the same again. Except places like
Port Rumor. Things rarely changed there, no matter
who was in power.

He'd wait another three months after that, give
things time to settle down. Then he'd contact her.
Through Neadi Danzanour, probably. He might be an
arrogant bastard, but at least he wasn't loathsome.

He swiveled his chair to one side, intent on a cup
of hot tea, when his office door chimed. He looked at
the overhead ID. Demarik and Jankova.

He shrugged. They probably were working on
some ideas of their own. "Come."

The doors slid open.

"More suggestions, Commanders?" He started to
rise, started to motion them into the chairs across
from his desk. But he stopped, half out of his seat, his
right hand in midair.

Demarik and Jankova looked like death. No, they
looked as if they brought news of death. They stood
stiffly, hands clasped behind their backs, bleak expressions on their faces.

He waited until the doors slid closed, then braced
both hands on the top of his desk. "Tell me."

A quick glance between the two of them. Neither wanted to tell him the news. Kasmov, he thought. Someone had assassinated the emperor. There'd been rumors . . . But, no, news of that would come to him first. Through Vanushavor's office—

Rafi. Rafi was—

Oh, Gods. No. Trilby.

"Tell me!" he ordered.

Jankova spoke first. "An Imperial fighter squadron intercepted the *Careless Venture* out by the Sachor jumpgate."

"What was she—she had no reason to head there!" He looked from Jankova to Demarik. He found it hard to breathe. He forced himself to speak. "On whose orders?"

"Kospahr's." Demarik's voice held an undisguised note of derision.

"Kospahr sent a squadron . . ." He felt as if something had just kicked him in the gut. "Status of the *Venture*!"

"She took a direct hit, sir." Jankova stepped toward him, her arms loose at her sides. "I'm sorry."

He'd never felt so cold and so raging hot at the same time. For a moment, his mind locked. He heard only Jankova's last words: *S'viek noyet*. I'm sorry.

Unbearable anguish flooded through him. He lunged past his desk, intent only on finding Kospahr. And killing him.

Trilby was gone. Nothing mattered anymore.

He felt Jankova tackle his waist. Demarik grabbed his shoulders, tried to block his mad charge.

Fools! I could snap both their necks right now. He ripped Demarik's hands from his shoulders, turned to wrench Jankova off him, but the woman was repeating something, over and over again.

It finally sank in.

Trilby might still be alive.

He swung around, leaned one arm against the wall for support, and grabbed Jankova by the elbow. He yanked her against him. "She's alive?"

"It's possible, sir. But you can't go after Kospahr now. You have to listen." She lay one hand against his chest, stepped back. "Please. Listen to what Zak found out."

She looked back at Demarik, who was gingerly lifting himself off the floor.

Rhis released her.

"Sit, Captain. Please." Demarik motioned to one of the chairs. It was skewed from its deck lock, its covering torn but still in one piece.

"I'll stand." He was breathing hard, the pain in his chest coming in long waves, crashing against that open space where his heart used to be.

Jankova retreated to the battered chair. Demarik stood behind her, one hand on her shoulder.

"We know about Kospahr's plans for Captain Elliot. We know you gave Captain Elliot the release codes," Demarik began. "And that you authorized departure clearance. However, Kospahr doesn't know you authorized it. He only knows, or rather he thinks, that Captain Elliot escaped."

"But Degvar ops—"

"A Lieutenant Lucho Salnay has confessed to assisting her escape," Jankova said. "You may not remember him, Captain. He's a good friend of Corporal Rimanava's, in station communications. They were seen talking to Captain Elliot in the station lounge earlier."

He met Jankova's level gaze. She knew he'd been there. And he knew Salnay's confession was a sham. To save him, Tivahr the Terrible.

"If Kospahr knew the orders came from you," Jankova continued, "you'd be facing a court-martial. At the very least, he'd order Zak to take over command of the *Razalka*. We'd have to do so, at least until an investigation was initiated."

He nodded. The stupidity of the blatantness of his actions came home to him.

"You wouldn't be able to help her from the brig. And if she is beyond help," she added, her voice softer, "I don't think she'd want you to throw your career away over someone like Durwin Kospahr."

"If he killed her?" His voice was raw. He couldn't believe he was saying those words.

"Then we'll deal with that. Trust us, Captain. Zak and I will deal with that."

"And this Salnay?"

Demarik gave him a ghost of a smile. "Major Mitkanos is handling Salnay. He's Rimanava's uncle, you know," he added casually.

Mitkanos. And people accused him of having his own little kingdom on the *Razalka*!

"Who told Kospahr the *Venture* was gone?"

"We're not sure yet," Demarik said. "Possibly Pavor Gurdan."

"Bastard! I'll see him and Kospahr in hell." He slammed his fist hard against the wall.

Jankova stood, stepped toward him, her face gentle with heartbreaking compassion.

He drew a deep breath. "Tell me everything you know about what happened. About Trilby. When will you know if she's still alive?"

"The squadron was based on Degvar. Mitkanos—"

"Let me guess. Has a brother in the squad."

"Sister-in-law, I believe," Jankova said. "But she's not squad leader. She's managed to leak the information that it appears enviro's still working on the bridge. But not the rest of the ship. They've got the *Venture* in tow now."

Rhis stood rigidly still. Thoughts, images played through his mind. He clasped his hands, threading his fingers together, and brought them up to cover his mouth. Did he dare voice his small hope?

He dropped his hands, motioned toward Jankova. "She does that. Cuts off life support when she needs extra power for the engines. She's got that ship rigged . . . well . . ." He shook his head. "You wouldn't believe how she's got that ship rigged."

He thought of a small toy felinar dangling from a red ribbon. His throat tightened. He had to turn his face away from Jankova.

"How long before the squadron returns?" he asked after a moment.

"At tow speeds, an hour," Demarik said. "But we could—"

"—meet her! Gods!" He barreled toward the door, shoving it aside when it didn't slide open quickly enough. "Mister Demarik," he called to the man hurrying down the corridor behind him. "I want us moving in five minutes. Plot an intercept course."

"Aye, sir!"

He slapped his comm badge. "Tivahr to sick bay! Tell Doc Vanko to get his ass out of that poker game and get a full emergency med team assembled on Shuttle Deck Six in fifteen minutes."

He slapped it off and was five feet from the doors to the upper bridge when Jankova grabbed his arm.

"Captain, remember. You knew nothing of this until we told you of her escape. You have to keep focused on that. You have to play it like—"

"I'm the usual arrogant, manipulative, loathsome bastard I always am? Yes, Commander, I think I can do that."

"I'll be on the bridge at my station, should you need me." She stepped toward the lift. Her station was on the lower tier.

"Hana," he said. "Thank you."

She gave him a soft smile, but no hopes. No hopes. Trilby might be alive. But he had to accept the fact she might not be.

He strode onto the upper bridge, bellowing orders, making sure everyone felt his anger at being made a fool of by a little no-account Indy freighter captain.

Hiding his fear that he'd never again see her alive.

They were moving away from the station in five minutes. In ten, Kospahr was by his side, gloating.

"See, Tivahr? You thought you knew it all. But she fooled you, fooled your whole team. If it wasn't for my close association with Lieutenant Gurdan, she would've gotten away."

"Gurdan? I'll remember that."

"Be sure I won't let you forget it. You owe all this to me." He waved his hand toward the enhanced images of the squadron, and a small, elliptical freighter, on the viewscreen. "All this."

"I won't forget, Kospahr. Don't worry about that."

He pushed himself out of the command chair as if intent on something on a console to his left. He stared over a bridge officer's shoulder, seeing nothing, then turned. The stairs to the lower bridge were before him. He forced himself to descend leisurely, as if waiting to pounce on an unsuspecting crew member errant at his duty. But he sought Jankova's station.

"Anything?" he asked her softly, pretending to stare in the opposite direction. He knew she was tied into the flow of chatter between the squadron fighters. And was, at the same time, now actively scanning the battered remains of the *Venture* for anything the best of Imperial technology could discern.

"She took two direct laser strikes to the stern. Starboard cargo holds and engine room took the most damage. Enviro must be running off an aux somewhere. I'm picking up a faint energy output amidships."

"She has a small generator there."

"Then that must be it."

"The bridge?"

"I'm showing a humanoid heat signature. More than that, I can't tell from here."

There was a body. But there was no way to know if the body was alive. He chanced a look at her. "Thank you again, Hana."

"I think it's a pretty good possibility she's still alive, sir."

"I think it would be damned, damned good if she were still alive." He stepped away before his voice could crack and betray him.

* * *

At three minutes to intercept he was in the small holding room outside Shuttle Bay 6-D. He splayed his hands against the glass wall. His CMO and emergency med team waited a few feet behind him.

The bay lights blinked twice, then turned to red. One minute warning. Vessel on final approach. All air was sucked out of the bay.

The great bay doors rumbled. Between them appeared a crack and the first glimpse of a large grayish mass being dragged in by his ship's tractor beams, above and below. When the doors opened sufficiently, a third beam would lock on and pull the craft forward. Landing pads would rise from the floor.

He watched his ship's tow systems perform with unerring precision. Throat dry, heart hammering in his chest, he'd never been so afraid in his life.

The *Venture* was dragged in at a crab angle, her bow tilted away from him. He could see only the starboard viewport. Dark. Lifeless. Then the bay's overheads flared and whatever else he could see there was lost behind the reflections.

Her starboard hull was blistered, scored. Her main exterior hatch door had buckled. He clenched one fist, would have shoved it through the glass if he could.

Her starboard cargo bay was . . . gone. Obliterated. A gaping chasm in its place, cables dangling. More damage on either side. Hull plates missing.

He looked quickly back at the bridge, at the lights still flashing red in the bay. *Come on! Come on!*

He pushed past the sliding door the second they turned green, squeezing himself sideways to get through.

The landing-pad hydraulics still hissed, the emergency ramp rising. He grabbed the railing with one hand, clambered to the top, and kicked at the exterior access.

"Captain! We can cut through with a—"

There! The panel gave way. He thrust his hand into the searingly cold metal, groped for the three levers he knew had to be there. One. He found one. Pulled. Then two. Pulled.

Where was three? His fingers stung, throbbing, from the contact with the icy metal. He shoved his arm further into the raw opening, felt something slice the top of his hand. The warmth of blood dripped through his fingers.

Three! He pulled.

The hatchway door slid open about six inches and stopped. He placed both hands against it and forced it sideways, then plunged forward, distantly aware of voices, clanking, clanging noises behind him. The corridor was dark and icy cold. He careened off a crooked wall panel, pounded toward the bridge.

The hatch was locked. She would have sealed it when she turned off enviro.

He dropped to his knees in the darkness, probed blindly with scraped and stinging hands for the emergency-access panel near the floor. Then a bright light illuminated the panel.

Demarik, behind him, with a crowbar and a light.

Rhis pried off the panel cover, found the three levers. But Demarik was in front of him, blocking his way, going in first.

Zak. You don't have to protect me. He lunged after his exec. The bridge was in shambles, but his gaze was riveted to the captain's chair. And the small blond head hanging awkwardly to the right.

A tangle of cables blocked his path. He ripped them from the ceiling, stepping over and through them. He wedged himself between her chair and navigation, sliding down almost to his knees.

She was still strapped in the safety harness. Her eyes were closed, her face pale in Demarik's handheld beam. Her right hand reached out toward him, toward nothing.

He grasped it. It was cold. His own blood stained her palm.

"Trilby-*chenka*?" He breathed her name.

He heard Demarik's datalyzer snap open and the pounding of footsteps from the corridor. Then his CMO bustled in, shoving Demarik backward. Medistats appeared in hands. Medical jargon barked back and forth.

He stared at her. She wasn't moving.

Someone touched his shoulder. Demarik. "Captain, you have to get out of here. You're in the way."

He pushed himself shakily to his feet, only part of him understanding what was said. Demarik grasped his arm, pulled him across the twisting debris and out into the corridor.

But he grabbed the edge of the hatch, hung on stubbornly. "I can't leave her. She's cold. It's so dark—"

"Khyrhis, listen to me. She's alive." Demarik shoved the datalyzer under his nose. "She's been beat up a bit. But she's alive. Let Doc handle her. For now."

Alive? It took a few seconds for him to understand, to see the life-form readings dancing across the small screen. She was weak. She was injured. But she was alive.

He stumbled away from Demarik, grabbed the

railing to the ladderway just aft of the bridge, and leaned against it.

She was alive. He felt himself sliding, his legs shaking. He landed on the top step, his knees almost in his chest.

Tears of joy and relief trembled through his body, spilling out of that great empty place where his heart had been. He buried his face in his hands and cried in relief.

Everything was dark and cold. And then everything was bright and uncomfortably warm. Prickly. Things poked her. Sounds drifted, garbled. She wanted desperately to sneeze.

Then she was thirsty. Gin. A tall iced gin. Double limes. Sounded good.

Trilby Elliot opened her eyes. Everything was dark again. No. Dim. Her vision hazed, then focused like her old binocs. Red-rimmed numbers. An annoying beeping sound.

She tried to turn her head, decided the effort wasn't worth it. She moved her gaze through the dimness. Red numbers to the left. Damned beeper over her head. On her right . . .

It took a moment. A chair. Empty.

Her nose itched again. She raised her hand to scratch it, bumped her wrist against something. She crossed her eyes and looked down.

A cylinder. Over her.

She was in sick bay. It didn't look like hers but, hey, maybe she'd made a big profit from that run to . . . to . . .

She licked her lips, swallowed. Tried her voice. "Dezi?"

A door slid open, sending a shaft of bright light into her eyes. She squinted, saw the outline of a stocky form.

Not Dezi.

"*Lutsa,*" a male voice said as the lights slowly came on.

Lutsa?

"No. My name's Trilby." Her voice sounded rusty. She really needed some gin.

The stocky form was at her side. She heard the snick of a medistat opening. She blinked as her eyes adjusted to the light.

The guy who thought her name was Lutsa was about sixty, broad-shouldered, and balding. She didn't recognize him, hoped she wasn't supposed to. She knew who she was. It would be hell if she didn't remember anyone else.

Like who she'd been out drinking with. That's the only way she would've ended up in some unknown sick bay. Pub-crawling.

"How are you feeling?" Baldy said. He had an accent. She couldn't quite place it.

He also had on a blue lab coat. Not a med-tech, like Chaser, whose white coat carried the GGA med-lab logo. So this one was a doctor.

Why did all doctors always ask how you're feeling? She thought it was a stupid question. "I don't know," she told him. "You went through med school. You tell me."

He seemed momentarily startled, then he chuckled. "Much better. I can hear that. This is good." He snapped the sensor shut. "Your head hurts, yes? And your shoulder. Right side. Anything else all my years in med school might have missed?"

"I'm thirsty. And my nose itches."

"Good! We can handle both those things, I think, Captain Elliot."

"Then you know who I am?"

He slanted a glance at her as he unlocked the regen cylinder. "But of course."

For a moment she tensed. Not because he said he knew her name. But because he was sliding the unit down, uncovering her body . . . covered by a thin but soft shift. Newer regen units could read through fabric. She relaxed.

"Then why'd you call me Lutsa when you came in?"

"Ah. *Lutsa* is Zafharish for *lights*. It is our command to increase room illumination."

Zafharish?

Zafharish. As in Zafharin. As in . . .

Tivahr.

She closed her eyes, a gasp of anger escaping her lips.

"You have pain? New pain?" She heard Baldy's sensor snick open again.

"No." She raised her hand, waved at the sensor, then gratefully rubbed at her nose. "I just . . ." She sighed. "I forgot where I was. I'm not sure I know what happened. I'm not sure I *want* to know what happened."

Baldy pursed his lips. "It is better for me to talk about your injuries. You were seriously hurt. But in the past three days—"

"Three days?"

"—you have recovered well. Due, of course, to my excellent care."

Ah, yes. Imperial arrogance.

And an Imperial fighter squadron. The alarms wailed again in her head. "Your ships attacked me."

"Not ours." He adjusted her pillow, raised her head so she could take a sip of water.

She swallowed. "I know Imperial fighters when I see them."

"I am sure you do. But they were not ours. Not from the *Razalka*." He looked at her for a long moment.

She wriggled up into a sitting position.

He raised the head of the bed another few inches. "Better?"

"Thank you. But if they weren't from the *Razalka*—"

"I am a doctor, Captain Elliot. I can answer any medical questions you may have. Anything else, well, they did not teach me such things in medical school."

She sipped her water, watched Baldy pull data from the regen unit that still covered her from the thighs down. It felt like the shift went farther than that. She ran her hand down its pale silver surface. Nice material. "Where's Tivahr?"

"Being a pain in the ass somewhere, I imagine."

She laughed, completely surprised by his answer. "I *am* on the *Razalka*?"

"You are."

"And yet you feel free to call your captain a pain in the ass?"

"I have known Khyrhis for more than twenty years. I think in that time I have gathered sufficient evidence to support my conclusion."

"I could probably give you some more, if you need it."

"My file overflows."

She laughed again. Her shoulder hurt like hell, but it didn't matter. If felt good to laugh. "Thank you, Doctor . . ."

She waited for him to fill in the gap.

"Vasilivankovich. But everyone calls me Doc Vanko." He grinned.

"Thanks, Doc. So who do I talk to about my ship?" And Dezi. Her heart suddenly plummeted. Dezi. "There was a 'droid. An envoy 'droid. He was my copilot. Would you know what happened to him?"

Doc shook his head. "Not my department. I am sorry. But I should be able to get Captain Tivahr to answer your questions. Or Commander Jankova."

She wasn't ready to see Tivahr yet. Not until she could throw a good punch at his face. "I'll take Jankova."

He nodded. "I will see what I can do. There is more water there, next to your bed. The emergency call button is here, by your right hand."

And my one working laser rifle? she wondered, but didn't voice it. She had more things to worry about.

Dezi.

Hana Jankova arrived five minutes after Doc left. "You gave us a good scare."

Trilby looked at the auburn-haired woman. She could see no deception in her blue eyes. "I could probably turn that around and say you—or, rather, the Empire—gave me one. But Doc tried real hard to get me to read between the lines. He wants me to believe the *Razalka* had nothing to do with the attack on my ship."

Jankova reached back, hit the palm pad for the door. It slid shut. "In time you will be told, and shown, everything. But, no, those fighters did not come from this ship. They came from Degvar. But the command to send them, yes. That did originate here."

"Tivahr." Trilby spat out the name.

"No." Jankova's voice was firm. "You must believe me on this. And yet you must, until I tell you otherwise, act as if you think it was Tivahr. Or else your life, and his career, will be in jeopardy."

"But that makes no sense!"

"Please." She leaned against the edge of the bed, her hand on Trilby's arm. "I know I am not Neadi or Carina. You have no reason to trust me. But you must. Lucho Salnay is being held as coconspirator in your escape."

"Lucho? Farra Rimanava's Lucho? But he—"

"Helped you." Jankova's gaze pinned her. "Lucho helped you."

Something began to work in Trilby's mind. If Lucho was covering for Tivahr, then it could only be because Farra Rimanava had asked him to. And Farra wouldn't ask unless Mitkanos approved. Trilby's gut told her to trust Mitkanos. "Oh, right. Lucho helped me. Tell me what else I've forgotten. I've been seriously injured, Doc says."

Jankova smiled, relaxed a bit. "Lucho helped you. He didn't know that Captain Tivahr altered your primaries. You told him only that you were having integration problems between your ship's technology and ours. Lucho manually released the docking clamps because you told him the mechanism wasn't accepting your signal." She heard echoes of Mitkanos in Jankova's recounting. Only Mitkanos knew Trilby had tweaked the clamp mechanisms.

"Right. What happens to Lucho because of this?" Sacrificing that handsome young man for Tivahr the Terrible didn't seem just.

"Because there was no hold order on your ship in Degvar ops, very little. His only crime, if you will, is that he didn't advise the *Razalka* of your departure. For that oversight, he is in Major Mitkanos's hands. I believe he is forcing him to study the history of the *Stegzarda*. Confined to his quarters, of course. Mitkanos's trusted niece, Corporal Rimanava, is the only one permitted to bring him meals. Poor man."

"So Lucho helped me and I escaped. What made Tivahr send the squadron after me?"

"Captain Tivahr was well aware that you were to remain on Degvar until Lord Minister Kospahr authorized your release."

"That's the certain someone who wants to kill me?"

Jankova cringed slightly. "Not exactly, no. Rather, I think he has little value for any one life when political decisions are made. We cannot prove that, of course. But he is someone who, if he knew Tivahr had deliberately let you go, would certainly see the captain stripped of command."

Well, it would do the son of a Pillorian bitch good if that happened. But Trilby understood Jankova's point. She made a rude noise. "Tivahr let me go? You're daydreaming, Commander. He's a Ligorian slime weasel. No, wait. I apologize. That's an insult to Ligorian slime weasels."

"Then who helped you escape, Captain Elliot?" Jankova fell into the part.

"I don't know. Some cute, hunky guy. Met him in the lounge on Degvar. Think his name was Luke, or something like that. He wanted to inspect my"—she wiggled her eyebrows—"auxiliary thrusters. Then I found out he worked in ops. Things fell into place after that."

"Yes. That is what he said also." She rose, but Trilby reached out her hand, delaying her.

"Dezi." Her voice caught, the silliness of a moment ago fading. "I have to know."

"He was in your engine room, yes. Portside. Your ship took considerable damage, but mostly to starboard. I do not know if your ship can be repaired."

Trilby's heart plummeted.

"But Captain Tivahr is working on Dezi." Jankova patted Trilby's hand. "We needed something to keep him occupied. He is being a royal pain in the ass."

Trilby leaned back against her pillow after Jankova left, let everything sift through her head and fall back into its proper place. Everything except Khyrhis Tivahr.

She had no idea what to do with him, nor where he belonged.

His quarters looked like a salvage shop. His dining-room table was covered with safety netting. Cables and coils of plasteel thread, small containers of bolts, stacks of thin interface panels were visible underneath. Two long tarnished-metal legs lay strapped to one of the chairs. A tarnished hand, its fingers curled inward, was netted on the serving table behind him.

A large metal torso lay open in the center. And a long black box rotated slowly in a holovise.

The high whine of a crystal splicer filled the air. Then his door chimed. He looked over the rim of his magnifying goggles, saw Hana Jankova's ID. "Come."

She walked in, the lower half of her body disproportionately large. He pushed the goggles off his nose and let them fall on their cord around his neck.

She looked normal again.

"News?"

"She's awake. And fine."

"Awake?" He jumped to his feet, fortunately remembering to flick off the splicer before he shoved it in his shirt pocket. He smacked his shin on the table leg but ignored the pain as he quickly strode into his small living room. He and Jankova met in front of his couch. "She's awake? She's fine?"

"Yes. And yes."

"You should have called me." He pulled the goggles over his head, tossed them across the room. They landed on top of a box of spare parts. "I could have—"

"You know our agreement." She poked her fingers in his chest.

"That was when she was unconscious. Kospahr would get suspicious if he caught me keeping vigil over her. But if she's awake and talking—she's talking?"

"Gave Doc an earful, I gather."

"Then I should be able to see her. To interview her. Interrogate her. Whatever the hell an arrogant, loathsome bastard like me would do." He looked around for his jacket. Where in hell was it?

"Captain—"

"I'll just be a minute. Let me get my jacket."

"Captain Tivahr."

He stopped. He was breathing heavily. He brought his right hand up, then let it fall in an exasperated gesture. "Hana, don't. It's been three days. Almost four. I haven't seen her in all that time. Damn it, she almost died! I almost lost her."

"Doc gave her a light trank. She needs to sleep for a while yet."

He collapsed onto the couch. "You're not going to let me see her, are you?"

"You're still . . ." She hesitated.

"Dravda gera mevnahr?" he supplied. Ass over teakettle.

"Yes."

He covered his mouth with his hand, then pulled on his mustache. "I know," he said softly. "I know."

"So will Kospahr." She sat next to him on the couch, patted his shoulder. "Another day. Give it another day."

"Just let me see her, a little bit. Today. That'll help. Make it easier. I won't be quite so crazy. I promise."

She chuckled. "Liar."

"Yes. I know." Dejection colored his words.

"Captain—"

"She's still angry over that, is she?"

"She didn't say. She was worried about Dezi. And I had to make sure she understood what she had to remember. That's all we really talked about. I didn't want to tire her."

"How'd she look?"

"A few bruises. But fine. Better than she did three days ago."

Three days ago she had been cold and lifeless, terrifyingly still. And had his blood smeared on her hands.

He looked down at his own. They were completely healed. No scars, not from the unbreakable lightpen he'd snapped. Not from the impenetrable metal he'd torn in half. Thank you, Imperial genetics and technology.

"Tomorrow?" He couldn't keep the hope out of his voice.

She stood. "Tomorrow."

He walked her to the door of his quarters, then leaned against the wall after she left.

Tomorrow was technically only six and a half hours away. But he knew it would be at least another six after that before any visit he could make to sick bay would be considered reasonable.

Twelve and a half hours. Thirteen, knowing Commander Hana Jankova. He found his jacket in the other room on his bed, on top of a large stuffed felinar that smelled like powder and flowers.

He'd go play Loathsome Arrogant Bastard Captain for a while with his crew. It would help pass the time.

Unfortunately, Durwin Kospahr caught up with him twenty minutes later, just as he left the bridge.

"Captain Tivahr!"

"What, Lord Minister?" he asked without caring.

Kospahr had to quicken his stride to keep up. "I've been reviewing Lieutenant Gurdan's report, as well as the data from Captain Elliot's ship. Her knowledge of the traders' lanes is quite remarkable."

Rhis stopped before the lift, palmed the button. "She's a freighter operator. It's part of her job." He decided to head down to engineering. Surely this idiot wouldn't follow him there?

"But some of these lanes haven't been used in centuries! And there are other routes into our Empire."

He'd seen Trilby's files on those, recognized a few of them. But Trilby had a few even he hadn't known about. As she'd told him, everything sooner or later ended up at Port Rumor.

"I'm aware of the routes in her nav banks. The old ones were abandoned because they can't support the faster, heavier ships. And newer technology. The guidance beacons, especially the Conclave ones, are weak. Or nonfunctional."

"Yes. Of course." Kospahr seemed disappointed he hadn't found something else to prove the fallibility of *the* Captain Tivahr. "But perhaps they could be put to some use in the commercial sector? I could bring this up to my cousin the emperor."

"They'd be of more use to the Imperial Fleet." The lift arrived. Rhis stepped quickly inside and swore silently when Kospahr followed.

"Engineering," he said.

"But you said the guidance beacons are weak? Old?"

"They are."

"But how then could we use them?"

Rhis glared down at the man. He'd been playing with just that theory for a while. He didn't need Kospahr's interference. "That, Lord Minister, is on a need-to-know basis. And you don't have a need to know."

"But the 'Sko! Grantforth!"

"I already thought of that. And have discussed it with Emperor Kasmov."

"But, but I didn't see any report."

"I didn't issue one."

The lift indicator beeped twice. "Engineering Deck," said a tinny autovoice.

Rhis turned. "I have work to do. If you'll excuse me." He nodded, then strode out into the corridor. And swore again when quick footsteps thudded behind.

"Captain Tivahr!"

Rhis stopped and counted to ten before turning around. Two engineering techs caught the look on his face and fled in the opposite direction.

"You talked to the emperor without speaking to me first?"

"Several times."

"I demand to know the content of those conversations!"

"You will if, and only if, I deem it advisable for you to do so."

"But we will be making a move on the Conclave within two weeks! We—"

"Kospahr!" Rhis grabbed the front of the man's expensive jacket, drew him up to his toes. He watched Kospahr's face turn purple, heard the man choke. *Gods, that felt good.*

He released him. Kospahr stumbled, his hand coming up to his throat. "You fool! You—"

"No. You're the fool. We're in an open corridor and you're blabbering about an upcoming mission. Against a neighboring system." Rhis's voice was a low, angry growl.

"But this is your ship! The *Razalka*," Kospahr whined.

"It is my ship. And on my ship, discretion is the rule. Either you follow this rule, or I will have you removed to Degvar. Do I make myself clear?"

Kospahr stepped back. "You don't have to tell me the rules, Captain. I am the second lord minister of defense. The emperor is my cousin." He turned on his heels and stalked away.

Rhis took two long deep breaths. *Well, that's an improvement. It's no longer 'my cousin the emperor.' Now it's 'the emperor is my cousin.'*

He pulled back his sleeve, glanced at his watch. Eleven hours, fifteen minutes to go.

He rearranged the scowl on his face and headed for engineering.

16

He called sick bay on intraship from his office at 0600. "Doc—"

"Jankova says no."

Hana Jankova, he wanted to tell the man, did not run this ship. He did. But Jankova ran his tactical team, his special-operations missions. He'd put her in charge of those areas three years ago.

And Captain Trilby Elliot had become part of a special-operations mission. So for now, Jankova was in charge.

Which was, Rhis knew, for the better. For the moment. He didn't get where he was in the Fleet by surrounding himself with stupid, incompetent people who didn't know their strengths from their weaknesses. Jankova knew his as well.

He paced the length of his office. Straightened some of the plaques and awards in his wall cabinet that had shifted when he'd slammed into it during his mad charge. Poked his fingers into the rip in the chair in front of his desk. He could patch it with duct tape. That'd give it a nice, familiar feel.

His door chimed. He looked up. Jankova and Kospahr.

Oh, joy.

He reached for his coffee, leaned a hip on the edge of his desk. "Come."

Kospahr bustled in. "The commander tells me I'll be able to talk to that Elliot woman this morning."

"At 1100 hours." Jankova met Rhis's gaze levelly.

Kospahr strode past the large desk as if it were his office and not that of the *Razalka*'s captain. He stood with his back to them for a moment, stared out the viewport. A portion of Degvar's upper levels was visible.

"I want you there, Tivahr," he said, turning. "She probably doesn't know enough about Imperial politics to appreciate who I am. But I'm sure she's afraid of you, especially after all that's happened. And if she isn't, I'm sure you can give her reason to be."

"She saved my life." Rhis ignored the warning look from Jankova.

"In exchange for reward money, your report said. Understandable, given the level of person she is. Port Rumor." A distasteful look crossed Kospahr's face. "Never been there, but I've heard."

"Why do you need to talk to her? You have the reports. The emperor and the Council are in agreement with our recommendations. Your job is done, Kospahr." Something in him balked at the idea of having Trilby and Durwin Kospahr in the same room. He didn't want her tainted by the man's sliminess.

Kospahr shot a quick glance at Jankova before answering. "Many reasons, but if nothing else, curiosity. I'll admit that. You may have been impressed by her technical skills. I was too. But I'd like to see for myself what a Grantforth whore looks like. Gurdan said she's a looker."

He was already moving before Kospahr finished his sentence, but so was Jankova. And he had to clear his desk to get to the lord minister. Jankova only had to step right in front of him, hand on his arm, delaying him as if she'd just thought of something.

"Oh, by the way, Captain Tivahr. As long as we're on the subject of Grantforth, I've some new information you might want to look at." She squeezed his arm, hard. He got the message. Don't go *dravda gera mevnahr* now.

He sat down in his chair as if that's where he was headed all along. He swiveled away from Kospahr, worked on composing his features back to a semblance of normalcy, and tapped at his screen. "It's in my private files, Commander?"

"Not yet. I just learned of it as I went to meet the lord minister at his quarters. I should have more details by the time we talk to Captain Elliot."

"You didn't tell me this!" Kospahr's tone was accusatory.

"I'd only have to repeat it twice, Lord Minister. I'm telling you and Captain Tivahr now."

Rhis admired her gumption at standing up to Kospahr. He began to understand that Hana Jankova was more than just an inquisitive mind and compassionate heart. There was a good chunk of gutsiness in her too. Not unlike his air sprite.

He leaned back in his chair, steepled his fingers over his face. Ignored Kospahr. "What's the nature of this information, Commander?"

"A communiqué from GGA offices."

"To Tril—to Captain Elliot?"

She nodded. "It carries Jagan Grantforth's transit code."

He raised one eyebrow. Another good-bye letter? Or a plea to resume the relationship?

"It's privacy-locked, however." Jankova glanced at Kospahr, who stepped away from the viewport, his fleshy face angled toward her in interest. "And as the *Careless Venture* took considerable damage, we can't use her own comm pack to open it. My team's working on it. We hope to have something before 1100 hours."

"Get on it, then, get on it!" Kospahr waved his hand angrily in her direction. "This could be important."

"I'm well aware of that, Lord Minister."

Rhis glanced at the time stamp on his screen: 0730. Three and a half hours. "I agree with Minister Kospahr," he said. "The message may contain something of import. I'll accompany you over to tactical, take a look at the code structure." He stood. He knew damned well he could unlock that message. So did Jankova. He didn't think she'd withheld its arrival but that it probably happened just as she'd said: she'd learned about it at Kospahr's door.

He knew now she would've told him about the transmit as soon as Kospahr left. His own stupid reaction to the lord minister's words had forced her to reveal it, to divert him.

"I'll go with you too." Kospahr was already trying to get into step with him.

Rhis bit back his original reply, changing it quickly to something he knew would work. "Fine. Then I'll contact the emperor myself about this new development." His office door closed behind them. "You can wait in the tactical division while the—"

"No, no! I'll talk to my cousin the emperor at once. You're not a diplomat, Tivahr. You don't know how to phrase things. You go take care of the minor technical parts. I'll handle the emperor." Kospahr walked down the corridor, puffing.

He thought it was time to show Jankova Trilby's *J* file. He got himself tea, then glared over the shoulders of her team while she watched the transmits in the privacy of her office, across the corridor from the tactical briefing room.

Ten minutes later he crossed the corridor again, waited a moment until her door slid sideways.

"Innocent enough," she said as he took the solitary seat across from her desk. "Until you consider the players."

"Just your normal love affair between an unknown, destitute freighter operator and one of the wealthiest CEOs in the Conclave."

"If she'd sought him out, it would make more sense."

"He sought her out. Right after Uncle Garold was appointed chief secretary."

"Coincidence?" She said it in such a way he knew she didn't believe that. "And now he wants her back. Zalia's not making him happy."

"Coincidence," he said. He finished his tea, then stood. "It's 1030."

She glanced up at him, her mouth opening, but he held up one hand. "I'm going to go down to sick bay and harass Doc and the med-techs. Promise I won't go to her room until you arrive with Kospahr. I leave to you the pleasant duty of escorting him."

"Making me suffer for making you suffer?"

He stopped in the doorway. "Something like that." He stepped through.

He knew the picture he presented, standing stiffly in the corner of the room. Military perfection. Imperial Arrogance on display. Shoulders level, back ramrod straight, chin high, hands clasped behind his waist.

Kospahr probably thought he was doing it to intimidate Trilby. In truth, he was doing it because it was the only way he could keep from reaching for her, dragging her into his arms. His hands were shaking.

He saw something flicker in her eyes when he followed Jankova and Kospahr in. But she looked away quickly and then studied the second lord minister of defense. He caught the hint of a wry smile curve on her lips as Kospahr introduced himself, listed his credentials.

Imperial Arrogance at its worst.

"If it weren't for the Empire's impressive medical technology," Kospahr told Trilby, "you might not be here."

"If the Empire didn't require its officers to be Gods damned liars, I wouldn't have to be here." She pointed at Rhis. "I pulled his ungrateful ass out of a swamp. So he tries to kill me, then takes my ship. Promising me reward money. Promising me I'm free to go once I get him back here."

Rhis heard the venom in her voice, had the feeling

that much of Trilby's ire was not feigned, in spite of Jankova's explanations.

"So what do I get?" She spread her hands. "Nothing. A cup of tea. A meal. And lies. Then a squadron of his fighters blows my ass into next septi." She glared at Rhis, then looked back at Kospahr. "Do you blame me?"

"Yes, Captain, I do!" Kospahr replied. "You obviously have no understanding of what has transpired in the past two months with the 'Sko. Nor do I expect you to. But we are engaged in some very serious business, and your petty needs will have to wait."

"You have no right to hold me here. I'm a citizen of the Conclave. If I file a report on what he did, you might find yourself in the middle of another untidy war."

Kospahr took a step back. Clearly, that glaring fact had escaped the sharp mind of the career politician. But it was something Rhis had been aware of all along. It was time for him to pick up his part of this drama.

"You might want to rethink your position on that, Captain Elliot. We have reason to believe an official in your own government has negotiated a kill order on you with the 'Sko. The Conclave may not be as concerned with your safe return as you think." Unfortunately, that was the truth.

Trilby shot him a haughty took he remembered well. "So you say. You know damned well I can't read Ycskrite."

"Believe me," Kospahr said, "we are not trying to protect you because we find your company charming!"

"Protect me?" Trilby turned quickly toward the

portly man, and Rhis saw her wince from the movement. "You damned near killed me."

"Because you departed a military outpost without permission," Rhis said evenly. "And you refused to respond to a request to power down." That, too, was true. If she hadn't run, Degvar's squadron would have towed her back unharmed.

"That was very foolish on your part," he added.

"No. The only foolishness on my part was not leaving you on Avanar to play tiddlywinks with the vampire snakes. They'd probably find your company charming."

Kospahr moved closer to her bed, gave her an oily smile. "Perhaps we should both admit there have been some misunderstandings. If Captain Tivahr has been harsh in his methods, you must understand it is because that is what he was trained to do. But I am here now. To take over, to rectify his mistakes. You should be thankful a second lord minister such as I takes an interest in your case."

Kospahr reached for her hand. Trilby snatched it away. Rhis started to snicker, then turned it into a cough when Jankova jabbed him with her elbow.

Kospahr didn't bother to turn around to see what the commotion was about. "The reality is, my dear, you need our help. And we need yours. There is no reason this cannot be a comfortable partnership."

"More lies?" She looked over his shoulder at Rhis. Her face was pale, her eyes looked larger than he remembered. Sooty with shadows. There was a bruise fading on the edge of her jaw. Another across the base of her throat where the safety harness had branded her. Her soft, pale hair looked like disheveled moonlight.

Yav chera, he wanted to tell her, but she had asked about lies. Not about what was driving him crazy.

"In any military operation, there is certain information that is restricted," he answered her. "However, if you agree to cooperate, I guarantee you will be apprised of all that we feel is pertinent at the time."

"Need-to-know, Tivahr?"

He nodded slowly, watched her mouth spread into a wry grin. Felt the corresponding warmth spread through him at the same time. The last time she'd thrown that phrase at him they were on the *Venture*. They were almost friends, about to be lovers. He wanted desperately to pick things up from that point.

He turned to Kospahr. "She will cooperate."

"Wise decision, my dear." Kospahr patted the edge of her bed. "I'm sure you'll find life on this side of the zone a bit better. Especially someone as attractive as you are." He leaned closer. "Not all men are fools, like Grantforth."

"No, Lord Minister," she said quietly as Kospahr turned away. "Some are worse."

Rhis followed them compliantly through sick bay but stopped just as the doors closed behind them. They took several steps down the corridor before Jankova turned, slanted him a glance.

"Commander, you'll accompany the lord minister back to his quarters. I need to speak with the doctor."

"You ill, Tivahr?"

"Obviously not, Lord Minister. But I must sign off on Captain Elliot's medical reports and make sure they properly reflect all we've done for her. Just in case, of course, the Conclave should ever request them."

"Ah! Yes. You must make sure they properly

reflect that we did all we could to prevent her being injured." He waved his hand over his head as he turned. "Carry on, Captain."

Jankova hesitated, then fell into step with Kospahr. He waited until they disappeared around the corner before spinning on his heels and striding back through sick bay's doors.

"Jankova approved this?" Doc intercepted him in the middle of sick bay.

"No. But she didn't disapprove it either." He put his hand on the shorter man's shoulder, nudged him out of the way. "Go hide in your office. I'm supposed to be in conference with you. Over Trilby's medical records."

He hit the palm pad, stepped through. She was still sitting propped against the pillows, a light blanket over her. But she'd pulled her knees up to her chest and crossed her arms on top of the tent made by the blanket. She looked startled to see him standing there.

The door closed. He thumbed the lock on. Fear flickered in her eyes, and in his chest, a corresponding pain at the sight of it.

"How are you feeling?" he asked softly. He slid his hands in his pockets. Better there than reaching toward her when that wasn't what she wanted.

"You came back to ask me that? Go ask Doc. He's the one with the medical degree."

"You are angry with me."

"No. I'm overjoyed to lose my ship and my best friend. To have damned near died. This has been great fun. We really ought to do it again sometime."

"Trilby-*chenka*—"

"Jettison that, Tivahr. Jankova told me you're on

the shit list if Kospahr finds out you gave me the release codes. I told her I'd cooperate. You don't have
to be nice to me anymore."

He pulled his hands out of his pockets, wiped them
over his face. "Jankova's concerns are not mine."
And he realized as he said it that it was the truth. He
didn't give a damn about his career. Not if keeping it
meant losing Trilby.

She glared at him. He sought the chair, sat in it,
rested his elbows on his knees. This might take a
while. "I did not send the fighters after you."

"She said that. I gather that was Kospahr's idea."

"He wants to use you to trap Grantforth."

"Which one?"

"Both."

"I hate to disappoint Chubby Boy there, but I
don't think either's interested."

"Jagan is. He's sent you a transmit."

"Jagan sent—you read my mail? Again?" She
shook her head in disbelief. "You're unbelievable.
You have no respect for anyone. I'd like to be there
the day someone finally says no to you. It ought to be
a sight."

"Someone in GGA is closely involved with the
'Sko. I decoded the transmit because it could help us
take action against them."

"And my transmit to Neadi? You read that too."

The efficient Corporal Rimanava. He wondered
what she'd told Trilby. "That was wrong of me, yes.
But you were so angry with me. I was looking for
anything that might tell me how to get you to talk to
me again."

"Locking me out of my ship's primaries was a big
step in that direction."

"I put that program in place when I was afraid you would go searching for Carina."

"Oh, yeah. The friend I don't care about. I remember now."

"Trilby—"

"Look. Captain. I'm not as stupid as your friend Kospahr thinks I am."

"He's not my friend."

She waved his comment away. "I know something pretty dirty is going on with the 'Sko and GGA. Maybe even Secretary Grantforth. And that you and your team think Jagan used me and the *Venture* to set all that up. I don't like it. I'm not even sure I buy it. I think it stinks. But I told Jankova, and I'm telling you again. I will cooperate. Which means," she said, holding up her hand as he leaned forward, intent on putting forth his own explanation, "that you have no right, outside of those parameters, to be involved in my life. You may be emperor on this ship, but I'm not one of your little peasants. Is that clear?"

He clasped his hands together. "You are very angry with me."

She fell back against the pillows, murmured something to the ceiling that sounded a bit like, "Why me?"

He could tell her, but he didn't think she wanted to hear it right now.

Trilby hated the look on his face as he left her room in sick bay. Disappointment under an "it's okay" mask. He was either a very good actor or her rejections really pained him.

Either way, it didn't matter. Because as far as she was concerned, there were only two ways to look at

Khyrhis Tivahr: as a liar, who felt that his continued attentions would guarantee her continued coopera-tion, or as a lover, one so far above her station and social circle—like she really had one of those!—that they stood no chance of success in a relationship. Someone was bound to get hurt, and that someone, she had recently learned from Jagan Grantforth, was Trilby Elliot.

But she'd work with him. In spite of what she'd told him just now, she wasn't totally sure GGA was innocent. Neadi's rumors still bothered her.

Plus, she owed it to Carina to find out the truth. And Mitkanos. And Farra. And the rest of them, in gray uniforms and black, right down to the crew of the *Razalka*. Because if the 'Sko got a foothold in the Conclave, life in civilized space would become a liv-ing hell.

Only a greedy fool like Jagan Grantforth would think otherwise.

Only a crazy fool like Trilby Elliot could stop him.

17

A middle-aged female med-tech brought Trilby's lunch on a tray. Doc trailed in behind, leaned against the open doorjamb after she left.

"I'm a really good cook," Trilby told him, between mouthfuls. "If you had a galley, I'd prove it. This is replicator, right?"

"One hundred percent balanced nutrition."

She flipped a few clumps of brown mush with her fork. "Tastes like rice that was ashamed of its identity."

He laughed. "It's our replicator's version of a Yaniran rice dish, yes. It is quite wholesome."

"Give me the original recipe. I'll make it delicious."

"There are a few personal galleys on board. But I would have to clear the matter with the captain."

She pointed the fork at him. "Ask him about my cooking. I never saw a man eat so much food in my life."

"You cooked for him, yes?"

"I cooked for us. My ship doesn't have replicators.

And as most of my runs are trikes, I stock up on fresh from station hydroponics when I need to." She thought for a moment. "You got a hydroponics on board?"

"A small one. Again, I would—"

"Have to ask the captain, I know." She took another mouthful. This stuff was pitiful. She might have to pull a favor. "Well, when I get out of here . . . By the way, Doc, when am I getting out of here?"

"Another day perhaps. You're healing nicely."

"And then?" She didn't know if Doc was in the information chain as far as her deal with Tivahr and Kospahr. For all she knew, he might believe she was going from here to the brig. Or to Degvar. She was sure he knew she had no workable ship to go back to.

"I believe Commander Jankova is in charge of arrangements after I release you."

That wasn't totally bad news. She liked Hana Jankova. Then she thought of someone she didn't like. Whose presence didn't quite mesh. "What do you know about this Kospahr who was here this morning?"

"Second Lord Minister of Defense. Cousin of Emperor Kasmov."

"So he informed me. But what do you know about him?"

"I take it you are not asking about his blood type?"

She grinned. Doc was okay. "No, but I thought you might know more about his species. Been a long time since I've seen a free-floating asshole with legs."

Doc had a deep, rumbling chuckle. It filled the small room. "Then you must not know too many politicians."

"One other comes to mind, and you're right: there are distinct similarities. So what's he doing on the *Razalka*? I'm surprised Tivahr tolerates him." From everything she'd heard about the senior captain, he wouldn't.

"The captain was absent when Kospahr came on board. There was a point, and this is strictly off the record, when we did not know if Captain Tivahr was returning. Jankova came back with the news the 'Sko had captured him."

"Jankova was on the raid?" This surprised her. The woman was smart, and tough, Trilby admitted. But she didn't look that tough. Must be something the Imperials put in the water.

Doc nodded. "She heads special operations. I thought you knew this."

"Probably, but it didn't sink in until now."

"So the captain told you about the raid?"

"He told me a couple of versions. The only consistent thing was that he got left behind in Szedcafar. I thought it was pretty shitty they abandoned him."

Doc frowned. "They didn't abandon him. He voluntarily stayed behind to facilitate their escape. He, out of all of them, is the best suited to survive unfavorable conditions."

"Avanar at noon is unfavorable conditions. Capture by the 'Sko is generally fatal."

"For most people, perhaps. But the captain . . ." And Doc hesitated. Trilby wondered if he thought he had said too much.

"Is not most people," she finished for him. She hoped he might volunteer more, confirm some of the rumors Mitkanos had talked about. But he only took her tray from her, laying her napkin across the top.

"I shall see about finding you someplace to cook, Captain Elliot. I think I might be able to justify it for the improved health of my patients."

He left her with orders "to rest," as if she could do anything else dressed in a soft silvery shift that hung past her knees. And no socks or boots. And not a laser rifle in sight.

But her body took Doc's command seriously, even though her mind labeled it *only a ten-minute nap.* When she woke, her door was closed and the lights in her room were dimmed. She glanced at the time panel on the far wall, saw it was 1830. Time for dinner and she'd just finished lunch.

Then she saw something else. Tivahr, in the chair.

She blinked, rolled over on her side. "Don't tell me. Studying my sleeping habits will help you defeat the 'Sko."

"No. Though it is a tempting suggestion." There was a smile in his voice. But whatever expression his mouth held was invisible under his dark mustache and the dim light.

She didn't want to discuss tempting suggestions lying down. She didn't want to discuss tempting suggestions at all. She pulled herself upright, plumped the pillow behind her, and leaned back. "What are you doing here?"

"Do you know that we have known each other for only eleven days?"

She did, but didn't want to admit she'd thought about it. About how on day four she'd thrown herself at him, torn his clothes off while he'd removed hers with equal enthusiasm. It had been an incredibly stupid move on her part, considering what happened on days five and six, and every one after that.

Back then, on day four, she'd seen him as a kindred spirit. A tweaker of wogs-and-weemlies, like herself. And, when she found out he'd survived capture by the 'Sko, a hero. Unlike herself. Those two things fed the attraction she'd felt for him since she first saw him lying on her sick-bay regen bed. Magnificently naked.

He'd made it increasingly clear that he wanted her, and it seemed so very okay. Because he was just a lowly lieutenant. And she, a lowly freighter captain.

But he wasn't a lowly lieutenant. And she was just a lowly freighter captain. She had to remember that. Had to forget day number four of those eleven days.

"In freighter lingo," she told him, pulling the sheet up around her and tucking it under her arms, "we call eleven days a 'single dex.' A deuce dex, what you'd call twelve, is a 'stinker.' "

"Why?"

"Because unless you got a real good enviro system, and most short-haulers don't, that's what your ship's going to smell like after twelve days in the lanes."

He laughed. Of course he would. He'd never experienced a ship on a twelve-day run with a failing enviro. Or no fresh water. Or no money for docking fees.

He didn't know what it was like to patch all your equipment, your clothes. His uniform was spotless, almost elegant with its fitted black jacket, tailored pants, polished boots.

And he'd gotten his hair cut. Probably had his own personal stylist.

"Doc says he might release me tomorrow," she said, as his laughter died away. "What then?"

"Then we take a look at what we know about the

'Sko and Grantforth. And we decide how you will answer the transmit from Jagan."

"He probably doesn't expect me to answer. We didn't part on the best of terms."

"I know."

It took a moment for his comment to sink in. Irritation flared in her. "All my personal transmits. Everything. You read them all, didn't you?"

"It was necessary."

Oh, Gods! They were so . . . intimate. The earlier ones. And the last few, the things Jagan called her . . . She was beyond mortification.

She grabbed the pillow from behind her back and flung it at him with all her might. It hit him square in the face. He let out a satisfying "oomph."

"You have no morals! No morals at all!" Damn, that hurt. She rotated her injured shoulder. "And damn you, stop laughing!"

He was laughing at her. Standing, clutching the pillow in his arms, and laughing.

She held out her hand. "Give that back. I'm sick and injured. I need it."

He sat down on the bed, facing her, and reached around her to tuck the pillow behind her back.

Wrong request, Trilby-girl. This was not where she wanted him to be. Not this close, with his breath in her hair, his arms brushing against hers. His mouth, hot against her skin, his mustache rasping against her cheek. He dusted her face with kisses of exquisite tenderness.

She was lost, and she couldn't afford to be. She squirmed away from him, brought her hands up to his shoulders, pushed him back.

"Don't, damn you. Stop it!" Her voice cracked. She hoped he thought it was anger.

"Trilby-*chenka*—"

A knock on the door. Three quick raps.

He pushed himself off the bed, ran his hand through his hair. He faced the door as it slid open. Doc's solid form blocked the incoming light.

"Time, Captain. I told you no more than thirty minutes. It's now forty."

"Yes. Of course." He stood by the edge of her bed. Trilby examined the hem of her blanket, knew he was looking at her. Out of the corner of her eye, she saw Doc step closer.

"We do not want to tire our favorite patient."

"No."

"Time to leave, Captain Tivahr."

"You are releasing her tomorrow?"

"I will let you know in the morning."

He stepped away. Trilby raised her eyes, saw him hesitate in the door.

"Vanko," he said to Doc. Then a long sentence in Zafharish. Her name. Some other words she thought she recognized, but she couldn't be sure. She'd have to get hold of a language program. There was too much at risk here.

Like being left alone in a small room with Khyrhis Tivahr. Risky, very risky.

Doc answered him, a few more sentences back and forth, and then he was gone.

She smoothed out the blanket and drew her knees up again. Wondered if Doc could see the flush of anger and shame on her face.

"*Lutsa,*" he said. The lights brightened. "You have a good nap?"

"Delightful."

"And your visitor?" Doc flipped open his medi-stat, ran it down her arms as he talked. "No, let me guess. A royal pain in the ass, no?"

"A royal pain in the ass, yes," she told him. "He doesn't seem to understand the word *no*."

"You'll have to teach him."

"Thanks, but I've already got a job."

He closed the sensor. "Two more hours in the re-gen. Then tomorrow I will issue your release. You may have some soreness in your shoulder for a few days. And, of course, do not enter any marathons for a least a week. But other than that, you'll be fine."

He patted her arm. "Ilsa will bring your dinner in a little while. Rest, for now."

Rest. She hugged her knees against her chest, stared at the closing door. She wasn't tired, didn't want to sleep. She was afraid she'd have nightmares. And Tivahr would be in every one of them.

Her breakfast arrived at 0800, along with clothing and a pair of boots. She picked up the familiar drab-green flight pants only to find the material unfamiliar. And unpatched. She examined the T-shirt and service jacket. All the same. And her ship's ID was gone from the jacket sleeves.

Even her underclothes were new.

Someone—she had a suspicion as to who—had replicated her uniform, matching her size but improv-ing the quality of the fabric. Far beyond anything she could ever afford.

She dressed, ran her hand down her jacket sleeve. Nice. Wow.

*   *   *

Nice. Wow. She turned around slowly, took in the appointments of her cabin, and only half-listened to Hana Jankova's apologies.

"This is not 'basic.' This is"—*compared to what I'm used to*—"very nice." A small seating area with a couch opened to a private galley on the left. On the right, a separate bedroom. With a door. A real bedroom. Access to the sani-fac from both the bedroom and the seating area.

Carpet. Wall insulation. Padded stools with armrests at the galley counter. Two viewports behind the couch. Big ones, not the small round ports that graced the *Venture*'s hull.

And not an inch of duct tape in sight.

The couch was soft. She sat, leaned back, patted the cushions. "Nice."

"I'm glad it pleases you. Most of our visitors complain."

"Kospahr, you mean?"

Jankova grinned wryly. "He's the latest in a long list."

"He should try living for five years in a sixty-five-year-old short-hauler. Or better yet, crew quarters on a Herkoid tanker. Herkoid would've crammed twenty people into here and expected a big thank-you."

"Do you feel up to meeting with my team in an hour?"

The message from Jagan. Jankova had given her an overview, but she'd yet to see it. "I'll meet with them now."

Jankova shook her head. "Take time to get settled. Have a cup of tea. Captain Tivahr wants to be at the meeting as well, and he's tied up with Lord Minister Kospahr at the moment."

"They deserve each other." She pushed herself up off the couch.

"He's not as bad as he used to be."

"Who, Kospahr?" Trilby deliberately misunderstood. She didn't want to hear nice things about Khyrhis Tivahr but knew she'd opened herself up to the subject with her remark.

"The captain. He's not the same man who stayed behind on Szed."

"A short vacation at Club 'Sko will do that." She wandered over to the small galley. Hot coffee and tea on demand. Top-notch replicator. But also a cooktop. Even better.

Jankova leaned on the counter. "He's very . . . concerned about you."

"I'm fine." As fine as anyone could be who just lost her ship, her livelihood, and was struggling with her self-respect. "So where do I meet you in an hour?"

"The Tactical Briefing Room on Deck Seven. But don't worry about finding your way. I'll send someone to escort you."

"Not Tivahr." The words escaped her mouth before her brain had a chance to edit them. Damn! She liked Hana Jankova but wasn't willing to let the woman into her own personal nightmares. She murmured a weak explanation. "I just . . . he's busy. I don't want you to bother him."

"I'll probably send Lieutenant Osmar, from my team. He needs to practice his Standard. It will give you a chance to get to know him. We'll be spending a lot of time together in the next few days."

"Sounds good."

Jankova left. Trilby saw a series of letters flash on the overhead ID panel as the door slid closed. *HN-JNKV*. Ident scanners on military ships evidently recorded both entrances and exits. She'd have to remember that, start memorizing the codes.

She didn't want any surprises on the other side of her door.

ADZSMR.

Okay, she thought. Doesn't look remotely like *Tivahr*, if Jankova's ID was anything to go by.

"Come," she said. Someone had evidently coded the cabin to respond to Standard. The door opened.

"Captain Elliot? Lieutenant Andrez Osmar." He saluted, stepped inside.

Andrez Osmar was about her own age, with curly black hair cropped close to his head, a wide nose, and a golden skin color that hinted at the possibility that someone in his past had spent some time on Bartravia.

"Come on in, Lieutenant. Let me just grab my jacket." She pulled it off the back of the stool in the galley and placed her empty coffee cup in the sani-rack.

She followed him down the corridor to the lift, looked up at him while they waited. He was tall, probably as tall as his captain. Good set of shoulders. Neadi would approve.

She made small talk with him in the lift. He'd been on the *Razalka* for two years. Before that, he was under Captain Rafiello Vanushavor's command. No, he'd never been to the Conclave. At least, not socially. Three years ago they'd been at war. Then he'd only seen the Conclave's Fleet. Not the worlds, or stations. But he'd heard stories.

"Port Rumor? *Vad!* Much interesting place. Much trouble. Good fun!"

"If you ever get the chance, there's a bar called Flyboy's. My friend Neadi and her husband, Leonid, run it. Leonid Danzanour."

"Zafharish name. Is good."

"Is great. Maybe I'll see you there sometime."

The tactical division on the *Razalka* spanned both sides of the corridor. Trilby followed Osmar through the double doors into the briefing room, where she met the other two members of Jankova's team: Grigor Cosaros and Cadrik Bervanik. Cosaros was about Osmar's age, but Bervanik was older. Late forties, possibly early fifties. He reminded her of Doc, squat and balding. Cosaros was wiry, more intense.

Tivahr stood at the head of the long table at the far end of the room, arms folded across his chest. A three-dimensional holochart hovered in front of him. He turned when she entered but said nothing while Osmar performed the introductions.

Then Jankova came in, followed by a man who was introduced to her as Commander Demarik. Gray haired, but prematurely gray, Trilby guessed. He had a likable face and gorgeous dark eyes. The *Razalka*'s executive officer, Jankova told her. She heard the pride in the woman's voice, noticed the slight brush of her fingertips across Demarik's arm as he turned.

More than pride.

She was glad for Jankova. They seemed right together somehow.

Jankova handed Tivahr a thin datatab. He pushed it into the slot in the table.

"Captain Elliot?" Tivahr motioned to the seat next to his at the table.

Reluctantly, she walked over and sat. The holo-chart disappeared, to be replaced by a wafer-thin screen.

Tivahr took his seat, leaned slightly toward her. "This is the message from Jagan Grantforth that we intercepted."

Pilfered, you mean. She noticed Jankova's team members were suddenly busy at their own consoles. At least they were willing to grant her privacy.

The message was longer than she'd expected. Jagan looked tired, harassed. And as if he'd been drinking too much. Marriage to Zalia was not bringing him happiness. He realized now that money wasn't everything. He needed to see her. He apologized for all his rude words. But he felt so strongly for her. It made him so afraid.

His life was falling apart. He was desperate. Could she at least contact him, assure him she was okay? He was worried. She hadn't been to Flyboy's in a while. If they could just be friends, he'd be happy. Maybe he could even offer her some work through GGA, to make up for the pain he'd caused her. They could be business associates. He knew he didn't deserve more than that.

"You'll always be the only woman I'll ever love." He ended his message with a weak smile.

She leaned back in her chair as the GGA logo winked off. She thought she was going to throw up.

18

"It's absolutely out of the question." Rhis knotted his hands together, rested them on the tabletop. He wanted to knot them around Kospahr's neck. "Captain Elliot isn't trained for a mission of this complexity."

"She doesn't need training," Kospahr replied smoothly. He lounged at the opposite end of the long conference table in the Tactical Briefing Room. Osmar, Jankova, and Trilby were on the lord minister's left, Bervanik, Cosaros, and Demarik on his right. "She's a freighter captain. All she has to do is fly the runs we tell her. The rest is up to the 'Sko."

Bait, Rhis knew. Kospahr wanted to use his air sprite as bait. They'd had this discussion before, and it'd almost killed Trilby. Now, at least, Kospahr was willing to admit the *Razalka* had to be involved. The minister's first plan had been to have the *Careless Venture* lure the 'Sko, then have the *Razalka*'s fighter squadrons move in. But Rhis's ship would have to be a considerable distance away from the *Careless*

Venture in order to avoid detection. An unsafe distance, in his estimation. In his expert opinion. And it would put Trilby and whoever else was on board in great physical danger.

The 'Sko were not particularly careful about whom they killed.

But Grantforth's pleading missive to Trilby hinted at a possible shipping contract with GGA. Rhis believed Jagan wanted access to her ship again. He toyed with several possible reasons. The trouble was, there wasn't much of the *Careless Venture* left to show him. And rebuilding her would take time.

He made that clear to Kospahr, who dismissed the objection with a wave of his hand.

"So scrap the idea of repairing that derelict ship of hers. I agree, it would take too long and frankly isn't worth the Empire's time or money. You can rig one of our new freighters, dangle that in front of the 'Sko and GGA. Add whatever weapons array you want."

Rhis saw Trilby's head jerk at this latest proclamation. Jankova evidently wasn't editing her whispered translations to Trilby. Which was just as well. He wanted to make sure Trilby understood Kospahr's priorities. And opinions.

Lieutenant Osmar looked up from his datapad, voiced his own concern. "The Conclave and the 'Sko might pick up on an unusual weapons array as well, Lord Minister."

"I can design around that somewhat," Rhis conceded. In fact he already had. "But it still doesn't lessen the risk. Nor does luring the 'Sko give us the connection to Garold Grantforth. I say we wait and see what develops with Jagan Grantforth. When he contacts her again—"

Kospahr slapped the table with the flat of his hand. "The entire Empire could be at risk if we permit the 'Sko to gain entry into the Conclave!"

"I don't think the situation has escalated quite that far," Rhis replied levelly. He picked up his lightpen from the table, balanced it in his fingers. "And dangling Captain Elliot before them without thoroughly preparing for all eventualities, and thoroughly protecting her safety, could precipitate even more complications. As I said, she's not trained—"

"Then train her. Or send a trained team with her," Kospahr said.

Rhis felt Jankova's gaze on him, saw Osmar look up again from his datapad. Cosaros and Bervanik said nothing, but he knew if he asked for volunteers, they'd all stand up in unison.

But that would be almost as foolish as sending Trilby out alone.

"Jankova's team just returned from an assignment. I'm not going to send them back out again. Cosaros and Osmar haven't recovered from their injuries. This was their third mission in six months."

And Jankova's absence hadn't done Demarik any good either. For the first time, Rhis sympathized with his executive officer.

"Then don't send Jankova's team. Lieutenant Gurdan's people are available. I've already spoken to him."

"But I haven't." Nor did he intend to. "And you don't have final say here, Lord Minister. I do."

"We don't have the time to waste while your people lick their wounds."

Rhis's eyes narrowed. The man was not only insulting, he was an idiot. "Sending injured personnel on a mission is the height of stupidity. The only possible answer is to delay a month while Commander Jankova's team recovers and Captain Elliot's ship is repaired."

"A month? We don't have a month. That young Grantforth's hot for her again. We can't afford to—"

The mention of Jagan sent anger sizzling through Rhis's words. "My answer, Kospahr, is no!"

"*Cordag merash!*" Trilby's voice cut between them, ordering him, ordering them all, to listen to her. In perfect Zafharish.

He glanced at her, caught Jankova's slight smile of surprise. Trilby was learning quickly. Too quickly, for Kospahr's liking. The lord minister started to rise.

"*Viek,*" Trilby added. Please.

Rhis noted her smile to Kospahr was as forced as the courtesy she added. He banked his irritation, let her continue.

"I think I understand pretty well, from Commander Jankova's translations, what you want to accomplish. And Lord Minister Kospahr is correct: I do know freighter operations. And for that reason, Captain Tivahr's plan won't work."

Kospahr, clearly pleased by her pronouncement, leaned back, eyes narrowed, fleshy lips curling into a half smile of self-satisfaction. But Rhis knew Trilby had more to say. He didn't think in the long run she'd be siding with the lord minister.

Trilby gestured to Cosaros and Bervanik, then nodded to Jankova on her right. "No offense to any of you. But on the freighter docks I've worked, you'd all stand out like a well-fed felinar in a mizzet colony. You say you want to create a fictitious freighter company, a Zafharin–Indy joint venture, with me as hired captain. And have this company agree to do business with GGA. Well, if you're going to do that, you're going to have to let me, as captain, choose my crew. And it wouldn't be any of you, because you're all too . . . respectable.

"And Gurdan's people," she told Kospahr, "all walk around like they have rods up their asses."

"You have a unique way with words," Kospahr said dryly.

"It's part of my charm," she shot back at him.

Rhis rapped his lightpen on the table. Trilby's comments were valid but only pointed out the problems. She didn't offer any solutions. They still had work to do. Before he could remind them of that fact, Osmar leaned forward, put his thoughts out in accented Standard.

"Captain Elliot is right. We do not have merchanter training. Not that we could not learn lingo, or methods. But it would take time. If we could delay this project, as Captain Tivahr says, work with Captain Elliot on some runs, then we are in better position to fit in at places like Port Rumor. We could be," and he grinned at Trilby, "less respectable."

And physically sound. Cosaros had taken two laser hits to the leg during their escape. Osmar had broken his left arm, suffered a concussion. Doc still had them on injured reserve.

Trilby was far from healed as well. Her injuries were more recent. Rhis saw the shadows under her eyes, saw her wince when she moved too suddenly.

But Kospahr wasn't interested in reasons for a delay. He started to object, but Jankova snapped her fingers.

"We might not have to delay. Mitkanos," she said.

Rhis saw Demarik look toward her, nod in agreement. "I didn't think of it until Andrez mentioned merchanter training. Mitkanos's family runs a depot in Port Balara. We could talk to him about filling in on our team."

"He's *Stegzarda*," Cosaros said. He didn't have to add "not Fleet."

That could be a problem, and not just because of the rivalry between the two branches. Rhis intended to be part of Trilby's "crew," whether she liked it or not. And whether Mitkanos agreed with it or not. He had a feeling Mitkanos wouldn't.

The major had already done Rhis one favor by deleting all records of his authorization for the *Careless Venture*'s departure. And had made it clear he did so only because Demarik asked. They had a tie from long ago. Rhis never asked what it was. Only that it was this history with Demarik and, his exec admitted, Mitkanos's fondness for Captain Elliot that engineered the ruse of Lieutenant Lucho Salnay's "assistance" and Trilby's "escape." Not because Mitkanos had any interest in protecting Captain Tivahr.

He admittedly owed Mitkanos for that. That didn't make the prospect of working a mission with the *Stegzarda* chief any more pleasant.

Yavo Mitkanos accepted Rhis's offer of a chair with controlled courtesy, listened to his brief preliminaries with a professional attentiveness. But Rhis clearly saw the expected: the man didn't like him. It was in the control, in the veneer of professionalism, in the way the burly man looked levelly across the wide desktop between them.

Rhis was used to people being, if not intimidated by his presence, at least deferential. But Mitkanos had been casually unconcerned when Rhis stood at his table in the officers' mess on Degvar. And was only marginally more cooperative now.

The only thing that seemed to motivate the man was Trilby's safety.

"She's willing to work with you?" Mitkanos asked.

"Yes."

"This surprises me. I'll overstep my bounds here and say you've treated her most unfairly."

Rhis sat back in his chair. "You're right. You're overstepping your bounds, Major. But I didn't send those fighters after her."

"I'm well aware of that. But I'm speaking of things that happened before that incident."

A wave of anger, then shame, washed over Rhis. He knew he'd hurt Trilby by not telling her who he was. He wouldn't have thought she'd cry on the shoulders of someone like Mitkanos. "I'm not interested in your opinions on my interaction with Captain Elliot. I asked you here solely because Commander Demarik believes you can assist us in an operation to force Grantforth and the 'Sko into the open."

"Zak Demarik is correct. I grew up on my family's merchanter docks. Spent six years working the freighter trade before joining the *Stegzarda*. That's what you wanted to know, correct?"

"How long ago was that?"

"Twenty-three years. But my family still runs the depot. I follow their business."

"I'm looking to create a believable, workable freighter crew of five. Myself and Captain Elliot are already part of that roster. I need three more. If Captain Elliot agrees, can you provide us with personnel with military training and freighter experience that fit those parameters?"

"You need two more, Captain Tivahr. If you're going to operate out of both Rumor and Saldika, you need me on board. And, yes, I can provide you with people who will fit the bill."

"I'd prefer someone from Degvar Fleet personnel—"

"I have several in mind, both Fleet and *Stegzarda*. But I think Captain Elliot has to have the final say. She has the most to lose out of all of us. And she's already lost more than is fair. Can she accompany me back to Degvar, or has she been confined to quarters?"

Rhis clenched his fist. "Do you always speak your mind so freely, Major?" So carelessly as well?

"When I feel it's necessary."

"I could also find it necessary to remove you from this mission." He knew Demarik had faith in Mitkanos, but if he had to, he'd find somebody else. Someone who'd remember who was in command.

"Your only other choice then, on this short notice, would be Pavor Gurdan. I don't recommend him."

And Kospahr would be gleeful to have Gurdan on board. No, Rhis was stuck with Mitkanos, and they both knew it. He stared hard at the man, made sure the major knew he wasn't pleased with the situation.

"Captain Elliot isn't a prisoner here," he told Mitkanos. "She's cooperating fully. You have an hour to assemble your best personnel for her consideration. Send a full dossier to me when you've made your choice. I'll present that to Captain Elliot, give her time to review it. Then at," he glanced at the time stamp on his desk screen, "1600 hours I'll accompany her to your office. She can meet with your candidates, make her final decision at that time."

Mitkanos looked as if he was going to say something but thought better of it. Rhis took it as a positive sign.

The *Stegzarda* major stood. "Dossier in one hour. My office at 1600."

He strode out the door. Rhis unclenched his fist.

Rhis waited while she read the dossiers. She sat in the same chair Mitkanos had occupied earlier. Mitkanos had filled it. Trilby simply perched on it, a slender form in dark green against the gray fabric. His office auxiliary screen was swiveled toward her. Her lightpen tapped, highlighted, selected.

He'd read the files before he called her to his office, entered his opinions on Mitkanos's six candidates. "You want coffee? Tea?"

She looked up, frowned at being disturbed. "Um, no. Thanks." Bowed her head again. Tap. Tap.

His office replicator was recessed in a corner. He requested tea for himself. She was reading his final notes when he walked behind her chair to bring the steaming cup back to his desk.

"Okay." She breathed the word, nodding more to herself than to him.

He adjusted his desk screen, pulled the data from hers.

Yavo Mitkanos. Of course. He expected that. Then three more names. Two from Fleet. Basil Enzio. Dallon Patruzius. And one *Stegzarda*. Farra Rimanava, the young woman with Mitkanos in the mess. Not surprising. All good choices, judging from a quick glance at their service records. Just one too many.

He tapped his own lightpen on the list. "You have four here."

"Yes."

"I don't want to use six. Just five—"

"I'm giving you five. Myself as captain. Patruzius as copilot. Enzio, Rimanava, and Major Mitkanos. That's five."

"And me." For a moment he thought his participation in the mission had slipped her mind. Then he saw the line of her mouth tighten. She was excluding him. "I am in charge of this mission," he said softly. He didn't want to sound overbearing. He wanted her to see that he valued her. Trusted her.

But she didn't seem ready to trust him. "That doesn't mean you have to be part of my crew."

"Trilby—"

"You asked my opinion." She leaned forward, pushed the auxiliary desk screen out of the way. "I'm giving it. Mitkanos, Enzio, Rimanava, and Patruzius. You don't belong."

He did. He had to. He was putting her back in touch with Jagan Grantforth. He had to be there. "I've spent a good part of my life doing intelligence work. I can belong and will. I am in charge of this mission," he repeated.

"Then let me make it clearer. I don't want you there." She leaned back, crossed her arms over her chest.

She was still angry with him, pushing him away every chance she got. He saw that, hoped in time she'd understand why he'd had to lie about who he was. It took some of the sting out of her rejection, but not all. A small cruel voice in his head whispered that it might not only be anger. That it might be something else. Something she had alluded to in the officer's lounge on Degvar.

Something that labeled him a freak. An unholy experiment. Or worse: how Malika had seen him. A curiosity to be conquered, bragged about, laughed at.

"I will be on board as copilot. And mission leader." He touched his screen, sent the list back to her. "And I think we both agree on Mitkanos. So the last two choices are yours. But only two."

She glared at him for a moment. "Rimanava," she said. "And Patruzius."

He tabbed down to their bios, scanned them. Patruzius was Fleet, currently assigned to the Degvar quartermaster's office. He'd worked Saldika, was fluent in Standard. That would've been one of his choices as well. Something flickered in his mind when he looked at Patruzius's image, something familiar. But he couldn't place the face with the neatly clipped beard, close-cropped hair.

Rimanava wasn't fluent in Standard, but then, their cover was that of a mixed crew. She'd grown up in Port Balara, worked for two years on the merchanter docks. He could find no flaws in her record, and perhaps her inclusion would placate Mitkanos.

"Good," he said. "I'll tell Mitkanos. We'll meet with him in two hours."

He recognized the man as soon as he and Trilby walked into Mitkanos's office. The beard was gone, the hair longer and now pulled back at the nape of his neck and secured with a black cord. Black, like his uniform. A Fleet supply-ship captain.

Patruzius. The man who'd sat so close next to Trilby in the officers' lounge, who'd placed his hand in such a familiar manner on Trilby's arm, was Dallon Patruzius. And Rhis had just authorized his placement on the mission team. On Trilby's ship.

Rhis suppressed a groan and wondered, not for the first time in the past few days, if a permanent place had been etched for him on the divine shit list.

He nodded to Mitkanos. The young woman standing next to him was the *Stegzarda* corporal, Farra Rimanava.

Trilby was already shaking Rimanava's hand, then Patruzius's. The bastard winked at her.

"Good to see you again," she told him.

Actually, no, it isn't. Not as far as Rhis was concerned. Things had been said at that table in the lounge, and Patruzius and Rimanava had been there to hear them. Suddenly he wasn't as pleased with his new crew as before.

But Patruzius was Fleet. One of his own people. His allegiance was to Senior Captain Tivahr. He'd make sure Patruzius didn't forget that.

★ ★★ 19

She couldn't bring herself to sit in this captain's chair. Not yet. The ache of losing the *Careless Venture* was still too new. But the pull of this ship, an Endurance Class freighter only a few years old, was enticing. The Empire was handing her this beauty. Tivahr had made that much clear. It was hers to keep after the mission. Regardless of how the mission turned out.

Helluva reward for returning their prized senior captain. Providing, of course, that she survived.

Shame Dezi was still in a hundred pieces and not here to see it.

She ran her hand over the back of the captain's chair. High-backed and cushioned, upholstered in a soft fabric that felt like woven leather. No duct tape. No lumpy welds holding the armrest to the frame. On the console, a microthin screen that slid noiselessly up at her touch, blinked on instantly.

She felt Tivahr standing behind her, waiting for her reaction. She'd kept herself in check all the way through the large freighter bay on Degvar. Not the commercial bay, nor the docks the *Stegzarda* used. But one that required them to pass through three security checkpoints.

She assumed, by that point, he wasn't leading her to a generic Imperial cargo ship. But it still took some discipline on her part not to let a well-deserved "hot damn" slip through her lips.

An Endurance Class short-hauler. Hot damn, indeed.

He grasped her elbow lightly, guided her to the front of the chair. "Sit."

She felt his touch like firewasps in her veins, jerked away. "In a minute."

She wrapped her arms around her chest, continued her methodical check of the command console. Then turned to her right and inspected the copilot's screens and, behind that, navigation.

This was a real bridge, with space—walkable space—between the stations. Not like the *Venture*, whose bridge hadn't been much more than an oversize cockpit.

Enviro. Communications. Weapons. As for the last, she could see the modifications still under way. Cables snaked over that console and into an open access panel underneath.

She heard him step toward her. Turned, because she didn't want to feel his breath on her hair again, or the heat of his body against her back.

"Where'd you steal this from?" And then a sickening thought. How many Conclave crew had died defending it?

He shook his head. "It's not stolen."

Oh, right. She forgot. During the war, the Empire labeled any captured ships as "transferred property."

"Okay, who involuntarily transferred this ship to you?"

A small grin crossed his lips. He reached for the back of the captain's chair, swiveled it around, then sat. "No one."

Why was he grinning like that? She didn't see anything funny in standing where some of her own people may have fought for their freedom.

"You really think this is an Endurance C-Two? Trilby, Trilby." He shook his head. "Come. Three more minutes. I'll give you three more minutes."

For a moment she didn't understand. Of course this was an Endurance C-2. She knew a C-2 when she saw one. She—

—uncrossed her arms, stared around the bridge again.

Then she stormed off the bridge and down the corridor. Tivahr's boots thudded behind her. She could hear him chuckling, damn him!

She clambered down the ramp, her hand sliding on the railing, grasping it just as it ended, and she used her own body weight to swing herself around. She darted under the thick landing struts and peered up at the belly of the freighter. Saw the square drain locks, red-ringed fuel ports, docking-clamp interfaces. The latter, especially, looked all too familiar.

Damn! Damn! Double damn!

She emerged on the starboard side, ran her gaze down the length of the ship, seeing now what she'd missed before. Differences. There were differences. Hull-plate size and configuration. Viewports.

She took a few steps backward, saw braking-vane patterns that didn't belong. And stumbled against something hard but soft and warm.

Tivahr locked his arms around her waist, pulled her against him, laughter still rumbling in his chest. She pounded her fists halfheartedly against his hands at her midsection. She was too intrigued by the ship to be completely annoyed at him.

"Okay, so it's not an Endurance C-Two," she admitted. She leaned her head back against his shoulder to get a better look. It wasn't even a Conclave-produced ship. "What is it?"

His voice was low and sexy in her ear. "I like to think of her as an illegitimate but well-loved offspring. You know, perhaps this *Dasja* Conclave freighter falls in love with a *Dasjon* Imperial huntership. This is the result of their liaison."

"Seriously, Rhis. Where'd you get her?"

His arms tightened around her, the fingers of his right hand threading through her own. She suddenly realized what she'd done. Rhis. She hadn't called him Rhis since she found out who he was. He'd been Tivahr since then. Or, preferably, Captain Tivahr.

"Tivahr," she said with a warning tone, as much to herself as to him. She damned her tongue and wished her brain wouldn't go into stasis every time he got near her. Her body certainly didn't respond that way.

She wriggled against him and he released her, reluctantly.

"She was built here," he told her when she turned. "No, not on Degvar. But she was constructed at an Imperial shipyard and, yes, to resemble an Endurance C-two. Oddly enough, your military has never been able to see through her deception. But I've yet to be able to pass her by a freighter captain."

Now she knew how the Empire, how Tivahr, conducted intelligence missions in Conclave space.

"What's her name?"

"She's had many. None of course can be used again once we cross the zone."

Changing a ship's sealed ID program was easy for the likes of Tivahr.

"She's got to have a name." It was almost sacrilegious.

"You're her captain. That honor is yours."

The thought immediately thrilled her, then alarmed her. Whatever she was, she was magnificent. Far too magnificent for the likes of Trilby Elliot.

Jagan had bought her bracelets, silk blouses, perfume. Tivahr was giving her a ship.

And just like the bracelets, silk, and perfume, she'd give this gift back too. But this one she'd regret for the rest of her life.

But for a while, just a little while . . . A name rose suddenly in her heart. Her throat tightened and she wiped her hand over her eyes, smearing the dampness there.

She stared at the ship, an Endurance C-2 but so much better, with systems and capabilities that bordered on brilliant.

"*Shadow's Quest,*" she said softly. It fit. Because in the end, she'd lose this Shadow too.

It was the second message she'd received from Jagan since she'd agreed to work with Tivahr. But the first to come to her on *Shadow's Quest.* She sat in her office—small, but it was hers—behind the bridge and listened to it twice.

Then she keyed in a request for a fresh cup of

coffee from the replicator—*her* replicator—and listened to it again.

Jagan Grantforth seemed greatly disturbed that she was no longer in command, and in possession, of the *Careless Venture*. "I'm worried about you. You must be devastated, Tril. You're all alone. I know how much that ship meant to you."

He didn't know diddly-squat. He'd never given a damn about the *Venture* before, except to make sure the mattress in her cabin was soft enough for him.

"Did this transport company let you transfer all your map files to this new ship? Make sure they know how useful all your years of experience in the business are. All those shortcuts you know."

Map files? The *Venture*'s map files? She couldn't place the term, thought for a minute it might be an acronym. MAP, with the *M* standing for Major, Minor something . . .

Map. Charts. Navigational charts.

The *Venture*'s nav banks.

She bolted out of her office, skipped down the stairs two at a time. The lift would probably be quicker, but she kept forgetting about it. Besides, her brain seemed energized by the pounding of her feet on the resilient decking.

Tivahr was in engineering. A real engineering room. Two techs from the *Razalka* and one from Degvar's ops were making a last-minute install. They had a deadline of 0600 tomorrow. *Shadow's Quest* would officially enter the freighter business at that time.

She spotted him kneeling on the floor, holding a small datalyzer into an access hatch. "*Vad*," he called in approval to the gray-clad tech at the far end of the console. "The signal's balanced now."

She barely noticed that she understood his Zafharish response to the tech. She squatted down beside him, grabbed his arm. "It's not me. It's my ship!"

He sat back on his haunches and stared at her.

She felt almost giddy with relief. And idiotic for not seeing it before.

"It's not me," she repeated. "Jagan. He's not, he's never been, interested in me. It's my ship. The *Venture*. He's having shit fits in his latest transmit because he thinks I junked her nav banks."

The same nav banks that held not only the data on all of her routes and runs but the routes and runs of every captain the ship had ever had in the past sixty-five years. All the old trade routes that no one used anymore because the guidance beacons were outdated.

No one, maybe, except the 'Sko.

Tivahr followed her into the lift and up three decks to her office. She turned her desk screen toward him. He sat on the edge of her desk, sipped the coffee that she'd gotten for herself, and watched the playback of the transmit.

"He could just be saying how sorry he is because he's trying to get back in your good graces."

Yeah, you'd know about playing those kinds of games, wouldn't you? She leaned forward in her chair. "Jagan doesn't even know a ship has nav banks. Trust me. Someone fed him that line. He refers to the short-cut in my map files. He couldn't even get the line right. He's an accountant, for the Gods' sakes!"

"His family owns GGA—"

"And he's an accountant. Has no military or merchanter flight time. He goes to the depots on his family's private yachts and takes inventory. He wouldn't know a star chart if it bit him in the ass."

She could see his mind working. He took another sip of her coffee. She wondered if he had come to the same conclusion she had. She couldn't be the bait because she wasn't what Jagan or the 'Sko wanted. The Empire could let her go now, if not in *Shadow's Quest*—and she didn't remotely think they'd just hand her this ship, especially if the mission were scrubbed—then at least with a one-way shuttle ticket in hand back to Port Rumor. Plenty of people there would be willing to help her find Carina.

But he shot her hopes down with his next sentence. "We can integrate the *Venture*'s nav banks onto this ship. It will take us only another six, eight hours." He slapped his hand against his thigh. "Bloody hell! I should have thought of that."

"But they're damaged—"

"The data's intact. Only the retrieval programs and some of the hardware integrators were lost." He put her empty cup down, then pulled his lightpen from his jacket pocket, tapped the end against his mouth while he thought. "We could trap them. Set it up so they obtain the nav banks. But I can put in a code, traceable by us. We can track who the data goes to and how."

He swiveled the screen back to her. "Compose a message. Send it in an hour or two. Praise your new employers, Vanur Transport, who had, of course, been more than happy to integrate your nav banks. And paid you well for it."

He was grinning, but his smile had distinctly feral undertones.

She voiced her supposition. "The 'Sko are looking to use the old lanes to move in and out of the Conclave undetected. And someone in GGA is supplying them with the means." She couldn't quite believe what she was saying. GGA working with the 'Sko. Is this what Carina, or maybe Vitorio, found out? Vitorio'd had contacts in GGA through Chaser long before Trilby had met Jagan. She pushed the ugly thoughts from her mind.

Tivahr seemed to sense her discomfort. "I suspected that for a while. Now I think we have proof."

"Then why all the attacks on Rinnaker, on . . ." She shook her head. Stupid, stupid, stupid! It was the one common thread she'd seen but ignored. She answered her own question before he could.

"Most of Rinnaker's ships are older." She pointed her finger at him as if lecturing him. "They've been in business for almost eighty years. Longer than Norvind or GGA. Only Herkoid was around longer." Over one hundred twenty. And their ships, when they still traveled the lanes, looked it. "When Herkoid folded, Rinnaker's nav data was the oldest in the lanes."

"Which the 'Sko want. And GGA wants." Tivahr repocketed his pen. "So they hit Rinnaker's old freighters, force them to sell them as scrap."

"To GGA. Which also graciously gives them low-cost loans to buy new ships." Things were starting to fall into place in Trilby's mind. But not everything. "But GGA's got Rinnaker's data. Why do they need mine?"

"We'll have to take a look at the data to answer that." He slid off the desk, then turned, planted his hands on top of it and looked at her. "You worked for Herkoid, didn't you?"

She nodded. "So did Vitorio. Carina's brother."

"You ever take nav data from their ships?"

Oh, Gods. She closed her eyes for a moment. "Shadow did."

"Shadow?"

She waved one hand in the air. "This ship's namesake. Shadow was a genius. Even when he was a kid, he could've run circles around the stuff you create. We grew up together—Carina, Vitorio, Shadow, Chaser, and me."

"And he took the Herkoid files from you, or Vitorio?"

"No. He worked with me and Vitorio on a Herkoid long-hauler. Died on it too. He started copying Herkoid's command files and nav files and the-Gods-only-know-what-else before he was killed. He had this beat-up old datapad. He listed me as his sister in his personnel file. Herkoid gave me his things, including the datapad, after he was killed."

"And the files?"

"When I got the *Venture*, I dumped everything into her banks. Not just Herkoid nav data. Everything. Everything Shadow ever created, every program he ever wrote. I got some fail-safes—"

"I saw them."

Hell, of course he had. Sometimes she felt so naked around him! In more ways than one . . . *Bad choice of words, Trilby-girl.* "The original fail-safe was his program. Some of my diagnostics were too. I just expanded them, customized them to what I needed. And the programs he didn't finish, I did."

"And Jagan knew about this?"

"He knew we worked for Herkoid." She was thinking hard now. "He's met Vitorio. Chaser. He heard some of the old stories. It was common for one of us to brag about what Shadow had done. What he could've been. But there's no way Jagan would know what to do with information like this."

"But somebody does." He pushed himself upright and ran a hand over his face. "And somebody still wants that data. Jagan's the link. Send him that message about the wonderful people at Vanur Transport. I am very interested to see how he responds."

He stopped as the door slid open. "And by the way, also inform Jagan Grantforth you're neither heartbroken nor alone. Tell him your fiancé is making sure you're well taken care of."

"My fiancé?" For a moment she thought he was going to recruit Dallon Patruzius for that position. Or, Gods forbid, Mitkanos. Then she saw his sly grin and wished she could wrench the screen from her desk and chuck it at him.

"Yes, your fiancé. Rhis Vanur, CEO of Vanur Transport."

She shot to her feet. "You are not!"

"Did I forget to tell you about my promotion, darling? Yesterday a mere lieutenant. Today, a corporate CEO. Hard work does pay off." He shrugged, then ducked quickly as an empty coffee cup sailed past his head.

There was a palpable hush in the Tactical Briefing Room. The overhead lights were dimmed, better to see the data highlighted on the holochart suspended over the middle of the table. Rhis strode quietly around the table, glanced down at Jankova's pad. She was linked with Demarik's. His executive officer had returned to his usual seat at the far end of the table. A seat Kospahr had occupied during their last meeting, four days ago.

But Rhis had somehow forgotten to inform the lord minister of this late meeting. Oddly, so had Demarik and Jankova. Of course, they were delegated the duty of fetching the new team on board: Mitkanos, Rimanava, and Patruzius. When the *Stegzarda* major offhandedly noted the lapse with an undisguised grin of pleasure, everyone exchanged glances and shrugs. Undoubtedly, they were all working too hard. It was an understandable oversight. And the general consensus was that the lord minister wouldn't want to be disturbed at this late hour.

They'd accomplished much in those four days. The transferal of the files to *Shadow's Quest,* and the implementation of the tracking codes, delayed them only six hours. Vanur Transport would be up, operating, and—barring any other unforeseen revelations—departing Degvar by 1200 hours tomorrow, with Captain Trilby Elliot at the helm.

And Captain Khyrhis Tivahr—Rhis Vanur—in command.

He stopped behind Trilby's chair, smoothed a wrinkled section of her jacket collar. She flinched away, but not as much as she had yesterday, when he'd wrapped his arms, briefly, around her waist. Or the day before, when he'd rested his hand on her shoulder, then touched her face.

One step at a time. He would get her back, one small touch, one small step at a time.

He was also sending a message. Not to Demarik

or Osmar or Cosaros or Bervanik. Demarik and Jankova had known what Trilby meant to him before he'd set foot on the *Razalka*. His executive officer often received information that no one else did.

And Jankova's team followed her lead. They had eyes, and brains, as well.

As did Doc Vanko, who had greeted Rhis's first appearance in sick bay after Trilby's accident with two words: *excellent choice*.

They'd known each other a long time. Nothing more needed to be said.

No, the message he was sending had two destinations. The first was to Trilby. He wasn't giving up on her, nor on what he knew they could have.

The second was to Mitkanos and Patruzius, seated across the table from her. *She's mine. Don't even think about trying to change that fact.*

He was having second thoughts about permitting Dallon Patruzius on the team. The same easygoing manner that marked the supply captain a natural on the freighter docks, and on this mission, also made him a natural flirt with Trilby. And Farra Rimanava. But Rhis wasn't concerned with Rimanava.

Nor did he think Trilby or Mitkanos would find his objection valid. And they had an ETD of 1200 to concentrate on, a little more than ten hours from now.

"It is something in Herkoid's data, there's no doubt." Mitkanos was shaking his finger at the holochart in the same way Trilby had wagged her finger in Rhis's face earlier. And in response to the same information.

"*Vad! Yasch*—Yes, I have examined these stats from Rinnaker too." Osmar gave a quick nod to

Trilby as he switched from Zafharish to Standard. "They all reference a Herkoid route. Here, so to save you time." Osmar tapped his pad, sent his summation to Mitkanos's team.

This was the first time Mitkanos's team viewed the total picture. Rhis was interested in their input, especially that of Patruzius, as much as he was reluctant to admit it.

Patruzius had come to Fleet out of the merchant sector five years ago. Before that he'd worked with Fennik Import–Export, based in Saldika and, when the war ended, with runs to Port Rumor.

Patruzius had even been to Flyboy's. That fact had surprised him more than it had Trilby, when Patruzius had mentioned it yesterday on the bridge. Though he'd never been in Neadi's bar when Trilby had been there.

"That's Herkoid's Black Star route." Trilby pulled up Osmar's summation from her files. Rhis leaned on the back of her chair, read over her shoulder.

"Strezza ebohr," he said in her ear. He knew she was learning more and more of his language. He wanted her to. She would need it.

Trilby touched her pad. The trade route shimmered into solidity to the left of the holochart. She dragged her lightpen, superimposed it. It went from Marbo to an empty spot in the Yanir Quadrant. Imperial space.

It should have gone somewhere else. Rhis slid into his seat, brought up Trilby's file, checked the coordinates. No, everything was correct. Except that it only had a Point A. Not a Point B. Not a station, not a planet, not even an intersection with another trade route.

He heard Rimanava and Cosaros arguing the same thing. In Standard, fortunately, for Trilby's sake.

"Mister Demarik, what are the oldest star charts we have on the *Razalka*?"

Demarik looked at him through the swirl of colors in the middle of the table. "Five years in our banks, ten in archive, Captain."

Bloody hell. Sometimes he was too efficient for his own good. Herkoid had ceased operations fifteen years ago, but this data looked to be at least thirty years old, if not older.

"We've got older than that on the *Nalika Gemma*." Dallon Patruzius leaned forward, looked at him past the bowed heads of Mitkanos and Rimanava, who were comparing data on their pads. "Let me borrow your ship's comm and I'll see what I can find for you."

Farra Rimanava's hand on his arm stopped him from rising. "Degvar ops—"

"Doesn't need to know what we're doing." Patruzius stood.

Rhis nodded his approval. Damn it! The man was good.

"Use my office, Captain Patruzius." Jankova swiveled her chair around, rose to meet him.

"Dallon," he told her, grinning.

Rhis waited until the door slid closed behind them before meeting Demarik's gaze. His exec shrugged. Rhis went back to the data on his pad, scowling.

His ship badge pinged. He answered with a tap to his pad. His screen shifted to a view of the duty officer at communications. "Captain, a Delta Priority One transmit from Admiral Vanushavor's office."

"Transfer it here." He didn't like Delta Priority

Ones, usually took them in the privacy of his office, where he could swear long and loud without disturbing his bridge crew. But he didn't think his bad habits would come as a surprise to anyone in the Tactical Briefing Room.

"Disturbing news, Tivahr. Unconfirmed at this point." Neville Vanushavor's dark eyes narrowed. He was in his formal dress uniform, had probably been called out of some elegant social function to deal with this latest development. Medals glinted on his chest, gold braid dripped down his left shoulder. He was in his late sixties, but still powerfully built. Still in control of the Imperial Fleet.

"Sources tell us that there is an 'open trade' agreement being negotiated between the Beffa trade cartels and the Conclave government. I know we've heard rumors before. I'm bringing this to your attention now because a name's been mentioned. Garold Grantforth."

Rhis saw Trilby stiffen in her seat next to him. The admiral's message was in Zafharish. He didn't know how much she understood, though he knew her vocabulary had grown in the past few days. However, Grantforth's name needed no translation.

"I'm sending a copy of our information with this transmit. So there's no need to go into the details at this point.

"This much, however, I will tell you. Whatever your schedule is with your current mission, it needs to go into double time. Now. There's no such thing as 'open trade' with the 'Sko. Once they devour the Conclave, they will be coming after us."

The screen shifted to an image of the seal of the Imperial House of Vanurin, then flashed off.

There was a palpable silence in the room. Rhis stood, jerked his thumb toward the door. "Get Jankova," he told Demarik, who was already rising.

He glanced down at Trilby, saw her eyes dark and wary, her mouth pursed in distaste. "Did you understand?"

"Some. Maybe too much. Grantforth's bringing the Beffa cartels in."

He pointed to the holochart. "When Jankova and Patruzius return, I'll bring up that transmit. Then we will talk about pushing up our departure time."

"We can be ready in two hours," Mitkanos said with a quick glance at Farra Rimanava.

"Two hours," Trilby agreed.

Rhis drew a deep breath, pushed down the sick feeling rising in his stomach. This was too fast, too soon. He had been so sure Grantforth would wait until his nephew met with Trilby, obtained the Herkoid data he now knew they needed.

Something had changed their minds. He didn't know what it was. And he didn't like that feeling one bit.

20

It would be a deuce to Port Saldika, then a trike to Port Rumor. A waste of five valuable days, in Rhis's opinion. But to head straight to Rumor would raise too many red flags. They needed Saldikan transit stamps on their manifests, Saldikan clearance codes in their personnel files.

Files that made Khyrhis Tivahr into Rhis Vanur. And showed Farra Rimanava as recently hired out of the Port Balara freight-consolidation office.

Patruzius and Mitkanos's profiles needed only a little muddying. Both had ties to the freighter community. And Mitkanos's contacts allowed Port Balaran origination codes to be added to the ship's registry, no questions asked.

But five days! A full hand, he corrected himself, knowing that's how Trilby termed it. He tapped the end of the lightpen impatiently against the desk. Even with the rest of the Herkoid files to unravel and then the addition of the final tracking codes, it was more time than he wanted to waste.

The door to the small office slid open. A flash of gray beyond it. They all had new uniforms: Vanur Transport gray. Trilby stepped in, laughing, then turned and took a playful swipe at a man just out of her reach. Patruzius. "You watch yourself, mister!"

"Aye, Captain!" Patruzius saluted her, stuck his head through the open doorway. "Captain." He nodded to Rhis, then disappeared. His heavy footsteps echoed down the corridor.

Rhis flipped the lightpen in his fingers, rapped it against the edge of the desk in a brisk staccato.

Trilby sat in the chair across from the desk, leaned casually against the armrest. "We're clear of Degvar's outer beacon."

He'd been on the bridge with her when *Shadow's Quest* had departed Degvar over an hour ago, wanting, if nothing else, to watch his air sprite handle her new toy. But there was little for him to do once the ship took a heading for Saldika. Via trader's lanes. Not military ones.

His time was better used on recording the Herkoid files. He'd told Trilby to join him in her office as soon as they hit the lanes. He just didn't count on Patruzius being her escort.

"You auditioning for the percussion section of the Imperial orchestra?" She pointed to his lightpen. "Or sending a message in code?"

He stilled the lightpen, then dropped it onto the desk. "Have you heard anything from Grantforth yet?" Another individual he wasn't keen on in Trilby's vicinity.

"Jagan? No. He probably figures he has time, knowing we've got a trike to Rumor."

"Not if someone else is dictating his timetable." He'd mulled over Trilby's earlier comments on Jagan's transmit. It did look like someone was feeding the man his lines.

"Do you think they'll try to intercept this ship?"

It was a possibility he'd considered, after learning of the sudden negotiations with the trade cartels. It was also why he'd ordered Mitkanos to have the weapons systems on a cold standby. No heat signature to pick up. But ready. Even though Grantforth had no way of knowing their exact location.

"Stage an ambush before we reach Saldika? It would surprise me. You know your answers to him show a Port Balaran code." Courtesy of the Mitkanos family and a touch of Rhis's wizardry. "More likely between Saldika and Rumor. 'Sko activity, if that's the route they take, is more prevalent there."

It wouldn't be a true kill order, he knew. They'd want the ship's nav banks intact. And her captain alive. They'd do a ram-boarding. Just like they had with *Bella's Dream*.

He had every intention of letting them have the altered nav banks. He'd kill every last one of them if they even looked in Trilby's direction.

Trilby tilted her head, peered at the data on the desk screen. "Is that Hana's report?"

Jankova had performed a thorough analysis on a small section of the Herkoid data from the *Venture*. With the change in schedule, there hadn't been time for her to do more. He nodded. "Your Black Star route integrated with the old charts from the *Nalika Gemma*." Old, but not old enough. Twenty-five years, with sections going back twenty-seven. "It is a place to start," he said.

"Agreed. Can I have my chair back?"

A small smile crossed his lips. The five days wouldn't be a total waste if he could enjoy himself with Trilby. He let a thick Zafharin accent lace his words. "You may share it with me."

"And you may get out of it, now." She mimicked his accent, wrinkled her nose at him. Her tone was light and teasing. Very much the Trilby he missed. Very much the Trilby he wanted to find again.

"Come to the ready room, then." *Shadow's Quest* had a small one, complete with workstations, at the opposite end of the corridor. "Work with me. We can trade a few wogs-and-weemlies."

He could tell immediately she didn't like his suggestion. He'd only been thinking of the camaraderie they'd shared on her ship. She was remembering, probably, what he'd done to her primaries.

She stood, dismissed his suggestion with a shrug. "Dallon's using the ready room. Go work with him."

Dallon. So Patruzius was Dallon now. Or had been for a while, judging from the teasing going on in the corridor. He reached for his lightpen. Tap. Tap. Tap.

She leaned over the desk, snatched the pen from his fingers. "Get out of my chair, Tivahr. I've got work to do. And I don't need an amateur drummer in my ear when I do it."

He saw his chance, wasn't about to let it pass him by. He stood, feigning a grab for his pen. His hands found her shoulders instead. He pulled her onto the narrow desktop as he sat down on it, covered her mouth with his own when she started to protest.

She wrenched her face to the side. "Damn you!"

She swore softly at him, tried to pull back from his kisses, but was off-balance and ended up sprawling awkwardly on one hip on the desktop. He yanked her against him, one arm solidly against her back, the other threading into her hair.

He had no intention of letting her go until he wiped all thoughts of Dallon Patruzius from her mind, until he branded her once again with his own heat, his own scent. He kissed her through her squirmings, through her hands pushing ineffectively against his shoulders, trying to break his hold on her.

Then her struggles ceased, her body arching against his. Her scent of powder and flowers intoxicated him. She nuzzled her face into his shoulder. He held her tightly, trailed kisses down her neck.

"Trilby-*chenka* . . . ow!"

She bit him, hard, sinking her teeth right through his shirt into his shoulder.

He jerked backward just enough to see her grin of triumph.

He was about to kiss that too, when the office comm pinged.

She twisted abruptly out of his arms, leaned in front of him, and tapped the flashing box on the desk screen. "Elliot." She sounded more than a bit breathless.

"Farra here. I, oh—!" Farra Rimanava's face tilted on the screen to match Trilby's odd angle.

"I'm on the other side of the desk. Wait." She swiveled the screen around. "What've you got?"

Rhis rested one hand on her waist, out of Rimanava's line of sight. She tried to push it away but he caught her hand, held it, knowing she wasn't about to get into any further wrestling match with him as long as the screen was on.

"I am checking through this septi's freighter schedule at Saldika. The data is now just in. Logs show a GGA wide-body scheduled in depot. First time"— Farra glanced back at her data—"in four months."

Coincidence? Rhis looked over Trilby's shoulder. Gods, he hated coincidences. "On-loading or off?"

"Off-loading, sir. But I do not know what. She is Conclave. Manifest details are not public—"

"Resource code," Trilby cut in. "Two alphas, one numeric. Right after their docking-bay assignment."

"EV-Seven."

"Spare or replacement parts for enviro systems," Trilby said. "Could be anything from link cables to containers of filters. Not a real profitable item for a wide-body. Short-haulers usually get those small runs. Or they piggy-back them to something else."

Farra nodded. "Very true. Does not feel right to me either."

"Send the whole schedule to the ready room." Rhis slid off the desktop, turning the screen with him as he did so.

"Aye, sir." Farra's image blinked off.

He held his hand out to Trilby. She flashed him a narrow-eyed look and hopped down from the desk. There was a telltale blush of color on her cheeks. She may not have wanted to respond to his kisses, but her body had.

He took that as a small point in his favor, for now. Changed the subject to the more pressing concerns. They had time, yet, for personal things. A deuce, then a trike.

He palmed open the office door. "Why would GGA use a wide-body for enviro parts?"

"They don't. Wide-bodies have a lot of mass, use a lot of fuel. Bulky as hell." She followed him into the corridor, her hands clasped firmly behind her back, as if she didn't want to chance brushing against him. "They're for moving big things. Prefab housing domes. The military likes them for moving armored ground tanks, like P-Ninety-fives."

He knew what the Conclave's platoon tanks looked like. Massive, turreted, heavily plated. He could house four fighters in the same bay as—

He stopped, grabbed her arm. "How many cargo bays does a GGA wide-body have?"

She shook him off, stepped back. "Six, if it's B-class. Four, if it's F-class. Why?"

"You tell me. How many 'Sko fighters could a wide-body haul?"

He saw her eyes widen, saw her mouth open in disbelief then close quickly, as if to let the words escape would damn them all.

"No," she said finally, sounding clearly unconvinced by her own denial. "They couldn't. Someone would notice on off-load. Customs inspectors, dockhands. Come on, Tivahr, you can't believe they could sneak—"

"Who said they're off-loading them on Saldika? Or any port? Why not drop them into the lanes, those lanes that Herkoid loved to use, and then continue on to their scheduled destination with the small, easily movable cargo of enviro parts?"

"Shit." She said the word softly, almost under her breath, then bolted down the corridor and squeezed through the parting doors to the ready room. "Dallon!"

Rhis strode after her. He stepped through the still-open doors. Trilby was in a seat at the end of the table and already had Farra on screen.

"Both of you, listen to me. I don't want to repeat it twice." She glanced at Rhis as he sat next to her. "Three times," she amended. "Yavo, you listening?"

"Here." Yavo's voice came from behind Farra's image. They were both on bridge duty.

"GGA might be hauling something other than enviro parts in that wide-body. Farra, pull from Saldika all GGA wide-bodies that logged through there in the past four—"

"Six," Rhis said.

"Six months. Then, Yavo, I need the same from your people on Balara. I also need arrival times and, especially, any delay advisories."

"Anything else, Captain?" Farra asked.

"Not for now. Thanks." Trilby tapped off the screen, looked at Rhis.

"They could also just figure their delay for the drop-off into the ETA," he told her. It's what he would do. Consistently late arrivals would eventually raise someone's curiosity. If GGA were doing what he suspected they were, they couldn't afford questions.

"Someone want to clue me in?" Patruzius asked.

Rhis swiveled toward him. "Grantforth's using wide-bodies to transport low-volume cargo across the border."

"Unprofitable."

"Unless they're transporting more than cargo." Rhis explained his theory briefly. Patruzius's previous experience with the freighter industry didn't require more than that.

Trilby tapped her fingers on Rhis's arm, drawing

his attention. "Bogus arrival times. You said they'd just schedule later ETAs . . ."

That's where their discussion had left off when Patruzius interrupted. He nodded.

"But they can't alter their departure. I know—*we* know," she made a small gesture toward Patruzius, "pretty accurately how long it would take a fully loaded wide-body to go from Rumor, or even Quivera, to Saldika. Or an empty one, for that matter. I should be able to pick up departure times, or at least out-system transits at the border beacons on my side of the zone. Then compare that to their arrivals."

"Without alerting the Conclave government?" Patruzius leaned forward. "You can't be positive Grantforth doesn't have someone watching for a pull on that data."

"The government," Trilby told him, folding her hands in front of her screen, "isn't the only one who tags that data." She arched her eyebrows slightly, looked at him with a patient expression, as if waiting for comprehension to dawn.

"In the Empire, the border beacons are all military," Rhis said, puzzled.

But Patruzius was nodding in agreement with Trilby. Rhis damned his own lack of familiarity with the commercial freighter industry. And the too-slick supply-ship captain's experience in it. It put Patruzius and Trilby on the same side of the fence, if only for a moment. He didn't like that at all.

Patruzius rapped his fist against his forehead. "Sorry. My lapse. Your Intersystem Commerce Department—"

"Sends all their data to the Freight Traders' Union as well. And as a member of IFCA—"

"Independent Freighter Captains' Association," Patruzius told Rhis.

"I'm aware of that," he snapped, fingers drumming lightly on the table. He'd just recently paid Trilby's outstanding dues, amending her license to Vanur Transport.

"As a member," Trilby continued, "I have a right to that data. For marketing purposes, of course."

"What's the downtime?" Rhis knew that if ships' movements across the border were collected only once a month, it might not be useful at this point. At least, not for this current "coincidence."

"A cycle," she said. "Twenty-four to twenty-six hours, depending on how you define your day. The FTU harvests the lists every shift change, then it's massaged and sent to their offices at all the ports and depots. At the worst, we'd be a deuce behind realtime if someone's late in posting it."

"Posting it?" The Zafharin military was an integral part of the Imperial government. Rhis wasn't used to the idea that what he considered government data might be hanging out there for all to see.

"Posting it," she told him. "FTU has a link in their grid. But I can get IFCA's link easier, hit their archives, backdate my autograb command. I should be able to get the past four to six months in a couple hours."

"Do it," he ordered, but she was already saying another word. A word that he didn't like.

"If . . ." She hesitated.

Bloody hell. What now? "If?"

"If the *Venture*'s comm pack still has my authorization codes. If they were lost in my little encounter," she smiled thinly, "then I've got to pick up a link from someone else through their code."

"Patruzius, get what you can from Rimanava and Mitkanos." Rhis stood. "Captain Elliot and I have to go perform some last-minute surgery."

Trilby recognized the tangled mass of data on her office screen as something that used to be her main comm-pack structure. Programs filled with direct links and passwords that facilitated the flow of information every time she made port or accessed a major beacon in transit. And that uploaded to her, simultaneously, everything she needed to know to get to her next run: changes in transit schedules, alerts on ion storms, new tax structures for certain classes of freight. Everything IFCA and the government thought she should know.

All, at the moment, totally unreadable.

She pointed her lightpen at the screen. "How'd you grab this?" She thought she knew but wanted to hear Tivahr's explanation. Wanted to keep him focused on the problem at hand and not that they were alone again in her office.

He leaned against the edge of her desk, one hand on the back of her chair. "Remember that invasive filter we discussed?"

So. Imperial technology wasn't flawless. She suppressed a grin of satisfaction and nodded. "That's what I thought you did. Tried it through an internal link, right?"

"Obviously it skewed a few things."

"Obviously you forget that competition for contracts is tough in my neighborhood. That same captain that's buying you beers is also pumping you for information on your runs, your agent's setup. And probably has some jumpjockey trying to tap into your ship's logs at that very moment. Which is why he's got you off ship and buying you beers in the first place." She shot a narrow-eyed glance up at him. "You're military. You're supposed to be used to espionage."

"You had a trap set?"

"We all have traps set. And we change trap keys at random. You never know who some dockhand's sister-in-law might work for." She tapped at the keypad, segued in a line of alphanumerics. The data on the screen shifted but was still muddled.

"But I had your primaries—" Tivahr began.

"Which I changed after I left Degvar. Of course." She scanned for a familiar line in the data, saw it, froze it with a tap of her lightpen. She entered the final sequence and this time permitted herself a wide grin at his hushed "Well, I'll be damned."

"We can pick up that FTU data now."

Or rather, Trilby knew as she entered the request into the ship's systems, she could reactivate her link to the grid. Hopefully they'd have something to work with in ten to twelve hours.

For now it was back to a waiting game. And Tivahr seemed intent to spend it by her side. She didn't want him there, didn't want to be with him any more than she absolutely had to. "Why don't you check and see if Dallon's got something more?"

"Patruzius knows where to find us if he needs us."

He wasn't taking the hint. "I've got work to do, now that I know you rescued my old files."

"I can help."

"No. Leave me alone, Tivahr." She jerked her chair around, tried to unsuccessfully to dislodge his hand.

"What are you so afraid of?" There was a quiet note in his voice that didn't match the tension in his body, the rigidness of his arm that kept her facing him.

You! She wanted to throw that at him. *I'm afraid of you.* But that wasn't quite the truth. More so, she knew that admission would open a flood of other questions, requests for clarification on her part.

She didn't want to say out loud why she was afraid of him. It was hard enough dealing with that in the relentless litany in her mind. And in her heart.

Something about Khyrhis Tivahr reached her, touched her deeply. She thought maybe it was because she still saw flashes of Rhis Vanur in him from time to time. But over the past few days she discovered it was more than that.

It wasn't the Rhis she saw in Khyrhis, but the Khyrhis in Rhis.

He'd always been there. Remote, aloof, in control. That was the unwavering dedication she'd seen in Rhis from the beginning, the competence. That rock-solid something that said to her, *Lean on me. I'll never fail you. I'll always be there.*

No jumpjockey gossip ever tagged Senior Captain Tivahr as unreliable. Or a quitter. Or a coward. If anything, it was acknowledged that Tivahr the Terrible didn't give up. *Impossible* wasn't in his vocabulary.

It was Khyrhis—not Rhis—who'd sidelined his physical pain to get the *Careless Venture* up and running. It was Khyrhis—not Rhis—who had flawlessly, expertly avoided the attacking 'Sko fighters.

And it was Khyrhis—not Rhis—who'd admitted to her that no one would believe he'd taken Trilby, a beautiful air sprite, to bed. Or rather, that such an air sprite had gone, willingly.

Mitkanos thought the *Razalka*'s captain had forced her into his bed. Dallon, Lucho, and Leesa assumed he took her ship by force as well. That fit with the image of *the* Captain Tivahr. He entered a briefing room or officers' lounge and chatter died, shoulders straightened, faces became serious.

The competent, dedicated, tireless Tivahr the Terrible. He wore those traits like impenetrable armor.

But Trilby's gotten through, and that's what scared her. She'd gotten through, and when she did, it was Rhis who had taught her to say *yav cheron*.

She avoided looking at him. "I'm not afraid. I'm busy. Now go away." She reached for the screen, tabbed down a line of data.

She heard his deep growl of frustration, like a rumbling sigh, then her chair shook slightly. He pushed himself to his feet.

She stared blankly at the screen after her office door slid closed behind him. A deuce to go to Saldika. Another trike at least after that. And then who knew how many more runs until they uncovered what GGA was doing with the 'Sko?

The last thing she needed was all that time with Tivahr. The last thing she needed was to fall in love again.

21

Saldika Terminal was noisy, crowded. So she didn't know he was there until he grabbed her, clamping his mouth, hot and wet, on hers, his tongue thrusting like some kind of convulsing snake. She heard Tivahr's harsh growl come up behind her, a string of untranslatable Zafharish words that questioned everything from Jagan Grantforth's lack of legitimate parentage to the location and inadequate size of his reproductive organs.

Only much more graphically.

She pushed him away and fought the urge to wipe her mouth on her sleeve. "Jagan. What a . . . surprise."

The sandy-haired man grinned lopsidedly down at her. "I've always loved surprising you, little darling."

Little darling. She'd forgotten he called her that. It used to bring a thrill to her senses. Now it only chilled her, colder than the snowy landscape outside the terminal's wide-spaced windows.

It had just started snowing when she brought

Shadow's Quest in on approach, not quite an hour ago. Cargo Hangar 47-L was covered and heated, a necessity on a frigid world like Chevienko.

Customs inspectors, thanks to Mitkanos's connections, were almost as warm as the large hangar. Ten minutes later they'd hopped a pod to the main terminal, intent on finding out what Grantforth Galactic Amalgamated was up to.

But it looked as if Grantforth had found them. A trike earlier than anticipated too.

"I didn't expect to find you here," Trilby said. But maybe she should have. Admiral Vanushavor's message detailed an unexpected move by Secretary Grantforth and the 'Sko. Yet she still had a hard time believing Jagan was in on any kind of conspiracy. Flirtations were more his style than political machinations.

Jagan's gaze traveled past her shoulder, then up and down. Tivahr was behind her. That would be the up. Mitkanos was next to him. A slight down in height. Off to her right, she heard Farra's lilting laugh over the chatter of freighter crew and dock techs moving hurriedly through the terminal corridor. Out of the corner of her eye she saw Farra and Dallon standing in line at a nearby newsstand that displayed local newsdisks the Imperial grid often didn't carry.

"I couldn't wait to see you." Jagan reached for her hand but Trilby turned away, hastily made introductions as Tivahr and Mitkanos flanked her.

"Yavo Mitkanos, Rhis Vanur. This is Jagan Grantforth, of GGA."

"Vanur, eh? You speak Standard?" Jagan had evidently caught, but didn't understand, Tivahr's opening diatribe moments before.

"The basics, yes," Tivahr said.

"*Vad,*" Mitkanos replied.

Both men spoke more than the basics, Trilby knew, but they wanted Jagan to think otherwise.

Jagan stepped closer to Trilby, held his hand out to Tivahr. "So you're the one funding your own little shipping company. Well, I for one am glad to see it. Risk-takers, that's who make a name in this universe." His smile was picture-perfect.

Trilby had forgotten how Jagan could do that, sound friendly and open while at the same time delivering small cuts and barbs. *Little shipping company.* A cut buried under the hearty professional patter of an entrepreneur.

If Tivahr picked up on it, she couldn't tell. It was Mitkanos who responded first, his accent even more pronounced than usual. "True. Very true. There are big, how you say, profits to be made now between Empire and Conclave. Little companies, as you put it, can open doors for you."

Jagan laughed, clasped Mitkanos on the arm. "And we want those doors open, don't we? Profit's profit. Credits glitter as bright in a palace as they do in a whorehouse." He winked at Tivahr.

"I bow to your knowledge of that." Tivahr's tone was clipped. She felt his hand rest on her shoulder in a move that was clearly proprietary. Maybe he was seeing the same Jagan she was, beneath the veneer.

Something dark flashed briefly through Jagan's eyes, but then Dallon and Farra stepped out of the crowd. Trilby shrugged off Tivahr's hand and introduced them.

"Market news," Dallon held up a thin disk for Jagan to see, then handed it to Mitkanos.

"Right on top of things," Jagan said. "That's good to see. That's what GGA needs now. Someone who knows trade on this side of the zone."

He sounded so sincere. Trilby could almost believe this was a genuine business meeting and not something with a deeper, hidden agenda. And one that possibly involved the 'Sko.

She studied the man standing next to her. He was still handsome, in his expensively tailored dark suit. Though now she clearly saw signs of stress and dissipation. His blue eyes were puffy and his usually well-maintained tan faded.

He seemed to notice her scrutiny, shoved his hands in his pockets, and tilted his head down toward her. His expression was sheepish.

"I really need to speak with you, Tril." There was a notable hesitancy in his voice. "I've made some mistakes. I'd like to change that."

"Jagan, I—" Next to her, Tivahr shifted slightly. She glanced at him, saw his eyes narrow. He'd heard, or heard enough. Best to keep the talk to business. They had to find out what was going on with Grantforth, and she didn't need the *Razalka*'s captain bringing his male ego online. "Your transmits said you were interested in a shipping contract."

"I am. But—" His glance went up again. Tivahr.

"*Dasjon* Vanur makes the decisions in that regard. I just fly the ship." She motioned toward one end of the corridor. "Should we find a bar and sit and discuss things? Or do you want to see *Shadow's Quest* first?"

He seemed to finally understand that he had only two options right now: business or business. The only choice she gave him was location.

"A bar sounds good. Better. I, uh, I could use a drink. You up for a beer or two?" Jagan gave a short nod to Dallon, Farra, and Mitkanos. He was trying, Trilby noticed, not to look at Tivahr.

She wondered briefly if Jagan recognized the *Razalka*'s senior captain. No, he would've said something, she was sure of that. She heard Dallon's enthusiastic response and a grunt from Tivahr.

"I know pub of decent quality, not far," Mitkanos offered.

"Lead the way, my friend. And, of course, I'm buying." Jagan held up one hand. "Won't hear any arguments about it."

Trilby had a feeling that if Tivahr had his way there'd be plenty of arguments, the least of which concerning who was paying for the beer.

The bar's name was also its location: Seventeen Blue. Saldika Terminal's corridors were color-tagged with a wide stripe on the floor and another on a wall, designating Blue and Yellow for commercial-freighter access, Red and Gray for passenger-ship travelers. The pod deposited them in Yellow, where Jagan had found them, not far from the intersection of Blue. Mitkanos was right in that it was only a short walk. But flanked on one side by Jagan and the other by Tivahr, Trilby felt as if she were on a forced march rather than a leisurely stroll in search of a beer.

The pub was T-shaped, the entrance narrow, but it opened to clusters of tables on the left and right. Farra spotted an empty, round table on the left, and there was a moment of jockeying for position when both Jagan and Tivahr made sure they sat next to

Trilby. Mitkanos reached for the center of the table, tabbed up the menu on a cylindrical holoscreen. Flyboy's didn't have such high-tech luxuries, nor did it have liquid-image walls that rippled colors and shapes matching the cadence of the music. The soft but upbeat tune filtered down through a ceiling covered intermittently with large panels of blue fabric.

Trilby looked around. Definitely not a freighter bar. At least not a freighter-crew bar. Those patrons in uniform looked like officers. Those out of uniform looked well paid and well fed. She leaned back in her chair, encountered Tivahr's fingers on her shoulder.

She glanced at him. He raised one eyebrow slightly. She sighed.

A 'droid server wheeled up, announced that the Iceberg was the drink of the day. Trilby understood but let Mitkanos translate the Zafharish for Jagan's sake, then glanced around the table. "Perhaps just beer for now?"

"Chevienko brews a good red ale," Dallon said, pointing to the cylindrical menu.

Mitkanos glanced at Jagan, who nodded. "Sounds fine by me. Two pitchers to start?" He handed the 'droid his credit chip while Mitkanos relayed the order.

"Got our banking interests already started in the Empire," he commented when the 'droid returned the chip to him. "GGA's always been aggressive in new territories, you know. Not as aggressive, of course, as your Imperial Fleet." He chuckled. "But then, you didn't win the war."

"No, peace was declared by a mutual treaty," Dallon put in.

Jagan tilted his head, seemed to look at Dallon as if

for the first time. "You speak Standard very well—Patruzy, is it?"

"Patruzius. Dallon Patruzius. I've spent a good amount of time in the shipping lanes. Been to Marbo, Port Rumor when I worked with Fennick IE."

"And now you're with Vanur, eh? Good move." Jagan turned toward Tivahr. "Got yourself a real fine captain in Trilby here. I hope you know that."

"I do."

"She knows Gensiira like no one else."

"I value Trilby more than you know, *Dasjon* Grantforth."

"Jagan. Just Jagan. After all, we're going to be partners."

Tivahr's smile was tight. "That is what we are here to discuss."

"Business first. Then later," Jagan reached over, patted Trilby's hand, "time for some pleasure. Tril and I go back a long way. That's why this is so important to me."

Tivahr leaned forward as Trilby pulled her hands away from Jagan into her lap. "What can Vanur Transport do for GGA?"

Jagan sat back, crossed his arms over his chest. "Heard some good things about you, you know. Reliable. Honest. Even here, GGA has a way of checking reputations. And that's important to us. We have our own reputation to consider, especially in something as new as this."

Trilby listened to the words flow from Jagan's mouth as if they were coated with oil. What an unbelievable liar he was! No. A very believable liar. He had the right tone, the right demeanor, the right smile. His only problem was the facts. Vanur Transport was totally fictitious and didn't even exist two septis ago, except for the falsified history created by Tivahr and Mitkanos. She knew damned well he hadn't checked out anything more than the fact that the *Venture*'s nav banks were now in the *Quest*'s.

"But we're not the only ones who know this," Jagan was saying. "That's why two things are important at this point: one, that we be the first. And two, that we be the fastest. GGA was built on efficiency and prompt delivery times. Once we bring a long-hauler into a depot, we need those goods out and on their way."

"Not always that easy," Dallon said, "when the workable routes between the Empire and the Conclave are so few."

"Right. My point exactly." Jagan nodded. "Now, Tril here—"

But the 'droid server rolled up with a tray and two pitchers, and for the next few minutes conversation stilled as beer was poured and frosty mugs were passed around the table.

Jagan took a large mouthful, then continued. "You know our problem. As my friend Dallon over there said, because of past political incompatibilities, trade routes are few. There's already complaints about delays at the major jumpgates in Gensiira. And more problems with faulty guidance beacons. Seems your technology just doesn't like ours sometimes." He laughed.

Trilby glanced at Tivahr. His face had a feral smile she'd seen before.

"But my little darling here," Jagan motioned to Trilby, "well, I know she's got some tricks up her sleeve. I worked some runs with her, you know. She can get from Point A to Point B quicker than anyone I know, when she wants to. Even with her old ship. Not the fastest thing in the lanes."

"*Shadow's Quest* is an Endurance C-two that I have personally modified," Tivahr said.

"You an engineer, then?" Jagan asked.

"I have considerable experience in that area, yes."

"You ever see her old ship?" Jagan's question would've sounded offhand, if Trilby hadn't known exactly what he was searching for. Her "map files." She held back a snicker.

"Yes." Tivahr paused. "I know her intimately." He stressed the last word.

Jagan shifted in his chair. Clearly, he was catching an undercurrent and wasn't sure what to do with it.

"*Dasjon* Vanur," Trilby said, making sure she stressed the formality of the Zafharish title, "worked with me on some last-minute upgrades to the *Venture* just before she was destroyed." She wished Tivahr would remember their primary objective: find out what was going on with GGA. Whatever relationship she did—or did not—have with him was not an issue here.

"She loved that ship," Jagan told Tivahr. "Put everything she had into her. Five years, wasn't it, darling?" He smiled at Trilby. "We had such good times, so many memories—"

"She took serious structural damage, but we were able to recover most of her databanks." *Let's get to the point here,* Trilby pleaded. Jagan's false sentimentality was starting to turn her stomach. "*Dasjon* Vanur and I amended all her data to the *Quest*. What the old *Venture* could do, the new ship can do even better."

"That's just what I wanted to hear." Jagan beamed and raised his mug. "This signals the start of a beautiful and profitable relationship."

The second pitcher of beer was poured, and numbers flew back and forth across the table. Percentages based on turnaround times. The cost of insurance recognized by both the Empire and the Conclave. Dock fees. Tivahr and Mitkanos lapsed into Zafharish for much of it, with Dallon translating. Trilby followed it all but let Jagan think she understood very little, save for *dharjas taf, viek*—cold beer, please.

Jagan drained the last of the ale from his mug. "I've got ten containers here in port, if you're interested."

Tivahr glanced at Mitkanos. The older man nodded.

"I am," Tivahr said. "To Port Rumor?"

"No. Syar Colonies. But for certain reasons, I want to avoid the beacons at Marbo."

Trilby saw Dallon tilt his head in interest. Her conversations with him over the past deuce told her he knew that many Marbo personnel had strong ties to Norvind. And that GGA wouldn't want their competitor to know what they were doing, just yet. Plus, if they had to deal with poke-nosies, better the ones at a GGA-friendly depot, like Syar.

At least, she hoped that was Jagan's reasoning.

"We can do that," Trilby said.

But Tivahr was frowning. "Syar is a seven-day run—"

"A full septi," Trilby corrected him.

"—in my ship. A long-hauler could do it in five. Why do you need us for that?"

Trilby wanted to kick him. Jagan was letting them

in to GGA, which was their sole purpose here. Trust Tivahr to want to be a stickler for regulations and details. She shot him a narrowed glance. "Because a long-hauler can't bypass Marbo like we can."

Jagan chuckled. "My little darling knows what she's talking about, Vanur."

Tivahr's face was expressionless. "You are willing to pay for the extra fuel, then?"

"I'm willing to pay whatever it takes to get from here to the Colonies."

Tivahr made a lazy gesture with his hand toward Dallon, posed a question in Zafharish. His voice was light. But his words, as Trilby translated them, were not. "The bastard is setting us up for something, and it's not just to avoid Marbo. Am I wrong, or is a run to Syar a bit unusual for a small ship?"

Dallon's smile was easy and, Trilby knew, false. "For a smuggler, no. But I can't see GGA working contraband. He has an agenda. I just don't know what it is."

"Problems?" Jagan directed the question to Dallon.

"We haven't worked that deep into the Conclave yet," Dallon replied smoothly in Standard. "Captain Elliot's clearance codes will get us past Marbo. But we'll need an authorization packet for Syar transmitted to us before we get there, or someone might realize we didn't go through Marbo."

Jagan answered Dallon with a wave of his hand. "Not required. You'll be flying GGA's flag. Plus, you'll have a GGA officer on board."

"A GGA officer?" Tivahr asked tightly.

Oh, no, Trilby thought. *No, no, no. Don't tell me. Don't say it.*

Jagan beamed. "Me."

* * *

Trilby leaned back in the captain's chair, listened to Farra at communications as she went over schedules with the portmaster's office looking for a preferable departure slot. While Trilby's command of Zafharish had improved, it wasn't sufficient for the kind of negotiations going on now on the bridge of *Shadow's Quest*. Vanur Transport not only had to amend their ETD but arrange for cargo transfer as well.

Tivahr, in the copilot's seat, turned a lightpen over and over in his fingers in undisguised irritation.

At least he wasn't drumming it on the console.

Trilby's ship badge pinged. She tapped at the square emblem on her collar. "Elliot."

"Patruzius here, Captain. We've got Grantforth's baggage. He's checking out of the overnight now. We should be back on board in thirty minutes, if the pods are on time."

"No rush," Tivahr growled out under his breath.

For once, Trilby was in complete agreement with him. "Acknowledged. Farra's finalizing a departure for early tomorrow right now. Looks like 0700's a go."

"I'll tell Grantforth. But there's something else you should know."

Trilby saw Tivahr straighten in his seat, the lightpen stilling in his hand. "Problems?" she asked.

"Not exactly. But while Yavo and I were waiting in the overnight's lobby, the local 'cast showed a newsvid. The Conclave announced that they're setting up meetings to finalize trade agreement with the Beffa cartel."

"Acknowledged. Thanks for the info, Dallon. Elliot out." She tapped off the badge, angled herself toward Tivahr. "You think Jagan knew about this?"

Tivahr thought a moment. "It would explain why he showed up here. We knew from his last transmit he wanted your nav banks. Now it looks like he wants to be the one who delivers the data. Perhaps Garold's deal with the 'Sko hinges on that. And if he is Dark Sword, that data will lead us right back to him."

It was hard for Trilby to believe that something she had could be so important to the likes of the 'Sko. Or be involved in destroying the career of Garold Grant-forth. But then, Shadow had often hinted that he had ways of making big money someday. He just died before he could explain what he had intended to do.

On their deuce run to Port Saldika, Trilby had examined the old star routes Shadow pulled from Herkoid. A few she'd known about. Many she didn't. She could definitely see their utility—especially, as Tivahr pointed out, their utility to an invading faction that wanted to move undetected. She didn't have to read between the lines as he, Dallon, and Mitkanos pored over the data. If the Zafharin had those charts, the war might've ended differently three years ago.

Or, at least, things would've favored the Zafharin for a while. But not forever. Even she could see that. Sooner or later, the Conclave would figure out that the old routes had been resurrected. Trilby wasn't the only one alive who still knew they existed. Thousands of people had worked for Herkoid.

But the only data the 'Sko wanted was that snatched by Shadow, the data she and Carina had. And aside from the obvious, neither she nor her ship-mates could yet figure out why.

"But this does," Tivahr said, turning the lightpen

between his fingers again, "make me feel somewhat better about having our friend Jagan on board."

Trilby frowned. "Why?"

"Because at least I know they're not planning to have the 'Sko ambush us between here and Syar." He rapped the pen twice against the console. "He's our babysitter, our guarantee of safety, if you will. It's only after he gets us to the Colonies that I am now worried about."

Trilby was too, though she said nothing for now. Tivahr's mission—the one that had dropped him in her lap on Avanar—had taken him from the Syar Colonies to Szedcafar. Now they were headed back to Syar again. She hoped Szed wasn't the next stop on their travel plans. The 'Sko were even more serious about finders keepers than she was.

22

Loading 'droids and antigrav pallets buzzed under and around *Shadow's Quest*. Trilby leaned against a set of servo-stairs and thought wistfully of Dezi. But it was Jagan's voice she heard, soft in her ear.

"You don't need to supervise the loading, Tril. How about you and I hop the next pod to the terminal, do some dinner, catch up on old times?"

Trilby turned. With all the clank and clatter, she hadn't heard Jagan come up behind her. Last she'd seen him, he was arranging his luggage in the crews' quarters, a deck below the bridge. Then Dallon was going to show him how to use the comm terminal in the *Quest*'s small mess so he could send out his contracts to GGA legal on Bagrond. She'd left the ship purposely to get away from him. But now here he was, still in his expensive dark blue suit and pale blue band-collared shirt. All very trendy. All completely out of place in a starfreighter cargo hangar.

She crossed her arms over her chest, her fingers

resting against the new ship's patches on her sleeves. "All of us will go over in a bit. But if you're hungry, go on ahead. Dallon will give you a ship badge. We'll call you when we're on our way."

The eyes that studied her face spoke of a different kind of hunger. He patted his left breast pocket. "Already got one. How about the others catch up with us later?"

"Thanks, but no, Jagan." There was the loud clang of a cargo-bay door shutting. She turned away, grateful for the distraction. She had no intention of going anywhere with Jagan Grantforth, alone. It was bad enough he'd be on the ship for a septi, tolerable only because, as Tivahr said, he was their guarantee of safety. At least until they got to the Colonies.

Tivahr and Mitkanos were talking to a loading 'droid across the hangar. They had their backs to her, but as if he felt her watching him, or as if, even more, he knew who stood beside her, Tivahr looked over his shoulder in her direction. He reached for Mitkanos's arm, leaned over, and spoke to the burly man.

Then he pivoted on his heels, heading toward her. He wore the same dark gray service jacket she did, the same type of dark gray flight suit. Basic, functional freighter clothing. Definitely not trendy.

Yet on him it looked somehow . . . different. As if the fabric knew it should also bear a set of bright captain's stars. Five of them. Senior captain.

"You don't want to go, or he won't let you?" There was a distinct peevishness in Jagan's tone. The last time Trilby had heard that, he was saying, *Mother always said . . .*

She glanced back at Jagan. "How's your mother? And while we're on the subject, how's Zalia?"

"You don't understand—"

"You're right, I don't," she snapped.

He dropped his gaze, chewed for a moment on his lower lip, looking decidedly uncomfortable. She softened her tone, even though she knew he deserved her anger. "You have your life. I have mine. Let's keep it that way, okay?"

"And is he, this Vanur, part of your life now?" He jerked his chin in the direction of the man striding closer.

"He owns the ship. And he's . . . a friend." She found herself struggling with the word. But she didn't know what term to use in place of it. "He understands my goals." That much was true. Khyrhis Tivahr understood her love of her ship, the lure of star travel, the freedom of life in the lanes. And her need to find out what happened to Carina, whatever the cost.

"He's probably just using you, Tril. I mean, look at the facts. He's got one ship, maybe a little spare money or some investor he's bamboozled. And where'd you meet him—doing runs to Degvar, you said, right? You're out of your element. Hell, you don't even speak the language. Then, after your ship's attacked, he's there with this offer. Am I right?"

As off base as Jagan's suppositions were, they still rankled her. Possibly because, while the facts were wrong, she remembered Tivahr pretending to be Rhis Vanur. She had felt used. Bamboozled. She pushed the hurt away. "It really doesn't matter—"

"You let him fuck you before or after he offered you the job?"

Her closed fist cracked hard against his jaw before she was even aware she'd swung her arm.

Jagan staggered backward, his flailing arms tangling in the servo-stair railing. Heavy footsteps thudded quickly behind her, coming closer.

"You bitch!" Jagan tried to jerk his arm free of the metal stanchion. There was a slight ripping sound. "You Gods damned bitch!"

"Grantforth!" Tivahr shoved Trilby aside, grabbed a handful of Jagan's suit jacket. Jagan struggled to stand and push Tivahr away at the same time.

Trilby was breathing hard. She sucked on her raw knuckles and watched Jagan try ineffectively to wriggle out of Tivahr's grasp. Shit, but her hand hurt!

Still, hitting Jagan had felt so good.

"What's going on?" Tivahr bellowed at Jagan. He had a two-handed grasp on the man's suit. The front of the jacket pulled away from the long tear in the sleeve, revealing the lighter shirt underneath.

Jagan glared up at Tivahr. "Bitch hit me."

Tivahr looked back at Trilby, his dark eyes glittering dangerously. "Explain."

She took her hand out of her mouth. "It's personal."

"Personal." He clearly didn't like her response.

"Leave it go, Tiv—Vanur." In the heat of the moment, she almost said Tivahr. Damnation! She had to watch herself. She drew in a long, slow breath.

Tivahr let go of Jagan, releasing his hold on the fabric as if he'd touched something slimy. Jagan took a step to his right, but Tivahr's arm shot out, blocking him. "Wait. I am not through yet."

"Hey, friend." Jagan twisted his mouth into a frown. "I'm the victim here, remember? I'm also," and he raised his fingers to gingerly touch the darkening bruise on his chin, "your employer."

"A contract to haul freight doesn't give you the right to abuse someone," Tivahr said through clenched teeth. He lowered his arm.

"She hit me!"

"But I guarantee you provoked her."

Jagan stared past Tivahr, directly at Trilby. She made sure she met his gaze, head held high. If he knew what was good for him, he'd shut up now. Questioning Tivahr over his employment methods, and his relationship with her, just might get his other sleeve torn.

Jagan seemed to finally realize that as well. He dropped his gaze and studied the tips of his boots, or the streaks and stains on the hangar floor, for all Trilby knew. "Yeah, well, there was something between us at one time," he said when he looked up. "I'm sure she told you."

Tivahr said nothing, but Trilby felt, for the first time, something very frightening in his silence. It was a condemning, accusatory silence. She could imagine whole squadrons of ensigns quaking in their boots.

"Maybe I had it coming," Jagan said finally. He massaged his jaw. "We were a pretty hot item for a while. Guess she hasn't forgotten that." He voice held a note of bravado.

Trilby wanted to throw up. Or clock him again. She spun on her heels and stomped back toward the rampway.

Rhis watched Trilby head for the ship, then turned back to Jagan. "Stay away from her." It was clearly a command, not a request.

The blond-haired man shrugged. "It was just a little lover's spat. She'll get over it."

Rhis read Jagan's message loud and clear: *I had her first. I can take her back again.* If he didn't need Jagan to find out what GGA and the 'Sko were planning, he would've gladly thrown him across the hangar. In pieces.

But Jagan also, he knew, needed Trilby and the information from Trilby's ship. He'd have to make sure Jagan wasn't planning any late-night rendezvous to gain her cooperation.

"I will not repeat myself. You will stay away from her. Or I will have you confined to your cabin."

"You're not the captain. She is." Jagan dismissed him with a slanted glance, strode back toward the ship. Back toward Trilby.

In three steps Rhis was behind him, his hand clamped on Jagan's shoulder. "Where do you think you're going?"

Jagan jerked back. "To change my jacket. Friend. And then to get myself a drink." His fists clenched, then relaxed. He shrugged. "Since Tril's not interested, I'm sure I can find some sweet little thing who is."

Rhis saw the shift in mood, the way Jagan's gaze darted impatiently over his shoulder. The man's anger simmered just below the surface. Hell, Rhis was clearly provoking him. Stupidly. He could blow this whole mission if he weren't careful. Because provoking Grantforth he was. But Grantforth wasn't rising to the bait.

He wanted to. The tense set of his shoulders, the clenching of his fists, the way he bit off the ends of his words. The way "friend" sounded anything but friendly.

Jagan Grantforth wanted to fight almost as badly as Rhis wanted to fight with him. But something held him back. He had, as Patruzius noted, an agenda. Rhis felt that strongly now. Almost as strongly as something else: that agenda was based on fear.

Rhis deliberately took a step back, gave Jagan some space. "Chevienko has many long, cold nights. You should have no trouble to find some Saldikan lady looking to stay warm, no?"

Jagan seemed to accept that as the closest thing he was going to get to an apology. "That's my plan. We have a seven o'clock departure?"

"Correct. But you will not be needed on the bridge, so if you choose to sleep late—"

"Just as long as I'm not in the captain's cabin, right?" He laughed, but it had a brittle note.

In spite of all his training, all his mental chastisings, Rhis tensed visibly.

"Just kidding." Jagan raised his hands in mock self-defense. "It took me awhile, but I caught on, okay? You and Tril. Who am I to say anything about that? I mean, she's a decent piece of ass. Just be careful when you finally get bored with her." He rubbed his jaw. "She's got a mean right hook."

In pieces. Torn, shredded, dismembered, and strewn about the cargo hangar. Flattened into the grit-covered floor by the wheels of uncaring cargo 'droids. Rhis held on to that image of Jagan for a moment while he froze a smile onto his face.

No, better yet, he'd drag Grantforth back to the *Razalka* somehow. His ship had a specially designed training chamber with holosims that exactly duplicated the harsh, jagged outcroppings in the mountains on Stegor. He wouldn't even bring a weapon.

Just his fists. The mountain sands were red. He'd work on Jagan Grantforth until the man's body and the ground were virtually indistinguishable.

His forced smile became almost genuine. "I am glad we understand each other. And your advice is noted."

He let Jagan trudge back to the ship, unaccompanied. Let him think he trusted him, believed him, or, at least, understood him, man to man.

But he'd watch him, very carefully. Jagan had an agenda. And Trilby was but a small part of it.

Rhis waited five minutes before climbing the ramp to *Shadow's Quest*. By that time Jagan should be down on the crew deck. He touched the CLS panel to the right of the main air lock on the cargo level and keyed in a request for Trilby's location. She was in her quarters.

He tapped his ship badge. "Vanur to Captain Elliot."

"Elliot." She sounded tired. No doubt dealing with Jagan was a strain for her.

"It's Rhis. I'll be there in five minutes. I want to stop by the bridge first." And his quarters as well, but he didn't mention that. He tabbed off, without giving her a chance to say no.

He took the lift up, found Farra in her seat at communications, with a clear view through the forward viewports of everything that had transpired between Trilby, Jagan, and himself.

"Dasjon," she greeted him. They all knew not to use any other title while Jagan was on board. Just as they all knew to pretend to speak less Standard than they did, with Patruzius being the exception.

They also spoke to each other only in Zafharish.

"Everything's a go for 0700?" he asked.

"Affirmative, sir."

"And the loading?"

"Uncle Yavo's code-sealing the last of the containers in Hold Three now."

He nodded. "Dinner in an hour, my treat. I leave where to you and your uncle. Tell Patruzius too. We'll seal the ship and meet at the ramp at"—he glanced at the time stamp on her screen—"1845."

"And *Dasjon* Grantforth?"

"I believe he has alternate plans."

"Probably for the best." Farra grinned, then motioned out the forward viewport. "Our captain has good reflexes."

In Rhis's estimation, Trilby Elliot had many fine qualities, reflexes notwithstanding. He stood in front of her quarters, one hand hidden behind his back. He touched the palm pad on the side of the door with the other. It chimed softly.

The door slid open.

"Don't start with me." Her eyes were shadowed underneath. She'd doffed her gray service jacket. It hung haphazardly over the arm of the small couch in her sitting area.

He fought the desire to pull her into his arms, surround her pain with his hardness, his certainty that nothing would ever hurt her again. But he had something to give her first. "May I come in?"

She stepped aside, nodding, motioned him in.

He hesitated. Tension and fatigue wrapped around her like a suffocating cloak. His timing with his surprise was either perfect, or abysmal.

He pulled his hand from behind his back, held the

small, plush felinar out to her. Its red ribbon dangled through his fingers.

She gasped softly, reached for it, but at the last moment she hesitated. Brought her gaze up to his. He could see a light film of tears shimmering in her eyes.

He tried to smile. His throat felt tight. "I thought you might want this," he managed to get out.

Her fingers closed around the small toy that had decorated her bridge. "Thank you." She clutched it against her chest, glanced up at him again. There was a tinge of warmth in her eyes now, and a small flush of color on her cheeks. She sighed. "I mean that. Thank you."

The thin screen on the low table in front of her couch was activated. He glanced at it as he followed her into the room: Zafharish vocabulary lessons.

The small smile he permitted to play across his lips was nothing compared to the warmth that spread through his chest. He hoped that learning his language meant she wanted to stay in the Empire. With him. Maybe his timing with the toy was better than he'd realized.

She propped the plush felinar against one edge of the screen, picked up her empty coffee cup. "Want some? I was just going to get a refill." Her tone was light, but without any real energy behind it.

"*Yav chalkon gara reling, viek.*" He casually requested a cup of tea, trying to sound, not teacher to student, but as if speaking Zafharish to her were an ordinary occurrence. He wanted it to be.

She was already turning. "Yellow tea or that black—oh! Sorry." She shrugged. "I understand better than I answer."

He stepped closer. "It takes practice." He wrapped his fingers over hers as she held the cup.

She pulled away. "I'm surrounded with it here. But I'll probably forget it all once I get back to Port Rumor." She pushed her cup into the replicator, ordered coffee. "You never said: black tea or yellow?"

"Trilby-*chenka*—"

"Don't, please."

He was silent a moment, tried to read her discomfort in the straight line of her back, in the set of her shoulders. She was pushing him away again. "I'm not." Asking. Prying. Condemning. "Black tea is fine."

She keyed in the request.

He waited until she handed him the steaming cup. "We will have dinner off ship tonight, 1845. I told Farra to choose where," he added, when he realized his first comment sounded too much like an order. "Grantforth's already left, for places unknown."

She relaxed a little, sat down on the couch in front of the screen on the low table. Picked up the little felinar again, smoothed its fur. "I don't know if I'll last a septi without killing him." She tabbed off the screen. It slid from sight.

He grinned, eased down next to her on the couch. "You'd not lack help."

"The best the Imperial Fleet and *Stegzarda* have to offer?" She leaned back against the overstuffed cushions, a wry smile on her lips. It faded. "It's none of my business," she said after a moment, "but can I ask you something?"

He forced himself to relax, to ignore the one question he feared her asking. At least asking now, when things were so tenuous between them. He didn't need anything else to drive her away. Or make her look at him with disgust, as Malika had.

"Ask," he told her easily, as if his very life didn't hang in the balance.

"What's the problem between you and the *Stegzarda*?"

He soundlessly let out the breath he'd been holding. The *Stegzarda*? That's all she wanted to know? He felt as if, for once, he'd received a reprieve from his habitual spot on the divine shit list. "The *Stegzarda* are primarily ground and security forces. The Fleet patrols Imperial space. When it comes to certain outposts and stations, we share jurisdiction."

"I know that. But what's the problem? And don't tell me it's just common rivalry."

Oh. That. He turned the cup around in his hands. "It's rather complicated."

"Then just give me the basics. I can probably figure out the rest."

She'd been talking to Mitkanos. He could hear that clearly now in the even tone in her voice, could see it in the slight tilt of her chin. She'd been given an opinion, a strong opinion. He tried to keep his recital impartial.

"The *Stegzarda* base and academy are in the Yanir Quadrant. Have been for over two hundred fifty years. The Fleet was much smaller then. We didn't have ships with the long-range capabilities we do now. As the Fleet expanded, especially in the last ten, fifteen years, we rightfully took over jurisdiction in Yanir, as we did with all the outlying quadrants in the Empire."

"We?" she asked, raising one eyebrow.

He damned Mitkanos. "The *Razalka* was assigned to

Yanir. Our authority then superseded the *Stegzarda*'s."

His authority, actually. That had been almost ten years ago. He didn't regard the transfer of powers as one of the sterling moments in his career. Looking back, he knew he wouldn't have done things any differently. But they could have been handled better.

She was nodding. "So they'd been very efficiently taking care of their quadrant for, oh, two hundred or so years, and then you come in with your brand-new, shiny huntership and tell them you're in charge now."

"The transition was not without its share of problems." He hesitated, not really understanding why he needed to be honest with her, but he did. "And yes, looking back, I probably contributed to a few of them. Fleet has always valued results over diplomacy. Perhaps in that situation, too much so."

She nodded slowly.

He sucked in a short breath, continued: "I've been guilty for many years of letting my position, my rank, dictate who I am, how I act. When we took over in Yanir, I knew that emotions, pride in the *Stegzarda*, ran deep. Instead of working with that, finding compromises, I ignored it. It was wrong. How I handled it was wrong even though the desired results were achieved."

Another thoughtful nod. "Did you know Mitkanos then?"

"Only by reputation, service record." But he should have, he knew. The man had been chief of security on station for three years, worked in security longer than that. The *Razalka* had stopped on Degvar dozens of times.

"But you trusted him enough to bring him on this mission."

Actually, he wasn't given much of a choice, as he remembered it. "He has an excellent record and the necessary contacts in Imperial shipping."

"I know that. I saw his record too. But I don't . . ." She hesitated. "I would've thought you'd insist on all Fleet personnel."

"Hana's team was overworked, still on the injury roster. And Gurdan's people had ties to Kospahr."

She wrinkled her nose at the name. "So you had no choice, is that it?"

"Essentially. Yes." He could tell she was sifting through his information. It was important to her, but he didn't know why. "Mitkanos tell you differently?"

"Mitkanos told me very little. Other than he called you an arrogant rimstrutter."

He'd heard worse. A year ago, though, that evaluation might've angered him. It would've warranted at least a mental check mark. Now he almost understood it. "I'm also a hungry arrogant rimstrutter. We're meeting them at the ramp in," he glanced at his watch, "ten minutes."

She grabbed her empty coffee cup, then his. "I need a few minutes to brush my hair. Powder my nose. I'll meet you there," she said as he followed her to the small galley area.

"I'll wait."

She hesitated. He mentally lined up a few more reasons to keep her with him. So he was surprised when she merely nodded, retrieved the felinar from the couch, then headed for her bedroom.

A few minutes later she returned, hair shining like pale moonlight, a touch of color on her cheeks. She stepped by him to retrieve her jacket from the couch. Powder and flowers.

She thrust her hand into the sleeve. "Who's securing the ship?"

"We are. We'll go to the bridge from here." He studied her as she straightened her collar. Some of the edginess he'd sensed in her since they left Degvar was dissipating. He couldn't say exactly how he knew that; it might be in the way she walked or held her shoulders. Or just the lights that now danced in her eyes.

Some of it was no doubt a result of her well-placed punch on Jagan's jaw. Revenge, his people said, was sweeter than the best Suralian honey. And maybe some of it was because of the toy felinar. A part of her past, returned to her safely.

But he also had a feeling that something in his answers about the *Stegzarda* played a part. He was glad of that. He just wished he knew what in hell it was so he could keep on doing it.

23

Breakfast the next morning wasn't an option, but whether it was because of the large and delicious dinner she'd had the night before or because her stomach was a bit in a knot over dealing with Jagan in the confines of the *Quest* for a full septi, Trilby didn't know and didn't care to explore. At 0645 she finished her coffee and left the lounge for the bridge. Tivahr was in engineering with Dallon. She'd comm him once she was ready to bring the *Quest*'s primaries online.

It was routine, yet it wasn't. She went through her preflight checklist as she always did: fuel mixture, pumps operative, aux generator synched in on standby, cargo doors sealed and locked. But there was other movement around her. Farra's soft voice talking to Saldika Departures. Tivahr's clipped accent answering her comm. Mitkanos's burly form ambling in with some last-minute updates on a troublesome ion storm by the border. Then he clomped off the bridge, down to the cargo deck, for one last inspection.

Tivahr squeezed her shoulder as he slid into the copilot's seat and strapped himself in. Strapped in herself, she couldn't move away from his touch. She wasn't even one hundred percent sure she wanted to anymore.

It was the oddest thing seeing him next to Jagan, first in the wide corridor of the terminal, then on the pod, and then later in the hangar, as he hauled the shorter man up by his jacket lapels.

She wondered how the hell she'd ever been attracted to Jagan Grantforth.

She wondered what in hell she was going to do about Khyrhis Tivahr.

Later. She'd deal with that, and him, later. And try to forget she'd slept with the small felinar on her pillow all night. "Full power active. Initiating systems check."

"Life support optimum. Filters online," Tivahr replied.

Dezi's voice. That should be Dezi's voice. But she knew if it were, she'd miss another voice, deeper, with a distinctly clipped Zafharish accent.

She went down her list by memory. Farra answered some questions, Tivahr others. Mitkanos's deep rumble replied over intraship confirming the status of the engines.

She heard footsteps and out of the corner of her eye saw Dallon slide into navigation. "He still alive?" She knew he'd checked on Jagan.

"Snoring and deep in hangover heaven. But had the forethought to strap in."

"Shame," Tivahr intoned. "Ship's afterburners have a nice kick."

Farra laughed, but added in Zafharish, "He's not

that bad, really. Typical bureaucrat. All strut and nonsense."

"Mind your tongue, Farra-*chenka,*" Trilby quipped back in the same language.

She caught Tivahr's wide grin and felt the heat rise to her cheeks. He seemed to take it as a personal triumph every time she spoke Zafharish.

"We are cleared for departure," Farra announced, lapsing back into Standard. She relayed taxi instructions.

Trilby fired the ship's heavy-air engines and eased out of the cargo hangar.

They were in the lanes within the hour, heading for Saldika's outer beacon.

"Rimanava."

"*Vad, Dasjon.*"

Tivahr was back to Zafharish again. Trilby took her attention from the stream of data on the distant ion storm and leaned back in her chair.

"What's the status on Grantforth?" he asked, and Trilby translated. His accent was easier for her to understand than Farra's or Mitkanos's.

"Still in his cabin, *Dasjon.*"

"Keep an eye on him. I want to update our conversation from dinner last night. I've thought about some of our theories. These are things he shouldn't hear."

"As soon as he moves, I'll tell you."

"*Jhevd'.*"

Trilby heard Tivahr use the informal term for thank you. Though he consistently addressed Farra by her last name, in military fashion, she noted that overall his conversations with Farra were more relaxed. With

Mitkanos or Dallon, he'd have said, *"Jhevdon."* I am grateful.

Tivahr glanced from Farra to Trilby but slowed his words down slightly to allow for Trilby's translation time. "I want to keep the conversation in Zafharish, just in case. Will you be able to follow?"

It took her a moment to form her answer, and she knew it wasn't perfect. "If I cannot, I can say this. Say something," she corrected.

"Patruzius?" Tivahr twisted around in his seat.

"Vad, Dasjon. Do you want Farra to bring Uncle Yavo in on closed intraship, or do you want him to come up here?"

Dallon said "Uncle Yavo" with a grin. There was a clear camaraderie between the two, in spite of the fact that Dallon was Fleet. But not, Trilby suspected, an arrogant rimstrutter like Tivahr. Though even the *Razalka*'s senior captain wasn't quite as arrogant as he used to be.

Tivahr thought for a moment before answering Dallon's question. "I don't want to risk intraship, even closed. I don't know how much Jagan knows about ship's communications—"

"Less than a mizzet's ass," Trilby put in, courtesy of an idiom she'd learned from Farra.

"Even so. Tell Mitkanos to get up here as soon as he can. But until then, let's go over what we know. Make sure we're not missing something important."

Garold Grantforth had announced the first trade agreement with the Beffa cartel and the 'Sko earlier in the day, which was, considering intergalactic distances and time considerations, more like a deuce past. A few things they agreed were notable. The Beffa were coming to the Conclave, the chief secretary said, because their own government, now controlled by the Niyil military, was unstable. The rim worlds of the Ycsko Empire, which were predominantly Beffan, were left out in the cold, more than literally.

The Beffan allied worlds and stations said they feared retaliation by the Niyil. Garold Grantforth's next project was to get them military assistance from the Conclave.

"And did you find out about the Dakrahl?" Trilby asked. There'd been no mention of the religious powers in the 'Sko Empire. Tivahr told them last night he had ways to get some quick information on the mysterious sect.

"I sent those queries out when we got back to the ship," Tivahr said, with a nod toward Dallon. "On the surface it appears they're staying out of it, for the moment."

"But you don't believe that." Dallon swiveled back and forth in his chair, as far as his safety straps permitted.

"No. That's their official posture."

"Where does this put Secretary Grantforth?" Trilby asked.

"Officially, as a peacekeeper." Tivahr pulled a lightpen from his flight-suit pocket and toyed with it. "But I think we have reasons now to suspect the link to Dark Sword is either in his office or GGA. I've put out a request to intercept all 'Sko transmits on this. Something feels very wrong."

"Everything involving the 'Sko feels wrong." Mitkanos stepped onto the bridge. He looked around, chose the empty chair next to Farra, pulled one strap across his chest, left the other dangling. "What of the Dakrahl?" he asked Tivahr.

"We were just getting into that. Right now they're saying little. But then, they've always played their power games silently. I'm more interested that my contacts say several high priests were seen on Szed recently."

"The Niyil," Dallon told Trilby, "have a well-known dislike of the Dakrahl."

Rhis jabbed the air with his lightpen as he spoke. "But if the Beffa are working with the Conclave, that could force the Niyil to consider the Dakrahl in a different light."

Trilby held up one hand. "Wait a moment, please." She formed her comments, translated them into Zafharish. "We believe Beffa works with Grantforth. And Grantforth talks to GGA. Then GGA uses wide-body haulers to help Beffa bring ships to the Conclave." Their earlier investigations into the movements of GGA ships near the border had showed, as they all suspected, some significant and inexplicable delays. "But the ships that attacked us out by Avanar were Niyil. What were they doing there?"

"Looking to attack Beffan ships, to halt the deal?" Farra suggested. "That's what the newsvid said. The Niyil don't want the Beffans allying with the Conclave."

"It's more than that," Rhis said. "If Grantforth's trade deal was legitimate, Beffa wouldn't need the old star charts. The Conclave would grant them entry. So we have to assume that something much larger, much deeper is going on."

"That Beffa's making the deal as a cover? That the Niyil are involved?" Dallon looked at Mitkanos, then at Rhis. "That would be suicide for the Conclave. The 'Sko would overrun them first chance they got."

"Us and them," Mitkanos agreed. "Especially if the Dakrahl get into the game. The Dakrahl would like nothing better than to be in a position to make a move on the Empire, take back Faytari. With the Conclave under their rule, they could do that."

"Faytari?" Trilby knew it was a section of Zafharin space that bordered the 'Sko. But it wasn't the only section. "Why Faytari?"

"The Faytari Drifts." Tivahr made a broad sweep in the air with his lightpen, as if delineating the asteroid belt deep in Zafharin space. "It's the Dakrahl's belief—the other factions don't hold to this—that the Faytari Drifts contain pieces of three sacred Ycsko moons. Their legends tell of an evil deity that cast the moons away, then challenged the Dakrahl priests to bring the moons and their supposed treasure troves back. It's nonsense, of course." He leaned back. "About fifty or so years ago, we gave a 'Sko science team access to the Drifts. Just to try to settle this claim of theirs. They found no proof of their claim. And there were no treasure troves. But the Dakrahl don't want to give up."

Trilby rearranged the words, translated, and arranged them again. Tivahr was looking at her. She nodded.

"So I think we have to consider," he said, glancing from Mitkanos to Farra to Dallon, "that they may be a part of this as well."

"But the trade agreement is pointing to the Niyil, not us, as the oppressors." Farra glanced at her panels, then back at Tivahr.

"Give them time," her uncle told her sagely. "Give them time."

A small light flickered on Farra's panel. She caught it, tapped her screen. "He's out. Heading for the lounge."

Jagan was awake.

Dallon flipped open the harness buckles and stood. "I'll go listen to what glory-stories our friend has to tell."

Tivahr rapped the lightpen on the arm of his chair. "Make sure he knows the bridge is off-limits. Then in an hour you're off duty. You too, Rimanava."

Dallon ducked his head, strode down the short corridor.

Trilby leaned back against her chair and closed her eyes. "How many days to go?" Maybe she could drug Jagan, make him sleep through them all.

"Seven," Tivahr's voice said. "Six and a half, truthfully. And then we see what Syar has to offer."

She groaned as she formed the words she wanted to say. "As long as it is not a one-way ticket to Club 'Sko, I am happy."

"I've been there," Tivahr replied. "Much over-rated. Can't recommend it."

She remembered the bruises on his body. Hell of a vacation memento.

Mitkanos unhooked his harness strap. Trilby had noticed the man rarely liked to sit in one place for long. After the wide corridors of Degvar, an Endurance Class starfreighter must seem very confining to him.

"You want me to take main or late shift?" he asked Tivahr. And there was no requisite *Dasjon*. Even last night at dinner, Trilby'd noticed that Mitkanos simply spoke to Tivahr. No name, no title. The rivalry between the Fleet and the *Stegzarda* was still apparent here. Though Tivahr seemed less bothered by it than he had on Degvar.

"I need you on a swing shift, because of our guest. At least for the next two days. I'll have Dallon relieve you after that. But I want to keep Grantforth always looking over his shoulder, not knowing who might be in the corridor, or when."

It was a good, workable plan that meant Mitkanos would be on duty for two hours before and after each shift change. But she had a feeling the *Stegzarda* major would make his presence felt a lot more than that.

They all would. With Jagan on board, the usual laxity of 'tween time wouldn't occur. Tivahr might feel Jagan was there to babysit them, but the reality was that they also had to babysit Jagan.

There were too many questions and too few answers.

An hour later, Farra logged off duty and left the bridge, but not before she offered, "If you need me . . ."

Trilby turned away from her console. "*Vad*. We'll call." Then she was left alone with Tivahr. She brought up the specs on her new ship and tried to look busy, tried to look like she didn't want any conversation with a man who occupied far too much of her thoughts as it was.

He seemed to sense that, excused himself a little while later, told her to lock the bridge. He returned with two wide mugs of soup, spill-capped and steaming. It was past lunch. She hadn't realized she was hungry.

If he'd encountered Jagan, he didn't say. But

Trilby's random glances at the ship's CLS showed their guest was spending most of his time in his cabin.

"Soup is okay good for replicator," she told him in halting Zafharish.

"Okay good?" He grinned. "Listen to me. Good. Better. Best. Very good." He went through the Zafharish words, pronouncing them carefully, making her repeat them in between spoonfuls.

Then he went through a list of negatives. Bad. Horrible. Disgusting. Worm fodder. She laughed at the last one.

The nav comm pinged twice. They were picking up the Yanir-3 beacon. Trilby secured her mug, keyed in course changes.

He wanted to work on verb tenses after that. I see. I saw. I will see. I have seen. It wasn't as difficult as Trilby thought, and having a real person to work with, instead of a program, helped.

The nav comm pinged twice again. Yanir-4 and a jumpgate. Tivahr primed the hyperdrive engines. Trilby ran through a prejump checklist, then opened intraship.

"This is Captain Elliot. Jump countdown starts in five minutes. Secure and strap down, kids."

Shadow's Quest took the jump flawlessly, with hardly a shimmer. A thrill ran through Trilby just to have her hands on the controls at the point, to feel the ship respond, to see systems data cascade down her screens with an almost artistic flow.

"Good, better, best. Good, better, best." She added a little tune to the Zafharish words, sang it under her breath as the ship settled in for its hyperspace transit.

"You. Want. Coffee?" he asked her in Standard, but matching her tune with his deeper voice.

"Thanks. And no more language lessons for a while. I think I'm a bit punch-drunk." It was more than that, she knew. She felt safe on the *Quest,* safe on the bridge, and in the past four hours she hadn't argued or fought with anyone. It was almost like an old 'tween time on a run with Dezi.

Tivahr leaned over her shoulder, pointed to a screen on her far left. "Pull up the last download we had on that ion storm. I want to look at it again when I get back."

"Think it's a problem?" she asked as he stepped away.

"If our friend were not on board, I might. It would be a good cover for an ambush when we come out of jump. But now I want to show you a way you can use it, make it into a wog-and-weemly you'll like."

"Sounds interesting." She heard the bridge hatch slide closed. The light on her panel showed it locking.

Five minutes later he was back, palm-coding past the lock. The pungent aroma of coffee wafted in.

He slid into the copilot's seat. "Now, let me show you how to use storm interference to make guidance beacons think you are someplace you are not."

Trilby stood, stretched, and leaned on the back of his chair while she sipped her coffee and drank in his methodology. It was intriguing, fascinating, and a bit humbling. Again she found herself thinking: *if Shadow had lived . . .*

He did, in a way, through this ship. If only for a little while.

Three pings from navigation.

They were through the jumpgate that quickly? She glanced at the time stamp, thinking enough time hadn't passed. But it had. And that, she knew, was a dangerous sign. She slid back into her seat, rehooked her harness.

She'd lost herself for several hours in Khyrhis Tivahr. In his energy, his intellect.

Dangerous. The man was dangerous.

"Initiating exit sequence." She ran her fingers over the controls, saw his movements complement hers. She opened intraship. "This is Captain Elliot. Five minutes to mass and velocity dump. Secure and strap down, kids."

Shadow's Quest streamed through the jumpgate at the Yanir–Gensiira border, all systems optimal.

The bridge hatch cycled behind her. Trilby glanced at the time stamp. It was just about swing shift.

"Mitkanos." Tivahr confirmed her supposition, pointing to the palm-code ID readout on the console.

Trilby loosened her harness, swiveled around. "You're a little early. Get a cup of—"

"Grantforth's missing." Mitkanos stopped in the hatchway, his broad face mottled in anger. He looked quickly from Trilby to Tivahr. "I have a transfer manifest that needs his signature. His ship badge is in his cabin. But the son of a Pillorian bitch is not."

She heard the snick of Tivhar's harness but she was quicker, already on her feet. "You checked his sani-fac? The lounge?" He'd been in the lounge with Dallon, earlier, a fact confirmed by his ship badge. She glanced at the comm console. Jagan, or rather his ship badge, hadn't moved from his cabin. "Dallon—"

"Accompanied our guest to his cabin hours ago." Mitkanos had already covered that possibility. "Grantforth complained of a headache. Too much *fedka*. And no, Dallon's not seen him since."

Tivahr stepped up to him. "Stay here. With her." He pointed to Trilby.

Damn it! This was her ship. "No! I—"

"We don't know where he is, what he is doing. I need someone—I need you on the bridge in case there is a threat to the primaries."

"Jagan's not capable—" she called after him as he strode off the bridge, but Tivahr was right. Someone had to be on the bridge who could make decisions, take countermeasures. It was SOP.

Mitkanos slid into the comm chair with a grunt. She tracked Tivahr's ship-badge icon down the ladderway, saw Dallon's in engineering. Farra was still in her cabin, answering Mitkanos's call.

She turned, automatically initiating security procedures as she climbed back into her seat, placing the ship on yellow alert. All entry passwords were closed access except to Tivahr and herself. The ship's primary system files went through double backup. Enviro was secured.

She restrapped her harness, chewed for a moment on her lower lip.

Where in hell was Jagan? *Shadow's Quest* simply wasn't that large. Sure, there were nooks and crannies under stairwell storage areas, in maintenance tunnels. Five cavernous cargo holds. Large compared to her old *Venture*. Still, it could be searched, thoroughly, in under an hour.

She turned slightly. "You saw his cabin, right?" she asked Mitkanos in Standard. Translating everything to Zafharish was too much of a strain at the moment. "Anything odd?"

He thought for a moment. "Suitcase open. Some

clothes inside. Bed slept in, not made. But nothing bad, like someone had a fight with him, no."

She didn't think that. The only person he'd be likely to fight with would be Tivahr. Or herself. They'd both been on the bridge.

Except Tivahr had gone to the lounge for soup. Then coffee.

No. She found herself shaking her head at the thought. Maybe Tivahr didn't like Jagan, or didn't like the fact that Jagan had been her lover. But harm him, kill him because of it?

It was ridiculous. Besides, they needed Jagan to get them to Syar, to get them into GGA where someone called Dark Sword was working with the 'Sko. . . .

Who else, Neadi had asked, *would be sleeping with the 'Sko?*

The Zafharin. Or, perhaps, one Zafharin in particular. Who had been left behind on the 'Sko world of Szed. Then miraculously escaped.

The thought made her hands feel icy, her throat tight. Tivahr had insisted on coming along. Even though she and Dallon and Mitkanos and Farra, or any of Mitkanos's other candidates, could've handled the run just fine.

Then Jagan showed up on Saldika. Showed up at her docking gate. Showed up at her docking gate at almost the exact time they arrived.

How did he know they'd be there? Sure, he knew *Shadow's Quest* had to stop at Saldika. He could have found that out from her flight plan. But ETAs varied widely. And gate assignments often changed at the last minute.

That's why all ports had public message boards: *I'm here now. At gate such-and-such. Come meet me.*

Common as mizzets in a cargo bay.

But she hadn't posted anything.

Damn, damn, double damn! She pinched the bridge of her nose. Were there two agents, both 'Sko double agents, working with each other? Against each other, for different 'Sko factions?

She'd had a hard time accepting that Jagan could be part of any 'Sko plot. He honestly didn't have the intelligence. The deviousness.

But Tivahr . . . He fit the profile perfectly. Brilliant. Powerful. With impeccable military training.

And a flair for deceit, for manipulation.

Her stomach churned, rebelling at her thoughts. For all that Khyrhis Tivahr fit the profile, he didn't. In the short time she'd known him, she knew that much. Knew it intimately. Innately.

Khyrhis Tivahr would never betray the Empire. More importantly, he'd never betray the people who trusted him, depended on him. Like Hana Jankova. Or Zak Demarik.

Or Trilby Elliot.

She forcibly stopped her thoughts at that admission. *Don't,* she told herself. *Don't even start thinking like that. Don't trust him. Don't depend on him. Don't fall in love with him. He's got the* plastered *in front of his name, Gods damn it!*

"Captain Trilby." Mitkanos was leaning over, touching her arm. "You okay?"

She had a death grip on her harness strap, her fingers almost numb from where she'd wrapped it around her hand. She released it, shook out her fingers gingerly.

"Just thinking about things I don't want to think

about." She gave him a halfhearted smile. "Any news?"

He shook his head. "We can very much tell you where he is not, however. The *Dasjon* is searching Hold Two. Dallon is in Three. Farra is—"

Their ship badges pinged simultaneously. Her hand moved quickly. "Elliot."

"Captain! This is Farra. I have *Dasjon* Grantforth. I need the team in sick bay at once!"

Tivhar's response growled through her ship badge. "On my way."

Dallon's acknowledgment followed.

She tapped her badge again. "Farra, give me status."

"He is alive, Captain. Breathing. But not conscious."

She closed her eyes for a moment. Had she misjudged Tivahr? Again? "He's injured?"

"I cannot tell. Appears not. But—" The sound of male voices rumbled in the background. The comm link clicked off and on.

"This is Tiv—Rhis."

Gods, Trilby realized, even he was forgetting who he was. Or wasn't supposed to be.

"As soon as I have answers, you'll hear."

The comm link went dead.

24

She was running down the ladderway again, forgetting her ship had a lift. Tivahr had commed her. "He's awake."

She sidestepped into the corridor, headed for sick bay. Tivahr stood outside, arms folded across his chest, brows slanting in a frown. His face relaxed when he saw her, but only slightly.

She stopped in front of him, caught her breath. "What happened?" It had been over two hours since Farra had found Jagan, unconscious, slumped at the base of the ladderway near sick bay.

"Overdose."

"Overdose? As in suicide?" That didn't sound like the Jagan Grantforth she knew. "Or did his late night partying finally catch up with him?" That sounded more like Jagan. He'd gone his own way on Saldika. He had the money, the looks and, even in the Empire, the Grantforth name. Maybe he'd dabbled in more than just *fedka*.

Tivahr pulled a small vial from his pants pocket, handed it to her.

For a moment she thought her supposition about mixing drugs and alcohol was true. Then she read the label. "Motion-sickness tabs?" She groaned. Space sickness. Jagan was used to traveling on his family's large luxury yachts. Not freighters, built more for cargo capacity than comfort. He'd had the same problem on the *Careless Venture*. But she'd forgotten.

"That's what the label says." Tivahr nodded. "That is not what the analyzer tells us."

She blinked. Hard. Looked at the vial again, then at Tivahr. The tension was back in his face. "What was in here?"

"Zalcafrenine rozide. Also known as Renzorca."

"Ren what?"

He shook his head. "It's an Ycskrite term."

At the mention of the 'Sko language, she tensed.

"It means *blood boil death*. Loose translation, of course," he added.

"Someone tried to poison Jagan? Why?"

"He doesn't know. At least, he's not telling me."

"Who gave him the pills?" Trilby briefly wondered if Jagan's wife knew he was meeting with her and was jealous.

"He said he has a standing prescription at the company pharmacy. He took it trying to dispel the effects of his hangover, something he said he's done before."

She glanced at the vial again, recognized the GGA Med-Lab logo. She'd seen it often enough on Chaser's transmits. "But you said this was 'Sko—"

"It is. Illegal in the Empire. I have to assume the same for the Conclave."

"But he's alive."

"He only took one. Half a dose." He took the vial from her fingers, put it back in his pocket. "Full dose and he would not be."

In the past few months she'd wished Jagan dead any number of times. But that had been a cathartic exercise. Not the real thing. Not like this could have been.

"When the pills made him feel worse," Tivahr continued, "he knew enough to head for sick bay. It was probably his last rational thought. Renzorca short-circuits the thinking process very quickly. That's no doubt why he didn't use the comm, didn't put on his shirt or badge. I would guess he even had no idea where sick bay was. Most likely he ended up in the corridor by happenstance. Fortunately for him, this ship's not that large."

Delusional, half-naked, aimlessly wandering the ship in pain while everyone searched for him. Tivahr was right. A larger ship, and they might not have found him until it was too late. "Can I see him?"

A moment of hard silence from Tivahr and then a noncommittal shrug. But his face wore that same closed expression she remembered from right after the 'Sko attack off Avanar. He was worried about something and wasn't in the mood to share it.

It wasn't Jagan, or the poison. It was her. A threat against her. Like the 'Sko attack off Avanar.

He knew more than he was telling. That almost stopped her, made her want to drag it out of him. Except that Jagan Grantforth had nearly died on a ship under her command—and she was still captain, in spite of whatever games Tivahr was playing. She felt a level of responsibility. And an odd pang of sentiment. They'd been lovers, friends. She realized now that if something had happened to him, she'd regret it.

Jagan was an incurable flirt and hadn't a humble bone in his body. But other than marrying Zalia—marrying the money and position Trilby knew Jagan's mother always intended he would—he wasn't a bad person. They'd had fun, lots of good times in the almost two years they were together. The restaurants, the clubs, the theater, the parties. He opened her eyes to a way of life she had only dreamed about when working the docks in Port Rumor.

With an unexpected clarity she knew he'd also opened her eyes to something even more important. That she was a survivor. He'd raised her up to the glittering heights and then dropped her down—and she survived. Was stronger for it. She found something inside herself that was indefatigable and—finders keepers—she'd never lose it.

She stepped in front of Tivahr, then turned, saw that hard, closed, worried but determined look still on his face.

What the hell. Maybe it was time to face another realization. Something else she'd found and wanted to keep. Nothing ventured . . .

She stood on tiptoe and, grabbing a handful of his jacket for balance, brushed his lips lightly with her own before leaning against him in a deeper kiss.

His arms locked around her immediately, his mouth branding her with his heated response. She felt as if thousands of fluttermoths spiraled through her body. She stepped back, reluctantly, and more than a little weak-kneed.

That closed, worried look was gone from his face,

replaced by one of surprise and hopefulness. His dark eyes were smoky with desire.

"Trilby-*chenka* . . ." He held on to her arms, tried to pull her back to him, but she held up her index finger, stalling him. Not without a mixture of regret and trepidation.

He was still *the* Tivahr. She was still taking a chance. "Business first."

His hand slid down her arm and he drew her finger to his lips, kissed it lightly. "I'll wait for you in the lounge. Dinner?"

Gods, they were supposed to be off shift two hours ago. She nodded, found herself smiling even though she was tired, and her emotions felt as if they'd been dragged out the drive vents and in through the aux thrusters again. "Sounds good."

She squeezed his hand, then stepped toward sick bay's door, activating its sensor. It slid open as Tivahr strode away.

Farra looked up from the medistat when Trilby entered. "Captain."

"Saved my life, that little darling did." Jagan's voice was hoarse but he was propped up in the regen bed, sipping a steaming liquid from a spill-capped mug. A med-broche was clasped to his wrist. His face had a pinched expression and he looked like he was fighting a three-bottle hangover. But his smile was genuine.

Hell, if she'd downed a 'Sko poison and survived, she'd be smiling too.

"You did good work, Farra." Trilby patted the young woman's shoulder as she stepped past her toward Jagan's regen bed.

"*Stegzarda* training in emergency medical procedures. Uncle Yavo would never forgive me if I did not."

Trilby leaned against the edge of the empty regen bed behind her, crossed her arms over her chest. "You look like hell, Grantforth."

"Feel like I've been there and back."

"I know Rhis asked you, but how do you think a 'Sko poison ended up in your medicine?"

Jagan let out a long breath. "I don't have any answers. Other than I don't know if I should be worried that someone's trying to kill me personally or trying to kill a bunch of us in GGA. What if my prescription wasn't the only one altered?"

Trilby's arms fell to her side. She hadn't considered that. What if the pills had been switched in GGA's main pharmacy? Hundreds of GGA employees would be facing death. The main pharmacy . . .

. . . was where Chaser worked. What if his meds were poisoned? What if he was the one—

She pushed the thought away. She'd known Chaser her whole life. "You discuss that with Rhis?"

"No. I . . . we . . ." He glanced at Farra. "We were playing with some ideas just now. After Vanur left to find you."

More good work, Farra.

"You think it's a plot against GGA?"

He shrugged. "I hope not. But in case it is, I think I should send a message. A warning."

And hope the warning's not too late, Trilby knew. "Agreed. Is there someone you know you can trust with this information? Someone who can act on it immediately?"

"Besides Mother, and I really don't want to upset her right now, it'd have to be Uncle Garold."

Secretary Garold Grantforth. Trilby frowned slightly, her mind still running over some possibilities that were less than savory. "Sure you want to bother him? The news said he's involved in trade negotiations." With the 'Sko. And Jagan's vial held 'Sko poison.

"I think he'd be insulted if I didn't contact him. This is a very serious matter."

She pushed herself away from the empty bed, motioned to Farra. "Can you get him a link here to record a message?"

"*Vad*. Is not a problem."

"I'm going to be in the lounge, having dinner. Call me when it's finished."

"*Vad*, Captain." Farra flicked off the medistat and reached for her portable datapad.

"*Jhevd',*" she replied automatically. Then saw Jagan's raised eyebrows. "I'm learning. Hard not to when it's all I hear these days." She lay her hand on his arm, squeezed it briefly. "I'm glad you're all right, Jagan."

"So you can take another shot at me with that mean right hook of yours?" He was grinning, his tone light. Then his smile faded. "I'm glad I'm alive too, Tril. And . . . I'm sorry. For a lot of things I did wrong by you. I mean that. I know I owe you an explanation. I—"

"You need to compose that message and get some rest right now." She put on her best "stern captain" tone. "We can talk, if you want, later. But you really don't owe me any explanations."

"Well, yeah, I really do, and you'll probably pop me one in the jaw again. But I deserve it. And . . . I had no right to say what I did about you and Vanur. So I deserved that one too."

"We'll call it even, okay? Farra's got the pad ready for you." She gave him a smile as she stepped toward the door, caught his answering grin and the small dimple in his cheek.

This was the Jagan she remembered. The charming one she'd fallen in love with. She watched him turn his smile toward Farra. Better watch out, Farra-*chenka*.

But, no, Farra had someone back at Degvar. A very special someone.

And I have a dinner date. With Khyrhis Tivahr. "The" Khyrhis Tivahr. But that's okay. I can handle that. Now.

The sick-bay door closed behind her with a muted whoosh as Trilby hurried down the corridor.

Rhis heard the footsteps approaching in the corridor. Short. Definitely female. He grinned, then hit the reheat button on the keypad. Dinner for two, coming up.

He would never understand women. At least, he probably would never understand one particular woman, but that was okay. As long as she was there, tantalizing him, intriguing him, making him crazy . . .

Gods, did she make him crazy!

Maybe he'd ask Rafi about it sometime. Maybe not. At the moment, he was more interested to see if the Trilby who came through the wide lounge hatchway was the Trilby who'd grabbed him and kissed him so delightfully outside sick bay.

He didn't realize he was holding his breath until she spoke.

"Smells good, Rhis. Maybe I should hire you as ship's cook."

He let out a slow sigh. *Trilby-chenka. Ahh, Trilby-chenka. Yav chera.* Tousled hair the color of moonlight. Impish smile. All soft curves under that zippered gray flight suit that he could tear off her in less than twenty seconds. Maybe fifteen.

But not yet. Take it slow. Don't spook her. "Anything smells good when you're hungry. Even Yaniran rice *bolaf*." He reached behind the counter, brought out the bottle of white wine he'd chilled, poured her a glass, then one for himself. "This should help."

The surprised look on her face pleased him. Well, he had other surprises for her. This would do for now.

She took the glass. "Getting fancy, are we?"

"We are off duty." He stepped closer, touched glasses with her for luck. "And I think we both deserve it."

He studied her face, her eyes half closed briefly as she tasted the wine. Maybe, he posited, something in jumpspace had miraculously removed her animosity toward him. Hell, the Dakrahl worshiped the Faytari Drifts for something close to that reason. Treasures notwithstanding, there were places in the Drifts, their legends said, that could cleanse a person, heal them, alter them.

She certainly had been all prickly and standoffish until they'd cleared the exit gate, and then she'd mellowed. Or was mellowing, he corrected himself. He could still see a slightly wary look in her eyes.

Just as she no doubt saw in his earlier, and bloody hell if she didn't know that he was worried about her and Grantforth. After all, she'd pulled him off the jungle floor, nursed him back to health. What if that same compassion now resurrected itself—toward Jagan?

What if—and he didn't totally discount it—Jagan's whole overdose was a stunt to get Trilby's sympathy? That was why he'd given Farra Rimanava strict orders in Zafharish before he'd commed Trilby: *don't leave them alone in sick bay together.*

He would take no chances.

But it looked like it hadn't been necessary. Her kiss told him that much.

Would it again? He tilted his face down, captured her mouth with his own. She leaned into him, answered his slow, lazy kiss with lips warm, willing, and tasting of wine. Then the processor pinged. Food was the last thing on his mind, but they needed the sustenance. They had a long ways to go before Syar. And the-Gods-only-knew what kind of trouble would greet them when they got there.

But more important, they had a whole six hours to themselves before they were back on duty. A lot could happen in that time.

They might very well need the sustenance.

He grinned down at her. "Join me for dinner, *Dasja?*"

"That's why I'm here." She took another sip of her wine, turned toward the table.

He brought out the steaming casserole, some vegetables, and two round Saldikan sausage cutlets. They filled their plates, then Trilby leaned toward him.

"Jagan thinks his prescription might not be the only one poisoned. He's putting together a warning message to send to GGA."

His fork stopped in midair. "He did not say anything to me—"

"Because it was Farra who got him talking," she

said. "I don't know if that's the answer. But it's something we've got to consider."

"A move against GGA in total?" A warning, perhaps, from an associate who didn't like Garold Grantforth's trade proposal? Possible, but to use a 'Sko poison didn't make sense. He was shaking his head and realized Trilby was looking at him questioningly.

He explained. "The only reason would be to stop Grantforth's dealings with the Beffa. But then, why not go after the secretary himself? And why with a 'Sko poison, if the 'Sko are the very group he's trying to help?"

"Not all the 'Sko. The Dakrahl? The Niyil?"

"The Niyil are more likely to shoot at GGA ships than use poison. The Dakrahl . . ." He thought on that while he chewed. The religious faction was often very creative in their methods. "Possible."

"Or? I hear an *or* in there."

He'd thought of this, when he wasn't trying to figure out what suddenly changed his air sprite's mind about him. "Someone wanted us to show up in Syar with a dead GGA accountant on board."

She stared at him. "For what purpose?"

"We know the purpose. Someone wants your nav banks. Your knowledge. What better way to get control of this ship, control of you, than to charge us with murder?"

"That's crazy!"

"Dark Sword hasn't been effective all these years because he's sane and kindly."

She took a quick sip of wine.

He lowered his voice. "Dark Sword is the one behind the kill orders. Which, until recently, were few enough to look like happenstance. But with trade negotiations now on the table, and with people like your friend Neadi questioning the unlikeliness of so many attacks on freighters, Dark Sword has no choice but to change methods.

"More attacks will push Conclave opinion against the trade agreement, no matter how influential Garold Grantforth is. So there has to be another way to ensure 'Sko presence in the Conclave and acquire those freighters with Herkoid data. An impound and a murder charge is a rather good way to accomplish the second."

"A ship under impound is sealed."

"And her logs, all her databanks, are copied into the court system as evidence, no?"

She nodded.

"And if Dark Sword is as well placed as we think, he might be part of that system in the Conclave. Someone whose access to such records wouldn't be questioned."

"So you think Jagan was set up?"

He nodded. "It is one possibility I've considered. I have been trying to figure out by what means they were going to take this ship, and her nav banks, without arousing suspicion. And if it turns out no other prescriptions were poisoned, it's a strong possibility."

"But if something happened to Jagan, his uncle would call off the trade talks. He'd take it as a direct threat."

"That's only if it looked as if the 'Sko killed his nephew. But all Uncle Garold would know is that Jagan was poisoned while on a ship operated by his ex-girlfriend. Who probably had told more than a few people he left her heartbroken. And that she'd like to see him dead."

"But I'm not in love with Jagan anymore!"

He was very glad to hear her make that statement, even if the circumstances eliciting it were less than savory.

"I haven't been since I—" And she stopped, bit her lip self-consciously. "Since I pulled your ungrateful ass out of the swamp." She leaned back, crossed her arms over her chest. But a smile played across her lips, and a challenging light danced in her eyes. "You just maneuvered me into admitting that, didn't you?"

He reached across the table, pulled one hand out of the crook of her arm. He threaded his fingers through hers. "Unexpected bonus. But I'm glad to hear that, yes."

He saw the color rise to her cheeks.

"So you think someone will be waiting to arrest me when we hit the Colonies?" she asked. But she didn't pull her hand away.

"I think someone is waiting for a message from *Shadow's Quest* about an unfortunate accident."

"That's not the message they're going to get."

"I know. All the more reason things will be very interesting when we get to Syar."

"Dark Sword's certainly going to be surprised."

"I learned a long time ago, Trilby-*chenka,* that it is much, much better to be the one giving surprises than the one receiving them." He thought of Kospahr on the *Razalka*'s bridge. No, he definitely didn't like surprises.

She pulled her hand out of his grasp, but it was only to stab at her dinner. "Are you going to tell Jagan any of this? Or do you want me to?"

"Not until after he sends his message and we know for sure if there are more poisoned prescriptions. If there aren't, I'll talk to him. Or we both can." He wanted Jagan to know without a doubt where Trilby's allegiance was. "I don't want any of our suspicions to be leaked through his message."

Her ship badge pinged. She tapped it at. "Elliot."

"*Dasjon* Grantforth's message is ready."

Rhis tapped his badge on, switched to Zafharish. He didn't know if Farra was still in sick bay and if Grantforth could overhear. "We're almost finished dinner. Bring it to the bridge in five minutes. Get Patruzius to stay with him."

"Understood, *Dasjon*. Five minutes. I'll comm Dallon." The connection clicked off.

"Not even time for another glass of wine?" Trilby stood, clearing the plates from the table.

"Bedtime snack," he said, and thought her soft laugh sounded very encouraging, indeed.

He watched Jagan's message twice before permitting its transmission. It was short, earnest, and about what he expected from a corporate accountant.

Nor was he surprised by its destination: Garold Grantforth. Go right for the top when you want to make things happen.

It would be several hours, if not more, until they had a response.

He nodded to Farra and Mitkanos, then laid his hand on Trilby's shoulder. "We're off duty," he said in Zafharish. Then, in Standard, he asked her, "Nightcap?"

She blushed. Mitkanos turned away, grunted, and busied himself with the bridge scanners. Farra swiveled around in her seat at communications and faced her console.

Rhis grinned, wrapped his arm around Trilby's waist, and pulled her through the bridge hatch lock. He nibbled on her ear as they walked toward the lift.

"Rhis!" she pleaded, laughing softly.

His name had never sounded so wonderful.

25

Trilby stood in the middle of the small sitting area in her cabin and watched Rhis as if she were seeing him for the first time. She watched the lines of his body as he uncorked the wine, then reached overhead for two glasses from the galley cabinet. His gray shirt pulled across the width of his shoulders, the curve of muscles in his back and arm.

He glanced at her, briefly, with a lopsided smile and a flash of something promising in his dark eyes. Then he concentrated on pouring the pale liquid. His face was relaxed but the line of his jaw was strong, his cheeks slightly shadowed where they'd not seen a razor since yesterday.

She remembered his face the first time she'd seen him, lying in the damp grass, the remains of a 'Sko Tark behind him. His dark lashes had rested against pale skin; darker bruises blossomed along his jaw.

On her regen bed in sick bay, his naked form showed the muscles of a man who pushed his body hard, to the limits. And in those terrifying minutes when he first grabbed her, she'd felt his power.

The Khyrhis Tivahr. *The* Senior Captain.

The man who had taught her to say *yav cheron*.

She took the stemmed glass he held out to her. He'd said barely two words since following her to her cabin. But then, she'd said nothing either. The air around them seemed to speak instead, charged with that primal energy she remembered feeling so intensely on the *Careless Venture*. Every time he came close to her. Every time his eyes met hers. Every time he touched her.

If the decking under her boots caught fire right now, she wouldn't be surprised.

She dipped her finger in the chilled wine, touched it to his lips.

A low groan rumbled in his throat. He brushed her palm with a damp kiss.

"Khyrhis." She said his name softly, tentatively. It was his real name, one she'd said over and over in her head, and her heart, but never before out loud.

He clasped her hand, his fingers strong and sure as they threaded through hers.

"*Yav cheron,*" she whispered.

He pulled her hard against him, his mouth claiming hers, their intertwined hands for a moment caught awkwardly between their bodies. Then their hands slid apart. Hers went down the taut planes of his chest, moved around his waist. His went up, his thumb against her jaw, and his kiss deepened.

Her wineglass fell to the floor with a hollow clink. She wanted to touch his face too, caress it as he was caressing hers. Then it was the thickness of his hair she needed to feel.

His fingers kneaded the small of her back, the swell of her buttocks. He pressed her into his hardness. He nibbled at her mouth, taking her lower lip between his teeth. Squadrons of fluttermoths soared up her spine.

Slowly, deliberately she moved her hand from his waist down his thigh, then up, feeling him throb against her fingers. He inhaled sharply, pressed against her hand.

She teased his mouth with her tongue. Her fingers sought the zipper on his flight suit, found it, tugged.

He stepped back and suddenly his arm was under her knees. He lifted her smoothly. Her hands grasped his shoulders as he turned. Four steps and they were through her bedroom's open door. Two more and she was on her back, in the middle of her bed, with a flushed and passionate Khyrhis Tivahr—*the* Khyrhis Tivahr—kneeling beside her, unzipping her flight suit, kissing her neck, pulling at the thin strap of her T-shirt.

She nudged off her boots. They hit the floor with a thud, and she had the presence of mind to reach blindly over her head for the console. "Cabin lock, on. Privacy Code—oh, Gods!—One!"

Strong but incredibly gentle fingers had found the heat between her legs. She arched into his hand. Her breath shuddered into his mouth as he kissed her.

"Trilby-*chenka*." His voice was as raspy as his mustache against her cheek. "*Yav chera*. I want you. I cherish you."

He moved his hands up her body, stroking, caressing. She grabbed a handful of his flight suit, now half on and half off. She wanted it off. It was an impediment. She needed the warmth of his skin, the roughness of his hair against her.

A louder clunk of his boots, then a slight chill for a moment as he lifted off her and stripped away the last of his uniform.

When his body covered hers, she wrapped her legs around his hips. He nuzzled his face in her neck, then trailed kisses over her breasts.

She moaned, pulled his mouth back up to hers, wanting every inch of her body to touch his. Sensation sizzled through her. His hands became more insistent, his kisses more frenzied.

She needed him inside her now. "Please, oh, Gods, please!"

She clung to his shoulders as he thrust into her. One hand cupped her bottom, lifting her hips as he stroked deeper. She could feel his muscles tremble as his control slipped. But hers went first, an explosion of fluttermoths and fireworks that left her gasping for breath.

And sent him over the edge. "*Dasjankira*. My lady, my love!"

She understood his words in Zafharish now. He was hoarse, his breathing ragged when he finally sagged against her. Their bodies were sweat-slicked. Her powdery perfume mingled with the heat of his male scent. She rubbed her face against the dampness of his neck, listened to his words.

"I love you, my *dasjankira*. My Trilby-*chenka*. You are from my dreams. You are what I cherish."

She raised her face. "Khyrhis." Passion still smoldered in his dark eyes. She couldn't remember how to say, in his language, that she cherished him, loved him too.

She kissed him, hard, instead.

He didn't seem to mind.

She woke with the feel of his lips on her shoulder, his fingers stroking her breasts. She was spooned against him under the tangle of covers. She peered at the bedside console. They had forty-five minutes before they needed to find coffee, perhaps breakfast. An hour before they had to be on the bridge.

She wriggled her bottom against him, felt his throbbing response against her skin. And his soft chuckle in her ear.

They ended up bringing coffee to the bridge. Breakfast wasn't an option they had time for. Mitkanos vacated the captain's chair when Trilby stepped through the hatchway, with Rhis right behind her.

Mitkanos moved to the communications station. But Dallon was in the copilot's chair, finishing a systems check. Trilby knew he should've been off duty long ago. He shrugged when she mentioned it. "I don't need that much sleep. Plus I was hoping a response from Grantforth might come in."

Rhis slid into the copilot's seat as Dallon stood, moving to an empty one at navigation. "Anything?"

Dallon shook his head. "Nothing. But it's been six hours. We should hear something soon, I think."

"Unless he's too tied up with the trade negotiations."

"Or," Mitkanos said, "someone else intercepted the message."

Trilby studied the command console, checking her ship's status as the discussion continued around her.

"How's our patient?" Rhis asked.

"Back in his own cabin." Dallon gestured toward the CLS board behind Mitkanos. "Recovering nicely."

Oh, Gods. Trilby caught Dallon's movement, realized that both her and Rhis's ship badges would have given away their location—in her cabin—during the past six hours. She felt the heat rise to her face and looked hurriedly back at her console.

Rhis brought up his supposition that Jagan was supposed to die on board so that Dark Sword, and whoever was working with him, would have access to the ship's nav banks.

"Devious," Dallon said. But Mitkanos disagreed. Too risky. They could have just as easily—if Jagan had died—changed their flight plan to the nearest port as an emergency measure.

Dallon leaned back in his chair, toyed with his half-hooked harness straps. "Perhaps that's what we were supposed to have done?"

Rhis voiced more theory. Mitkanos dissented. Dallon added questions. Trilby stayed silent, listening to it all. Even if she hadn't known the voices, she could've picked out "Fleet" from *Stegzarda.* Rhis's questions, and answers, were broader in scope. He wasn't satisfied until he had examined every possibility, played out every scenario.

Mitkanos was more linear. His answer was the 'Sko were a violent people. Subtlety and subterfuge weren't their style.

"Ah, but the Dakrahl," Dallon said. He was the middleman, in Trilby's opinion. But his responses still heavily bespoke Fleet.

The subject changed a few minutes later. "The sublights are handling well since you resynchronized them." Rhis nodded at Mitkanos.

The burly man shrugged slightly. "Factory specs are usually overcautious." The fact that the *Razalka*'s captain paid him a compliment didn't appear to interest him much. But it told Trilby something about Khyrhis Tivahr. As Hana had said, he's not the same man who'd gone on the mission with her team.

Trilby checked the drive readouts. Fuel optimization was improved. She glanced again at the scanners, enviro, weapons. Online but showing cold. Mitkanos again.

And no response yet from Garold Grantforth. Or GGA.

"Okay, boys." She motioned with one hand to Mitkanos, then Dallon. "Back to your cabins. We'll take it from here. And, yes, as soon as we know . . ."

She left her voice trail off. They were all anxious to hear about the altered prescriptions. And if there was anything left of GGA personnel at HQ on Bagrond.

Her thoughts flew to Chaser standing next to her and Carina in the holo from Flyboy's. It was inconceivable that he'd be involved. It was equally chilling that he might've seen something and been killed. She hadn't heard from him since before Avanar.

But she had heard from Neadi. If anything were wrong, her friend would've said.

"*Vad. Vad.* I need dinner. Then sleep." Mitkanos patted the back of Trilby's chair, then ambled through the bridge hatchway.

"*Dasjon.* Captain." Dallon gave them a respectful nod, followed the *Stegzarda* major into the corridor.

The hatch door clanked shut. Trilby keyed the lock. Rhis grabbed her hand, squeezed it.

She gave him a wry smile. "They knew. The whole time. They knew you were in my cabin." She jerked her chin toward the now-empty comm station, with its CLS panel to her left.

"That was unavoidable."

"I don't think Uncle Yavo was very happy about it."

He sighed. "Uncle Yavo is *Stegzarda,* through and through. But that's not my concern." His thumb stroked her fingers. "Are you okay?"

Actually, yes, she realized with mild surprise. Better than she thought she'd be. There'd been those regrets born of uncertainty the first time. Then, when she found out who he was, sheer panic, fueled by anger.

Now . . .

She squeezed his hand in answer. "Very okay."

He let out what sounded like a sigh of relief. "Good. Now all I have to do is save the universe from the evil 'Sko and life will be perfect."

She laughed. "It all rests on you?"

"But of course!" He raised on eyebrow. "I am—"

"Zafharin. I know, I know. You're Zafharin."

"And an arrogant rimstrutter. Don't forget that."

"And the embodiment of perfection," she added.

"Actually," he said, his voice dropping to a sexy growl, "I much prefer your body."

"Do you? If you're nice to me, I may let you play with it from time to time."

"Tell me how to be nice to you, *Dasjankira.*" My lady love.

She pulled her hand out from under his, reached for his console. She keyed in the nav link. "Course change coming up. Be nice to me and handle it."

"No task is too great . . ."

She groaned and turned back to her monitors.

They'd crossed Gensiira's border into Lissade

while she and Rhis had slept in each other's arms.
With Jagan's authorization codes they were bypassing
the customs checkpoint on Marbo, heading directly
to the Colonies. She pulled up her charts. They were
about thirty-five minutes from a secondary beacon. If
a message waited, they might find it there.

She also toyed with the idea of sending one to
Chaser. Or Neadi. Or both.

Rhis had his lightpen out, flipping it between his
fingers. Should she add to his worries? She had to be
wrong. Chaser had no motives, no reason to work
with the 'Sko.

But he had known about Shadow's files. He knew
about her and Jagan. He was often at Flyboy's.

She took a deep breath. "Jagan's not the only one
at GGA who knew about the old star charts."

Rhis caught the pen in midair, regarded her levelly.

"It didn't . . . I didn't even think of him until you
found the poison in the prescription. Chaser works
for GGA Med-Labs."

"Chaser." He frowned slightly, then his eyebrows
lifted. "The red-haired man in the holo with you."

"With me and Carina."

"How long—"

"My whole life. Our whole lives. We grew up together in Port Rumor: Carina and Vitorio, Shadow,
Chaser, and me."

"Chaser ever work for Herkoid?"

He was the only one who hadn't. She shook her
head. "He went into med-tech training with the Port
Authority, worked as a paramedic for a couple years
before he signed up with GGA." She could see him
processing the information. "But he knew about the
charts Shadow took. And the ones Carina had."

"Did he ever ask to see them or ask you about them?"

She shook her head. "Chaser hates to fly, hates space travel. He's like Jagan. He's got to take meds or he makes the whole trip with his head in the sanifac." She grimaced. "I don't know if I'm more worried that he might have been poisoned or that he . . ." She let her voice trail off. She couldn't say it.

"Or that he might be part of the plan," Rhis finished quietly for her.

She nodded. Damnation! Not Chaser.

"Could he have done it, or helped?"

Trilby sighed, watched the data flow over her monitors for a moment. "He works in the pharmacy building. He probably has access codes, sure. Or knows someone's codes. But he's just a big, lovable, goofy guy. I can't picture him ever wanting to harm someone."

"The promise of power, and money, changes a lot of people."

Or the threat of blackmail. "He had a problem a couple years ago. With recreational drugs." She glanced at Rhis. He was nodding. "Spent six months in rehab. GGA could've let him go. But they didn't. I mean, it was pretty amazing, because he's just a medtech and Garold—"

She stopped, hearing her own words.

"Go on," Rhis said.

She swallowed. "Chaser said Garold Grantforth personally took an interest in his case. He was really flattered." She closed her eyes, let her head fall back against the headrest. Chaser. Garold Grantforth. Jagan. The 'Sko.

They all had one thing in common.

Trilby Elliot.

"Secretary Grantforth, not Jagan, helped Chaser?" Rhis asked.

She opened her eyes, stared at the starfield dotting the forward viewport but saw nothing. "He wasn't Secretary Grantforth then. Just a minor politician. Commissioner of something or other. But Chaser was still flattered, because Garold is synonymous with GGA."

"Did he know Jagan before you became involved with him?"

"Chaser? Not that he ever said."

Rhis picked up his lightpen, twisted it in his fingers again.

"Chaser wouldn't hurt anyone," she protested.

"If his addiction resurfaced, or it was made to resurface, he might do a lot of things." He reached for her again, enfolded her hand in his. His touch was warm, reassuring. "And he also might not. There are, what, hundreds of people in GGA Med-Labs? How many hundreds more in GGA itself? But it's good to play with these theories, Trilby-*chenka*. Because any one of them, or none of them, may be necessary when we get to Syar. It's how we prevent unpleasant surprises."

She squeezed his hand in answer.

It couldn't be Chaser. Not Chaser.

The secondary beacon brought no answer to Jagan's message. Trilby clicked off the incoming link, watched Rhis scroll through the usual news briefs and market downloads. "Think maybe I should talk to Jagan?"

The look on his face told her he didn't like that

idea. Or, rather, still didn't like her with Jagan. "When the time comes, we both question him."

Trilby let it go at that for the moment. She wasn't really sure what she'd say, anyway. How do you ask someone if they're a traitor or if one of their family's a traitor? And knowing Jagan's penchant for numbers and propensity to avoid politics, she wasn't sure he'd see any kind of deal with the 'Sko as traitorous. Especially if it meant profit.

And they wouldn't come to another beacon for three more hours. Close to the end of their shift. Less than a deuce away from the Colonies.

She felt Rhis's fingers massage the back of her neck. She hadn't realized she was so tense. She closed her eyes, heard him unhook his safety harness then hers.

She opened her eyes and he pulled her to her feet. "Come here."

He sat back down in his chair, settling her in his lap. "I don't know if you need this. But I do."

She wrapped her arms around his neck, letting his warmth sink into her. "I don't imagine this is acceptable behavior on the bridge of the *Razalka*."

"I may consider an amendment to regulations."

"Hana would approve."

He chuckled softly. "Well, yes, Jankova has never been reticent in pointing out my faults."

"I didn't know Imperial Arrogance was permitted faults."

"It's not." He was silent for a moment, his fingers tracing patterns in the small of her back. "Trilby-*chenka*?"

"Ummm?" She could fall asleep so easily right now.

"You were very afraid of me."

She remembered Imperial Arrogance striding through the dingy corridors of the *Careless Venture*. Standing stiffly at the base of her ship's ramp on Degvar. "You did try to kill me."

"No. Render you unconscious perhaps, because I didn't know where I was, what was going on. But after that. You were so afraid of me. Why?"

Why? Why. She had a hundred answers. And she had none. How do you explain an inbred lack of self-worth to Imperial Arrogance? How do you explain a hard-learned distrust of authority to a senior captain? "Because I was named after a blanket."

His fingers stopped. "What?"

"A blanket. Trilbyham Looms. When the Iffys picked me up, cataloged me, I didn't have a name. But I was carrying this tattered blanket with a label that said *Trilbyham Looms*. So they tagged me in as Trilby."

The massage resumed, slower this time.

"And you think that would matter to me?"

"You have *the* in front of your name."

"The?"

"*The* Khyrhis Tivahr."

He gave a short, harsh laugh. "I thought that was after it. Tivahr the Terrible."

"That too."

She felt him take a deep breath. "And our . . . friend. He's not *the* Jagan Grantforth?"

"Of *the* Grantforths? Absolutely. I swore, you know, I'd never get involved with another guy with a *the* in his name."

"And this made you afraid."

"This made me angry. At you. But really at myself."

"Because a woman named after a blanket does not . . . what—fall in love?" He gently pushed her back so that she was facing him. "Can I say that? That you love me?"

He didn't know. She could tell by the trepidation in his eyes that he honestly didn't know what she felt for him.

Well, she hadn't been terribly straightforward. Or consistent. She gave him a lazy smile. "Yeah, you can say that."

A grin spread slowly across his face. A corresponding warmth grew inside her. "So now you're not afraid."

"Of you? No."

"Of us?"

She had concerns. Normal relationship concerns. But she didn't feel anymore she'd be facing them alone. "No. I'm not afraid of us."

His thumb traced her jaw. "You should never have been."

"I had to figure that out for myself." Which was true. She didn't know that until she saw that the Rhis she hated was the same person as the Rhis she loved. She was the one who'd changed, placing labels on him, interpreting his actions because of a lack she thought was inside herself. A lack he didn't know about, and didn't care about.

"Of course, Hana and Doc Vanko did try a bit of persuasion on your behalf," she added.

"I'll be sure to add commendations to their files when we get back." He drew her forward, kissed her lightly.

She let herself enjoy it for a moment, then put her

hands against his shoulders. "You make it sound so easy."

"Commendations?"

"No. Getting back. You don't seem terribly concerned about what's waiting for us in Syar."

"Honestly, I'm not. Or I would never have permitted you on this mission. Surely you know that by now?"

"But this man you call Dark Sword—"

"Or woman. Or group of people. All of whom need you alive. And your nav banks intact. The only risk I see—and Demarik and I went over this rather thoroughly—would be resistance. Which is why I structured this as I have. Cooperation with GGA. I fully intend to hand them your nav banks—your altered nav banks—quite willingly. It would be the height of stupidity on Dark Sword's part, or the 'Sko's part, to harm us after that. It would raise too many questions."

Rhis's plan was almost reverse logic. Falling into their trap with a trap of his own.

"So when we get to Syar—"

"We accept whatever reasons GGA gives for acquiring this ship. Then we look for a tri-hauler called the *Cosmic Fortune,* which will just happen to be needing crew with our experience, and we go home. Tracing all the while, of course, the data we gave to GGA." He gave her a satisfied grin.

He had the whole thing planned, right down to a ship waiting for them. "I should've known," she said wryly.

"Yes. You should have."

Imperial Arrogance. She kissed him quickly, then pulled out of his lap. "There's one flaw in your great plan so far. We missed breakfast. And are about to miss lunch."

"It was worth it."

Her heart did a little flip-flop at the undeniably sexy tone in his voice. But her stomach was also rumbling. "I'll bring something back to the bridge." She ruffled his hair. "Don't get us lost now, okay?"

"Last time I got lost, you found me. That turned out rather nicely," he told her as she palmed open the bridge hatch lock.

Well, yes, it had. After a few twists and turns. "Finders keepers. Remember that." She stepped into the corridor and the hatch cycled shut behind her.

She strode into the lounge just as the incoming alarms erupted through the ship. She pivoted, dashed back into the corridor, and pounded up the ladderway, her heart thumping wildly. Her throat was too dry to bark questions through her ship badge.

The hatchway was open and she could see Rhis in the captain's chair. Red and yellow lights blinked in a familiar crazed staccato.

"What is it?" Her voice was raspy. She almost fell into the copilot's chair as he banked the ship hard to port. She raked the straps across her chest.

" 'Sko." His voice was deathly flat. "Mother ship. Two squadrons."

She slapped off the alarm, keyed the console mike to intraship. " 'Sko incoming. One plus two. Red alert stations, now!"

She heard Dallon, Farra, and Mitkanos confirm through the comm board behind her. She keyed the mike again. "Elliot to Grantforth. You're confined to quarters. But if you know anything, *anything* about this, mister, you tell me now!"

Jagan's voice was a plaintive whine. "I swear, Trilby, they're not supposed to—"

But the rest of his explanation was lost as an overhead panel exploded. And intruder alarms kicked back on, filling the ship with a deafening wail.

26

Strained voices shouted orders in a mixture of Standard and Zafharish. Rhis was in command, but Dallon translated whatever he seemed to believe Trilby needed to know.

That helped, but for the most part Trilby reacted on instinct. Keeping the ship in one piece, all systems operating, needed no translation.

"Torpedoes, incoming, portside." Dallon barked out heading and speed. Rhis initiated evasive maneuvers. Trilby monitored shield status, still holding at one hundred percent despite several direct hits.

But the 'Sko hadn't fired torpedoes at them before.

Farra, at communications, sent out repeated SUAs on both Conclave and Imperial channels. And monitored for any answer from the *Cosmic Fortune*. Which was, Trilby guessed, a bit more than an average tri-hauler. But she could also be as much as a deuce ahead of them.

The torpedoes veered away.

"Sloppy shooting," Mitkanos grumbled in Zafharish.

"Don't count on it." Rhis didn't take his concentration from the board. "That might just be a warning. Farra?"

"*Nav.* Nothing yet, sir."

Trilby answered his question before he asked it. "Comm pack still online. We're sending." *But no one's answering.*

"Bloody hell." Rhis's curse was hushed, tense.

The ship shuddered slightly as Mitkanos fired their weapons. Not the ion cannons, not yet. That, Trilby knew, would be for the mother ship. If she got close enough.

"They're pulling back, regrouping maybe," Dallon advised.

Rhis shot a quick glance over his shoulder at the younger man. "Jumpgate?"

"None in range yet, sir. We're in one of those dead areas."

Trilby caught Rhis's gaze, and his unspoken command. Her fingers flew to the nav link on her console. "Which one is the real file?" She was looking at the Herkoid data Rhis intended to give to GGA.

He reached over quickly, highlighted a minor file tagged for enviro. "Here. Bring it up. I'll decode it."

She scanned the old star charts as they filled her screen. Lissade. Syar. She grabbed all references to the Colonies, ran through them quickly.

The ship rocked again, lights flickering. She glanced to her left. "Shields holding at eighty percent."

"Jumpgate?"

"Not yet." She paged through another chart. Damn it! There had to be something. She didn't care where it went, as long as it took them into hyperspace

and gave them time to have someone meet them—
and the 'Sko, if they followed—when they exited.

The long-range scanner in front of Rhis beeped.
Trilby looked at the board. Maybe the *Cosmic
Fortune*? Or a Conclave patrol?

But Rhis's mouth hardened into a thin line. "Second mother ship. 'Sko. Thirty-five minutes out."

That meant two more squadrons of 'Tarks.

"Why?" Trilby asked, feeling it was a foolish question even as she voiced it.

"Jagan's message is my guess." But Rhis didn't
sound like he was guessing.

Mitkanos swore. "Damned bastard."

Another sickening shimmy, another flickering of
lights.

"Shields at eighty and holding. Generators online," Trilby said, and opened the next star chart.
Two squadrons of 'Tarks were big trouble. Four were
certain death.

"Watch starboard flank," Rhis called out to
Mitkanos.

"On them. On them. In range."

Trilby saw the cluster of ships part on the scanners.
Rhis saw it too. "The newcomers are splitting up—
damn it! Class-Five destroyer! They're screening a
Class-Five destroyer!"

He banked the ship, hard. Engine-overload signals
flashed. Trilby was wrenched against her harness
straps, then something slammed into the back of her
seat with a harsh cry. She jerked forward.

"Bloody fucking . . ." Rhis switched to Standard.
"Get the hell off the bridge, Grantforth!"

Trilby twisted around. Jagan's hands were locked
onto her headrest. He was half kneeling, half sprawling

on the floor behind her. His face was pale, sweat-streaked.

"No! Wait," he croaked.

Rhis jerked his thumb at Dallon. "Get him off here! And lock the bridge this time!"

Jagan clawed at Trilby's arm. "Tell them I'm on board! They can't . . . they won't . . . they just want those map files."

"Get below, Jagan!" Trilby told him tersely.

"Uncle Garold needs those map files to seal the agreement!"

"Those are Niyil ships, Grantforth." Rhis turned in his seat, tried to push Jagan backward.

"Yes! We're working with them too."

Trilby caught Rhis's quick look of disgust. Then Dallon grabbed Jagan under the armpits, yanked him upright.

"They've got ion cannons primed," Mitkanos said in Zafharish.

"Bring full weapons online!" Rhis ordered. "Destroyer is primary target. Fire at will."

Jagan wrenched against Dallon, reached for Trilby. "What's he saying? What's happening?"

She looked up. "We're in trouble. Big trouble. Strap him in at second nav, Dallon." There was no time to drag Jagan below to his cabin. She needed Dallon on the bridge.

And Rhis needed her attention. "Jumpgate?"

She turned back to the charts. "Working on it." But there was nothing. Nothing. The 'Sko couldn't have picked a better spot to ambush them if they'd known. . . .

She glanced at the code trailing down the side of the file. Shadow's notations and a comment by

Vitorio. This was one of the charts Carina had. Trilby felt as if her heart stopped. "Khyrhis." She said his name softly.

Dark eyes turned to her. She didn't try to disguise the fear in her voice. "This is the same chart *Bella's Dream* had. There are no jumpgates here. They know that."

He held her gaze for a very long moment, then turned away. His deep voice was emotionless, held the hard tone of undeniable authority. "Rimanava. Open a channel to Admiral Vanushavor, Code Delta Priority One. Copy to Captain Rafiello Vanushavor on the *Vendetta*, Commander Zakar Demarik on the *Razalka*. Transmit all logs.

"Append note to Demarik. On my orders, engage the First Fleet. Objective: Syar."

Trilby understood. Rhis was authorizing an invasion of the Conclave.

But Jagan didn't, though he evidently recognized some names. "Vanushavor? *Razalka*? What in hell are you doing, Vanur? I told you, they just want—"

"In range. Firing!" Mitkanos bellowed.

Rhis held the ship steady, then turned back to Jagan, his eyes narrowed. "Our nav banks? I already tried that. They declined. Answered with two squadrons of 'Tarks instead. They want you dead. All of us dead. Probably your beloved uncle as well. Only fools think they can make deals with the 'Sko."

Jagan strained angrily against his harness. "Who do you think you are to call me—"

"Tivahr. Senior Captain Khyrhis Tivahr of the *Razalka*. That's who I am, Grantforth. Now shut up or I will let you talk to the 'Sko. In person. Out the air lock." Rhis swung around. His fingers flew across the command console with a vengeance.

And he missed the sight of Jagan's mouth dropping wide open. But Trilby didn't. Nor did she miss the flicker of fear in his blue eyes.

He finally noticed her scrutiny. "You knew this?" His voice rasped.

"Yes." She went back to her star charts. But an unexpected pride surged through her. *The* Khyrhis Tivahr. It sounded very, very right.

"Mother Two, ten minutes," Mitkanos intoned.

The 'Sko destroyer had pulled back, gathered its shield of 'Tarks around it again when Mitkanos returned fire with their ion cannons.

Shields were down to seventy-five percent, but comm pack was still online. That was critical. Someone had to hear them. Someone had to answer their distress call. They might outrun a mother ship, even two, but not the 'Tarks, which could refuel from the mother ships. Time was not on their side.

They needed a safe haven, but without a jumpgate Trilby couldn't find them one. There was nothing out here in this section of the Syar Quadrant, not even an asteroid field. It was, as Dallon said, a dead zone. The description chilled her. No. It would not be her dead zone. She refused to accept that.

"Trilby." Jagan's voice hissed across the bridge, through the beeping of the monitors and curt commands in Zafharish. "Link me to the 'Sko. I can—we can trade his life," he pointed at Rhis, "for ours. They'd love Tivahr the Terrible."

Trilby flashed him a disarming smile. "Fuck you, Jagan."

"Bitch!"

She shrugged, caught Rhis shaking his head at their exchange.

"Captain Tivahr." Farra switched to Standard. "I am picking up a Norvind convoy, forty-six minutes out. They acknowledge our SUA."

Hope blossomed in Trilby's chest. Forty-six minutes. They could hang on that long, couldn't they? A freighter convoy wouldn't be heavily armed, but they might have an escort. It was better than nothing and might buy them time until the Fleet—either Fleet— could find them.

Rhis was already relaying instructions, altering course to intercept.

"Coming in range. Targeting." Mitkanos's commands brought her back to the closer problem. The 'Tarks. In a different formation.

There was something odd about it, but she couldn't peg what exactly, and reasoned that she could well be misreading it due to stress and inexperience. She wasn't military. She went back to her duties. "Shields down to seventy. Unless—" Hell. Jagan was on the bridge. Who needed enviro belowdecks if no one was there?

She looked quickly at Rhis. He nodded. "Cutting off life support to crew deck," she announced. "Thirty seconds. Segueing power to shield generators."

"In range. Firing!"

She glanced at the screens, saw two 'Tarks splinter apart. "Good shot, Yavo."

Then something slammed into the ship. Trilby wrenched sideways, the chair's armrest digging painfully into her ribs. She heard Mitkanos grunt over the screeching of alarms. A panel sizzled behind her, punctuating Rhis's litany of curses in Zafharish and Standard.

"Bloody Gods damned ion cannon! Direct hit, starboard flank. Mitkanos!"

"Star . . . starboard torpedo tubes inoperational."

Her screens were no more encouraging. "Shields down forty percent."

"Recalibrating lasers," Dallon said. "I need five minutes—"

"We don't have five minutes. Brace! Incoming cannon fire!"

Trilby's skin chilled as she tugged her harness secure with one hand. She raised the other arm over her face, locked her feet against the lower panel. Only at the last minute did she glance under her arm and catch Rhis's dark and weary gaze as it flickered up briefly from the command console.

"*Yav cheron,*" she told him.

His wistful smile was the last thing she saw as the bridge exploded.

She woke to a red-tinged darkness and a bitter, metallic taste in her mouth. She recognized both. Power was down. Enviro had kicked off, long enough for her to lose consciousness. Dezi must have gone down to engineering—

But Dezi wasn't here. This wasn't the *Careless Venture.* She struggled against something heavy, found it wasn't her safety harness holding her into her seat but a thick braid of conduit, cascading through the ceiling.

She coughed, pushed it aside. The ship was eerily quiet, save for an ominous hissing noise from the corridor. Ruptured enviro conduit. Her eyes adjusted to the dim light, caught shadowy forms, silent, around her.

"Rhis!" She unsnapped her harness, lunged for his seat. It was empty.

Oh, Gods! She dropped to her knees, felt along the floor, her fingers finding debris but nothing more.

"Rhis!" She heard a clunking noise, but it sounded distant. Way belowdecks.

She pulled herself to her feet, shuffled to her right toward two forms. They were warm. She heard a groan as she ran her hands over the smaller one. Farra. "Farra? Yavo?"

"*Vad, vad.* This is you, Trilby?" Mitkanos answered first.

"It's me."

Farra was coughing. Mitkanos worked on releasing her harness.

"Where's Rhis?" Trilby asked.

"Here." He was leaning in the hatchway. "Bloody Gods damned generators—"

She nearly sprang into his arms, tripping over cables and warped panels on the way. He caught her tightly against him. His face was wet and covered with something gritty, but she didn't care. She kissed him until Mitkanos stumbled into them, bumping her sideways.

"*S'viek noyet.*" The large man grabbed a skewed section of bulkhead, tried to twist it sideways.

Dallon. Gods, no.

Rhis moved, braced his arms against the tall panel, pushed with Mitkanos. Behind them, Farra worked on the command console.

The red-tinged emergency lights brightened. Two

small overhead white lights flickered on. Trilby could see Dallon slumped in his harness. Mitkanos grabbed his arm, felt for a pulse.

Dallon stirred, raised his head groggily. "Bloody hell."

"Don't move yet," Rhis ordered in Zafharish, and drew out a small medistat.

"*Vad yasch.* . . . I'm okay, Captain. Just blacked out. Enviro must have quit."

"It did." Rhis ran the unit down Dallon's side. "You're a tough one, Patruzius."

"Captain." It was Rhis whom Mitkanos called to, but Trilby turned as well, stepped toward him. And saw Jagan's form pinned awkwardly in the chair, a metal rod protruding from his chest. Blood stained the front of his pale shirt. His eyes were open, as if in surprise.

She closed her eyes, felt her head start to spin, then Rhis's arm was around her waist. He lifted her into his chair. "Put your head down. That's it. Deep breath. Deep breath. It's all right."

All right. Was it all right? Jagan was dead, impaled by a conduit casing that must have shot through the ceiling in the explosion. A foot to the left and it would've hit Dallon. Or, at another angle, herself. Or Rhis.

She stopped staring at her boots—they were scuffed—and raised her face. "I'll be okay."

He kissed her forehead.

"Ship's status?" she asked.

"Well, enviro's working." He glanced over his shoulder at Mitkanos, whose arm was wrapped around his niece's shoulders. "I don't know about the hyperspace engines. Or the drives."

"Only emergency systems respond on the boards," Farra said. "Lights, enviro. That is all."

Dallon had moved to Mitkanos's station and leaned over the monitors, one arm clasped painfully against his side. "Weapons are not responding. Not that I'd expect—"

The ship jerked suddenly, followed by several loud thunks. Farra tottered against Mitkanos. "What was that?"

"Tractor beam, maybe." Rhis frowned, glanced over Trilby's shoulder at his console. Most of the screens were dead. His hand moved to the small pistol holstered to his hip. "Or boarding ram."

Mitkanos and Dallon mimicked his movement. Trilby patted her utility belt, felt her pistol and tools.

Another series of jerking movements and more thunks.

"Boarding ram," Dallon said, nodding. "Can we lock the bridge?"

Farra tapped at her console. "Nothing is responding."

"We have to make a stand here," Rhis said. "That convoy's on its way."

"How many will board at once?" Farra asked.

Trilby heard the muted click as Rhis unlocked his pistol. "I have no way of telling. But they have to come through that hatchway one at a time." He motioned to Dallon and Mitkanos. "Either side of the doorway. Then silence. Let's not give them any advance warning."

Trilby sat at communications, listened to her breathing, listened to the creaking and groaning of her ship. Rhis stood next to her, leaning one hip against the console. His pistol was in one hand, his other lightly massaged her shoulder.

Farra was at Mitkanos's station: weapons. Useless now.

Only command and copilot chairs were empty. They were the first things anyone would see coming through the hatchway.

Sounds. Thumping. Then voices, high-pitched, nasal. Jarring. 'Sko voices. Ycskrite words. Trilby snaked one hand up to her shoulder, squeezed Rhis's fingers. He squeezed back, hard. Then released her.

No distractions. Not now.

Boot steps, clearly boot steps now. Coming quickly, but not as quickly as her heart thudded double time in her chest. How many of the 'Sko had boarded? How many could they kill before their pistols went cold?

What if the other mother ship took out the Norvind convoy before it got here?

Forms suddenly appeared in the hatchway. She raised her pistol as Rhis fired. She took aim, squeezed the trigger in rapid succession. Laser fire singed through the air. Red-suited forms, tall, thin, flailed, screamed. Behind them, others fired back.

Ycskrite words were shouted. Rhis pushed her to the floor, snugged her up against the console. She saw Dallon drop to one knee, fire around a thin body jerking under impact.

Mitkanos backed up, drew Farra behind him. She fired over his shoulder.

The red-uniformed 'Sko kept coming. She could see gloved hands grab the wounded and lifeless bodies. Muted thumps followed as they were shoved out of the way, down the stairwell.

Trilby saw a flash of red, fired again.

"We need cover!" Rhis barked harshly in Zafharish.

Dallon jerked his head toward the bulkhead panel skewed across the nav station.

Trilby understood. They had to move the long metal panel diagonally across the bridge. It would give them a four-foot-high wall. They could wedge one end at the copilot's chair, the other at communications. They wouldn't be trapped on the flanks, like they were now.

Their shots would be more accurate.

Trilby understood something else. They needed accuracy. Their pistols were running low on power.

"Mitkanos!" Rhis pointed to the communications chair. "Lock it down. Patruzius and I will shove the panel toward you."

Mitkanos scrambled sideways. Farra adjusted her crouch, tapped off two more shots as he moved.

Rhis shifted his weight. He was going to dash across the open bridge, right through the 'Sko's direct fire. Trilby drew a deep breath. "Say when. I'll cover you."

"When."

She sprayed the hatchway with laser fire. Streaks of light blurred by in answer. She couldn't watch Rhis, couldn't take her eyes off the hatchway and the edges of red uniforms as they came into view.

But she listened and permitted herself a broad smile when she heard his trademark "bloody fucking hell!" from across the bridge.

He made it.

She pulled back, looked toward navigation, saw only his boots moving behind the skewed panel.

But so did the 'Sko. Laser fire sizzled against it.

She saw Dallon duck behind it, where Jagan's body still was.

Then a low growl from Mitkanos. He snapped open his pistol's power chamber and shook his head. The first of their weapons to go dead. And spare charge packs were below, on crew deck.

A 'Sko pistol, its power light green, was wedged against the bottom of the nonfunctioning hatch door. There was no way she could reach it.

The panel tilted. But Mitkanos must have seen the direction of Trilby's gaze.

"Wait!" he called, rising. He lunged for the 'Sko pistol. Trilby raised her own to cover him, but two forms surged through the doorway, clear body shields in one hand, laser rifles in the other.

She fired at the shields just as Farra did. Their charges splattered, ineffective.

"Yavo!" Farra screamed, reaching for him.

A 'Sko whipped around, his rifle pointed at the *Stegzarda* major. He fired. Mitkanos jerked backward, blood spurting from his arm, his shoulder. He roared in pain.

The other shielded 'Sko turned as Rhis rose from behind the panel, his pistol firing rapidly with deadly aim. He caught the closest one in the head, and the 'Sko's body wrenched backward.

Then it was Rhis reeling backward, his pistol flying from his hand. Two more 'Sko had barged in, shielded, firing. A dark stain blossomed in the center of Rhis's gray shirt. His body twisted as he slammed back against the nav console.

A harsh, keening cry rose in Trilby's throat, but she

clenched her teeth and fired at the 'Sko. Her vision blurred as tears flowed down her cheeks.

No. No. No. She repeated the words, firing faster with every syllable. No. No. Nonono—

Her pistol clicked. Cold. Empty.

Oh, Gods.

There was silence on her right. Farra shook her head, her pistol drained.

Only Dallon kept firing. Then a shielded 'Sko raised a rifle, pointed it at Farra's head.

"Your. Choice." The words came out tinny through a translator.

Dallon's weapon fell silent.

Trilby was breathing hard, her knees aching from kneeling on the hard decking. The narrow barrel of a laser rifle was inches from her face.

"Up. Stand."

She glared up at the 'Sko. Sallow-skinned. Elongated face. Yellowed eyes. Bright red uniform covering an equally elongated, thin body. The head was bald, save for a thin braid of hair in the middle. It could be male or female. She couldn't tell.

She didn't care.

"Fuck. You," she told it.

"Up. Stand!" The voice whined insistently through the translator. The thin face jerked over one shoulder.

A rifle still pointed at Farra. Now one was against Dallon's head too.

She steeled herself, turned her head a little further. Rhis.

Oh, Gods. A sob escaped her lips.

His body sprawled across the nav monitors. The hooded screen of the tachyon sensor had caught under his arm. It was the only thing that kept him from sliding to the chair, to the floor. His shirt was a dark stain, charred over his left pocket from the heat of the laser. His face was pale, his head hanging at an odd angle. His eyes . . .

. . . moved slightly. A blink?

She struggled to her feet, pushed away the barrel of the rifle as it was shoved against her shoulder.

"Rhis! Oh, Gods, Rhis!" She groped her way past the captain's chair, reached the copilot's station, stumbled.

The barrel of a 'Sko rifle slammed hard against her chest. She gasped for breath, felt her knees buckle. She grasped for the back of the chair.

And saw Rhis's eyes unfocus, his features go slack. His head dropped forward. Then, in what seemed like an eternity to her, his body slid slowly to the floor.

Something cold trembled violently through her. She dug her fingernails into the palms of her hands. Her arms shook.

The 'Sko grabbed her, wrenching her toward the hatchway. She tore her gaze from Rhis's crumpled form and saw Farra standing near Mitkanos's body. Blood pooled around his shoulder.

Trilby unclenched her fist, reached for her. Wordlessly, Farra took her hand.

Dallon was already in the hatchway, blood dripping from a long gash on his forehead, his long hair, now untied, hanging limp from sweat. His dark eyes blazed angrily. He limped toward her.

"*Dasjas.*" His voice was soft and full of pain. "I am so sorry."

Tears welled up behind her eyes. She shook her head, unable to speak. She only held Farra's hand tighter.

The 'Sko shoved her forward. "Now! Go. Move."

She stepped into the corridor and forced herself not to look back.

⋆⋆⋆ 27

The cell was small and on a lower deck of the 'Sko mother ship. She could feel the thrumming of the drives through her body as she sat on the floor, knees drawn into her chest. There were no benches, no beds.

It surprised her that the 'Sko had put them together: Dallon, Farra, and herself. She didn't argue about that. The cell was well lit but cold. She needed the warmth of Dallon's arm across her shoulder as they huddled together along the wall. His other wrapped around Farra's waist.

The force field shimmered a sickly orange-red across the front of the cell. 'Sko officers stood on the other side for a long time, talking in Ycskrite. If they were waiting to see what their three prisoners would do or were waiting to hear what was said, well, they'd have a long wait.

By tacit agreement she, Dallon, and Farra had adopted near total silence. Wait, watch, and see.

She wondered if the 'Sko knew who she was and wanted her alive.

She wondered if Rhis knew how much she loved him.

She started trembling again, steeled herself, angry at her reaction. She was senior officer. She couldn't permit herself to fall apart.

Two of the three 'Sko watching them strode away. Finally the third left, slowly, glancing back a few times before she heard the buzz of a force field activate in the corridor.

The brig was secure.

She turned toward Dallon. The blood on his face was dried hard, crusted, with long strands of his hair caught in it. His dark eyes glittered. She knew he was in pain. His limp had grown worse as the 'Sko forced them through the corridors and into the brig.

"Your leg," she asked softly. "Broken?"

His grin was strained. "Not completely."

"Farra?"

"Only some cuts and bruises." Her voice shook. But she was *Stegzarda*. Trilby knew she wouldn't break down.

"Captain?" Dallon's dark gaze searched her face.

Was it only a trike ago they'd sat in the lounge on Degvar, sipping tea?

"Same. No serious injuries." Her chest ached, though. She wouldn't be surprised if the 'Sko had cracked one of her ribs when it shoved the rifle barrel against her chest. "I can use my jacket, bind your leg. But I don't have anything to make a splint."

"You'll freeze in here without a jacket. And my leg's not an issue unless we have to run a marathon."

"Perhaps they'll bring a blanket, something we can use."

"Don't count on it" was his terse reply.

But they did, about an hour later. Three blankets. A bucket with water.

She stood as the force field shimmered back on. "I need a brace. Something to bind his leg. It's broken." She faced the 'Sko squarely, her eyes never wavering from its face. She knew she should feel fear. But she felt nothing. Only emptiness.

Rhis was dead.

The 'Sko chattered at her in its language, then reached for a small object clipped to its collar. "Repeat."

"I need a brace. A leg brace. His leg," she motioned behind her but still stared directly at the 'Sko, "is broken."

"Medic?"

"I am trained," Farra replied.

The 'Sko's thin face twisted quickly from side to side. "Can relay information. Not more." It departed.

"Think it will bring something?" Farra spoke softly.

"I didn't think we'd get the blankets," Dallon admitted. He wrapped one around Farra's shoulders before pulling another across his outstretched legs.

Trilby was still standing in the middle of the cell, arms folded tightly across her chest. *They want us alive. I don't know why. But they want us alive.* She wondered if they'd found Jagan's body. Realized this was the ship Garold Grantforth was waiting for. Realized that maybe they'd made a mistake.

Jagan had thought it was. She could still hear his

voice on intraship: *I swear, Trilby, they're not sup-posed to—*

Supposed to what? Attack, obviously. So he knew they'd meet up with the 'Sko mother ship. He knew they were involved in a deadly and dangerous game when he'd met her on Saldika. But he thought he'd be spared because of the nav files.

Rhis said he'd offered the 'Sko the nav files. They hadn't wanted them.

Maybe they were a different faction of the Niyil? Not the ones Jagan said were working with his uncle?

It was painfully clear that Garold Grantforth was working with the 'Sko. Working with the Niyil and the Beffa. But admitting to his agreements with only one. His deals with the Niyil were in secret. And, Trilby guessed, more than likely treasonous.

She turned, saw the crooked outline of Dallon's leg under the thin blanket. The dark stain of blood smeared on his face. "Close your eyes, Patruzius." That's what Rhis had called him.

"Huh?"

"Close your eyes." She stripped off her jacket, be-gan unzipping her shirt. "I need something to clean the cut on your forehead and I don't want to get the blankets wet."

He closed his eyes. She took off her uniform shirt, then pulled her T-shirt over her head.

The same T-shirt Rhis had slid over her body be-fore they went on duty. Eight, ten hours ago? He'd dressed her, lovingly, teasingly, from her socks to her shirt, her jacket. Brushed out her short hair.

She was trembling again. She thrust her arms through her sleeves, yanked the shirt zipper up, then donned her jacket. She wadded her T-shirt into a ball.

"Okay." She couldn't say more. She didn't trust her voice.

The water in the plastic bucket was clear and cold. She soaked part of her T-shirt, then knelt in front of Dallon and pressed it against his forehead.

Farra reached for her hand. "I can do this, Captain. Uncle Yavo"—she swallowed hard—"he made sure I learn medic tech. *Stegzarda*. We are *Stegzarda*. There is nothing we cannot do."

Trilby handed her the wadded shirt.

"*Vad*. Lean back, tilt your head," Farra told Dallon in Zafharish. "I need to soak through the blood to see how deep your wound is. Brave boy, ah, Dallon-*chevo*. Such a brave boy. You've done this before, hmm? Promised a candy for being good?"

Trilby heard Dallon's low chuckle. Farra Rimanava was a wonder. Yavo Mitkanos had treasured her for good reason.

Then the 'Sko was back, a rodlike contraption in its hand. Another guard stood behind it, rifle aimed at Trilby. The first 'Sko keyed off the force field from the panel in the middle of the corridor and tossed the brace into the cell.

"Brace. For. Leg." It shook its thin face rapidly.

That had to mean, Trilby decided, either yes or no. She refrained from nodding. If she didn't understand its body language, she doubted it understood hers.

She also refrained from thanking it. She wasn't in the least bit grateful. Nor would she ever be to a 'Sko. "If it's not what we need, I'll let you know."

She picked it up and brought it to Farra, not bothering to watch the guards leave.

Farra spent a few more minutes sponging Dallon's

face, then inspected the wound. "Not too deep. But at least it's cleaner now."

"Thanks, Doc."

"Hold your thanks, Dallon-*chevo*. I have to work on that leg of yours next."

"Need me to take my pants off?" He was grinning at her.

"Regrettably, I must deny myself that pleasure."

Trilby found a small smile creep across her lips at Farra's quick retort. She must have teased the shy Lucho mercilessly back on Degvar.

Which was where Farra belonged. On Degvar with Lucho. Uncle Yavo was gone. Farra needed Lucho. And he needed her.

I will get you back there, somehow, Trilby promised her. *I will get you back there.*

It was cold. And dark. Someone must have turned out the lights. He rolled over, or tried to. Found he couldn't. Something hard pressed into his back. His chest ached, felt as if it was split in half.

Oh. That's right. He'd been shot.

Rhis blinked his eyes again, hard. His vision wavered, then cleared. It was still dark, but a red-tinged darkness. Emergency lighting.

His ship. The 'Sko.

Trilby.

He forced his mouth open, unstuck his tongue from the roof of his mouth. Two harsh, breathy syllables emerged. "Tril-by?"

Nothing. Then a groan, low and guttural. From the far side of the bridge.

He dragged his elbow under his side, pushed. Pain

seared through him, almost blinding him. "Bloody fucking hell!"

"Tivahr?"

A voice, weakly saying his name. He sifted through memory, tagged it. "Mitkanos?"

"*Vad.*" A gasping, wheezing breath. "*Vad.*"

"Hang on." Stupid thing to say. He had no idea how far apart they were. He had no idea if he could even walk. Or crawl. He moved his head, looked down. Legs still there. Good. What he could see of his chest was a dark stain.

Oh, right. He'd been shot.

He tried rolling over again, found the problem was not so much his uncooperative body as a chair and a goodly portion of the nav console wedging him in. He wriggled slowly down toward the copilot's seat. Where Trilby had been sitting when—

Trilby. He saw her now, eyes wide with horror, hand reaching toward him, cheeks streaked with tears. And the red-uniformed 'Sko, slamming the hard barrel of the rifle across her chest.

Bastards! He'd promised himself if they even looked at her, they'd die. They'd done a lot more than look.

Yet she'd grabbed the chair, still tried to come toward him.

He was dying. Well, she thought he was dying. The 'Sko, he had to assume, thought he was dead.

Surprise.

It took him a few more minutes to untangle himself from the collapsed console and crawl out from under the copilot's station. He could hear Mitkanos breathing raggedly. His medistat was still clipped to his belt. If it hadn't been crushed by his fall, he'd need it.

He crawled over the debris, found the *Stegzarda* major flat on his back. "Where're you hit?"

"Chest. Shoulder."

He felt for the medistat, flipped it open. It hummed on. Good old reliable Imperial technology. "You've got a collapsed lung. Collarbone's shattered. Significant blood loss."

"This thrills me."

"It should. You're not going to die." There was an emergency med-kit on the bridge. Communications station, he remembered. Convenient.

He leaned back, felt for the wall panel, popped it open. Emergency hand beam. Antibiotic med-broches. Painkillers. Synth-flesh compound. Bone regenerators. Good old reliable Imperial technology. He dragged what he needed back to Mitkanos.

"Tivahr."

"Um?" He placed two broches near the man's neck. Antibiotic and painkiller.

"I saw them shoot you."

Rhis raised his hand to his chest, touched it gingerly. It ached like hell. In a little while, that damned itching would start. He imagined that what Mitkanos could see in the light of the hand beam looked pretty bad. "They did."

"Then . . . it's true. What you are."

He slid his hand carefully under Mitkanos's back. "I need you to sit up slightly. This might hurt a little. I want to get the bone regen strapped on before I look at your lung."

Mitkanos grunted. Rhis quickly ripped off the remains of the man's shirt, angled him up. He strapped on the regen, securing it under his armpit. He lowered Mitkanos back down.

Mitkanos gasped shallowly.

"Hurts like a bitch, I bet."

"You." Mitkanos raised one arm, pointed at Rhis's chest. "And you don't?"

"Not as bad as you, no." Good old Imperial technology.

Mitkanos nodded, closed his eyes.

Rhis opened the medistat, scanned the damaged lung. There wasn't much he could do about that right now. He needed to get Mitkanos to sick bay—if his ship still had one. If not, he could probably rig something.

He stood, stepped carefully over to the command console. The computers were dead. He stared out at the blackened viewport and wondered, for the first time, why he saw no starfield.

Was he really, finally, dead and didn't know it?

He couldn't be. He needed to tell Trilby how much he loved her. He needed desperately to hear her say she loved him. He needed to hold her, kiss away her tears. . . .

Two lights suddenly flared through the viewport. Instinctively he ducked down, wrenching the wound in his chest. Shit! Pain constricted his breathing for a moment.

He eased himself up, peered over the top of the console.

Bloody hell. He was in a fighter bay.

Two red-uniformed 'Sko trudged across the wide expanse of floor, dragging a servo-stair behind them.

They must have tractored the ship in. He remembered a mother ship. No, two. One of them had tractored *Shadow's Quest* into a fighter bay.

They must still need the nav banks.

Which told him Trilby was alive.

Which told him the 'Sko would be coming back on board. The ones dragging the servo-stair stopped at the wings of a small heavy-air recon craft. They weren't coming here now.

But they would.

He had to get Mitkanos off the bridge to a place of safety. He had to find Trilby, tell her he loved her. Then all he had left to do was save the universe from the evil 'Sko, and life would be wonderful again.

He picked his way back through the debris to Mitkanos, lay his hand against the man's good shoulder.

"Yavo."

His eyes fluttered open. "*Vad*, Captain."

"We're in a 'Sko mother ship. Hangar bay. I need to move you belowdecks. Sick bay, if it's still there. Then I've got to find Trilby."

"And Farra. Dallon."

"And Farra and Dallon, yes."

Mitkanos struggled to push himself upright. "I think I can walk—"

"Wait. I'll need help getting you down those stairs."

"Help?"

But Rhis was already moving through the hatch lock, over the bodies of the dead 'Sko. He picked out a few pistols, still showing green, shoved them in the waistband of his pants. He had two laser rifles in his cabin.

And help.

"Yavo? Think you can stand now?"

Mitkanos opened his eyes. Blinked. "This is help?"

"This is Dezi. Dezi, Major Yavo Mitkanos. We need to get him down to the captain's cabin." Sick bay had taken considerable damage.

The 'droid cocked his tarnished head. "A pleasure to meet you, Major," he said in flawless Zafharish. "Though I must say these are unfortunate circumstances. Here, let me assist you. I'm much stronger than I look."

Rhis grabbed the burly man around the waist, careful of his damaged shoulder. Dezi pulled Mitkanos's arm across his shoulder, braced himself against the man's side.

"Ready?" Rhis asked him.

"Of course, Captain. It feels so good to be useful again."

They made the first landing of stairs before Mitkanos could insert a comment. "You built this 'droid, Tivahr?"

Rhis shook his head, grinning in spite of his pain. "He's Trilby's. I just was putting him back together for her after he had a slight accident."

Mitkanos grunted. "Did you have to hook up his mouth?"

Trilby dozed fitfully, blanket wrapped around her. She watched the 'Sko come and go through her lowered lashes. They never stayed long. They'd tap at something on the console in the corridor, then leave.

She glanced at her watch. Almost six hours had passed since they were brought on board. Dallon was asleep, his head cradled in Farra's lap. The young woman caught her gaze, nodded slightly. Dallon was doing okay. She lightly stroked his hair.

Trilby was exhausted, but sleep frightened her. She'd see Rhis, his shirt stained, his dark eyes staring lifelessly. She didn't want to remember him that way.

Rhis was Khyrhis, and Khyrhis was tall, commanding, gentle, challenging. With night-black hair and a body—

Her eyes jerked open. Someone said her name. A form stood in front of the force field.

"El. Li. Ot." 'Sko.

She leaned her head back against the wall, regarded the 'Sko impassively. "I'm Elliot."

"Elli. Ot." It raised one hand. The other held a rifle. "Up. Stand."

"Trilby—"

"It's okay, Farra." She stood, dropped the blanket at Farra's feet as she passed by. She'd wondered when the 'Sko would get around to asking her questions.

The force field hazed. The 'Sko motioned her through. "Come."

She followed it down the corridor. They stopped at the second field. The 'Sko touched something at its waist and the field dropped.

"Come."

For a moment she thought of disobeying, just for the sheer obstinacy of it. But she wanted to see more of the mother ship, wanted to find some way to get out of the brig. She followed the tall form, glancing left and right. There were other cells, all empty save for an orange glow ahead on her left. She slowed her steps slightly as she came alongside, looked quickly down.

And saw a pair of dark blue eyes meet her gaze.

Her heart thudded and it took all her strength not to let the name escape her lips.

Carina.

She almost stumbled but caught herself. Her escort didn't seem to notice.

They were near the end of the corridor. There were no other orange-tinged cells she could see. But Carina was here. Carina!

And Vitorio . . . She hadn't seen Vitorio. But he had to be alive. Carina was.

Carina was alive.

Three more 'Sko joined them in the lift. They stared openly at her, making low comments in their high-pitched tongue. She still couldn't tell the males from the females. Or officers from crew.

But they were Niyil, Rhis had said. That meant they were military. She wondered how he knew.

The other 'Sko exited a few decks later and she was left alone with her escort.

Then the doors slid open and she was led into a wider corridor, still bulkheaded and functional like the ones below. Like the ones on her ship. Instrument panels dotted the walls at irregular intervals.

Doors here were painted blue. The *Razalka*'s doors were color-coded, signifying division and location. She belatedly realized the lift doors on the brig deck were green.

She'd been too stunned by Carina's appearance to take note of it.

The 'Sko stopped before a set of wide blue doors and spoke a rapid series of harsh-sounding words. The doors parted. "In," it told her.

Her escort followed her in, surprised her by bowing to her, and then left.

An angular 'Sko sat behind a low black desk, its wide shoulders stretching the red fabric of its uniform like a wire clothes hangar trying to force its way out. Its hands, resting on the desktop, were long-fingered, and it toyed with a round, spiked ball of some kind of soft plastic material. It had the same braid worn by every other 'Sko she'd seen, but its hair was darker and flecked with bright green.

It was staring at her, just like the 'Sko in the lift. She realized that it was also one of the ones that had stared at her through the orange-hazed force field in the brig.

Finally, it spoke. "Captain. Elliot. Sit." It motioned to a sling-type chair.

She perched warily on its edge. She didn't want to lean back. It would be too difficult to get out of, should she have to move quickly.

Not that she thought the 'Sko had brought her here to harm her.

Not that she thought it hadn't.

"I am Kalthrencadri. Thren. Easy more to say."

If it was hoping she'd say "pleased to meet you" it was going to be disappointed. "Thren," she repeated. "What do you want?"

Thren's mouth twisted. It could be grinning or it could be a rude gesture for all she knew. "You. Know. Grantforth."

"The whole clan? No. Just two." She'd never met Jagan's mother.

"Clan?" Thren repeated. The translator on its collar clacked something at him. "Yes. Family. You know Grantforth."

"I know two Grantforths."

"Lord Chief Secretary?"

The Conclave didn't use titles like Lord. Maybe the 'Sko were looking to promote him for his loyal service to their cause. "Garold Grantforth. Yes."

"And blood-kin?"

Nephew, probably. "Jagan Grantforth."

"Lord Chief talk Beffa. Beffa talk Niyil-Pry. Lord Chief has blood-kin. Blood-kin talk Elliot. Elliot has charts. Much old. Much secret." Thren paused. "Want."

Anger surged through Trilby. "We offered you the damned charts!"

"Niyil-Pry. Ship talk Niyil-Pry." Thren touched one bony finger to its chin. "Dakrahl," it said, identifying itself. The finger next tapped the desk. "Niyil-Day."

The *Quest*'s scanners had seen two 'Sko mother ships. But evidently even the best of Imperial technology couldn't discern they were from competing factions, though a hazy memory came back to her of an odd formation just before Mother Two arrived. Niyil-Pry. Niyil-Day, the latter allied with the Dakrahl. She'd long known the 'Sko were deeply factionalized, had heard rumors of interfaction battles. Now she was in the middle of one. And not the one Garold Grantforth had chosen to befriend.

"Want charts," Thren repeated.

Trilby would gladly give them the real charts, if it would bring Rhis back. It wouldn't. But it might free them. And Carina.

Only fools think they can make deals with the 'Sko, Rhis had told Jagan. She knew that. But using the charts was also the only option she had.

"You are Elliot?" Thren repeated.

"Yeah, I'm Elliot. I have the charts," she said

tightly. "Both sets. One's false. One's real. I'm the only one left alive who knows which is which. And how to decode them."

She waited while the translator interpreted her words.

Thren's head moved rapidly side to side. "No two sets! No two sets! Niyil-Pry data says Elliot woman has all. Woman! Kill blood-kin man, kill all men!"

Kill blood-kin. Trilby's suppositions were confirmed. They'd wanted Jagan, and anyone working with him, dead. It was possible they didn't even know what Jagan Grantforth looked like. *Kill all men* would assure their chances of success.

Kill all men had ended Rhis's life. Because of Jagan.

But Dallon was still alive. They hadn't killed Dallon; in fact, they responded to her requests for a leg brace. . . .

Dallon Patruzius wore his hair long. Farra's was long too. Even her own short hair was longer than Rhis's military crop. And Yavo's.

The 'Sko couldn't tell human males from females. Any more than she could with them.

She kept her face impassive. "I have two sets of charts," she repeated. "Both locked in code. I die, they die with me. You want the real one, we make a deal."

"Deal? Deal?"

"Bargain. Agreement."

Thren sat back, rolled the spiked ball under its hand. She fought the urge to grab the ball and cram it down its throat. "A ship. Freedom," she continued. "For my crew back in your brig. And another woman you have. Carina, from *Bella's Dream*."

Thren rolled the ball, back and forth, back and forth.

Trilby waited. For once, time was on her side. The SUAs had gone out. Someone in the Conclave had picked them up.

And Rhis had ordered Demarik to engage the First Fleet, head for Syar. Imperial ships could follow a 'Sko mother ship's ion trail. Someone had to be coming after them right now.

"You free. You break agreement. You tell military. 'Sko have charts."

She shrugged. "But it will be too late to stop you by then, won't it? You'll have the complete charts, Thren. All the lost jumpgates. All the hidden meetpoints. The Conclave can guess, but they won't know where you are."

Thren switched the ball to the other hand, rolled it in a circular motion.

"Conclave not problem. Grantforth. Niyil-Pry. Beffa." The thin lips grimaced. "Empire problem."

The star charts showed meetpoints in the Empire too. Demarik had a copy of the real ones from her ship. But not Carina's. "Compromise. Free us, give us a ship and supplies. You can escort us to a small world in Gensiira. I'll give you coordinates. You can disable the ship's engines. No one uses the place. Poisonous. We'll never contact anyone. But with a ship, we can survive. That's all I'm asking. Four lives for the charts."

The ball stopped rolling. "Thren think much on this."

"Think all you want." She pushed herself out of the chair, shoved her hands in the pockets of her flight suit. She glared at the sallow-skinned creature, which toyed with the spiked ball on the desktop just as it had thoughtlessly toyed with their lives. "But every day you wait is another day you can't get control of the Conclave. You have maybe a deuce, a trike before Lord Chief Grantforth realizes you killed his blood-kin. He'll issue a kill order on the Dakrahl. The Niyil-Day."

"Conclave not strong—"

"It's not just the Conclave anymore. My ship, the people on my ship"—Trilby hesitated, sucking in a short breath to keep her voice from quivering—"the men you killed were Imperial officers. From the *Razalka*. And with the *Stegzarda*."

The spiked ball stilled in Thren's fingers. The small translator clacked in short, intense spurts. The 'Sko hadn't known Khyrhis Tivahr was among the dead. She read that in Thren's tense silence.

"The Empire *will* pursue a kill order. And you'll be facing the Conclave and the Empire, allied against the 'Sko." She raised her chin a little higher. "Think on that, Thren. Think on that."

28

Rhis winced slightly as he slipped his black Imperial-issue service jacket over his flight suit. Underneath the jacket was his shoulder holster, with a pistol snugged against his right side and his left. He tugged on the weapons, making sure they were secure, then reached down to adjust the pistol strapped to his right thigh. His utility belt held four stun grenades. He tossed a spare belt with pistol and grenades to Mitkanos, sitting propped in a makeshift regen bed in Trilby's cabin—the captain's cabin, designed with a hidden emergency access to the cargo holds one deck below.

Mitkanos caught the belt, lay it across his lap. Some color had returned to his face, but his breathing was still labored. He wheezed when he spoke. "I should be going with you."

"This is strictly recon. You know the Fleet never makes a move until it's studied all angles to death."

Mitkanos snorted. "Invasion by committee consensus."

"Usually lack of," Rhis agreed. He knew the *Stegzarda*'s big complaint about the Fleet was its propensity to minutely review every possible detail before taking action.

Fat lot of good that had done him this time. He'd have to add one more dictum to his team's review process when he got back to the *Razalka*: *You're not as smart as you think*. He'd put it right next to: *I don't like surprises*.

He grabbed the two short-barreled laser rifles, slung them over his shoulder. He glanced at his watch. "Two hours. Maybe not even that." He'd been on 'Sko mother ships before.

"Captain Tivahr."

Something in Mitkanos's tone told Rhis this delay was important. That and the fact that, for the first time, the older man said his name with a touch of respect. He waited.

"Should you . . . ever decide to leave the Fleet, the *Stegzarda* would be proud to have you in our ranks."

"I'll keep that in mind." He grinned.

"And, Captain—"

"Major?"

"May the Gods be vigilant."

That, Rhis knew, would be nice. But he'd prefer if they simply took him off their shit list once and for all. "Dezi, you ready?"

"Absolutely, Captain Tivahr. I'm anxious to try out my new invasive accessing programs. It should be quite a challenge locating 'Sko primaries, don't you think?"

No, that wouldn't be the problem. The real problem would be keeping the 'Sko from noticing he'd accessed their primaries until he could take total control of their ship.

He slid through a small maintenance hatch still operative in the ruined engine room and shimmied down a landing strut into the darkened hangar bay. Dezi followed, joints well lubed and barely squeaking. His metallic skin was coated with a nonreflective layer. If he stood still, in the shadows, he might pass for a pylon.

Rhis hoped the 'droid wouldn't have to. He intended to have them avoid ship corridors and stick to maintenance tunnels. Even if he were to acquire a blood-red 'Sko uniform, his muscular build would give him away.

Hangar bays were traditionally cavernous, honeycombed with maintenance pits and tunnels. This one was no exception. Some of the hatchways were locked, others coded. Dezi spiked in at the first panel they saw.

If his programs were flawed, they'd fail now.

It was the longest six minutes of Rhis's life.

"Six minutes, fourteen seconds," Dezi told him. "We should not encounter such a delay again. I now have their root security-code system in my databanks. Rather ingenious, actually. Based on an obscure musical theory that—"

"Lovely, Dez. Later."

The tunnel was cramped, dimly lit. He half-crawled, half-sidled down its length, his chest aching. The skin surrounding the med-broche on his side itched. New skin matrix regeneration always did. Annoying. He should be used to it by now.

The tunnel widened at a cross juncture that held three square panels of databanks. Good, very good. Dezi activated the screen and found the directory. Subdirectory, really. The 'Sko would never have the ship's main computers so easily accessible.

He looked for blackout areas in the schematics, had Dezi note them. That's where he needed to go. That's what he needed to find.

As soon as he found Trilby.

He'd lied to Mitkanos. This wasn't recon. This was the mission. He'd come up against the 'Sko enough times to know he wouldn't get a second chance.

"Deck diagrams?" he whispered harshly to the 'droid.

"Accessing. A moment, please."

Rhis eased down on one hip, reached under his jacket, scratched at his stomach. Damned matrix.

"Partials only," Dezi said finally. "This is a secondary dataport."

"Display."

The monitor on the wall flickered, changed. Lower decks only. Recyc. Six hangar bays. Brig.

Brig. That had to be where they were holding her.

He sent a small prayer to the Gods, risked bringing their attention to his plight. "Are you into their intraship?" He had to infiltrate the 'Sko's communication systems to do what he needed next.

"Affirmative."

He reached into his jacket, pulled out a small datapad, flipped it on. "Send out a low-level power pulse, on my signal."

"Standing by."

He prayed she still had her ship badge. That the 'Sko would know it was useless with his ship's comm system destroyed in the attack, the CLS lifeless. They wouldn't think to remove it from her, as they no doubt had her utility belt.

The badges should respond to a small ping, keyed to a narrow frequency. At least, they'd been designed to do so, for emergency locate purposes.

"Now."

A tiny beam of energy, almost imperceptible, cascaded through the 'Sko comm system.

One ping. Two.

He drew in a quick breath, read out the IDs. FR-RMNV. DLPTRZ. Farra. Dallon. In the brig, as he thought.

No Trilby.

Where in hell was she?

He looked at Dezi. "I've got Farra. Patruzius. Not Trilby."

"Perhaps her ship badge is defective?"

Or they'd split them up, moved her to the other mother ship.

Bloody fucking hell. That would make life a bit more difficult for a while.

"Shall I send another pulse?"

He studied the monitor. "No. Not yet." There was a third option, one he preferred. She was on this ship, but not in the brig. The diagram before him was truncated. Lower decks. If Garold Grantforth was involved—and Rhis had no doubt he was—Trilby would be the one the 'Sko would deal with.

She was, after all, ship's captain. And should the 'Sko forget that fact, he also had no doubt his gutsy air sprite would be the first to remind them.

*   *   *

Trilby sat at the long table in the conference room and tried not to look at the dark stains smeared across the remnants of the *Quest*'s nav station. She'd told Thren where the datafiles were stored, in a subunit on the bridge. But, perhaps intending to impress her with their efficiency, the 'Sko had hauled back not only the small subunit but most of the damned nav console as well. Its warped frame, complete with the dark splatters and smears that could only be Rhis's blood, was propped along the far wall. Conduit and optic lines trailed across the decking. Monitors sagged in their cases. Keypads were buckled.

But the stains were what she focused on.

She wondered, briefly, painfully, what they'd done with his body. Maybe she could add that to her request list. A proper burial. The 'Sko, except for the Dakrahl, had no such traditions. A dead body was a dead body. They trampled over their own crew when they attacked the *Quest*'s bridge. Tossed the dead and the injured alike down the stairwell.

Mitkanos's body too. She'd ask for that as well. Bring them both to Avanar, bury them there. Rhis would be with her then, forever. In the large cave in the jungle where she first met him.

She swiped at a tear trickling down her cheek, turned her attention back to the screen inset in the conference table. The *Quest*'s nav banks were scrambled in the attack, but she expected as much. Told Thren it would take a while to untangle them. A careful while. There were, she warned, fail-safes.

She'd put them in herself.

"I'll need a destination directory, a large area of blank file space to start downloading to." She pasted her most innocent, blank look on her face. The same one she always wore when she'd look at Conclave customs inspectors and ask, "What illegal cargo?"

She saw Thren hesitate. She was asking for access to its ship's computer banks, and the 'Sko knew it. It leaned back in its chair, at the far end of the table. The spiked ball lay motionless in front of it.

"Why not old unit?" It pointed to the wreckage in the corner.

"Because, number one, it's damaged. Number two, that damage has severely limited its capacity. And number three, the files are larger than the remaining capacity. I could load them compressed, but then we're risking major data corruption if I run out of space."

It was one of the few things she told Thren that was true. If it didn't believe her, it could have its techs scan the unit.

It had, she knew, two options. It could let her load directly to the ship's computers. That's what she wanted. Or it could wait, dig up a portable unit with sufficient capacity, and lock her out of the systems.

She didn't want that.

She needed in to the 'Sko's computers. In to their primaries. She was going to give them Herkoid's star charts, suitably customized by the late Captain Khyrhis Tivahr. But she was also going to give them something else.

Surprise.

Thren chattered on intraship. High-pitched, grating Ycskrite noises answered back. Trilby waited, stared at her hands, at the tabletop, at the wide starfield through the circular viewport—anywhere but the broken nav console.

They were moving on the sublight engines now, after one brief hyperspace jump. She didn't recognize the stars, but then, 'Sko space was not her territory. Thren had requested Avanar's coordinates. Evidently they had their own ways of getting into Gensiira.

Carina's presence on this ship proved as much.

She had no idea why the 'Sko had kept Carina alive. Or Dallon and Farra, for that matter. Generosity and leniency were not words associated with the 'Sko. If they did something, it was because it benefited them, and only them, in some way.

And when something no longer did, they were brutal. Ruthless.

It was questionable whether the 'Sko would release them, leave them alive on Avanar. She felt they would only if they were sure—and once they saw the corrosive atmosphere of the jungles, who wouldn't be?— that they'd never leave. Their survival would depend on whatever ship the 'Sko gave them as shelter. Even *Shadow's Quest* would do. With the spare parts she'd accumulated over years of salvage and had carefully sealed and stored in the cavern, she knew she—with Dallon's, Farra's, and Carina's help—could rebuild the *Quest*. Definitely get her comm pack working. Someone, sooner or later, would find them.

But if the 'Sko didn't, if they reneged on their agreement with her—

It wouldn't matter. Rhis was dead. But his handiwork, and hers, would live on forever in this ship's systems, destroying it and, she knew, every other 'Sko ship it communicated with.

Thren stood suddenly, shaking its long face side to

side. "Chance? Chance. Trust. Need charts." It walked down the length of the table, leaned over her screen. It inserted one finger into an ID slot, then stroked three lines of code that appeared.

She watched the symbols flow by.

Ycskrite! Damn it, it was all in Ycskrite. Bloodbat droppings, for all she knew.

Thren pointed. "There."

She shook her head. "I don't read your language. I need to work with binary addresses. That's the only way I can get the charts to interface with your systems. At the binary level."

It spun around, slapped at the intership on the table, clacked out a long, angry-sounding sentence.

Within minutes, the conference-room doors slid open. Another tall, thin, red-uniformed 'Sko hurried in. Its braid, a yellowish-green, bobbled.

Thren screeched, clacked, screeched some more.

The tech—Trilby assumed it was a tech—whined in response.

Trilby shut it out, practiced saying *good, better, best* in Zafharish in her mind. *Good, better, best. Good, better, best.* She looked at Thren.

Worm fodder.

The tech wriggled its thin face, scurried toward her. It motioned her out of her seat, slid in when she vacated it. One finger in the side of the monitor, ID confirmed. Stroke, stroke, stroke.

Second ID input. More stroking.

Thren screeched.

The tech looked startled. Stroked the screen faster.

Trilby stood behind it, arms folded across her chest.

And saw numbers. Lovely, beautiful, need-no-translation numbers.

The tech screeched happily, looked at Thren.

Thren looked at her. "Now? You do."

The tech stood, moved out of her way.

Trilby sat. "Now. I do."

She began to slowly, methodically open and decode the charts. Deliberately, she chose the longest, most complex ones. Thren watched over her shoulder, and she hummed the tune to "good, better, best" while she worked.

After a while Thren began to fidget, shifting from foot to foot. Then, a short walk to the viewport, look out, walk back, look down at the screen.

Trilby continued her soft, hypnotic tune.

"Done? Done?"

She shot it the same look she'd bestowed on Rhis when they first met, clearly questioning his intelligence. Thren seemed to catch that, walked back to the viewport.

Finally, it stalked back to its chair at the other end of the table, brought up another screen. She heard the screen beeping and chirping and didn't know if Thren was busy with ship work or playing intergalactic poker. But it wasn't, she knew, aware of what she was doing.

Or what she was about to do.

She moved files quickly now, tagged and hid two in a bogus directory. Then she looked for a routine file link, found it, and rode it to the mother ship's main banks.

Good, better, best!

It took her a few minutes to find the primaries. She had to keep switching back to the star charts, unpacking into the 'Sko nav banks at the slowest possible rate.

Then she had them, but there was something she needed to do first.

"Thren?"

It looked up. "Elli. Ot?"

"Got a real old chart for you. Want to see it?"

The thin face wobbled anxiously.

"No, sit." She waved one hand as he started to stand. "If I bring it up here, it'll slow me down. I'll send it to you. What's your terminal ID code?"

It took her a few more questions, and screeching translations, to get from Thren what she wanted. Its personal ship link. She keyed it in, tagged it *worm fodder*.

She sent it a chart showing a multitude of hidden jumpgates in and around Lissade. Big money, that. She knew that would keep it drooling for a while.

If 'Sko drooled.

A hissing sound came from its mouth as it stared at the screen. Probably the 'Sko's way of denoting pleasure.

Always knew the lot of them were full of hot air.

She went back to her screen, pulled up the primaries. And saw at the top of the file something she never thought she'd see again.

Yav chera.

Her hand trembled as she reached out and touched the words on the screen.

Yav chera.

It wasn't a hallucination.

She glanced quickly at Thren. It was hissing, its yellowed eyes transfixed on the screen.

Her heart pounded. She moved her hands to the keypad and for a moment her fingers fumbled, her skin slick. She wiped one hand down her pants leg, started again.

Yav cheron, Khyrhis-chevo.

A line appeared immediately after it: *Dasjankira. Trilby-chenka.*

Her breath was coming in short, rapid gasps. She didn't believe in specters. Had Rhis keyed something into his programs on board *Shadow's Quest* to tease her? As a joke? Was this nothing more than an A-I interactive program, unfolding for amusement?

She keyed in a sentence an A-I might not be programmed to respond to. Something Rhis couldn't have anticipated. *Carina's here.*

Nothing. So it was a program. Her input wasn't part of its response loop. Her spirits sagged.

Bloody hell. Where?

She stifled a whimper of joy.

Brig. Dallon, Farra too.

Confirmed. I have Uncle Yavo.

Yavo? Alive?

Grumpy as usual.

She wanted to clap her hands, stand up, and cheer. *Where are you?*

Coming through your back door in about five minutes. Shall you finish scrambling their primaries, or shall I?

Gods. She had a sudden understanding of what had been going on, though it was beyond comprehension. Somehow, Rhis was alive. And on board and probably crawling around in the maintenance tunnels, looking for a data-access panel. Found a data-access panel. Found her doing the same thing. Duplicate efforts.

She had to trust he was armed. She wasn't. Let him concentrate then on that aspect. She could do hers.

I'm in the mood to scramble, she told him.

Good. I'm in the mood to kill.

He was definitely armed. And very pissed off.

She accessed the primaries, her hands shaking, called up the two hidden files, coded them to Thren's ID. Then she closed the primary and skipped down to the system's backups, threw in an answering parameter.

Back to the main primary. She scanned for a sequence of numbers Rhis had taught her to look for. They were further apart than she anticipated. She'd have to create bridges.

Bloody hell.

Five minutes, Rhis said. She had five minutes to disable the 'Sko control of the ship. She couldn't write all those bridges in that time.

But she didn't have to. *Sproings.* Shadow called them sproings because that's the sound he said they'd make when they jumped, replicated, and jumped again.

She could create a bridge, sproing it, and let it go on its way.

Damnation! This was almost fun.

Thren's nasal voice disturbed her. "Good! This is good!" It pointed to its screen.

No, you motherless son of a Pillorian bitch. This is best.

Her screen flickered briefly. Thren's head jerked up, its eyes wary, cautious.

"Oops," she said. "Really big chart. Total overlay of the Conclave. Sorry. Maybe I should delete it—"

"Total? Total? One chart? All Conclave?"

"Yeah, but it's unpacking too fast. It's going to drain your system resources for a while unless you shut something down."

"Tell!"

She glanced at the screen. "Closest resource is mechanical. Can you shut down the ship's lifts for two minutes?"

A screeching translation. Thren barked into the intraship unit. "Two minutes," it told Trilby. "No more."

She smiled. Touched a key. Impenetrable blast doors—"airtights"—groaned into operation. And locked down every deck on the ship.

Except for a code only she and Rhis knew.

Good. Better. Best.

29

Rhis was sliding through a maintenance panel on bridge deck when he heard the airtights grind into action. She'd done it. His air sprite was in the primaries, controlling all functions of the ship.

Every deck would be partitioned, sealed. Lifts inoperative. 'Sko crew would be trapped in their sections.

And he could let the air out, a section at a time or whole decks at once. It was his, and Trilby's, to control. He grabbed Dezi's hard shoulder. "Come on." The wide blue doors of the conference room were just ahead.

A noise behind them, a clacking screech. He turned, both rifles at hip level, firing. The 'Sko's body jerked, fell. Another appeared through a doorway, just opening as his laser fire burned down the corridor. He shot it in the head.

"Move!" he ordered Dezi, and sprinted toward the conference room.

Dezi's loping steps followed.

Rhis stopped at the side of the blue doorway, rifles raised against his shoulders. "Code in."

Dezi inserted a metal finger in the wall panel. The doors slid open and Rhis heard two sounds simultaneously.

One was an annoying, clacking screech.

The other was a woman's voice that was the sweetest he'd ever heard. "Dezi!"

And he knew, from the sounds, exactly where each was.

He stepped in, rifles spitting white streaks of death.

The tall 'Sko was caught halfway out of its seat. Bolts of energy impacted against its chest, its shoulders, its head. Dark blotches exploded over its red uniform. Its face skewed, its green-tinged braid whipped up and, for a moment, seemed to stand straight over its head.

Then its body arched backward and tumbled, crookedly, over the arm of the chair.

Then, and only then, did Rhis permit himself to look at Trilby. She'd dropped into a defensive crouch behind her chair, a protective posture that would make any *Stegzarda* major proud.

Or Imperial Fleet senior captain.

"I am," he told her as she rose, "a lot better shot than you're giving me credit for."

She ran toward him and threw herself against his chest, her arms wrapping tightly around his neck. He let the rifles fall on their straps, closed his own arms around her. He held her tightly and managed to bark out, "Lock the damned door!" to Dezi.

She was sobbing, laughing, kissing him.

His hands framed her face and for a very long moment he stared at her, drinking in every sparkle in her eyes, every soft curve of her lips, every sooty shadow of her lashes. Every tear glistening down her cheeks.

She trembled under his touch.

He whispered her name. "Trilby-*chenka*. You have my heart."

Then he kissed her, letting passion explode like a star going nova, searing her, branding her with everything he felt. Everything he was.

Everything he wasn't.

"Khyrhis. Khyrhis." She was crying, softly murmuring his name into his mouth.

He clasped her against his chest, his fingers threaded through her moonlit hair, and he held her, held her. Held her.

He squeezed his eyes shut.

She wasn't the only one trembling.

He let out a long, slow breath. "Trilby-*chenka*. We still have work to do."

She nodded, backed away from him, wiped her hands down her face. But when she looked back up, she was grinning.

He saw the screen at the far end of the table where she'd crouched, pointed to it. "You've got access from there?"

She nodded but was already turning away from him, reaching for Dezi. The 'droid took her outstretched hand, pumped it in a hearty handshake. "It's very good to see you again, Captain Elliot."

Rhis slid into the seat in front of the screen just as Trilby grabbed Dezi in a hug. Then she was behind him, still sniffling, one hand on his shoulder.

He tapped at the screen. "You excluded the brig.

Good. This hangar bay too. Or Uncle Yavo will be most upset."

"I didn't know where the *Quest* was."

"Not to worry. I've got it." He looked over the top of the screen, at the slumped form at the end of the table. "Who's your friend?"

"Thren something. Or something Thren."

Thren? His mind played with the name as he shut down enviro, deck by deck. The 'Sko should be feeling extremely woozy right about—

Thren. "Kalthrencadri?"

"Something like that, yes."

But he knew the answer before she even said it. Should have known. He saw the prayer ball sitting on the table.

"Dakrahl," he told her. He glanced up, made sure she saw his nod toward the spiked object. "High priest. Unusual on a Niyil ship."

But then again, knowing the 'Sko, maybe not. He'd puzzle it out later. He looked back at the screen. Engineering, crew quarters, galley were shut down. Life forms flickering out. They must be going crazy on the bridge. Probably trying to cut through the blast doors with their pistols. Fools. The 'Sko built ships almost as solid as the Zafharin.

He absently scratched at the prickly itching on his side. He'd shut down bridge enviro in a minute. But part of him wanted them to know, to watch their ship die. Deck by deck.

"What's that toy have to do with it?" She pointed at the ball.

"Prayer ball. Official toy, as you say, of a Dakrahl high priest. Helps them commune with," he waved one hand through the air, "whoever they commune with."

He looked back at the screen. He'd have a dead ship, save for the brig, the *Quest*'s bay, and this section of the bridge deck, in about three minutes.

"This one's been communing with the Niyil-Day—"

"Obviously—"

"Niyil-*Day*," she repeated. "Niyil-Pry cut the deal with Grantforth."

He wrenched his attention from the dying 'Sko. The Niyil-Day. Bloody hell. Of course. Much of what he'd risked his life to learn when he and his team had infiltrated Szed had centered around the factionalizing of the Niyil and who'd come out on top. This time.

"At least, that's what Thren told me," she continued, then outlined the rest, including the kill order on Jagan Grantforth and any male associated with him. A female named Trilby Elliot was the key.

Rhis suddenly saw the full picture. The Niyil-Day, the most ethnocentric of all the factions, would be the least well-equipped to differentiate one Trilby Elliot from any other human female on board.

Kill the males. Herd the females. One of them, sooner or later, would have to be Captain Trilby Elliot, finder of lost Zafharin officers, keeper of long-lost star routes.

"We're going to have to start taking the 'Sko a lot more seriously when we get back to the Empire," he told her. "With the Dakrahl siding now with the Niyil, they're not a fractured, divided force anymore."

The Dakrahl would press for recovery of the Drifts. The emperor was not going to be happy.

"We *are* going back, this time?"

The screen showed no viable life forms on the bridge. He reached for her hand, squeezed it, then pulled her to her feet. "We're going home, Trilby-*chenka*. This time, we're really going home."

Rhis watched over Dezi's shoulder as he spiked into a datapanel on the conference-room wall. Images, icons blinked on, underscored by Ycskrite writings. He pointed to two flashing glyphs. "We've got two crew, probably officers, still alive. Locked in their offices. But alive."

Rhis stroked the screen, read their names off to Trilby, standing next to him. "A commander in navigation. And a division chief. Tactical. I can't shut down enviro in their section without us losing it in here. But that's okay. They're not going anywhere, and they'll make interesting prisoners once we cross the zone."

"They can't get through the maintenance tunnels like you did?"

"Not unless they're three inches wide. When 'Sko blast doors go into lockdown, all maintenance tunnels seal with barred gates. You could slip your hand through, but not much more."

She leaned against the wall, reached out tentatively, and touched his chest.

Bloody hell. He should've changed his flight suit. But there hadn't been time. And he had other things, more important things, to deal with. Like finding Trilby. Like keeping them all alive.

"You were shot." Her voice was soft. "More than once. I saw them. I saw you."

He clasped his hand around hers, brought it to his lips. "I will explain everything. I promise. But later.

We need to get on the bridge, get this ship moving. The *Razalka*'s out there somewhere. And Jankova gets nervous when I'm late."

He keyed in one more sweep of the bridge and, satisfied no one there could put up any resistance, told Dezi to activate enviro again.

Five minutes later, he and Dezi unlocked the wide bridge doors and stood aside for a moment, letting the stale air and smell of death filter out.

He kept Trilby behind him, ordered her to wait in the corridor until he said otherwise. Surprisingly, uncharacteristically, she obeyed.

He definitely should have changed his flight suit. There were questions in her mind now. He just hoped she liked his answers.

Malika hadn't.

Red-clad bodies were strewn around the bridge in various poses of collapse. He and Dezi moved them to the semicircular room's shadowed edges. A 'Sko flag and a Niyil one hung from two long beams. He ripped them down, threw them over the two largest piles of bodies.

It would have to do. Though he didn't know why he was doing it. Trilby Elliot had seen worse. She'd worked for—no, been abused by Herkoid. She'd fought for her life on the grimy back streets of Port Rumor.

She'd watched Khyrhis Tivahr get shot and die.

And that's why he did it. She'd seen enough. Too much. He could at least spare her some of this.

When he returned for her in the corridor, she was clutching the prayer ball. "Has it revealed all its secrets to you yet?"

"No. But then, I haven't asked it."

He guided her onto the bridge and began the sequence to unlock the primaries.

"I threw a replicating weemly into the comm pack," she told him as the monitors in front of her flickered to life. "It's keyed to Thren's ID, but it may activate on its own."

"A weemly?" He was delighted.

"It would ride on all outgoing messages, link into the receiving comm pack, and replicate again."

"And?" he prompted.

"The only thing they'd be able to see on their screens would be a copy of my potato–cheese casserole recipe."

"Everyone has always enjoyed that casserole when I've served it," Dezi said. "Though I don't think the 'Sko—"

"Will get a chance to taste it," Rhis finished for him. "Can you disable it?"

She shot him a look that clearly questioned his intelligence. "Of course."

He returned to the command console, grinning.

More screens flickered to life.

"Intraship's on," he told her. "I think Farra and Dallon need to hear from you. And Carina."

He caught the bright glisten of tears in her eyes. Then she turned, keyed the closest unit. "Dallon? Farra?"

"Captain?" It was Dallon's voice, sounding distant. "You okay?"

"I'm fine. Ship's secure. Rhis is . . . Rhis is alive. Here. He's fine. He says Yavo's alive too. Listen, I'm dropping the force fields. The brig's blocked off by blast doors. We cut enviro everywhere else. I can't let you out onto that deck yet. But go down the corridor, to your left. A friend of mine's in the cell there. Her name's Carina. She might be ill or injured. I'm not sure."

"Farra's going now." Dallon's voice sounded stronger, closer. "Tivahr's alive?"

Rhis flicked intraship on at his station. "That I am. And be sure I'm still the same arrogant, loathsome bastard I always was."

A large blip suddenly appeared at the edges of long-range scan. Rhis clicked off intraship, got Trilby's attention with a wave of his hand.

She looked at the scanner and fear flickered across her face. "What's that?"

He forgot she couldn't read Ycskrite. "The *Razalka*. She'll be alongside in an hour."

Her expression of fear changed to one of relief. Then she grinned, threw a haughty look at him from over her shoulder. "You just don't listen, do you, Tivahr? I told you before. I never said you were loath-some."

He remembered. But then, she hadn't heard his explanations yet.

The senior captain's quarters were nice. Very nice. Trilby ran one hand over the soft fabric on the couch. In her other she held a tall tumbler of iced gin. And two limes.

She heard the sani-fac door slide open in the room behind her, heard footsteps on the carpeted floor. The shush of closet doors, the rustle of fabric.

She thought of her own cabin on the *Careless Venture*. Threadbare. Empty closets. And a man standing there, surprised when she shoved a pile of towels against his chest.

The same chest 'Sko lasers had burned into.

Later, he told her. He'd explain everything later.

But then there was the bridge to unlock and the *Razalka* to dock with. Demarik to confer with. And quick, insistent transmits between Imperial and Conclave admirals until it was clear to all parties that the *Razalka*'s appearance through Gensiira and into Syar was on behalf of a rescue operation. Not an invasion.

Not yet, Admiral Vanushavor said later. They needed the data from the captured mother ship first. To prove Garold Grantforth's part in all this, to show how he'd used Jagan to seduce Trilby in order to learn more about rumored old star charts that the 'Sko wanted. But his plans had gone awry when Jagan's mother intervened, forcing Jagan to marry the woman she'd chosen for him.

That's when Garold Grantforth had pressured Jagan to contact Trilby again, apologize, and get back in her good graces. Effectively signing his nephew's death warrant. Because the competing 'Sko factions had no intention of leaving live witnesses behind.

In the midst of the politics and machinations, Mitkanos, Dallon, and Carina were transferred, carefully, into Doc Vanko's care.

Not Vitorio. Her friend's drug-hazed recounting rambled, but Trilby understood and filled in what she knew Carina didn't understand. Working with information stolen from the Niyil-Pry faction, the Niyil-Day had kidnapped Carina and Vitorio, recovered the nav banks from *Bella's Dream*. Told them they'd let them live in exchange for the charts.

But when Carina had refused, they'd killed Vitorio and wrenched Carina away from her brother. And from the inside pocket of her service jacket tumbled an envelope of holos she'd forgotten was there.

More than one had been of Trilby and Carina at Port Rumor's freighter docks, the *Careless Venture*'s name clearly visible on the side of the ship behind them. The 'Sko had recognized her ship's name. So they'd let Carina live, keeping her sedated, hoping this Captain Trilby Elliot that the other Niyil faction desperately wanted would come looking for her. And bring the missing star charts along.

Another shush of a closet door.

Khyrhis.

Unsure of what to tell her.

But that, too, she already knew. Lots of rumors surrounded Tivahr the Terrible. More terrible to his own people, to whom family lineage decreed acceptance.

A *boulashka*, Mitkanos had called him. A genetic manipulation. No family, no name, no lineage—

She knew what that felt like.

—only, incongruously, he had power.

That she didn't know. Nor did it interest her.

His fingers slid across her shoulders as he moved around the side of the couch and sat down next to her. His short hair was still damp. He wrapped his hand over hers as she held the tumbler, brought it to his mouth, and took a sip. Then he lowered his hand, but didn't release hers.

"Feeling better?" she asked him.

"Immensely."

"Good. I much prefer you alive to dead."

He hesitated only a second. "I've done dead. It's overrated."

"You want to tell me about it?"

He looked down at their hands, locked around the tumbler, then brought his face up. "You thought your medistat on the *Careless Venture* malfunctioned, didn't you?"

Well, that was the normal state of affairs for most of her equipment on that ship.

"You couldn't get any true readings on me because there's a biosymbiotic layer, a matrix, in my chest and back. Sections can migrate anywhere I'm injured. It also skews medistats. Unless Doc Vanko's customized them."

All she could think of was that it must have hurt like hell to have something like that inserted under your skin. "What did they do, graft it in pieces?"

He was silent. "No. It grew, it grows there. It's part of me. I've always had it."

It took a moment for her to comprehend what he'd said. A continually regenerating protective layer. Useful for an Imperial senior captain with a penchant for pissing off the 'Sko.

"There's more." He closed his eyes briefly.

She wanted to put down the tumbler, stroke his face with her hands, but he had a tight grip on her fingers. He needed her touch. She didn't want to break that contact.

"Because of this matrix, my body has a greater muscle mass, strength, density. Faster recovery ability, not only from injury but poisons. Drugs. And I can memorize and record large amounts of data. In some ways, I'm not dissimilar to Dezi."

He stopped. She knew he waited for her reaction.

"Because of this layer that lives inside you?"

"Because of what I am, genetically."

"Which is?"

His mouth twisted into a wry smile. "Depends on who you ask."

Pain. She heard it clearly now. He was talking about abilities, attributes he had that had saved her life. And hundreds of others. His voice was tinged with shame. And loneliness.

"Is there anyone else like you?"

"No. The lab was destroyed by people who were afraid they were creating not a new breed of soldier but soulless monsters that would eventually dominate them."

"But they let you live?"

"I survived. They figured there was a significant amount of money already invested in me. And they were curious."

Bastards. Worse than the Iffys. "And have you met their expectations?"

He crooked one eyebrow in a self-deprecating gesture. "The 'Sko hate me."

"For good reason." She snatched her hand from under his, let the gin and the glass tumble to the floor. He jerked back. She could see from the look in his eyes he was misinterpreting her actions as anger, rejection. She framed his face in her hands, brought his mouth to hers, and kissed him, hard. Then kissed him again, drawing herself up on her knees till she was almost in his lap. She kept kissing him, pushed him backward onto the soft cushions of the couch. She straddled him. He looked up at her with eyes wide in amazement.

"I love you, Khyrhis Tivahr. I don't give a mizzet's ass what anyone else says or thinks. I love you. I found you. I'm keeping you. And there's not a bloody damned thing you can do about it." She braced her hands against his shoulders. "So you damned well better get used to it."

He grabbed her by the elbows and pulled her slowly down toward him, stopping only when her mouth was inches from his own.

"Trilby-*chenka*?" he whispered.

"Umm?"

He kissed her slowly, with almost heartbreaking tenderness. "*Yav chera.*"

about the author

A former news reporter and retired private detective, Linnea Sinclair has managed to use all of her college degrees (journalism and criminology) but hasn't soothed the yearning in her soul to travel the galaxy. To that end, she's authored several science fiction and fantasy novels, including *Finders Keepers, Gabriel's Ghost,* and *An Accidental Goddess.* When not on duty with some intergalactic fleet she can be found in Fort Lauderdale, Florida, with her husband and their two thoroughly spoiled cats. Fans can reach her through her website at www.starfreighter.com.

Be sure not to miss

GABRIEL'S GHOST

the next exciting novel of adventure
and romance from

LINNEA SINCLAIR

On sale November 2005

Here's a special preview

GABRIEL'S GHOST

On sale November 2005

Only fools boast they have no fears. I thought of that as I pulled the blade of my dagger from the Takan guard's throat, my hand shaking, my heart pounding in my ears. Light from the setting sun filtered down through the tall trees around me. It flickered briefly on the dark gold blood that bubbled from the wound, staining the Taka's coarse fur. I felt a sliminess between my fingers and saw that same ochre stain on my skin.

"Shit!" I jerked my hand back. My dagger tumbled to the rock-strewn ground. A stupid reaction for someone with my training. It wasn't as if I'd never killed another sentient being before, but it had been more than five years. And then, at least, it had carried the respectable label of military action.

This time it was pure survival.

It took me a few minutes to find my blade wedged in between the moss-covered rocks. After more than a decade on interstellar patrol ships, my eyes had problems adjusting to variations in natural light. Shades of grays and greens, muddied by Moabar's twilight sky, merged into seamless shadows. I'd never have found my only weapon if I hadn't pricked my fingers on the point. Red human blood mingled with Takan gold. I wiped the blade against my pants before letting it mold itself back around my wrist. It flowed into the form of a simple silver bracelet.

"A Grizni dagger, is it?"

I spun into a half-crouch, my right hand grasping the bracelet. Quickly it uncoiled again—almost as quickly as I'd sucked in a harsh, rasping breath. The distinctly masculine voice had come from the thick stand of trees directly in front of me. But in the few seconds it took me to straighten, he could be anywhere. It looked like tonight's agenda held a second attempt at rape and murder. Or completion of the first. That would make more sense. Takan violence against humans, while not unknown, was rare enough that the guard's aggression had taken me—almost—by surprise. But if a human prison official had ordered him . . . that, given Moabar's reputation, would fit only too well.

I tuned out my own breathing. Instead, I listened to the hushed rustle of the thick forest around me and farther away, the guttural roar of a shuttle departing the prison's spaceport. I watched for movement. Murky shadows, black-edged yet ill defined, taunted me. I'd have sold my soul then and there for a nightscope and a fully-charged laser pistol.

But I had neither of those. Just a sloppily manipulated court martial and a life sentence without parole. And, of course, a smuggled Grizni dagger that the Takan guard had discovered a bit too late to report.

My newest assailant, unfortunately, was already forewarned.

"Let's not cause any more trouble, okay?" My voice sounded thin in the encroaching darkness. I wondered what had happened to that 'tone of command' Fleet regs had insisted we adopt. It had obviously taken one look at the harsh prison world of Moabar and decided it preferred to reside elsewhere. I didn't blame it. I only wished I had the same choice.

I drew a deep breath. "If I'm on your grid, I'm leaving. Wasn't my intention to be here," I added, feeling that was probably the understatement of the century. "And if he," I said with a nod to the large body sprawled to my right, "was your partner, then I'm sorry. But I wasn't in the mood."

A brittle snap started my heart pounding again. My hand felt as slick against the smooth metal of the dagger as if the Taka's blood still ran down its surface. The sound was on my right, beyond where the Taka lay. Only a fool would try to take me over the lifeless barrier at my feet. A fool, or someone not intent on harming me. At least, not right away.

The first of Moabar's three moons had risen in the hazy night sky. I glimpsed a flicker of movement, then saw him step out of the shadows just as the clouds cleared away from the moon. His face was hidden, distorted. But I clearly saw the distinct shape of a short-barreled rifle propped against his shoulder. That, and the fact that he appeared humanoid, told me he wasn't a prison guard. Energy weapons were banned on Moabar. Most of the eight-foot-tall Takas didn't need them, anyway.

The man before me was tall, but not eight feet. Nor did his dark jacket glisten with official prison insignia. Another con, then. Possession of the rifle meant he had off- world sources, and probably wielded some power among the other convicts as well.

I took a step back as he approached. His pace was casual, as if he were just taking his gun out for a moonlit stroll. He prodded the dead guard with the tip of the rifle then squatted down, ran one hand over the guard's work vest as if checking for a weapon, or perhaps life signs. I could have told him the guard had neither. "Perhaps I should've warned him about you," he said, rising. "Captain Chasidah Bergren. Pride of the Sixth Fleet. One dangerous woman. But, oh, I forgot. You're not a captain anymore."

With a chill I recognized the mocking tone, the cultured voice. And suddenly the dead guard and the rifle were the least of my problems. I breathed a name in disbelief. "Sullivan! This is impossible. You're dead—"

"Well, if I'm dead, then so are you." His mirthless laugh was as soft as footsteps on a grave. "Welcome to Hell, Captain. Welcome to Hell."

We found two fallen trees, hunkered down and stared at each other, each waiting for the other to make a move. It was just like old times. Except there was the harsh glow of his lightbar between us, not the blackness of space.

"I never pegged you for an easy kill," I told him. Which was true. The reports of his death two years ago had actually surprised me more than his reappearance just now. I balanced the dagger in my hand, not yet content to let it wrap itself around my wrist. "When I heard what happened at Garno it sounded too easy. I didn't buy it." I shrugged and pushed aside what else I'd thought, and felt, when I'd heard the news. My opinions and feelings about the death of a known mercenary and smuggler mattered little anymore.

He seemed to hear my unspoken comment. "It wasn't planned to fool anyone with a modicum of intelligence. Only the government. And, of course, their news-hounds. But tell me the news of my passing pained you," he continued, dropping his voice to a well-remembered low rumble, "and I'll do my best to assuage your fears."

A muted boom sounded in the distance, rattling through the forest. Another shuttle arriving, breaking the sound barrier on descent. He turned toward it, so I was spared answering what I knew to be a jibe. Regardless, I had no intention of telling him about my pain.

Patches of light and shadow moved over his face. Sullivan's profile had always been strong, aristocratic, dominating the Imperial police bulletins and Fleet patrol advisories. He had his father's lean jawline, his mother's thick dark hair. Both were more than famous in their own right, but not for the same reasons as Sully. They were members of the Empire's elite; he was simply elusive.

The lightbar reached full power. It was almost like shiplight, crisp and clear. He turned back to me, his lips curved in a wry smile, as if he knew I'd been studying him.

He'd aged since I last saw him, about six months before his highly publicized demise. The thick, short-cropped black hair was sprinkled with silver. The dark eyes had more lines at the corners. The mouth still claimed its share of arrogance, though—as if he knew he'd always be one handsome bastard.

However, something else had changed, something deeper inside him. It was nothing I could see, sitting there under the canopy of the forest. It was something I knew. Because I *was* sitting there with Gabriel Ross Sullivan and I was still alive.

All the more reason to ignore his attempt at taunting me. His existence had been far more troublesome to me than his purported passing. "What went down on Garno? You cut a deal?" Moabar or death had been offered to a lot of people, but not to me. Most chose death. I hadn't had that luxury.

He snorted. It was a disdainful sound I remembered well. He shoved the rifle almost to my nose. "What's this look like? How long have you been here, three weeks?"

I knew what it was. Illegal. Damn difficult to come by. A rifle didn't wrap around your wrist like my dagger, or fit in the sole of a boot.

A thought chilled me. Maybe the Taka weren't the only guards the prison authorities used.

"Yeah, three weeks, two days, and seventeen hours. You know what they say about how time flies." I held his gaze evenly. His eyes were dark, like pieces of obsidian, unreadable. "That's a Norlack 473 rifle. Sniper model. Modified, it appears, to handle illegal wide-load slash charges."

He laughed. "On point as ever, Bergren. Dedicated captain of a peashooter squad out in no man's land. Keeping those freighters safe from dangerous pirates like me. And even when they damn you and ship you here and every inch of you still belongs to Fleet Ops." He shook his head. "Your mama wore army boots, and so do you."

"What do you want, Sully?" I jerked my chin toward the dead Taka. "You cleaning up after him? Or finishing what he didn't?"

He turned the rifle in his hands. "This isn't Fleet

issue. Or prison stock. This is mine. Contraband, wasn't that how your orders phrased it? Stolen. Modified." He paused and pinned me intently with his obsidian gaze.

We'd had conversations like this before, most often with me on the bridge of my small patrol ship. He'd be on the bridge of the *Boru Karn*, his pilot and bridge crew flickering in and out of the shadows behind him. He rarely answered anything directly. He threw words at you, phrases, like hints to a puzzle he'd taunt you to solve. Or like free-form poetry, the kind that always sounded better after a few beers. He loved to play with words.

I didn't. "Okay. So no deal was cut and you're not working for the Ministry of Corrections. Don't tell me you've added Moabar to your vacation plans?"

He laughed again, more easily this time. But not easily enough for me to put my dagger back around my wrist.

"A resort for the suicidal but faint at heart? Don't bother to slit your own throat, we'll do it for you." He gestured theatrically. "It could work. If I couldn't market it, hell, no one could."

"Not a lot of repeat business."

"Ah, but that is the operative word. Business."

"Is it? What are you funding here, prison breaks?" If he wasn't with the M.O.C., then he had to be working against them. But I'd never heard of any successful escapes from Moabar. There was no prison, per se. No formal structure. Just an inhospitable, barely habitable world of long frigid winters that brought airborne viruses, and bleak, chilled summers. Like now. I was lucky my sentence started when it did. I'd have time to acclimate. Others, dumped dirtside in the midst of a blizzard, often died within hours.

"If I'm funding anything, it's freedom for a cause. I've found, since my untimely but useful demise, that this place can provide me with a source of cheap, willing labor."

"Willing being the operative word, I take it?"

"Willing being the operative word, yes."

"Doing what?" I knew many of Sully's operations before Garno: stolen cargo, weapons, illegal drugs, ships, and everything that fell in-between. I just couldn't see why he'd chosen to seek me out. My expertise lay in none of those areas. Unless he'd lost his pilot, needed someone to captain a ship for him. But why come to me? He could have his pick from those who lined the barstools in any spaceport pub.

But then, I'd ignored his all-important earlier comment: my mother wore army boots.

"You know the system," he told me. "You were born and raised in it. As were your parents, and your parents' parents. I know your personnel file, Captain Chasidah 'Chaz' Bergren. Daughter of Engineering Specialist Amaris Deirdre Bergren and Lt. Commander Lars Bergren. Sister of Commander Thaddeus Bergren, currently second in command at the Marker Shipyards. Granddaughter of Lieutenant—"

"I know who I am."

"So do I."

"Good. Then you know my mother's been dead for almost twenty years and I haven't spoken to my father in over ten. And my brother, since the trial, won't permit my name to be mentioned within earshot. What's the point?"

"The point, my lovely angel—and no, don't look so skeptical. Though I may be a veritable walking list of negative personality traits, the one thing I am not, and never have been, is a liar. It's my great downfall,

Chaz. So if I say you're lovely—" He reached as if to touch my chin with his fingertips. I jerked back and almost fell off my log. I dragged my boot heel in the dirt to keep my balance.

"Don't tumble for me yet, darlin'." He laughed. "We have business to attend to first. As I was saying, death has afforded me a new perspective. A new maturity, if you will. While my goals haven't changed, my methodology has. That's where you come in."

"A mere captain of a pea shooter squadron?"

"That's Fleet's appraisal of your talents. Not mine."

"No, you always called me an interfering bitch."

"If you must quote me, please be accurate. A beautiful, interfering bitch. And now that I find I'm in need of one particular beautiful, interfering bitch, I can't think of one better. So tell me, my angel, are you ready to leave this veritable paradise and make a pact with the ghost from Hell?"

I turned the dagger in my hand, watched the light play over the blade. I'd been willing to sell my soul earlier for a nightscope and a laser pistol. On Moabar, that would guarantee survival. But Sully was offering me more. He was offering me a way off Moabar. Freedom. On Hell's terms, but freedom nonetheless.

I nodded, stuck my hand out. "Officer's agreement."

He clasped my hand firmly, then went down on one knee and brought it to his lips.

I pulled my fingers away from his mouth, angry at the invisible firemoths that seemed to dance across my skin at his touch. "This is a business deal, Sullivan."

He sat back on his heel, grinning. "Whatever you say."

"Damn straight." I pushed myself to my feet, transferred the dagger to my right hand and started to let it wrap around my left wrist. Then stopped. He'd retrieved the rifle and now stood towering over me, his dark eyes glinting brightly from the lightbar in his hand.

I let my fingers close around the hilt of the dagger, kept it between us as I followed him into the forest. Maybe I'd hold onto it this way, for a while. Just in case my ghost's good humor dissolved like mist from the moons.

Sully tabbed the lightbar down to half-power, just enough to guide us over fallen logs and rock-filled ditches. He held it low, our bodies blocking its telltale glow. I lengthened my strides to match his.

The only sounds were our footsteps crunching against the carpet of brittle twigs, the occasional slap of a branch against our jackets. His, like mine, was black, spacer-issue plain.

We slipped like shadows between the shaggy trees. It was as if I were twenty-two years old again, back in basic training, on a dirtside recon exercise. Sully moved that way too, with a cautious grace. A bright patch of moonlight cascaded through an opening in the forest canopy. As one, we edged around it.

I caught a wry, half-smile on his face. He angled his mouth down to my ear, echoing my thoughts. "Feels like boot camp."

I hated boot camp. But it had taught me some invaluable lessons. Apparently, Sully had learned them as well—though I couldn't remember any stint in the military on his dossier. I was about to ask where he'd trained when something glinted ahead of us, far off to the right.

Instinctively I flattened against a tree. My fingers tightened on the dagger. The lightbar blinked out as my heart rate picked up. Then my face was in Sully's chest as he clasped me protectively. I flinched back involuntarily, surprised not only by his action, but by a rush of heat. Then it was gone and I tagged it as nothing more than adrenaline fighting against a severe lack of sleep. He pushed me to my knees, crouched down with me. He flicked the safety off the rifle, angled it up.

His left hand cupped the back of my head, drew my face against his shoulder again. "Damned redhead," he whispered. "You glow like a jumpgate beacon. Now, hush. Be still for a moment."

A rush of wind rattled the leaves around us. I ducked my head further down, even though I knew my hair wasn't that red. It was dark auburn and, after three weeks on Moabar, far from glowing. I doubted the color was Sully's real reason, anyway. I didn't know if there was something out there he didn't want me to see, or he was simply feeding his ego by playing hero. Either way, I wasn't about to argue. My strange lightheadedness had returned. I needed a moment to steady myself, find focus.

His breathing was deep and even. He turned away from me, his gaze locked on something on the right. As I was hunkered down between him and the large tree, I could only see the outline of his hand on the rifle and the dark, skewed shadows of the forest floor.

"What is it?" I asked as quietly as I could. His fingers threaded into my braid as if he wanted to unravel it. Or, I realized with a blinding flash of stupidity, as if he searched for a way to get a strong and painful grip on me.

I remembered what had been on that Takan guard's agenda and tried to jerk my head back. Then I heard it.

A wheezing noise. A crackling. The sound that tissue paper would make if it were composed of glass. And another rush of wind, air pushing past me.

My mouth suddenly went dry.

Sully shifted his weight, brought the rifle up to eye level. The faint greenish glow of the nightscope reflected back on his face.

The crackling stopped.

I smelled something foul. My stomach clenched in response. A jukor. A vicious, fanged mutant beast with the distinctive scent of rotting garbage. A breeding experiment by the M.O.C., jukors were a distorted, hideous version of ancient, imaginary soul-stealers. They'd been bred to combat the more current, very real telepathic Stolorth *Ragkirils*. The government halted the jukor experiment ten years ago, when it had become apparent the creatures couldn't be controlled. Not like Takas.

I knew the smell because I'd had escort duty with a ship hauling a pack of jukors to be destroyed. It was a smell I'd never forget.

It was one I knew I shouldn't be remembering now.

A long wheeze, closer. My heart thudded at the sound. It was scenting for something. Us, most likely. Or its mate. Either option was a bad one. If it chose us as prey, its powerful hind legs and winged upper forearms would make it damn near impossible to evade.

If it were scenting for a mate, it would kill any other creature in its path in its lust.

A frightening thought. If it *were* scenting for a mate, that meant jukors were alive, breeding again, for M.O.C. purposes. Perhaps even new and improved?

Either way, we were dead unless Sully killed it first. My dagger would barely be able to pierce its hide.

Fingers tugged at my scalp. He *was* unraveling my

braid. I mentally questioned my ghost's sanity and jerked my head away, frowning.

He yanked it back. His breath was hot against my ear. "Your hair wrap. I need it. Now."

I swore silently, slapped the dagger back around my wrist then as quickly, and as quietly, as possible, unraveled the leather and fabric laces. My hair fell almost to my waist, drifting over my arms as I shoved the cords into his outstretched hand. My mind still questioned his sanity.

He thrust the rifle at me. "Keep a lock on it."

As I brought the nightscope to my eye I caught a glimpse of Sully grabbing a stout, broken tree limb from the ground.

Two moons dotted the night sky, adding their light. The jagged form of the jukor almost jumped through the eyepiece at me. It was twenty-five feet from us. Upwind. Its long snout moved slowly side to side. I heard the crackling again as it flexed one wing. Barbed tips, like tiny razors, glinted sharp and cruel.

Its lower arms and legs were furred A hide formed of rock-hard scales covered its chest and back. Only the base of its throat was vulnerable. A soft spot, unprotected.

Damned small.

I moved the rifle slightly as it moved its head.

Sully's hand covered mine, traded rifle for a leather and fabric-wrapped tree branch.

"It will see it, scent it." He put the eyepiece to his eye again, the greenish glow like a small alien moon on his face.

I understood. The leather and fabric held my scent.

"Beer toss," he said.

I understood that, too. Wasn't a station brat in civilized space who didn't. Old pub game.

"On three." He adjusted his balance slightly. He'd have to move the moment the jukor sprang.

"One." The word was a soft rustle of leaves.

I rose slowly, becoming part of the tree on my left.

"Two."

I started my windup.

"Three."

I hurled the branch high, arcing it upwards in the clear moonlight. The dark form lunged. Powerful wings snapped out, pushed downwards. An unbearable stench rolled toward me just as three flashes of light erupted on my right.

Sully: springing, moving, firing.

The dagger snapped into my hand. If he missed, or only wounded it, it would be here in seconds.

A roaring sound. An enormous blot of darkness descending from the air at an unbelievable rate of speed. Wings beating, fingered forelimbs yanking itself through the trees at us.

Sully, firing. "Run!"

He hadn't hit the jukor's throat.

I bolted sideways, headed for the thickest brush, hoping it would snag a wing, entangle an arm.

Branches whipped at my face, but the only pounding footsteps I heard were mine.

I stopped, spun about. Saw Sully drop to the ground, roll, come up firing again as the jukor's barbed wing slashed inches from his body.

Shit! I plunged back through the trees just as the jukor roared and slammed Sully to the ground.

DON'T MISS

SPECTRA PULSE

A WORLD APART

the free monthly electronic newsletter
that delivers direct to you...

< Interviews with favorite authors
< Profiles of the hottest new writers
< Insider essays from Spectra's editorial
  team
< Chances to win free early copies of
  Spectra's new releases
< A peek at what's coming soon

...and so much more

SUBSCRIBE FREE TODAY AT

www.bantamdell.com

SF 3/05